Peeper

Also by William Brinkley

Quicksand
The Deliverance of Sister Cecilia
Don't Go Near the Water
The Fun House
The Two Susans
The Ninety and Nine
Breakpoint

William Brinkley

Peeper

A COMEDY

THE VIKING PRESS
NEW YORK

Library of Congress Cataloging in Publication Data
Brinkley, William, 1917–
Peeper.
I. Title.
PS3503.R56175T4   813′.54   81-65288
ISBN 0-670-69751-6   AACR2

Printed in the United States of America
Set in Linotron Baskerville

For Jean

The nakedness of woman is the work of God . . .
                                —William Blake

Especially in Texas.
                        —amplification by the author

Contents

Peeper

1.

Help

N o wonder we name so many towns after women. Texas has such an abundance of good-looking ones, it's only natural. This is one such town. Martha, down on the Rio Grande.

My name is Daniel Squire Baxter and it was Thursday, February 10. Press day for the *Clarion*. The phone rang. A baby had been born. I hung up and it rang again. Someone was getting married. It continued to ring. Preparations were under way for next month's main event, the Bloomer Girl Ball. The Gun Club would meet on Monday night, the Ladies' Aid Society on Friday afternoon, the Domino Club also on Monday, the Baptist deacons on Thursday, the banker's wife was flying to Dallas for a day of shopping. I have been here long enough to learn how much the life of a small town revolves around its newspaper. It is as if the townspeople can't do anything without telling the paper first. Usually they wait until Thursday to tell it.

I took it all down and between calls wrote it up. Above me, the old ceiling fan which I use to save money on air conditioning rasped away, and the ancient Mergenthaler Linotype *clack-clack*ed through the swinging door to the composing room. When there was a moment I wrote head-lines and went out there and hand-set them. I dealt with the people who came to the counter. The town clerk brought in a citation about a suit for a bad debt which a statute required to

1

be published in the newspaper. Reverend Billy Holmes came in with the Church News. And then the classified ads. A Santa Gertrudis cow in calf for sale. A lost Irish setter that answered to the name of Red had got into the back end of the wrong pickup by mistake. A "lawyer's bookcase," the kind that was used on the frontier to add one shelf on top of another as you accumulated books, for sale. The ten cents a word included the fee of the author. I composed these ads to the customer's satisfaction and made change from the counter drawer. The phone rang. It was Mrs. Thomas Browning with an item for Social Notes. Her son Billy had been admitted to Southwest Texas State University at San Marcos.

"It's LBJ's old school," she said proudly. "Could you say that?"

"I'd be happy to say that, Mrs. Browning," I said.

I looked out the window onto Cavalry Street. A family group was standing there looking in at me, taking in the sights: the father, wearing a cowboy hat and a string tie, the nicely dressed mother under a parasol, and three stair-step children. They had that look people have when watching the animals at the zoo. I waved, and one of the children shyly waved back. The other two had their fingers in their mouths. The phone rang. I stayed at it. I had been at it since 6:00 A.M., and only now, nine hours later, was I able to start in on the page-one stories: the weekly vegetable-production piece, the new officers of the Daughters of the Republic of Texas, and the forthcoming Town Council meeting, whose principal business would be whether to allow the town bar Here-Tis to stay open until 1:00 A.M. on Sundays, instead of having to close at midnight, a considerable issue in Martha, since that extra hour fell on the Lord's Day.

Actually I liked it, except now and then on Thursdays. Even though I had never worked so hard. It had been softer covering the United States Senate and a lot softer covering the White House. Anyhow, tomorrow at this time I would be out on the blue Gulf in my Grand Banks 36, and I'd stay there until Monday.

And besides, help was on the way, at sixty-five dollars a week. That's more than I can afford but I had no choice.

3
PEEPER

When I first came here I thought I could do everything. I found out differently. This would be the last issue of the Martha *Clarion* I'd have to do all by myself.

The way I got her was that I received a phone call from an associate professor of journalism at Southern Methodist University in Dallas. We knew each other pretty well when he was a member of the working press in Washington, and when we'd last talked I'd told him I was looking for someone. Someone who wanted to work hard and was cheap. He said he had this girl whose mother he was shacked up with in a place she had taken in Highland Park for that purpose and who wanted to be a reporter—the girl, not the mother. Would I take her on as a personal favor to him? I was getting desperate. Try finding someone these days for sixty-five dollars. Nonetheless, with this *curriculum vitae,* I think he detected a certain hesitation on my end of the line and he pressed on.

"She's from Odessa, Texas," he said, "which with all that oil has a bigger per-capita income than Kuwait. When I affirm that her folks are Big Rich, sport, I'm understating the matter. The kid—well, she's been in and out of three or four fancy schools. She's very bright, very. I had her in a couple of classes, and the fact is, she was the sharpest thing in them. A little difficult but . . . look, the important part is, you can have her for practically nothing. Actually I'm doing you the favor."

"That's why we've always been friends," I said.

"You better take an offer like this, sport." Whiteside —that's my friend—has never recovered from reading F. Scott Fitzgerald. "She wants to be one of the great reporters. Washington, New York, Paris, Dar es Salaam, some-place like that. I told her no one could show her better how to go about it than you. I told her she could learn more from you in two months than she would here in two years. I told her that with you, sport, she'd be learning under the best."

"I hardly think you overstated it."

"I may have laid it on just a bit. She wants to sit at your feet."

"Listen, I'm worried about you," I said. "This thing about

the mother. Don't they let you screw the students these days? I thought that was part of the deal."

"Not unless you've got tenure. Well, sport, do you want her?"

I had just been forced to work six days in a row from being so short-handed and had actually missed a trip to the island.

"Ship her down," I said. "Sixty-five dollars. Make sure she understands that. Are you familiar with the phrase *razor's edge*? That refers to my profit margin. Also tell her we don't have any time clocks."

That was two weeks ago, and Monday she would be here. I sighed, looking forward to that. Through the window a huge, redheaded, open-bed truck, taking up well over half the road, was moving down Cavalry Street, headed from the fields to the packing sheds. Carrots. The phone rang. It was Mrs. Stanley Whitman with the news that her daughter Prudence in Sweetwater, Texas, a graduate of Martha High School, had just given birth to twins, making Mrs. Whitman a "double grandmother," she told me with a giggle, on Prudence's first try. I took it down for Social Notes. Prudence in her time had been a Bloomer Girl.

Texas' best product is not really oil or cattle, it's girls. There is something about Texas girls. They are different from girls elsewhere. I've been all over the United States and I know about these things. They know who they are and what they have. There is a visible aura to them. Something special, some instinctive, sassy, tart, flirtatious, lofty, pert, almost brazen yet curiously soft air of femininity and confidence. It starts at about the age of five and makes them marvelously appealing. Makes them, it seems to me, what a girl or woman is all about. I've spent a considerable amount of time wondering how this happened. It must have begun in frontier days when a woman, rarer than gold, was sought after as earth's most precious treasure: the air and assurance this gave her. Anyhow, the small towns of Texas are filled with them. I like girls and they have as many of them here in the Rio Grande Valley as any place I've been in Texas.

If you should drive due south from San Antonio on

Highway 281, you would come presently into ranch country, a brown landscape continuing mile after mile, beautiful to certain eyes in its unrelieved way. After four hours of driving through this, you would see through your windshield a startling thing. Suddenly the countryside will be green. It is as if a line had been drawn across the land. Then you become aware that it is not one green but many, every conceivable shade of that color—different greens for different vegetables. Far as you can see, the serried greens unfurl until they run up against the great wash of blue. You have entered the Rio Grande Valley. This is a misnomer, for no hills rise. It is an alluvial plain. The Rio Grande is to the valley people what the Nile is to the Egyptians. The river is everything. It created the delta, and now the irrigation from it grows the vegetables. As earth is measured, the delta is small. No more than seventy miles west to east and thirty north to south, ending where Texas ends, one way in the Gulf, the other in Mexico. But that parturient patch, with its three crops and 340 growing days a year, is one of the wonders of the North American landmass and one of the principal dinner sources for the multitudes of the North. For anyone who loves green countryside, for anyone who loves vegetables—their colors, feels, tastes, smells—here is paradise.

Still, I'm not here for the vegetables or even for the girls. I wouldn't be here at all but for the three days a week my job leaves me for my boat down on the island. One day—it was in Washington, D.C.—I decided nobody should work more than four days a week, ever. Less, if possible. Life, as they say, is short, and though I may be a preacher's son I haven't seen any written guarantees by an unimpeachable source for a second trip around. I'm not trying to find out what it means. I just want to learn how to use the time I've got. A lot of people think I copped out, but I know life is better for me here, away from bigness and crowds of people. I might have gone to south Florida, except the tourists haven't eviscerated this place yet, it's a lot cheaper here, and I like the fact that everyone didn't come from somewhere else. You can leave your doors unlocked, you can breathe the air and drink the water, and you can drive across town in four minutes. Also, I grew up in a town much like Martha, farther up the Rio Grande.

There was a weekly newspaper, the *Clarion,* for sale here, so I bought it—that is to say, I bought about a fifth of it and got a mortgage on the rest. Padre Island and the Gulf being just sixty miles away had a lot to do with it. I put the rest of my life savings into a 36-foot Grand Banks trawler—paid for about a fifth of that, too. So you might say my life is rather heavily mortgaged.

"Hey, boss. When are you going to have that page-one layout?"

Beto had come through the swinging door from the composing room. He was my only employee so far. Even in his printer's striped apron Beto, with his lean hipless build, licorice-black hair, tobacco-brown skin, and carefully trimmed mustache, cuts quite a figure and knows it. He always moves with an air, as if to say, A man is a man. He had asked that question twice already.

"Quién sabe? If you'll leave me alone, possibly even sometime today," I said briskly. "I only have two hands and one brain, Beto."

"That's true, boss."

I was just finishing up the Town Council story when I heard a big noise. I looked up through the sign on the window that said "The Martha Clarion." A red, rather beat-in sports car had pulled up in front. The driver was sitting there, revving the motor, looking up at the sign. I watched, annoyed. I dislike intentional noise. Then the driver got out, swung around the car, and headed for the door. I couldn't tell whether it was a boy or a girl. It was wearing jeans with a man's white shirt that was much too big hanging down over them. Then I realized it was a girl. I wasn't certain how I had come to that conclusion.

She stood at the counter and I got up and went over. She looked about eighteen, and I wondered whether she had come to place a classified ad or to ask directions to somewhere in town, most likely the historic old Cavalry Post. She appeared barely five feet, and I would have placed her weight at about ninety-eight pounds. She looked like some kind of waif, or stray. Maybe she was a runaway kid from upstate headed for Mexico.

Then I became aware that she was scrutinizing the room. She had huge brown eyes and they peered all around as if sizing up the place, taking in the abiding clutter and general disorder and creaky ceiling fan. She seemed even to be noting the raucous sound of the Mergenthaler coming from the composing room. She had said not a word, but something in her manner suggested distaste and acute disapproval. I felt my back go up. After all, the *Clarion* was my paper. Then her inspection appeared to move from the operation to me, and just as analytically.

"Young lady, I'm extremely busy," I said. "This is press day, if you don't mind. May I help you?"

"Don't call me young lady. Holy Christ, is *this* it? You must be Baxter. I'm Jamie Scarborough, your new reporter."

At once my teeth went on edge. I took a long deep breath and looked at her again. This time it was I who did the inspecting. The shirttail hanging out over the jeans. The dirty sneakers. The rather impudent, aggressive gamine face, the nothing of a body, the hair cut shorter than many a boy's. I looked through the window at the sports car. It was an MG, and it had a huge dent in the right front fender. No car like that belonged in Martha, Texas. If her inspection had produced disapproval, mine brought disgust and an alarm over what Whiteside had sent me.

"You're early" was what I said.

"You must be glad of that. Looks like you're the one who needs the help. Well, let's go to work. You said it was press day."

Both because I had a paper to get out and because I learned long ago to sit a spell on severe anger and hostility, I gave her the briefest possible explanation of our Social Notes column and put her to answering the phone while I went back to writing the copy and headlines for the page-one stories. I made up page one for Beto. I went out and set some headline type. I came back and did several short items. It must have been a couple hours later that I looked up to see her standing at my desk. Out the window, twilight was beginning to come to Cavalry Street. I had been at it dark to dark. I could see the Bon Ton Cafe across the street lighting up. You pronounce it Bawn Tawn. She was holding a sheaf of copy paper that had typing on it. Well, at least she had kept the phone calls off me for a couple of hours.

"Here they are," she said. "Mrs. Earl Hancock's son Alfred has made it through boot camp at the Great Lakes Naval Training Center. Miss Sally Carruthers will be attending a harp festival in San Antonio. The Orville Jenkinses are celebrating their twenty-fifth wedding anniversary by redoing their living room in wallpaper of small pink roses. Mrs. Henry Milam is going to Idalou this week to take care of her sick sister. . . ."

She took a deep breath.

"What a big bunch of nothing. Is that what this job is going to be like? Do you expect me to do this sappy bullshit every week?"

I gave her a long careful look. "Keep your voice down, will you? I don't have a hearing problem. Yes, that is exactly what this job is going to be like."

"Je-*sus*. You mean this is all that ever happens in this town? What in God's name ever brought you here? Whiteside said—"

"Will you shut up?" She jumped a little. "Stop asking all these questions. I don't care what Whiteside said, and I'm not interested in your observations. If you like, you can walk out the door, get in that heap out there, and go back where you came from. Otherwise, you'll do as I say. Starting right now with taking this copy out to the composing room and leaving me alone, girl. I'm busy." I put the copy on the desk and waved her away with both hands. "Get. Get."

"Don't call me girl." She hiccuped. She waited, glaring at me, her eyes as big as moons and flashing.

"It's too late to drive back now. It's dark."

She reached down, grabbed the copy, and flounced across the room to the swinging door to the composing room, her hair bouncing, the tail of the oversized man's shirt flapping behind her.

"And to answer one of your many questions," I said across the room. She stopped with her hand on the door. "That's what brought me here. The fact that nothing ever happens in this town."

PEEPER 1
The Bloomer Girls

Standing, he punctured the cellophane, lifted out the black pantyhose, and let them fall full length. He held them that way and studied them for a bit, put his hand inside and ran it down into one of the legs, pulling the stretch cloth taut, then slowly back up, observing the hand through the fabric. It was too transparent. He brought his hand up into the panty portion and held it near the lamplight and looked through. It looked as though it would do. He picked up the manicure scissors and carefully cut off the twin "hose" segments of the garment. He carried the panty section and the scissors into the bathroom, switched on the bright light, and from the medicine cabinet got out a lipstick that had been there a long time.

He slipped the panties over his head and arranged them. With the lipstick he marked out his eyes. Then he removed the panties and carefully scissored around the elliptical lines. He cut some more around the garment, tidying it up. Then he put it back on and looked at himself in the mirror. A smile, inadvertent, parted his lips. He looked rather like a black rabbit. But it could not have been more ideal. The stretch material made a snug, comfortable fit. The elastic of the waist anchored the garment around the neck. It was a good job. His grandmother would not have recognized him through it. And it actually felt good against the skin. He understood now why women liked them.

Leaving on the panties to become accustomed to them, he gathered up the discarded fragments of nylon, returned to the bedroom, picked up the cut-off stockings, and stuffed these remains in a paper bag. He looked out the window.

Dusk was coming on. He had to decide now. He turned on the light and sat down in the darkening room and began to reason out, just one more time, whether he really wanted to go through with it. He looked out across his yard to the street and, as the shadows fell and night neared, thought about the Bloomer Girls.

If there was a better-looking group of girls anywhere, he had not seen or heard about them. The town of Martha was a basketball town. It had the ritualistic high school football team that every little Texas town has to have, but basketball was the town's true love, in no small part because of the Bloomer Girls. All the boys aspired to be basketball players. You could drive around town on a hot August day and see little tads learning the fundamentals of the game from fathers and older brothers under hoops hung above dozens of garages. All the girls aspired to be members of the organization that cheered the boys on during time-outs and half times, though it had long since transcended this subordinate status. Becoming a Bloomer Girl implied a great deal more than just jumping up and down at basketball games. It carried with it the town's highest social prestige, something that continued through one's lifetime. There were grandmothers in town who had been Bloomer Girls. Alumnae meetings, teas, and dances were important events in the town's social calendar, and the annual Bloomer Girl Ball at season's end was the premier event of all. No higher honor could come to a girl in Martha. Personally, he went to the games as much to see the Bloomer Girls as the basketball players. The same, of course, could be said for most of the townspeople.

The routines performed by the Bloomer Girls—they were known as "sketches"—were not the rudimentary arm and leg flapping associated with the genre. They were minutely choreographed movements, rituals of considerable precision and skill, some of them deliberately comical, rehearsed over long hours. They were designed to display both the talents and the figures of the performers. The town had every right to be proud of the organization, and its sketches were regularly received with enthusiastic applause, often exceeding that given a timely hook shot by one of the boys. In most places if one wants to get a hot dog or go to the bathroom during a sporting event, one does so during half time. In Martha, one did these things during the game itself. No one wanted to miss the Bloomer Girls.

The costumes in which these entertainments were executed were themselves special and distinctive. They were not ordered from some sporting goods catalog. They were fine achievements of local seamstress art. The materials were the finest, everything was hand-sewn, and each costume was fitted precisely to the girl who would wear it. You could trace the passage of time in the town by looking at group photographs of Bloomer Girls over the years and observing how the item which gave them their name, along with the rest of the costume, had steadily become more curtailed and more giving of the girlish figure. Today's costume, while eschewing the vulgarity seen in cheerleader attire in certain other parts of the country and even farther north in Texas, was a snazzy, saucy presentation. It conveyed the quintessence of the young girl about to flower into womanhood. Short black satin bloomers displayed a goodly portion of white thigh; soft pink socks rose to just below the knee; pleated shirtwaists matched the socks in color and were secured by small pewter buttons, with the top button left rakishly unfastened to permit just the suggestion of blossoming breasts. Even the pink slash of ribbon in the hair seemed to contribute to the impression of gay impertinence. The sight of the ten Bloomer Girls with their high and confident air, accompanied by a faint and knowing smile, a smile that spoke of what they were about to become, invariably gave one a sense of joy, mixed with wistful longing. When the high school drum and fife corps struck up "Yellow Rose" or "The Girl I Left Behind Me" at half time and the line came high-stepping out from around the corner of the stands and onto the floor, people leaped to their feet and burst into cheers. Whoever won the game, the Bloomer Girls never lost.

The Bloomer Girls. It had been coming all along, he knew, sitting there in the darkness; coming to this. The long winter of looking, from his seat in the high school gym, at lissome thighs, at firm bosoms briefly in view, at an epiphany of fresh young bodies thrusting at him. Coming down to last night, to the season's last game, to making his selection. Coming down to the purchase this afternoon at Carruthers Mercantile, the town's quality department store. He was a lover of life's ironies.

Sally Carruthers had strawberry-blond hair and a complexion of pearl. Her five feet five inches and one hundred and five pounds seemed as dewy as a Rio Grande Valley dawn. He imagined her always as having just stepped from her bath. She was eighteen. She was an only child and a student of the harp, which she played on Sunday at the First Baptist Church. Able, because of the family business, to maintain a bountiful wardrobe and given to wearing ensembles of coordinated colors, she made a lovely picture sitting at the harp playing "Holy, Holy, Holy." People would say, "Sally is in lavender today," or, "Sally is in pink." He had seen her from a pew there, clad in long performing dress, her movements all graceful, her fingers plucking the harp's strings, the long flaming hair held back demurely in ribbons. The horn-rim glasses she wore when playing—she was almost humorously astigmatic—only added to the air of studious maidenhood. He had seen her again and again in the Bloomer Girl uniform, no glasses needed now, watched the daring kicks of now unshielded young legs, watched the waist-long hair of that stunning shade of red now tossing in abandon, sweeping to the floor. So lovely was her hair, so pure the color, that there were those who doubted that it could be real. Indeed, he knew, this question had been the subject of keen speculation by more than one session of boys—and older men too.

Waiting on him at her father's store, she showed no surprise that he should want such an item. Carruthers Mercantile had been established in 1878, and commerce must have been bred in her bones. Business was business.

"Let's see. We have natural, nude, white, black, pink, beige. . . ."

"Pink? Whoever would wear pink? And whenever?"

A smile, a flash of the eyes. "You'd be surprised. On both counts."

So other men, for whatever reasons, must have purchased this same item from her. It was a comforting thought.

"Black. I was instructed to get black."

"Black it is." She giggled. "Excuse me while I get my glasses. I'm practically blind without them."

The horn-rims.

"That will be a dollar seventy-nine." Smartly. "A dollar eighty-eight with tax."

As change was being made, he made conversation. "I expect you're all excited. The Bloomer Girl Ball tonight."

"Yes, sir. *All* excited. We deserve it, the way we slave." She gave a laugh of cool, self-confident gaiety, her voice that of a young girl mocking something very important to her.

"You do indeed. No one gives us more pleasure."

"Why, what a nice thing to say."

As ever, she was dressed precisely: navy linen slacks, white man's-type shirt, always a ribbon in the strawberry hair, this one navy like the slacks. He fancied there was a scent of clover about her.

"Do you go off in September?"

"Oh, yes. The University, where else?" The young mocking again.

He smiled. "Where else?"

A smile back. The entire transaction was smart and crisp, efficient and pleasant.

"Here's your twelve cents. Have a nice evening, sir."

He smiled at her. Carrying the weightless package he had gone out onto Cavalry Street—it was named in honor of the men who had once protected the town and was the only street not named for a flower or a tree. It was a gallant March day. Not a cloud scarred the blueberry sky, the air off the fields breathed clean and fresh, and the sun came down, warming but not too hot, on the late-afternoon shoppers. Most of them he knew, and he spoke quite often as he walked down the street. What a nice town they had.

Now in his room, his hand reached up and by chance

touched the pantyhose. He had forgotten he had them on. Out the window, night was closing in. The room was nearly black. If he was ever going to do it, it would have to be now. He would feel foolish to have come this far only to stop. He didn't mean the purchase or the preparation of the mask. Nor even the small, neatly wrapped gift package on the bed. He meant the winter of looking at them. He meant the unnamed longing, like some kind of ache in him. No harm could come of it. Just this one time.

He got his tennis shoes from the closet and put them on. He had already blackened them with India ink. He was already dressed for it: dark slacks, dark polo shirt. Out for a night walk. He put the pantyhose mask in one pocket, the present in the other.

It was one of the pleasant nights with which the town was often favored, a sky free of wind and cloud, an air he would have judged as close on the nose of 70 degrees. He regularly took walks at night, when in some ways the town seemed at its loveliest. The white stars were beginning to arrange themselves in their ordained patterns across the heavens. Here on the Rio Grande they shone out of a vast display case, in an endless sky arching above the boundless land. They gazed down on the prosperous white-wood and red-brick houses, set back, well separated from each other, so self-assured-looking, each with its one hundred and fifty feet of frontage, on green lawns, lawns deep in front, deep in back. More than anything else, it was a town of trees, dense-leafed trees like the ebony, the hackberry, and the huisache, and they stood like clusters of open umbrellas on the lawns, casting pools of blackness, shielding even from the light of stars. Tonight they would be his way stations. Flowering bushes in abundance stood also on the lawns, and the whole look was one of fecundity, of an earth which gave forth in generosity, even eagerness, like a fructuous woman holding nothing back.

The streets of the town were alphabets, east and west for flowers, north and south for trees. He moved down the sidewalk to Katsura, right a block to Goldenrod, continued to

Daffodil, left another block to Laurel. The friendly buzz of the cicada was heard, and now and then the tenor call of the nighttime songbird. There were growing things in bloom the year 'round but especially now, for spring came a month early to this subtropical land. The town was filled with scents and he walked casually, on a stroll, tasting the fragrances of the night, the honeysuckle and the yellow rose, the Confederate jasmine and the gardenia. The gardenias—the bushes were heavy with blooms now, and no lawn was without one or more of them. He had always associated the flower with women, with the fragrance only women had. It must have come from his first teenage dates, from their corsages. The back lawns were separated by alleys which were almost like streets. He entered the alley between Daffodil and Camellia, his tennis shoes soundless on the caliche.

He moved along, walking between the unbroken rows of oleander hedges which lined the alleys. It was a sturdy bush, nearly always in bloom, tall, thick, and concealing. A perfect enforcer of the privacy which lay at the heart of the town, but a town which, in the tradition of this country, disliked forbidding things like walls and locks. In the darkness he was aware now and then of a light beyond the oleander, and occasionally of a dog's bark, the squawk of a grackle, but otherwise aware only of the silence and peace which embraced the town at night. The oleander wall was broken now and then by a latch gate. He came halfway down the alley and stopped. He stood in the silence and looked at the large slanting black roof beyond the hedge which rose toward the stars.

How many men's suits, shirts, hunting jackets, boots must have gone across counters to give Gerald Carruthers a house like this, he thought, how many women's dresses, hats, how many nightgowns, sets of lingerie . . . pantyhose? He opened the gate, went noiselessly through, and closed it behind him. He stood on thick Saint Augustine grass. Trees rose from the yard, in the very center a tall jacaranda bloomed like some giant flower—lavender, he knew, though the color was not now apparent—and he moved across and stood in its deep shadow. Beyond him he could see the white-board dollhouse, a replica in miniature of the main house. Everyone knew Sally Carruthers still used the dollhouse to practice the harp. He looked at the main house.

It sat large, solid and brightly white in the night, encircled by rich bushes. Virtually every house in Martha was clasped in shrubbery, intended like the oleander hedge to give privacy. It would give privacy, all right. To him. The house stood dark save for one room, a corner room at the back of the house, perhaps thirty feet from where he stood. The windows on both corners were open. A room with a small, higher window next to it was also lighted—that would be the bathroom. From a faint glow far on the other side of the house he knew that the porch light was on. That would be for her date: Orville Jenkins, Jr., he knew. He smiled. Otherwise all darkness. The Carrutherses would have left early; they had been chaperones at the Bloomer Girl Ball for as long as anyone could remember. Fittingly so. They had clothed all the dancers, boys and girls, in their finery. He took the mask out of his pocket, pulled it over his head, and arranged it snugly.

He emerged from the jacaranda's shadow and, beckoned by the light, moved across the thirty feet of Saint Augustine carpet and implanted himself in the bushes surrounding the corner room. Silently he parted the thick foliage and looked through. He had been in the house but never in this room. It was a large pretty room, neat, clean, and impeccable like its tenant, all in light blue, conveying a certain frilliness, conveying essences that belonged only to girls. His eyes moved around the room and stopped at the bed. It had a canopy of blue and a blue-and-white-checked counterpane. On it was laid out a long white evening dress, the bodice embroidered with beads, surrounded by those objects of fragrance and mystery, a woman's undergarments: white slip bordered with delicate lace, white brassiere and white panties, both lace-adorned, white pantyhose. He could hear the steady sound of water, the sound of a shower pulsing. He wished he could see into the bathroom, but the wicked angle of the half-open door made this impossible. He crouched where he was and waited.

Then the sound of water stopped and there was only the sound of the night, of cicadas making their whining song. He kept his eyes fixed on the open door, and presently a girl came through it, applying a towel to herself. No more than a dozen feet separated them. He caught his breath. The drying went on, meticulous and thorough, and then abruptly the towel fell away, simply dropped to the carpet. Sally was in nothing tonight.

The whole body white and fine, a tone poem of pearl whiteness, glowing from the shower. The hair in wanton abundance, fluffy from the toweling, a flame falling down over the body. The bathed young breasts surprisingly full, the nipples pale pink, erect from the shower's warmth. "Rose petals floating in milk." Atop the whiteness of the young thighs, planted there like a fiery crown—the boys need never have doubted—a blaze of red hair. She turned and walked toward the bed, giving a moment's view of coaxing pearl orbs. She picked up the panties, turned back, and sat down under the canopy facing him. The legs were spread a little, the pristine satiny flesh of the inside of her thighs offered to him, the strawberry patch sitting down now between them like a flower resting there. His perspective granted him that most secret and softest of all woman's flesh, set at the very crest of the inner thighs, stroked by a blush of hair. In the sweetness of the view a wave of dearest fondness swept over him. He looked on in adoration, and feasted.

She lifted a leg, put a foot through the panties, the strawberry patch rising slightly. Then the other leg. With a remarkable, comical agility, all in one instantaneous movement, she was on her feet and the panties were on her. She wiggled her behind to bring them tight, sat again, picked up a hairbrush, and with long rhythmic strokes began brushing her hair. He watched the ritual in fascination. Her head tossing back impertinently as the hair, under expert management, began to arrange itself in a luminous fall, wide and rich, long to the waist and below. Her back straight, the breasts stretched and thrust forward so that the rose nipples were looking at him.

A raucous noise from somewhere in back of him! A flight of grackles alarmed by something took wing from a tree. Her head came cocked like a doe startled, the brush poised in midair. Instantly he sank into the bushes, then slowly raised his head. She waited, then stood and walked directly toward him. She peered out, squinting hard without her glasses, as though to focus. Then shrugged, a young girl's shrug, and returned to the bed. She sat again and resumed brushing.

It was time to go. He reached up, placed the small package on the windowsill, and walked back across the yard, through the jacaranda's shadow and out the latch gate, closing it quietly behind him. He stood and looked around. All was darkness and silence. He glanced up at the stars, in a gesture of enjoyment and appreciation of their unselfish beauty; they shone bright and serene over the town. He felt remarkably at peace. A sense of liberation, almost of redemption, came over him. He took off his pantyhose mask, stuffed it in his pocket, and went down the alley to the street. He hesitated, then, instead of walking straight through and going by the alleys, stepped out briskly onto the sidewalk on Laurel Street. He walked to Forsythia, turned left to Juniper, and started down the last blocks toward home, moving with a light, almost jaunty step, his Keds nearly soundless on the sidewalk.

It had been so easy, so pleasant, so sweet—so transporting —the thought occurred to him as to whether he should do it again. Certainly not. Nevertheless, as he walked along he idly amused himself by running through in his mind, like a man pondering over a sampler box of chocolates containing vanilla cream, nut crunch cup, caramel cordial, liquid cherry, malted milk nougat, and maple pecan fudge, the complete roster of Bloomer Girls, recalling how each looked in satin bloomers, pink hose, pink shirtwaist, during various sketches. Sissy Jo Conrad, Tammy Lacey, Betty Oakes. . . .

Suddenly in the distance the bells of the First Baptist Church struck up, and he knew it was eight o'clock. From the church's tower a hymn played on the hour from noon to

midnight. As he strolled home, hearing the sweet and
ancient chords flood out over the town, he joined in, whis-
tling its stirring strains.

> *Rock of Ages, cleft for me,*
> *Let me hide myself in Thee.* . . .

2.
Freight Train

She had been here a month.

When I got back from the island Monday after my traditional three days away, I dropped by the paper and was at once confronted.

"I have to talk to you," she said in cross tones. "I have something urgent to discuss."

She always wants to talk, and "urgent" is her only classification.

"Why don't we have supper tonight at the Bon Ton?" I said. "And we'll talk. It'll help us digest our beef stew."

"The Bon Ton? Gee, are you sure you can afford it?"

"I can afford mine. I'll be at the Cavalry Post if anything happens."

"Are you kidding? Jesus, I wish *something* would."

She is quite young.

I went over to see Freight Train Flowers. The first thing I always do on getting back to town is call on the chief of police, and then the mayor, to find out what has been going on in our metropolis during my absence.

The town government is situated in the old Cavalry Post—"the Cavary," as everyone in town calls it. The place still seems to have a ghostly smell of horses and saddle leather and harness. The inside is dark and cool. I went up the stairs and down the hallway. Both could have taken three horses abreast. I walked through the open door into the chief's office. It's a marvelous place for an office. It opens onto a wide veranda—"piazzas," as the Cavalry ladies called them—with a high ceiling and overhead fans. The Cavalry knew about these things, and those piazzas are the coolest place in town in summer. From them you look across the parade ground where Union horse mustered before setting forth to look for Comanche. Lt. Col. Robert E. Lee once commanded the Department of Texas from this office. It was empty now. A yard-long sign in letters three inches high hung across the wall: ONE AGGIE EQUALS TWO ORDINARY MEN. A moose, a deer, and a bear, all taken by the present occupant, looked down in bug-eyed moroseness at the desk. The desk has dents all over it from the cowboy boots parked there by that occupant.

I like visiting with the chief. He has a natural shrewdness and integrity that make him a good chief of police for a town that scarcely needs one. The town means everything to him. His dedication to its welfare is total. He knows where every scrap of power lies and exactly how to deal with it. I always felt the chief stood to the Town Council like a good chief petty officer to commissioned officers. The CPOs really run the Navy. The officers only think they do, because the chiefs astutely permit them to take the bows.

The chief of police is an Aggie, a graduate of Texas A&M University. Aggiehood is a very special state of mind, and being an Aggie is a lifetime undertaking. For example, if San Jacinto Day, the Aggie holy day, finds an Aggie in Paris, France, he will stop everything he is doing to search out other Aggies who may be in that city in order to be with them. It's called "Aggie Muster." The Aggie creed has guided the chief's life from college days, and it has never let him down. The thing about the chief is that he kids about being an Aggie more than anyone. Most of the Aggie jokes I've heard were told me by the chief, always followed by a detonation of laughter. Nonetheless he knows that nothing in life is so important as being an Aggie.

From the fact that the gun cabinet was open and a weapon missing, I knew where he was. The cabinet houses two rifles, a Remington .30–06 and a Weatherby 300, and an over-under 12-gauge Winchester. None of the weapons has ever been fired at a man, but the chief is a great hunter. I walked through the office and out onto the piazza.

He was standing by the railing with his back to me, the Weatherby 300 in firing position. It's a beautiful thing, its stock covered with rich filigree. He was drawing a bead on the statue of Lee which commands the center of the parade ground.

"Be right with you, Ace," he said without turning around. The chief always knows when I am there, even when his back is to me. Instinct, I guess. When you mix that with a kind of fine slyness, you have a formidable human being. It's a visceral combination, indigenous, a Texas thing. Something you're born with or learn very early on your own. I don't think you can teach it. "Soon as I get off a couple."

Martha not being a violent town, the chief's job gives him little opportunity to polish his eye and trigger finger for his hunting. He handles this problem by dry-squeeze practice on the piazza. He squeezed the trigger slowly.

"Got the Colonel," he said happily. "Right between the eyes."

The chief always refers to Lee by the rank he held when he occupied the chief's office. It is as if Lee had never made it to general and nothing he did after commanding Texas was of much importance. Using him for target practice was in no way against Lee. Actually the chief liked Colonel Lee a lot and certainly was the authority on everything he did in Texas. He lowered the Weatherby and stood a moment, gazing out over the prospect.

It had rained during the night, and there was a freshness and sweetness to the air. A few big snow-white clouds stood high in the clear blue sky. A bright March sun flooded down onto the parade ground, sown now in rich green Saint Augustine grass, and washed the old white-board Cavalry buildings standing neatly and cared for around it. You could almost hear the distant bugle call and see the dim columns of horse troops marching out in column line, their guidons fluttering before them.

"Nice place, ain't it?" the chief said. "That's the double

truth. When you get down to it, I reckon this job wastes the talents of a fine police officer like myself. Let's take a load off."

We went back inside, and the chief sat at his desk beneath the stuffed animal heads and the Aggie sign. He overflowed the chair on all sides. He pulled open the top drawer, reached in, scooped up a handful of peanuts, and threw his head back and the peanuts in, all in one movement like an adept elephant. *Crunch-crunch.* He once told me that he thought better while chewing peanuts. He keeps a large supply in the drawer, not in any container but loose there, using the drawer itself as a huge bowl. They are cheap but of splendid quality. The chief buys them in number 10 cans across the Rio Grande in Las Bocas, nine miles away. He parked his Justin cowboy boots on the desk with a solid clump to add a new dent to it. *Crunch-crunch.*

"Got a new Aggie joke. This Aggie is up at Port Aransas, and he walks in a bait store and sees this sign, 'Special, all the worms you want, one dollar.' The Aggie reads the sign, thinks a moment, then looks at the proprietor and says, 'I'll take two dollars' worth.'"

The roar hit me like a blast from a cavalry cannon, the chief's big belly shaking like a run of sea waves. Aggies aren't really dumb. It is their conceit to pretend stupidity, and that pretense is their biggest edge.

"Well, Ace," he said when he had recovered, "here we are. Monday morning. Bright-eyed and bushy-tailed. How was the three-day pass this time?"

Why the chief calls me that I've never asked, but I assume it's for ace reporter and is his form of humor.

"Never lovelier," I said. "The sun was shining and the water was blue."

"Hail, if I didn't know better, I'd say you was running Mexican brown down there, 'mount a time you spend. The drugs boys tell me they's more of it comes in by sea than by land nowadays."

"Yeah. I hear the same thing."

"I don't know how you do it. Sure sounds like a winner. I wish I could spend my life screwing off at the beach."

"Why don't you? There's nothing to keep you here."

He sighed. "They's something in what you say."

We passed the time of day, and he told me there had been a speeding ticket on Cavalry Street after the Bloomer Girl Ball and a fight in the Here-Tis bar. He had solved the fight by holding the two combatants, one in each hand, and having them kiss and make up.

"I think they liked that part," he said.

"I didn't realize we had anything like that in Texas."

The chief gave me a sly look. "You didn't?" *Crunch-crunch.* "Well, it ain't generally known, but between you and me, Texas has always had its share of queers. I don't find that so peculiar. From my experience on the subject, I'd say they's a direct connection between being a queer and being a macho, and we surely got our share of machos."

"I'm shocked. I'll have to watch my step. Someone as pretty as I am. You ever try it, Chief?"

"Yeah. When I was five. Didn't relish it too much."

I sighed. "You mean there's nothing else you can give me to fill the columns of the *Clarion*? A speeding ticket and a bar fight?"

The chief gave a minor belch. He belches fairly often, on various decibel levels, some almost inaudible, like a baby's burp, some like a clap of thunder exploding right above you. I blame it on the peanuts. Actually the chief's belch is one of his friendliest traits. It's nice and warm, a sign that he likes you. He never does it in front of strangers.

"Naw, I reckon that's it," he said. "Our usual week of high criminal activity. Sometimes I do wake up in the short hours with a nightmare that the Town Council fired me, figuring this town don't require a chief of police. Not that I'm complaining, you understand."

The chief looked at me thoughtfully. He has large ears with long lobes, a prominent nose, and keen brown eyes. You feel they don't miss anything. But it is Freight Train Flowers's voice which identifies him. It has a decided rhythm and pace to it, ritualistic, as if language were an important thing, not to be hurried over. It takes him about the same amount of time to say ten words that an ordinary person would take to say twenty. I have always found it a soothing voice. I have never heard him raise it or even alter its mensural cadence. At the most he will emphasize words during moments of conviction, like italicizing them on a written page. He is characteristic of a type in this part of the world. He can talk quite grammatically when he wishes—that is, speak the language learned during schooling—but usually he speaks another, preferred language, learned and burnished outside the confines of the classroom.

"They was one other thing," he said. "Something a little different for Martha. We had us a Peeping Tom."

"Well, *that's* something anyhow. Who'd he peep?"

"The Carruthers girl. Sally Carruthers."

I whistled low. "A nice choice. You catch him and have them kiss and make up?"

The chief gave a medium belch. "The offender has not been apprehended."

"Sally Carruthers," I reflected. "Any idea who'd want to do that?"

Crunch-crunch. "Well, if you talking about *want*, I'd say just about every man in Martha over twelve."

The chief told me it had happened an hour or so before the Bloomer Girl Ball.

"Probably some Mexican drifter wanting to see some Anglo nooky," he said in that slow-motion voice. "They like it too, you know."

"Yeah, I've heard somewhere they do."

"Maybe he figured it was turn about. After all, we go to Boys' Town."

"Yeah, you're probably right. Some Mexican." I waited a moment and looked at the chief. "Mexican drifters know all about when the Bloomer Girl Ball is. Come on, it had to be some high school kid, Chief."

The chief recrossed his Justins and looked at me. "Hailfire, I've thought of all that, boy. I don't need no *former* big-city, Washington, D.C., newspaper reporter to tell me that. You probably right. Kids sure know about the Bloomer Girl Ball."

He chewed some peanuts and spoke thoughtfully.

"In my tenure in office we never had nothing like a

Peeping Tom in Martha. Damn serious business. A felony, I'm sure. I'll have to look it up."

"What's so serious about a kid looking through a window at Sally Carruthers?"

The chief reached in the drawer, scooped up a fresh feeding of peanuts, tossed his head back, and threw them in. *Crunch-crunch.* He spoke solemnly.

"Well, pussy is private property, for one thing. I reckon it's about the most private property we got."

I looked up at the big Aggie sign. "Well, maybe. I don't think Peeping Toms are taken that seriously anymore. All this liberation. You've got these magazines and everything and they show it all. I doubt if anyone anywhere gets that excited now if someone gets a quick peek at a little fur."

The chief gave me that shrewd look of his. "Well, for one thing, we not talking about magazines. We talking about *live* pussy. For another, we not talking about anywhere. We talking about Texas. And we talking about *Martha*, Texas."

The chief pulled his Justins off the desk and stood up. When he stands, Freight Train Flowers dominates any room. He is a big man in every way, six feet one inch and a beefy two hundred and thirty pounds. An acre of belly overhangs his Mexican-silver belt buckle, which weighs two pounds and is engraved with Quetzalcoatl, the sacred Toltec bird-serpent. Someone seeing him for the first time might think of the word "fats," but this would be misleading, as younger and supposedly stronger men have realized on occasion from a position flat on their backs. What looks like pure lard is as solid as a Santa Gertrudis bull. He has arms like ham sides and hands that could hide a cantaloupe. His skin is the color and texture of rawhide and his hair the color of nails left out in the rain. His uniform is gabardine "summer serge," a heritage of his undergraduate days in the Aggie Corps. Like that of any good Aggie, the chief's hair could be mistaken for a pair of military bristle brushes laid side by side, though it is seldom seen, since he keeps his Resistol kicker hat on virtually all the time, especially indoors. It was off now only because of his target practice. As if to correct this oversight in manners he stepped over to the filing cabinet where he had left it and put it on.

"You been away too long, boy," he said, looking down at me from all that bulk. "For all I know, in Washington, D.C., the women, they walk down the street shaking their tits and the men playing with themselves. But we ain't in Washington, D.C., are we?"

The chief opened a drawer of the filing cabinet.

"Yeah, like you said, Ace, it was some kid. No class, these kids today. I'd never a dreamed of just looking. No, sir, that's not the Aggie way."

"The way I hear it, any way is the Aggie way."

The chief paused over the cabinet drawer and gave me a solemn look. "Well, they's something to that. Anywhere they'll let an Aggie in, an Aggie's likely to go."

I could see the faded football just beyond him. The bookcase contained only four books, but resting on it, atop a kicking tee, was the football that was involved, twenty-four years back, in one of the most famous plays in the annals of Texas sports. The game was the historic Thanksgiving Day meeting with the hated "University," whose students are referred to as "tea-sippers" by Aggies. It had been played in a virtual monsoon on a field so muddy the players at times seemed submerged in it. With A&M trailing by a score of 3–0, and with the University punting from its own fifteen against a clock which showed but twelve seconds remaining, tackle Claude Flowers had broken through the two linemen prudently assigned all afternoon to block him, slid savagely toward the kicker, and not merely blocked the kick but, leaping high, caught it on the fly in his gut as it came off the kicker's toe—thereby completing perhaps the rarest of all football plays, an intercepted punt. Despite a gait which permitted half the Texas team to catch up with him, he dragged four tacklers across the goal line as the gun sounded. In the Friday papers, the prose of the Dallas sports editor had taken flight and rechristened the Aggie tackle. The yellowed clipping was preserved under glass in a picture frame hung above the football: "On a dying Thanksgiving afternoon in Austin, a freight train named Claude Flowers roared out of South Texas to geld the proud Texas Long-horn, raise high over the slop and slime of Memorial Stadium the A&M maroon and white, and blazon his name into Aggie immortality. . . ." The sportswriter wrote in Old Style. That play was surely the biggest moment in the chief's life, so far.

From the file drawer he got out one of those enormous cans of Mexican peanuts, brought the can back to his desk, got a can opener out of his middle desk drawer, opened the can, and emptied the contents into his peanut drawer with a sound like a dump truck discharging a load. He threw the can in his metal wastebasket with a crash that would have awakened the Second Cavalry had it still been quartered below. He sat, parked his Justins on the desk, and shoved back his Resistol.

"How did Miss Sally and the Carrutherses take the dese-cration?" I said. "Are they hospitalized?"

He gave me a crafty look and pulled at one of his long ears. I knew something was coming. Though I have always found Freight Train Flowers to be a man of integrity, this is not to say he is above cunning.

"Well, Miz Carruthers, her and I had a little talk and she waxed my ass. Said she considered it a serious breach of our law-and-order atmosphere. She's the only cow I know don't know what tits is for. Asked me what the town was coming to. You know how parents are. But Sally was pretty cool. She hasn't had a collapse or anything like that. Of course she didn't know she'd been visited till the next day."

"How did she find out?"

"She thought she heard this noise. Wasn't sure. Except that next morning she found these tennis shoe tracks outside her window. Also a cigarette butt in the grass. But the main way she knowed was she found something else."

The chief paused. I felt he was deliberately drawing this out. As if he had a case, for a change, and meant to make the most of it.

"Found what, for God's sake?" I said.

"Take a even strain, boy. She found a little present on her windowsill."

"A present?" I said in exasperation. "What do you mean, a present?"

"A little box wrapped neat as can be. Carruthers Mercantile couldn't a done it better."

I sighed. "All right, Chief. What was inside?"

"A strawberry."

"A strawberry?"

"A red enamel strawberry. Right pretty thing," the chief said in his deliberate tones. He slumped back in his chair. "I don't know why we talking about it. You can't print any of this nohow, that's sure and certain. I don't think the mayor or my employers the Town Council would relish any story in the *Clarion* about a Peeping Tom in Martha. No, sir."

He was right. It doesn't bother me, except now and then. I knew it when I bought the paper. I'm not down here to win any Pulitzer prizes. I gave all that up. I'm in Texas. Not that it amounted to anything anyhow. If I had been living in a free society I probably would have given it two paragraphs, without the strawberry. You couldn't print that anyhow, and it was the best part. Still, I would have a little talk with the mayor about running *something*. I had to keep a few principles, just for the principle of it. Screw it. All I really wanted was to get through my four days and back to my boat. The one just made the other possible.

"One thing they do in Washington besides walk down the street and play with tits, they have something that vaguely resembles a free press." I sighed and got up. "Well, I've got to drop in on his excellency. Thanks for so much news, Chief. I'm not sure we'll have room for all of it in one issue."

The chief's eyes held a far-off look. "Imagine seeing that like God made it. Musta been mighty nice. I always felt Sally Carruthers had about the prettiest red hair I ever seen. If nothing else comes of this, it's reassuring to know finally it's for real. Somehow makes you believe they's some honesty left in this world."

He came out of it.

"Yeah, it was a kid all right." He was pleased with his little triumph. "A kid would think up a gift like that, get a box, wrap it real neat. Just like you said, Ace. Some kid."

"All right, Freight. One for the Aggies."

I started out, then waited.

"You know something? Anybody who would leave a present like that for Sally Carruthers, that shows a touch of class."

"Yeah. Well, we got a couple a those around too. You looking at one of 'em." He gave a minor belch. "You behave, now."

He's probably right about that. I went out of the building with its cool shadows, into the warm sun of the parade ground, and back to the paper and phoned the mayor to tell him I was on my way out for our regular Monday session. Holly Ireland answered and said they'd had an unexpected "dressing" and Brother Ireland couldn't be disturbed.

"Mrs. Byram crossed over Jordan this morning," she said. "Why don't you drop out after supper and I'll give you a piece of fresh rhubarb pie? I know how you relish rhubarb pie."

I also relish seeing Holly Ireland. I said I'd be there and would look forward to the pie. I reminded myself to skip dessert at supper and told my employee to telephone the Byrams and get some material for a story on Mrs. Byram's crossing. I told her she could write the story herself, an assignment which did not provoke the enthusiasm you might reasonably expect from a recent journalism student.

3.
Jamie

The Martha *Clarion* is a two-room establishment and now a one man–one boy–one girl operation. The front room is the city room and the room for everything else concerned with filling the columns of the paper, both editorial and advertising. Entering the composing room is like going out of the sunlight into a cave. It is dark and dungeonlike, a place where unearthly creatures perform mysterious rites. If one squints and looks around, one sees peculiar stalagmite shapes: the Miehle flatbed press, a "stone" for making up the paper and another one to hold type, cabinets of fonts containing headline type. Also a V-50 letter press where I overprint labels for the Orville Jenkins canning plant and a small Chief 17 offset press, also for job printing. The whole effect is one of inkiness and blackness, and so is the smell, which I have loved since I was fifteen and went to work in such a place as a printer's devil. There aren't many papers left with the kind of equipment to be found in that room. Especially the pipe-organ-like Mergenthaler Linotype, five feet wide by five deep by seven feet tall and two tons of weight, with its repertory of sounds, grunts, roars, and little tinklings. When Mr. Mergenthaler invented his Linotype in 1886, it was one of the greatest breakthroughs since Gutenberg. Body type could now be set on "hot-type" slugs instead of by hand. Most papers used the Mergenthaler Linotype to set copy clear up into the 1950s, when this hot-type method began to be succeeded by computers and other cold instruments. The flatbed press itself has been pretty much done away with by the offset process. But the *Clarion* still has the old equipment and it still works, most of the time—thanks largely to Beto, the other member of the *Clarion* force and the master of the cave.

Beto, who is twenty-four, came with the paper. He learned the Linotype trade from his father, who was a Linotype operator on a San Antonio newspaper, and he learned about flatbed presses from the editor I bought the paper from, and of course he knows the V-50 and the Chief 17, which are kindergarten stuff by comparison. He loves the old Mergenthaler the way a true seaman loves a tall sailing ship. He knows its idiosyncrasies and those of the flatbed, and when they break down he can somehow get them running again. He is a hard worker. When he isn't using the machines he's caring for them with his physician's bag of oils and greases and odd-shaped tools—a geriatric care, since the Miehle is pushing fifty years of age and the Mergenthaler sixty-five. He has great pride in his trade. I think his attitude is that no matter how good the copy I come up with, it won't have any value if it's not printed, and he, Beto Rodriguez, is the one who makes that possible. Sometimes I think he looks upon my function on the paper rather as a driver of racing cars might look upon the man who puts gas in his tanks. Great pride. But we understand each other. I grew up with people like Beto. We understand wherein we are different and what we have that is alike, and that enables us to be together. It may be that we like the differences in each other more than any similarities. Besides setting the paper in type and getting it off the press, Beto does the outside printing that enables us to stay alive. He is his own man but he has good manners. Since I am his boss he would never say to me what Jamie told me he said to her not long after she came.

"Beto thinks you're a real flake-off," she said. "He told me that if you would get out and hustle, instead of going off to that island three days a week, there could be a lot more ads in the paper and a lot more printing jobs. Then we'd all make more money and the business would grow. That's what Beto says."

"Yes. Well, that only confirms one of my worst suspicions: We're corrupting the Mexican Americans with this work ethic."

"We agree you know your stuff as a newspaperman, but he wishes you weren't so lazy. Other than that, he thinks you're okay. For a boss. Beto says—"

"All right, all *right*. I don't want to hear any more. But after this if you talk about me, see that you do it on your own time. That goes for both of you. Otherwise you're going to be comprehending some new and vibrant meanings of the word 'boss.'"

"Oh, I never see Beto except here. It's the only place we could talk about you. He has no interest in me that way. I think I look too much like a boy to him."

That's a fact anyhow. At first I noticed that Beto looked her over carefully a couple of times as he does anything in her twenties. Then I could see he had decided she wasn't sexy enough for him. Beto likes long hair, large breasts, swaying hips, and a decent-sized ass. Jamie doesn't have even one of these requirements. I am just as glad. It would have interfered with the paper's operation. I could tell Beto liked having her around because she worked hard—she didn't "flake off" like certain other people did—and was interested in his work and eager to learn what he did on the Mergenthaler and the flatbed and that was that. They were friends.

One man, one boy, one girl. People peering through the window. Working dawn to dusk, dark to dark, at least on the four days I'm here. But you could never get me back to Washington. Even though I am at the mercy of businessmen, and my life is lived on the sufferance of dry-goods merchants, drugstore proprietors, hardware, feed-store and grocery-store owners, bankers, and undertakers, of everyone whose advertising dollars hold a bullwhip over me. And on the sufferance, too, of all local politicians, who always think they know what is best for the town.

* * *

At least twice a week I've thought about firing her, except that she's taken to doing so many things, without her I'd never be able to get out of the place.

We ordered the Bon Ton Monday-night special of beef stew, okra gumbo, homemade bread, and a salad of sliced cucumbers and tomatoes. A few hours earlier these last two had been growing in the earth, and the beef stew is so good that the ranch hands come to town for it. It's better food than I'd usually got in New York or Washington. I had hardly sampled the stew when she lit into me.

"Listen, Baxter," she said, "don't you think it's about time I covered something mildly important? I do everything but sweep out."

"That's the way it is in small-town journalism. It's a hallowed tradition. I've known editors who sweep out."

"I type up ads. I take those asinine Social Notes from those sappy women. I take down the classifieds. I do those little piss-ant stories over the phone on the Garden Club and the American Legion Auxiliary and the Literary Club. I've been here a month and I haven't been out of the *office*. Isn't it about time I covered a *story*?"

"In Martha those *are* the stories. No, I'm afraid you're too important a reporter to be taken off them. You've been coming along fine. I'm keeping my eye on you."

"Don't give me that bullshit, Baxter."

Angry, she leaned across the table. The pupils and irises of her eyes are the one brown color, with the effect of making you look at them. Her short, toast-colored hair bounces around when she moves her head, which she does a lot of. Her forehead is wide above the wide-set eyes, but then her face, with its high cheekbones, narrows down to a determined little chin. Good bones, as they say. She claims to be twenty-one but looks a lot less. If she sat on your lap I don't think you would know anything was there. Her jeans show a tight little rump that could give change for a dime. You can't even tell if she has breasts. She was leaning half across the table, almost in the bread basket.

"Sixty-five dollars a week! My mother pays her maids twice that, and they get room and board and color television.

Okay, and I don't even mind that this place is like the Roman galleys. But I do want to be able to cover a story now and then. So you better give me one. Otherwise I just might split. First, though, I'd report you to the wage board. You're in violation of a federal statute."

"I'm going to be in violation of another if you don't shut up and eat your beef stew. It's called infanticide. Unless they get me on the child-labor law first. I don't *have* any good stories."

"You better stop saying things like that about child labor. You better stop treating me like a child. There're a lot of things in this town we could cover and expose if you'd turn me loose."

"Turn you loose! Jesus God. That's all I need."

"Where's your initiative?"

"I left it in Washington. I came here to get away from initiative."

She looked at me. "You're chicken."

"Yes, I am. Please pass the bread."

She shoved it at me. "I mean it. Either you come up with a good story for me, or you may have to start looking for another slave."

I needed her but I didn't need this. I could hear a note of irritation enter my voice. "I've been under a serious misapprehension. I didn't realize you were sent down here to teach me how to run a newspaper. I thought the idea was for you to do what I gave you to do, mind your manners, look up at me, and say yes, sir, now and then. In short, to sit at my feet, I believe the operable phrase is, and learn."

"How can I sit at your feet when you're gone half the time? Every Friday or Saturday you just disappear. What do you do down on that island? I bet you go down there and sleep with women. You probably have one living aboard that boat of yours."

I stopped eating and looked at her. "What I do or don't do on that island is none of your business."

"Can I go down there with you sometime?" she said in abruptly dulcet tones. She can change direction like a sandpiper. "I'd be pretty useful around boats too, I imagine. We could talk about journalism and newspapers and reporting, things like that. I could sit at your feet. Can I go with you?"

"No."

"Then I'll go by myself."

"Your privilege. It's a big island. They let anybody on it."

She sat back and tacked away in another direction. That is, back on course.

"Well, what about it? Are you going to let me start doing some stories or not?"

She gave a distinct little hiccup. A look of annoyance came over her face.

"I get hiccups when I get nervous or uptight. You're making me uptight by not promising to give me a story."

"Swallow some water." I shoved a glass across the Formica, and she drank some.

"You're *using* me, Baxter." She leaned across the table. "Well, I'm going to use *you*. You wait and see."

"Then you shouldn't talk so much. That's your first lesson in how to be a good reporter. God gave you one mouth and two ears."

"Oh? Very witty. However would I have known if you hadn't told me?"

She gave that giggle of hers, a short, derisive little giggle, as if the world, and everything in it, starting with herself, was faintly ludicrous. I liked that part of her.

"How old are you, Baxter?"

"Forty-one."

"You're not bad-looking for someone that old."

"For God's sake, will you stop asking these personal questions and let me eat? You're here to learn the newspaper business. Period."

"All right, then. Let me learn. Give me a story to cover."

I put my fork down. It banged against my plate.

"Enough. That's *enough*."

I must have really raised my voice. She almost jumped. When she spoke it was in a little voice.

"I'm sorry. I was just trying to—"

"I know. I *know*. And I'm trying to help you."

"You don't have to be such a bear," she said shyly.

"Now if you want to listen to me and do as I tell you, I'd like to have you stay. You help out a lot, okay? If that's not good enough, you'd better go back to that school of journalism."

"I *hate* schools," she said with sudden fervor. "*All* schools." Then her voice turned meek again, almost respectful. "Besides, I figure I can learn more from you in two months than I can there in two years."

I fancied I heard the echo of Whiteside's pleasing words. "All right, all right. But if you want me to make a newspaperman out of you, you've got to do as I say. I'm not going to ram it down your throat. You've got to be ready, willing, and eager." I looked at her. "Is that clear?"

Her small lips pressed together. "I'll be that. Ready, willing, and eager. I want to be a newspaperman more than anything."

I shoved my plate away and pulled up my coffee. "Now that you've ruined my meal, pass the sugar and cream."

"But this town," she said. "God, it's like the walking dead."

I swallowed some coffee. "You'll be pleased to know something has happened. A Peeping Tom visited us."

"A Peeping Tom?" Her large brown eyes got larger. "Can I cover it?"

"There's nothing to cover," I said. "It's all over." I told her about it.

"Baxter," she said, "there's more to this than meets the eye."

I smiled. Sometimes she does amuse me. "From the amount he saw of her, I doubt it," I said.

She sat back and looked at me with those big eyes, and I could see her swallow.

"I'm going to learn from you and sit at your feet and all that, but . . . you've got to promise me." She swallowed again. "About that story. A real story. Either you do that or I'm leaving."

She hiccuped. She waited a moment and added, "Tomorrow."

I looked at her sitting there in that oversized man's white shirt. Now that she'd said it, I thought she looked scared. She hiccuped again. I suddenly laughed.

"Have some water." I shoved it in front of her. "All right. Except we don't have any real stories at this moment. If and when one comes along I'll think about it."

She pressed her lips together. "No, that's not good enough. Not think about it. You'll assign me to it."

"All right, all right. I'll *assign* you. Are you satisfied?"

I'd have to come up with something. I had no idea what. I looked at her sitting there. Now that she'd won everything, she was sitting very straight with her hands crossed in her lap, very prim, ladylike, and innocent-looking as a young lamb. Some lamb. I'd fix her at least a little bit.

"There's just one thing," I said. "If I'm going to let you out of the office, you'll have to buy a dress. I can't imagine what you look like in a dress, but the people in this town will expect to be interviewed by a young lady."

"Young lady!" Her hair bounced. "In Martha, Texas?"

"When a woman comes around asking a favor of them —which, in effect, a reporter is doing—they're not used to seeing her in jeans with her shirttail hanging out. And dirty sneakers. You wouldn't want to embarrass me or the *Clarion,* would you?"

"Je-*sus.* All right. I don't suppose you have a Neiman's here?"

"Not even a Saks."

"I guess I'll have to go to that garage-sale place on Cavalry. What's it called?"

"Are you speaking of Carruthers Mercantile? Ask for Sally Carruthers. She's the one who got peeped."

"Why do you think he picked her?"

"She's got red hair."

We finished our coffee and walked back in the night across the street to the paper. I had left the lights on. Her old MG was sitting in front. It looked as though it hadn't been washed in a year, and the dent looked about that old.

"Have you ever thought about having that front fender fixed?" I said.

"Yeah. I've thought about it."

We went in and I started to turn out the lights.

"I think I'll stay awhile," she said.

"You don't have to."

"The floor needs sweeping out."

Across the street I stopped and looked back. Nothing on the street is over two stories, and most places are one. All up and down it, except for the Bon Ton, the paper was the only lighted place left. It looked lonely sitting there with everything else darkened. I could see her through the window, beyond the large inscription, "The Martha Clarion." She wasn't sweeping the floor; she was seated at her desk, bent over it in concentration, going through a stack of something. She looked very tiny and determined sitting there. Suddenly I had a terrible feeling. Not from anything she'd told me—she hadn't told me a word—but just a sense of something. Her parents passing her around, shoveling her from one expensive school to another—I know that kind of family. Big Rich. Too Rich, I call them. A terrible feeling that she never had a father, a real father, or anything like it, and that I was in danger of being elected. I didn't want that. That was the last thing I'd come down here for. The very thought of it scared hell out of me. Absolutely negative, as we said in the Navy.

I walked out to the Irelands'. Nothing is very far away in Martha, Texas. On my way I took a little detour past the Carruthers house. I stopped a moment and looked at it. There was an unusual thing. The yard light in back was on. I like walking in the town and I was early, so I took a turn down this pretty block and that one. I looked up at the sky full of stars and listened to the branches of the trees murmuring in the soft night breeze. I have never seen the stars shine with the glory and numbers that they display here. Mountains, even hills, diminish the sky, and there was none of that. It is as though all that sky space lured out members and even galaxies of the great star family that hid themselves in skies elsewhere. By the time I had coffee at the Irelands' and walked back, the moon would be up. I was looking forward to hearing what the mayor had to say about the peeping of Sally Carruthers, to the rhubarb pie—and to seeing Holly Ireland. I always look forward to her. She is one of those few persons whose company I am always reluctant to leave. Every time I see her I violate another Commandment: Thou shalt not covet thy neighbor's wife.

Brother Ireland's honorary title derives from his profession of town undertaker. Also from his having been chairman of the board of deacons of the First Baptist Church more often than anyone else. He occupies this position at present, presiding over the deacons' monthly meeting at eight on Thursday as well as the Town Council at seven every Tuesday. The earlier start of the Council is to allow time for the poker game which follows.

Esau Ireland, at age sixty-three, is a toy soldier of a man. He carries his five feet five inches and one hundred thirty-five pounds with an erect, military bearing. He has a nickname, acquired late in life at the time of his marriage and used by the town boys: "Tit-High" Ireland, a reference to the fact that he gives away half a foot to his wife. He has a small, shining bald head and a round jowl-less face, pink and fresh as a baby's, with a more or less permanent look of disapproval, and penetrating bottle-green eyes. He is a dandy, a spiffy dresser. He is the only man in Martha who wears waistcoats. From October 1 to May 1 he wears blue serge and carries a black cane. From May 1 to October 1 he is all in white Palm Beach, matching shoes, and straw boater. And always, whatever the season, a fresh flower in his lapel—the town florist feels indebted to him. Despite his size he possesses a celebrated strength. He can turn the largest individual over on his table without assistance. On one occasion six strong men were carrying a two-hundred-pound Ireland client out of the First Baptist Church when the lead man stumbled on the steps, tripping up all but the rear bearer. In a moment the man inside would have been a second Lazarus had not Brother Ireland leaped forward, seized the container, and literally held the main weight of it on his shoulders until the fallen recovered.

He is the bitchiest individual of his sex I have known. He is wonderful company. He has a short fuse with fools, of whatever rank, and with stupidity of all kinds. He doesn't take any mouth from anybody simply because he's the big town banker or the big town produce man. He has a reedy voice that somehow is commanding and can put the fear of God into people. He is surely the most powerful man in Martha. Part of this comes from his deep roots in the town. No one's family goes back further. But mainly it is his strength of purpose. He has a way of making his views prevail when he has really made up his mind to something. It is almost as if other men of power are afraid to disagree with him, afraid his querulousness, his sheer mulishness, will turn on them, ostracize or destroy them in some fashion.

Some townspeople feel his talk is too free and easy, too bawdy for his somber profession. But what can they do? He has a monopoly. Everybody in town sooner or later has need of his services. Brother Ireland has a great outspoken fondness for women. "Women are what it's all about, Baxter," he once said to me. "Everything else is just to get through the day so you can be with them." He often says, "Once she reaches my parlor I treat the body of every woman as if she were my own wife," an expression many people find cryptic.

Esau Ireland is important to me in a number of ways. Ireland's Funeral Home is one of my best advertising accounts. Fortunately, Esau is a thwarted writer, like about three fourths of the population of the country. Only in his case he has the means to do something about it: a full quarter-page ad, every week of the fifty-two. It helps. The ad does not list any of the services offered by Ireland's Funeral Home. There's no need for that, since you take what you can get. Rather the ad is what in national publications is called a "prestige" or "image" advertisement. It consists of a column of about five hundred words which Esau writes every week under the title "The Quick and the Dead," giving his thoughts on life, philosophy, horticulture, or any other subject you care to name. Actually it isn't as bad as it sounds, sometimes.

People often wondered why Brother Ireland married after

doing without this state so long. They wondered even more what would induce Holly Pringle to marry him. Brother Ireland first met her on the day of her birth, at which time he was thirty-five years of age. Brother Ireland and the Pringle family had known each other all their lives. Holly grew up comfortably on a farm near Martha, well cared for by her parents, who, when approached by Brother Ireland, placidly had no objections and in a civilized manner left this important decision to Holly. She apparently could find no great argument within herself against the marriage. Perhaps it was that Brother Ireland lived in one of the nicest houses in town, that she wanted to live in town rather than in the country, and that he would take care of her, as her parents always had. A lot of marriages bring a great deal less than that.

Holly Ireland has a sense of languor, almost lethargy, about her. She seems rather like a fond pet, petted and pampered. Brother Ireland gives her anything she wants. "If Holly wanted a carriage pulled by six live reindeer right here on the Rio Grande, Esau would give it to her," someone said once. When Holly said one day that as a little girl she had always wished for a treehouse, he built her one in a splendid hackberry in the back yard right next to the main house. It is no ordinary treehouse. It is built of cypress and has a skylight. I have no idea how often she uses it, or what she does up there.

With all her sense of lethargy, Holly Ireland can come up with some sharp insights. I have sometimes speculated whether there was some depth in her that has never been brought out. Probably not. She's probably just what she seems. I think she lives in a dream world. But what world is more pleasant?

One gift from her husband has been taste, style in dress. Brother Ireland has an unusual interest in women's clothes.

"It began professionally," he once told me. "The clothes women wear, from the outside in—believe me, Baxter, I am a true authority on this subject, for I have undressed and dressed hundreds of them. It is a fascinating field, with many ramifications and bypaths. They do not just put on things like you and me. They *adorn* themselves. It became a challenge to me to have them leave better dressed than when they came in. If I may say so, I acquired a certain expertise. From there it was but a step to a general interest in the subject of female raiments."

His wife has benefited from his knowledge. She is always turned out pleasingly, often exquisitely. She has the structure for it, a model's body: tall, slender, with lanky legs. Her dresses tend to the soft materials, such as chiffon and challis, and the soft colors, mauve, apricot, and lavender. She wears broad-brimmed, sweeping hats, replete with feathers and veils. As a couple the Irelands make a fashion plate, coming into the First Baptist Church on the Lord's Day or strolling down Cavalry Street with her on his arm. It doesn't seem important that she towers over him.

She has that particular strain of extreme blondness of certain Scotch-Irish stock: the hair a shimmering white-gold, the skin almost translucently white. Those who possess it must shield themselves from the sun as from fire. It is sometimes marred, at least in the eyes of those with this genetic strain, by freckles, and this is the case with Holly Ireland. She told me once that she would give anything not to have freckles and not to be so tall. I don't think she believed me when I replied that I felt freckles gave a life to beauty and that tallness meant there was more of that beauty. She simply smiled her slow-forming, languorous smile. Her eyes are blue-green with a washed look to them. There might seem a virginal quality about her were it not for her mouth. It seems to give it all away. It is slightly large and the lips seem always just a bit open, ready to give some rare nectar. Everybody in town figures that Brother Ireland has a great thing going with his wife.

I had walked around enough. Soon, down the street I could see the Ireland house, a big, two-story structure of many high gables, planted like a battleship, heavy, solid, and dark gray, on two hundred feet of lawn. The first floor was Brother Ireland's place of business. The second floor, the living quarters. I walked up the circular driveway, past the hearse which is always parked there, at the ready. It may be the oldest hearse in Texas. Brother Ireland kept it pristine, its black exterior and its wire spokes glistening, its long windows spotless, to provide an unimpeded view of the contents. I moved past it onto the wide stairway, cresting on a deep porch spanning the length of the house, and rapped the knocker in the form of a large angel. I suppose this was the one who, it was hoped, bore you on the long flight from this house to heaven above. Holly Ireland answered.

"Come in," she said in those humid tones that made you know you wouldn't think of doing anything else. Her dress fluttered slightly in the soft breeze let in through the door. "Brother Ireland is working. Come on upstairs. I'll just give you a piece of rhubarb pie and see if he can get away from Mrs. Byram for a spell."

Few things in life are more satisfying than a fresh rhubarb pie. After letting myself be persuaded into two generous slices, I went over some items for the paper with Esau. Then, to my surprise, Brother Ireland brought up the peeping. We were seated over coffee around the table in the Irelands' spacious dining room. Chairs and table were of darkest mahogany. They would not have moved in a Force 10 gale.

"Well, it's something new for Martha," Brother Ireland said with the grave air of taking up the case for serious dissection. He sat like a ramrod in his chair. "It has to be connected to the Bloomer Girl Ball, of course. Do you suppose it could have been the Jenkins boy, Sugar? He had a date with her that night. I checked into that."

"Orville Junior?" Holly Ireland asked. "You're suggesting he went around and looked at her dressing, then came back and picked her up as his date?"

"That wouldn't be cricket, would it?"

"What a way to behave on a date," Holly said humorously. "Orville Jenkins surely brought his boy up better than that. That boy sings in the church choir."

"Are you saying that the fact he sings in the church choir means he doesn't like to look at the unclothed female figure?" Brother Ireland said. He was not one to let faulty logic pass. "Personally, I wouldn't put it past Saint Orville himself. It's something a pharisee would do. Two did in the scriptures. The Apocrypha. Susanna and the Elders. To my knowledge they were the first Peeping Toms."

"Oh, now, really, Esau. Orville Jenkins?"

"What kind of young lady is Sally Carruthers, Sugar?"

"What kind of young lady?" Holly Ireland has a habit of repeating a question asked of her, especially if it is asked by Brother Ireland. "A very proper young lady, I would say."

"All Martha young ladies are proper young ladies, Sugar," Brother Ireland said dryly. "Personally, I always had the feeling that behind all that Little Miss Muffet play-on-the-harp was a real little bitch who knows exactly what she has to sell and what a seller's market it is. She's not of a mercantile family for nothing. She may have enticed him. Whoever he is."

"Oh, now, Esau," Holly Ireland said in mild protest. "I've always found Sally Carruthers very sweet whenever she waits on me at the Mercantile."

"Anyone can be sweet if they're taking your money," Brother Ireland said.

"She's got such a nice figure," Holly said pleasantly. "I can understand someone seeing the Bloomer Girls and picking Sally to peep. I mean, if men are that way."

When she crossed her legs, as she did now, you heard the slightest whisper of her garments, the mystery of them.

"There's a considerable body of evidence men are that way," Brother Ireland said in judicious tones. His round pink face brightened, like a baby that has just thought of its rattle. "But I hadn't seen you in a Bloomer Girl uniform when I picked you."

"You hadn't peeped me either," Holly Ireland said.

"How do you know?"

"What a tease you are, Esau."

They both seemed to be making a game of this. Maybe this was one of the things that kept the shine on their love. I had a curious feeling that Brother Ireland was using the incident of the Peeping Tom as an aphrodisiac. He was a man of ardor. Also he had that bawdy streak to him.

"I surely think I could understand it if someone wanted to

look at you that way, Sugar, and succumbed to the temptation. Couldn't you, Baxter?"

I shifted in my chair. I think Brother Ireland enjoys the
knowledge that other men are jealous of what he has.
Indeed, I think that knowledge is one of his proudest
possessions. All the same, I would not be accountable for his
response should their admiration lure them across a certain
line.

"Indeed I could," I said. I was trying to strike the right
note, which would be admiration without undue eagerness.
"I can well understand someone having the temptation to see
Holly even without those lovely clothes she wears. And
succumbing to it."

"What a nice thing to say," Holly said. "About the clothes, I
mean."

Brother Ireland gave me a penetrating look, and for a
moment I was afraid I had gone too far. Then he pounced.

"Another suspect! You walked right into it, Baxter. So you
admit you like to look at the disrobed feminine form? Add to
that the fact you don't have one of these at home to gratify
this rabid urge of yours. Follow? You may well be the Peeping
Tom."

"Wasn't that an interesting present our visitor left,
Mayor?" I said.

"I think it's rather insulting," Brother Ireland said. "You're
a woman, Sugar. Wouldn't you agree?"

"No, he sounds romantic to me," she said.

"Romantic?" Brother Ireland said in surprise. "What's
romantic about it?"

"It just is," she said placidly.

Brother Ireland looked at his wife carefully for a moment,
then sipped his coffee. "Well, whether it's insulting or romantic, what we have here is very simple." He had the manner of
a man who had solved the case. "That little present gives it all
away. He had to prove something to himself, and now he's
proved it. I'm assuming it checked out or he wouldn't have
left the present," he said astutely.

I was careful not to look at Holly Ireland, that being my
reading too.

Esau drained his coffee. "We know why, but we'll probably never know who. He found out what he wanted to find out, and that's the last we'll ever hear of it. After all, how many redheads do we have in Martha?"

He stood up.

"Now I've got to go downstairs and finish dressing Mrs. Byram. She's waiting for me, and we mustn't keep a lady waiting. Not that the old bitch didn't keep me waiting often enough." Mrs. Byram had been postmistress. She had had a way of handling people who complained about the mail service: She held their mail a few days. As he prepared to leave, I was glad I wasn't Mrs. Byram. "Stay and have another piece of rhubarb pie if you'd like, Baxter."

"I may do that," I said. "Oh, Esau. I'm planning to run a little item in the paper. Nothing much. Just saying the peeping took place. Nothing indelicate. Not mentioning the strawberry, of course."

He paused, standing there in his very straight, toy-soldier posture, and reflected. "I'm not sure we should say anything. Speaking as the mayor, I don't think it'd be good for our community if Martha got a reputation for Peeping Toms."

"For Peeping Toms? You mean because someone looks in a window once?"

"That's just the point. It was a one-time thing, and now it's all over and done with. Why keep it stirred up?"

"Stirred up?" I was becoming like Holly Ireland, repeating questions. "Listen, Esau—"

"I shouldn't think the businessmen of Martha would relish seeing their town portrayed as a sanctuary for Peeping Toms."

"A sanctuary?" I said. "For God's sake, Esau. I'm talking about *two* paragraphs on *one* peeping."

"Shouldn't think they'd relish it at all." Relish is a terribly important word down here if you're speaking of whether important people do or do not favor something. "Don't ever forget, Baxter, that the advertisers are of some importance to the *Clarion*. Follow?"

"I appreciate the delicate way you put it, Mayor," I said.

"Journalism," Brother Ireland said. "I've never understood that particular profession, how those fellows' minds work. As far as I can tell, they're all oddballs. Always wanting to ruffle calm waters."

The phone rang and Brother Ireland picked it up.

"Ireland's Funeral Home," he said. "What can we do for you?"

Brother Ireland always came right to the point. He listened for a bit.

"Oh, my Lord."

I watched his face get tougher and colder as he listened. He listened for quite some time. The only thing he asked was "How long ago?" At the end he said, "All right, Freight Train. You and I better meet first thing tomorrow morning."

When he had hung up he stood there a moment, his hand still on the phone, then turned to us.

"Betty Oakes. A couple of hours ago. She saw him out the window and screamed so loud the neighbors came running. He got away. He was wearing some kind of mask."

The mayor looked at his wife and then at me.

"Another Bloomer Girl. What have we got on our hands in this town?"

I stood a moment in the darkness of the porch. The moon was up and the big Saint Augustine lawn shimmered in its light. I went down the stairway, past the sparkling hearse and along Hibiscus Street. At the intersection of Juniper I stopped and waited a moment. It was only three blocks out of the way. I turned right and walked up to it and stood looking at it in the moonlight. Every light in the Oakes house was blazing. The Peeper was certainly turning on the lights of the town.

PEEPER 2
Licorice and Raspberry

He had scarcely been able to wait for night to fall. The last shreds of twilight were leaving the sky and the stars just coming on station when he swung along Jonquil Street. It was a night of sweetness, of spring fragrance that seemed to envelop the town and him as he strolled along, his tennis shoes scarcely audible on the sidewalk. The scents of the lawns fell over him like kisses: the gardenias, the roses, the Confederate jasmine, even the mown grass. He could hear the first cicadas tuning up for their nightly concert.

He turned left at Ebony, walked three blocks and turned right at Goldenrod, walked a half block, and entered the alley between Goldenrod and Forsythia. He carried the wrapped gift for her. It was too large for his pocket. He walked down the alley between the high oleanders on either side and came to her latch gate set like a welcome mat in the hedge. He looked up and down the alley. All was clear, all was quiet. He went quickly and silently through the gate and across the grass to a Rio Grande ash tree. He stood in its dark shadow and looked at the small clapboard house that belonged all to her. It was a classic old Texas bungalow which she had restored and kept painted and pristine. It rested like a little jewel in its setting of shrubbery, gleaming white in the darkness, seeming the smaller and more charming for the large green lawn surrounding it. Light shone from the windows of two rooms: a corner room and one next to it with only a single small window, higher than the others. The latter light told him that his timing appeared excellent but that he had not a minute to lose. It was synchronized to her jogging stint on the banks of the irrigation canals—so many women in Martha cherished their fair complexions and timed their exercise to the hours of shadows. He slipped on his pantyhose mask, pulling it snug and comfortable, and moved swiftly from under the ash tree in a hunched position across to the high window and crouched in the schefflera shrub which rose tall outside it. With infinite care he brought his head up until his eyes were just over the sill. He parted the leaves.

She was lying back in the tub, sweetly recumbent. It was an old-fashioned tub with iron claws and now graced with a coverlet of foam. Only her head was above it, the extreme blackness of her hair, pinned up by some sort of device, a contrast against the whiteness of the foam. She lay in pure sensuous enjoyment, luxuriating, then sat up, reached into the soap dish, and began soaping her breasts. They were generous but not grossly so, quite widely separated. She moved the bar of soap over them in easy, circular motions, bathing and lathering them individually with care and gentleness as if they were a set of precious stemware. Now and then he could see the frictioned nipples, dark as raspberries, blessedly erect, aim through the froth. She took her time, nothing in haste. To some a bath is something to make you clean and get over with and out. To others it is a ritual of enjoyment and luxury. He was delighted that she belonged to the latter group.

At last she stood up, covered with the foam, and reached for a hand shower. She began to direct it over her body, the froth falling away, down her breasts, down her rounded belly; front and back she directed it, the water flowing down her body and removing the last shielding remnants. She replaced the shower and stood wet and glistening, her breasts thrust forward proud and cleansed. He looked and now saw her milky whiteness accented strikingly by the licorice burst between her legs. She bent and reached into the soap dish again, buried the bar of soap in the black corsage and began to move it circularly until the pubic hair was a bonnet of white foam. He could see her push the bar down into the foam and move it gently around until the froth flowed down the insides of her thighs. She replaced the bar, reached again for the shower, and, holding it close, sent its spray surging against her pubis. He watched her face. Its expression held a quiet satisfaction, a glimmer of lubriciousness. She replaced the shower and shut off the water, stepped out, and reached for a towel. At the same time he reached up, placed the wrapped, beribboned box on the windowsill, and left. He would be interested to see if she would be seen in them on the banks of the irrigation canals. It would tell him a lot, if she were. He reached in his pocket, found a cigarette butt, and dropped it on the grass.

He walked across the night-cloaked yard, under the ash tree, out the latch gate, closing it softly, and continued down the alley along the oleander hedge, taking off his mask as he went. What exhilaration he felt. What a fine schoolteacher she was. How foolish he had been to let the Betty Oakes experience scare him off for over a week. Who would have thought that such a dainty, well-behaved young girl would scream like that? Perhaps it was just a matter of the town's getting used to it, of realizing, based on experience, that the very last thing he wanted was to alarm or in any way hurt or give concern to the women.

He emerged from the alley onto Ebony Street, walked a block down it and entered another alley, went through two blocks and came out onto Gumwood Street, walked a block, and entered the alley between Hibiscus and Iris. He followed the alley until he came to another latch gate set in another stand of oleander, entered the yard, walked across the grass, and stood under an anacua tree and looked across the yard at the house. Its battleship-gray silhouette sat like a fortress on the lawn, its many high gables seeming like gun turrets reaching up to aim at the stars. The enormous hackberry tree held itself almost against the house. Suddenly in the distance he heard the bells of the First Baptist Church chime a hymn, and he waited until it was through.

> *Abide with me;*
> *Fast falls the eventide;*
> *The darkness deepens;*
> *Lord with me abide. . . .*

The chimes meant it was ten o'clock. There was plenty of time, but he should step lively. He looked up and saw the light he wanted, put on his mask and adjusted it snugly, and walked, hunched, crouched, over to the hackberry tree. He stood a moment in its shadow, looking up. Then he began to climb toward the treehouse there.

4.
The Men

The news was all over town. The Bon Ton, where I had breakfast, was abuzz with it. I had been able to lock up the paper ahead of time Thursday evening, with the idea of getting an early start Friday for Padre Island and the Gulf. After my huevos rancheros I stopped by the paper before shoving off and heard from Beto that Mayor Esau Ireland had called with an urgent message. I phoned back and was told in rather stern tones that he was calling an emergency meeting of the Town Council for that evening. Martha had never had anything like an emergency meeting. I felt a considerable annoyance thinking of my Grand Banks just waiting there for me. But I could not afford to miss that meeting.

"How's Holly, Mayor?" I asked discreetly. "How is she taking it?"

There was a pause. Then the stern tone again. "My wife is a very resilient woman," he said. "She is carrying on. I'm extremely busy now with all this, Baxter. I'll see you at the meeting."

"Will there be the usual poker game, Mayor?"

"It's just like you to ask a question like that, Baxter," he said, even more stringently. "Naturally there is always the poker game after any Town Council meeting."

Early that evening I was getting ready to go over to the meeting when I looked up to see the small figure of Miss

53

Jamie Scarborough, late of Odessa, Texas, and the Southern Methodist University Department of Journalism, standing at my desk. She was dressed in her uniform of jeans and oversize man's shirt hanging over them.

"I'd like to cover that meeting," she said.

"I was planning to cover it myself."

"Can't I at least go with you and help you cover it?"

"They wouldn't let you in."

"Well, they *have* to. They can't keep out women any longer. That's all gone. You probably haven't heard down here, but they've got women reporters in locker rooms now."

"Yes. Well, I'm sure the town councilmen will find that very interesting. I'll tell them."

"They've *got* to let me cover it. We've got a Constitution, remember? This is the United States."

"This is Texas, kid."

"How about if I just showed up?"

"They'd find some way to keep you out. Like shutting the door. I guarantee you, they won't have any women covering that meeting. It's a male enterprise. Besides, you wouldn't like it."

"Bullshit. I grew up with people like that."

I looked at her. I still hadn't got used to it. "Besides," I said, "we play poker afterwards."

"Poker!" Her eyes lit up. "I learned poker when I was five. I'm *very* good. I bet I could clean you all out."

"Well, we can't have that. I'm the big winner. Move your legs, will you? I want to get in this drawer."

"They probably let you win. It sounds to me like they've got you in their pocket, Baxter. If I were you I'd be careful they didn't make me their house nigger. You ought to take me along for that reason alone. They wouldn't pull any wool over *my* eyes. Just let them try to suck up to *me* like they seem to be doing to you."

I thought of my advertisers and how they controlled, one way or another, almost everything I printed.

"Some sucking up."

I opened the drawer and found a notebook.

"You *promised*." She leaned halfway across the desk. Her

brown eyes were snapping. "You said I could cover the first story that came along. Are you going to go back on your solemn *word*? Are you going to be a *liar* on top of everything else?"

"Lower your voice fifty decibels, will you?"

The little bitch really wore me down. But my God, she was useful. She had cut my workday from twelve hours to nine or ten, and I hadn't missed my three days on the island since her second week at the paper. She went beavering all over the place. To all the editorial side of the paper, plus the classified ads, she had now added proofreading and bill-making and has begun to follow Beto around to see what he did.

She must have seen I was counting up a few virtues. Sometimes I think she can read every thought I have. Uninvited, she perched her little rump on the desk as if to make sure I didn't get away.

"Well?"

"I think I have something," I said. "This story concerns men and it concerns women. The women might tell you things they wouldn't tell me. Why don't we both work on it."

She looked at me suspiciously. "Where do I start?"

"The first thing you do is interview the women who have been peeped."

Her eyes lit up. She knew a good assignment when she saw one. "Well, I must say, that's more like it. Do you promise to run the interviews?"

"I'll have to see them first. No editor is going to commit himself to running stories he hasn't seen. Especially if he's dealing with total inexperience."

"Fair enough." She looked closely at me. "If they read okay, you won't hold them out for any other reason?"

I really didn't know the answer to that. Something was just starting, ever so slightly, to build up in me.

"Listen, you've *got* your assignment." I could hear my voice rising, with that warning note in it. "You claim to be such a great poker player. Hasn't anyone ever told you to quit when you're ahead?"

"Okay," she said meekly, doing one of her sandpiper

changes. "I'm grateful, I really am. I'm going to do you a good job. You'll see."

It has been said that the best poker players, in no particular order, are the Chinese, the Jews, and the Texans. Whatever the reasons for this excellence, there is scarcely a town in Texas where poker is not important. I often have the feeling when covering a meeting of the Martha Town Council that the principal object is to get the town business over with in order to get to the really important matter of the evening, the poker game that follows. One of the chief inducements to running for town councilman is that with it goes membership in the game. The chief of police and I are the only non-councilmen allowed in it, simply because we are always present for the council meeting itself. Although a game would still follow, the emergency meeting was different. This time the town business was a matter of importance.

The town council room in the old Cavalry Post has the same favored prospect as the office of the chief of police, which it adjoins. French doors open onto a wide piazza overlooking the parade ground. The room itself is singularly bare. Its centerpiece is an exceptionally large round oak table, at which both town business and the poker game are conducted. It is dented from shoes and cowboy boots, scratched by poker chips, burned by cigarettes, stained by the rims of cans of Lone Star beer. A shade light hangs just over it for the purpose of seeing poker hands more clearly. A small staff in the center of the table flies the flags of the United States and Texas. The flags flutter slightly from the ceiling fan which whirs over the table. The only other items of furniture are wooden armchairs and a noisy old refrigerator in one corner. I have never seen anything in it but Lone Star and Dr Pepper.

The bareness of the russet wooden walls has only a few interruptions: an oval-frame portrait of Robert E. Lee, in honor of the time he functioned in this building; a neck collar said to have been worn by his war-horse mare, Grace Darling; a smaller photograph of Black Jack Pershing, in honor of the time he chased Pancho Villa across the border around Martha, and a pair of spurs said to have been used by him; and, inevitably, a stuffed animal head, this one a Longhorn with prodigious horns sticking out into the room far enough to constitute a traffic hazard. Even the horns have dents in them.

Brother Ireland, in his no-nonsense fashion, brought the meeting to order.

"Councilmen, we all know why we're here," he said. "Freight Train, bring us up to date."

"Troops," the chief of police said, "let me see if I can just pull this situation together for you."

The chief's habitual use of this form of address carried no tone of superiority, such as that of an officer addressing enlisted men. Everyone understood that "troops" simply reflected the chief's years in the Aggie Corps.

"To date we have had a total of four peepings. The first was Sally Carruthers, the night of the Bloomer Girl Ball. The second was Betty Oakes, also a Bloomer Girl. At that stage I figured the Peeper was after the Bloomer Girls, and my thoughts turned to throwing some kind of protection around them. After all, it only involved them ten girls—eight, if he didn't go back for seconds."

The chief pushed his big Resistol hat back and went on in his slow cadence.

"Then he threw us a curve. He peeped a non–Bloomer Girl, Kathryn Shields, the schoolteacher, and then his first married woman, Esau here's wife."

The other four councilmen looked solemnly at Brother Ireland. The mayor showed no change of expression but kept looking steadily at the chief of police, who continued.

"We don't have much what I reckon you would properly call evidence at this point. I went out to all the places afterwards—Carruthers, Oakes, Shields, Ireland—and had a look around. They was some tennis shoe tracks. And he smokes. One butt each at Carruthers', Oakes', and Shields'. Two at Ireland's. Camels."

"Does that suggest he looked longer at Holly Ireland," Councilman Bert Hooper asked brightly, "than at the other young ladies?"

"It could suggest such a thing," Freight Train said gravely.

"Please proceed, Freight," Brother Ireland said somewhat stiffly.

"But they's something more important than the physical evidence. Betty Oakes was peeped the night her folks was out of town. The thought occurred as to whether the Peeper knowed that. So I checked the *Clarion*. Sure enough, they was an item in the Social Notes last week that the Oakeses was going to San Antone for a few days."

From their posts at the round table the councilmen all looked at me, almost as if I were responsible for the peeping of Betty Oakes.

"Mrs. Oakes phoned the item in herself," I said. "All of you and your wives have contributed to that column dozens of times. Voluntarily. Not to say eagerly."

"So the Peeper, he musta seen that item," the chief continued, "and it likely had something to do with his choice of Betty Oakes for Number Two. Betty was the one who got a glimpse of him, mask and all, and screamed like a wounded ki-o-tee. Musta put a scare in him, because he waited over a week before starting up again. Then it was Kathryn Shields, taking her regular bath after jogging. Inside knowledge again. We come now to the case of Miz Ireland."

The chief paused. He tilted his hat forward, didn't like it that way, and pushed it back again.

"Thursday night was the regular meeting night of the Baptist Board of Deacons, whose chairman is Esau here. It's also the night Miz Ireland was peeped. Obviously the Peeper, he knowed if he wanted to get a good look at her alone in the house, the time to do it was Thursday night. He also knowed the Irelands got a treehouse, so that looking at Miz Ireland on the second floor didn't present no problem."

The chief paused to let all this be digested. Everyone must have seen the implications, but he summed them up.

"The Peeper, he had detailed knowledge of the town. He had *specific* information. He planned each peeping, picking the suitable night and the suitable hour of the night. After looking at them various ladies, he left a present on the windowsill. Betty Oakes probably missed hers account of all that yelling she done. Nicely wrapped up presents. The strawberry for Sally Carruthers, the jogging shorts for Kathryn Shields, the book of poems for Esau's wife. Whatever they mean, he sure wasn't peeping at no strangers."

From the chief's great belly came an almost inaudible belch. His belches had many meanings. One of them, in my experience, was to signify something portentous.

"Troops, all this adds up to just one thing. The Peeper ain't some Mexican drifter or some kid wanting a quick one. He's someone that knows this town real good: the people in it, their habits, what they do, and when they do it. He's someone *we* know. He's someone we see every day. He's a citizen of Martha."

I expect by now everyone had reached this same conclusion. Nevertheless, a sense of shock settled over the room to hear it put on the record so flatly. In the profound silence I was conscious of the buzzing of the cicadas on the Cavalry parade ground through the wide piazza doors. I'd never seen the councilmen so somber.

"Well, I'd say we have a Grade A crisis on our hands," Orville Jenkins said. "I can figure an outsider coming here and trying to get a look at our women. We've got some of the best-looking women you'll find anywhere, even for Texas. It's hard for me to believe it's one of our own. I'm not sure I believe it even now. But assuming it is, what are we going to do?" Councilman Jenkins believes in making decisions and executing them.

"That's what we're here for, Orville," Brother Ireland said. "To decide that question."

"It's what comes of this anything-goes attitude," Jenkins said. "They see everything in these magazines, then they want to see the real thing. I know we've banned that trash here, but what good does it do? You can get it all just nine miles away across the river."

"Yes, we know," Esau said, a trace of impatience in his voice at the prospect of another of Councilman Jenkins's sermons. "We know what you can get across the Rio Grande. The point is, he's amongst us and we can't just ban him."

"It's cowardly," Jenkins said. "In my book, when you go

after defenseless women, you've crossed over the line. I've never believed in lynch law, but I might make an exception."

"First you have to catch him," Councilman Hooper said with his bright air.

"Yes, first you have to catch the scoundrel," Councilman Jenkins said grimly. "We will, never fear. Even if I have to turn out every man in my employ to scour every alley in town."

That would be a small army of men. Orville Jenkins is the town's biggest produce man, and produce is by far the biggest industry of Martha. He ships trainloads and truckloads of vegetables to the north. He has his own fields and he buys the crops of others, here and in Mexico. His complex of block-sized packing sheds stands like some huge army depot on the edge of Martha. In addition, he owns a large canning factory. One of my chief sources of revenue at the paper is overprinting his canning labels, part of the *Clarion*'s jobprinting sideline. It is quite lucrative and is just about the difference between the paper's staying in business and folding. Anyone listening to Orville's conversation, even on weekdays, would know soon enough that he is an active church man. Some people call him Saint Orville. If he had been present when Jesus, defending from the mob the woman taken in adultery, suggested, "He that is without sin among you, let him first cast a stone at her," Orville would have started looking around for a rock. He doesn't smoke, drinks only beer, and then only while playing poker, and, he makes clear, sleeps only with his wife. He is fifty-two. He stays very fit, both from his work, which keeps him on the move through the fields of vegetables, and from his religious principles about the care of the body as the temple of the Lord. Both body and face are square and sturdy. His thick, handsome, neatly barbered hair goes back in steel-gray waves. He stands foursquare straight, shoulders back, a legacy of the two years he spent at the Texas Military Institute in San Antonio. He is not a bad man, only a self-righteous one.

"I was just thinking, by God, they were good choices," Bert Hooper said. "Sally Carruthers, who I consider the Number

One Bloomer Girl. Betty Oakes and Kathryn Shields, both good lookers. And then Holly Ireland. I hope I'm not out of line, and begging your pardon, Esau, but he picked the best-looking wife in town."

Brother Ireland looked thoughtfully at his fellow councilman. "No pardon needed, Bert."

Councilman Henry Milam spoke up. "Strictly between us, I never thought Betty Oakes was all that much."

"Personally," Hooper said, "I would have picked Holly for the very first one."

"Well, after all, she was the first *wife* picked," Brother Ireland pointed out, as though in the interests of accuracy. I felt his reaction to the turn of events was quite complex —outrage over the actual peeping mixed with considerable pride.

"So we know one thing already about the Peeper," Bert Hooper said. He had the eager air of a man who was on to something. "Where women are concerned, the fellow has taste. He goes first class. I wonder who'll be next."

This speculation brought a solemn silence over the meeting, in which everyone seemed to be reflecting on the question raised by Councilman Hooper. He is the town banker, by inheritance; a Rotarian, by natural selection; a college graduate, by generosity of the University of Texas. He is the same height as Freight Train—six feet one inch —but this frame carries only a hundred-sixty-five-pound body, kept in splendid condition by daily swims in his pool. When he smiles, only his lower teeth show. Sandy red hair sits above a smooth tanned face adorned with a carefully cultivated carrot-red mustache of the guardsman species. I am sure he fancies himself as dashing. He is thirty-eight. He knows for a fact that he cuts quite a figure with the pretty tellers in his bank, and I would lay fine odds he's had a selection of them over the years, both Anglo and Mexican. Bert Hooper is not terribly bright but he doesn't have to be—his family has so much of the money in town. In one area he is bright enough—in getting the edge in any business dealing. His bank holds the mortgages on both my paper and my boat

"What kind of man would do a thing like that?" Council-man Henry Milam was asking. "You have any thoughts on that, Freight Train? Might start us thinking about who it could be."

The chief waited, his creased face set in careful thought, as if recognizing the importance of the question and wanting to give it his shrewdest answer.

"If you thinking, can we start looking around for someone who acts kinda peculiar, Henry, I don't think so. My guess is he's probably about like anyone else during the day. After all, what he likes doing ain't all that unusual. Just about every man I know enjoys looking at naked women."

"Most of us don't hide in the bushes and look through windows at night to do it," Milam said. "Most of us manage to find other ways to look at naked women."

Henry Milam has the Lone Star beer distributorship, which his family has held since the founding of that eminent company. It is like owning an oil well that will never go dry. Henry really needs to spend only about an hour a day on his job but usually spends more. "I have to test each shipment," he says with his dry humor. "Quality control." The Lone Star Company has a certain importance to me. Like Ireland's Funeral Home, they run a quarter-page "image" ad every week. At Trinity University in San Antonio, Henry was a high hurdler. He was nothing like the jock Freight was—after all, *nothing* is as big as football in Texas—but he was not bad. He placed second in his event in the Texas Intercollegiate Track and Field championships and would have placed first had he not knocked over the last hurdle, an incident that I have an idea he has never forgotten. He has maintained his wiry, lean, angular body in good condition ever since, so much so that he appears slightly gaunt. Every dawn he jogs down the silent streets of Martha—I have often seen him doing it, usually when I was coming in at the other end of the night—smelling the yellow rose and hearing the green jay and the grackle fussing as they come awake. As Marthans go, he is well read. He and I even discuss books now and then, at the counter of the Bon Ton Cafe. Out of a genetic inability to say no, plus all that free time his Lone Star patrimony leaves him, he gets trapped into town projects such as running the Kiwanis Club pancake supper and organizing the Martha Children's Home. He is good at these things, and the refrain has long since been established, "Let Henry do it." Henry always does. His real love is choral singing, and he sings tenor in the church choir. If tenors are the rarest of male birds, Henry is suprisingly good, and it is no embarrassment to hear him head for the high notes in "A Mighty Fortress Is Our God." Now close to fifty, he is the hardest-working member of the Town Council and the best, after Esau. The other members have a protective, kindly feeling toward Henry. He supplies Lone Star beer free for the Town Council refrigerator.

"I agree with Henry," Orville Jenkins said. "I think it takes a most peculiar man to do a thing like that."

"I'm not saying he ain't a bit peculiar *inside*," Freight Train said gravely, weighing his words. "All I'm saying is that he can carry on his regular business, whatever that is, and still do this other thing at night. That's my guess. Matter of fact, I'd go so far as to say that makes it a pretty intelligent man we're looking for. Not every man could do that. Not to mention all that careful planning on when to practice his hobby. I figure he's probably cooler than the average, more self-controlled, certainly cleverer than most. A shrewd fellow all around. Likely handles himself real well in a tight situation. I think we'd make a serious mistake, troops, if we underestimated our quarry. If you ask me I'd say he was double-smart."

The mayor turned to Councilman Sherman Embers, who had not spoken since the meeting began. The lawyer was neither shy nor inarticulate. But as he once explained to me in his cynical way, "If you keep your mouth shut till last, everybody will think what you say is important."

"What do you make of it, Sherm?" Esau said.

"Do you men know what's the biggest problem we're going to have? It's even suggesting who it might be. Accusing a man of something like that. . . . He'll sue you from here to Big

Bend and back. As a lawyer I'd advise all of us against naming names. Unless you see him some night looking through a window."

"But he's not necessarily abnormal?" Councilman Milam said.

"Hell, Henry, who's to say what's normal and what isn't? All I know is we can't have it." He gave that laugh of his with little or no mirth in it. "He isn't following the rules. We can't have another man playing by an easier set of rules than we ourselves have to obey. Looking at all that nooky free. If I have to work for it, why shouldn't he have to work for it?"

"That's an interesting way to put it, Sherman," Saint Orville said. "Very humorous. The Bible has something to say about men who look on women to lust after them." I wasn't certain whether the reference was to the Peeping Tom or a veiled reference to some of Sherm Embers's own well-known habits. "Matthew five: twenty-eight."

"Yes, I've read it, Orville," the lawyer said. "I've also read that the devil can cite scripture for his purpose. Shakespeare, *The Merchant of Venice*: Act One, Scene Three."

Sherman Embers is the most independent man in Martha. He came here twenty-six years ago right out of the University of Chicago law school and has been here since. Although genuinely liked by most people, he has never been fully accepted by the town's upper stratum. He drinks more than most. Everyone knows he screws around. It is hard to find anyone in Martha who has even one divorce, but Embers has been married three times. One of his wives was a girl he brought with him from Chicago, one was a local Anglo girl, and the third a local Mexican girl. Now he is not married to anyone, but everyone in Martha knows that Sherm Embers has to have women. He takes no known exercise—"Sherm screws for exercise," people say—but he is fit-looking, flat-bellied, keen-eyed, handsome, clean. Flecks of gray sprinkle the temples of his black hair. There is a sardonic cast to his mouth. He dresses well, and differently from almost any man in Martha, in expensive sports jackets and slacks. He is now fifty. At that age he ran for the Town Council and was surprised to get elected, he once told me over his Ezra Brooks. But then he has done legal chores and favors for a lot of people. If on the personal side he is what is called lecherous, it has yet to be determined by the evidence of centuries whether lechery is a vice or a virtue. I have known a number of women, a sex which after all ought to be considered the final word in the matter, who viewed it as, on the whole, the latter.

Freight Train Flowers was summing things up in a meditative tone. "I hate to say this, troops," he said, "but the way I see it, every man in Martha is a suspect."

Put that way, a sober quiet fell over the gathering. Brother Ireland cleared his throat.

"While we're trying to figure out which one he is among that considerable list of suspects," he said, "one thing I'm sure we can all agree on is that we've got to keep this thing quiet. Lots of reasons, but I can think of a couple right off. One is, it's an insult to our women to have this thing going on in the first place, and dragging it out in the open would only make it more of an insult. Also, it would be bad for business if it got around that Martha is a town where this sort of thing goes on."

"Amen," Orville Jenkins said. "My produce boxes go all over the country. Every one of them says Martha, Texas, on it in big letters. Let's keep a good reputation associated with that name, gentlemen. It's had it up to now."

Brother Ireland turned pointedly to me. "Follow, Baxter?"

"For God's sake, Esau, it's all over town," I said. I was beginning to feel I had a story on my hands. It would be the first in a long time, and whether I willed it or not, old juices were starting to flow. "Everybody in town knows about it. What do you mean, keep it quiet?"

"I don't care if everybody knows it," Brother Ireland said. "We just don't want it in print."

He glared at me and I glared back. He took his watch out of his vest pocket.

"The ladies should be here," he said, "and we mustn't keep them waiting. Freight Train, three of the four have consented to give us their testimony, I believe. I understand Betty said she couldn't do it."

"That's correct, Mayor. She said she'd be just too embarrassed in front of all you councilmen. The thing itself was enough of an ordeal, she said, too scary. But her and I talked, and I took some notes. So we got three. Which one you want first?"

"In the order of peeping," Esau said. "Let's start where the Peeper did."

All of us stood. Sally Carruthers was in blue. She wore a pleated blue skirt, a white blouse with old lace at the collar, blue shoes, and a sleeveless blue vest with covered buttons, and she carried a blue purse. Her hat was a little blue thing which sat on the back of her head, and that flaming glory that was her hair burst from beneath it and fell to her waist. She presented a picture of modesty and self-assurance. She said hellos around the table. Every one of us had been waited on by her across the counters of Carruthers Mercantile. Every one of us had heard her play the harp at the First Baptist Church, every one seen her perform dozens of times with the Bloomer Girls.

"We're much obliged you could come, Sally," Brother Ireland said. "We need your help. Won't you sit here?"

She took a seat at the round table between the mayor and the chief of police. She brought with her the propriety that women bring to men in male settings. The councilmen, who had been sitting in various leisurely positions before her entrance—slouched in their chairs, feet on the table sometimes—now sat up like proper councilmen. The chief even took off his hat. She gave a fragrance of freshness and girlish youth to the old cavalry room. I felt a dashing young lieutenant might have come riding back for her, perhaps after tying a yellow ribbon in that gorgeous hair.

"Miss Sally," Freight Train said, "this thing, it's got a lot more serious than any of us thought. When it was just you we thought it was a prank. Well, it's no prank. It ain't no one-time thing."

"I'll help any way I can, Chief Flowers," she said brightly.

She seemed entirely in control of herself and of the situation. "I can't tell you very much."

"Yes, ma'am," Freight Train said discreetly. "Ah, if I could just ask this, Miss Sally. Looking back, how long do you think he looked at you?"

"How long?" she repeated. "I have no way of knowing. I just know that he must have been looking at me when I heard that noise."

"Ah, yes, the noise. I wonder if you remember what you was doing when you heard that noise. What we're after here is, if we can figure how he operates, maybe it'll help us to nab him. Do you recollect?"

The chief's huge frame shifted a little in his chair, his impressive belly coming out confidently to meet the table. I had cause again to admire the big man's skills. His bearing toward her was one of circumspection and understanding over a difficult experience, his manner quiet and easy. The differing sounds of the two voices—her soprano, spirited and girlish, his bass, lingering and rhythmic—made a pleasing counterpoint.

"I was sitting on the bed brushing my hair."

"Ah-h, yes. Do you recall what you was wearing at that particular time?"

"Why, yes. My panties. I had just put my panties on."

"Yes, ma'am. Nothing else?"

"Nothing else."

The chief of police nodded. It was perfectly normal, the nod said, for a girl to be sitting there like that brushing her hair. Certainly it was in Martha, Texas.

"Right before that—I hope you don't mind these details too much, Miss Sally. They's a purpose."

"I understand," she said. "Not at all."

She smoothed down her skirt. She was sitting very straight, hands folded neatly in her lap, head up, all ease and confidence.

The chief pushed his hat back. "Right before that—right before you heard the noise, at which time you was sitting on the bed in your panties brushing your hair—what was you doing right before that?"

She took a breath. "Well, I'd taken a shower and I came out of the bathroom drying myself, and then I went over to the bed where I'd laid out my things—"

"The towel still around you?"

"No, sir."

There was a little pause.

"Please continue."

"I went over to the bed and sat down—"

"Was you facing the window where you was to hear the noise?"

"Yes, sir."

The chief cleared his throat. "At that time, not wearing nothing?"

"I'd just taken a *bath*."

"I wasn't criticizing, Miss Sally. Just establishing the circumstances. So you sat there like that on the bed facing the window? Nothing on at that particular time?"

"For just a little bit. Then I put on my panties and sat back down."

"Ah-h, yes. So from here on out you in your panties. And commenced brushing your hair, when you was interrupted by that noise."

"I went over to the window and looked out. I guess I should say I *squinted* out. I can see about two feet without my glasses. I heard some grackles fussing. I *thought* that was what I'd heard. So I went back and sat down and finished brushing my hair."

"You didn't pull down the shade?"

"Why, no. Nobody ever does that in Martha. I didn't think it would hurt what the grackles saw."

She smiled, and there was quiet, appreciative laughter around the table.

"Real nicely put, Miss Sally," Freight Train said. "I don't reckon grackles specially like to look, at that."

"Only at other grackles, I imagine," the young lady said. Everyone laughed again. Brother Ireland looked around the table as if to say that was about enough of the levity. A proper solemnity returned as Freight Train continued the interrogation.

"So you don't rightly know whether he stayed on after the noise or got scared and left, do you?"

"I haven't the remotest."

"So he could of been there five minutes or he could of been there thirty. Being as how you was in your panties and nothing else all that time, I'd lean to the last figure."

The chief looked down at his Justins, then back up.

"I hope this ain't been too much of a ordeal for you, Miss Sally. Oh, they's just one other thing. Who was your date for the Bloomer Girl Ball that night?"

"Why, it was Orville Jenkins." She looked across the table at Councilman Jenkins and giggled a moment. "I mean Orville Junior."

"Chief," Councilman Jenkins interrupted, "what is the intent of this line of questioning?"

"No intent," the chief of police said agreeably. I looked at him and wasn't sure. "Just trying to get all the facts on the table. I think that's about it, Mayor."

Brother Ireland looked around the circle of councilmen. "Any questions?"

"I have one. Sally," Bert Hooper said. He gave his lower-lip smile. "Your caller left that little present on the window-sill, the package with the strawberry. You have any idea what it signifies?"

The banker likes to make people squirm. She didn't.

"I haven't the remotest," she said distinctly.

There was a rather long silence, during which the council-men mainly looked down at the table.

"Well, Sally," Brother Ireland said, "on behalf of the Council I want to thank you for your cooperation. We're trying to stop this person from seeing more Martha ladies the way he's seen four of you already. Four are enough."

"Anything I can do to help, Brother Ireland. I understand your problem," she said sympathetically.

We all stood with her. She smoothed down her skirt. " 'Bye now," she said and went out smartly. We all watched her leave, the long strawberry-blond fall following her like a train.

One expected almost anything from the next witness, Kathryn Shields, the English teacher and maybe the best teacher in the high school. She is bright and outspoken. "Sometimes I think Kathryn is out to change the whole relationship between Texas men and their women," someone once said. Kathryn was delighted when the remark got back to her. "It could stand some changing," she said. "Like from top to bottom." Actually people have an admiring attitude toward her, though there is some head shaking. People around here admire spunk. They admire even more the underdog, especially if it is a bitch. She has striking aspects. A crisp and purposeful stride with a very slight twist to the hips, high firm breasts, a complexion of milk, black hair, and, especially, terrific legs. She probably came with these, but her daily jogging on the banks of the irrigation canals that crisscross the town helps keep them that way. There is a saying in town that every girl in her classes adores her and every boy is in equal parts scared of her and wants to get in her pants. About as much chance of the latter, the saying further goes, as of the Rio Grande freezing over.

Even with Kathryn Shields, the members of the Town Council were a little surprised when she appeared for her testimony in the jogging shorts the Peeper had left her. They were very good-looking, as was what came out of them. The shorts were a soft material with slits up the side and a brilliant red piping. Her testimony took about two minutes.

Freight Train: "You didn't get a look at him, Miss Kathryn, or hear anything?"

Kathryn: "Nothing. He was completely sneaky, like so many men."

Freight Train: "Yes, ma'am. Now—"

Mayor Ireland: "You must not be too outraged, Miss Kathryn. You're wearing his present."

Kathryn: "Well, they're the best jogging shorts I've ever had. I couldn't afford them myself, not on what you people pay schoolteachers."

Freight Train: "Yes, ma'am. Now, Miss Kathryn, you wouldn't have any idea how long he was at your window. I believe . . . that is to say, I think he seen you in your bath."

Kathryn: "No, I don't know how long. What difference does it make?"

Freight Train: "We just trying to get at the facts here, Miss Kathryn."

Kathryn (a sharp note coming into her voice, rising, turning into belligerence): "Well, the *facts* are as follows: I was taking my bath. He saw me taking it. How much of it he saw, I have no idea. That's the sum total of the facts. Except that it scared hell out of me when I found out about it, and made me wonder what kind of men we've got running this town, to let a thing like that happen. Now I have to go around town guessing which one of you men saw me take my bath. If you're through, I'd like to do my jogging."

Freight Train: "That's a very efficient summation. Yes, ma'am. We want to thank you, Miss Kathryn, for dropping by."

Kathryn: "I didn't drop by. You summoned me."

Freight Train: "Yes, ma'am."

She got up, and we all rose as she sashayed out. All seven of us stood looking thoughtfully at her going away in her jogging shorts. When she had gone, Freight Train said one more thing.

"Well, they sure fit, don't they? He musta knowed her exact size."

We remained standing to greet Holly Ireland. She was tall, slender, and handsome in a soft mauve jersey dress which brought out her white-blond coloring. She moved with a natural grace and sinuousness of which I felt she was entirely unaware. She knew everyone present well. She gave us all that soft, languorous smile. She took the chair offered her between her husband and Freight Train.

"Mayor," the chief of police said, "shall I conduct the questioning? Or would you prefer to do that yourself?"

"Why, you conduct it, of course. This is official business." Brother Ireland looked at his wife. "Isn't that so, Sugar?"

"Well, it isn't a party," Holly Ireland said and proffered us that smile again. It was like a nice, warm gift, freely given. It helped ease the tension natural to the situation. Freight Train began, gently as before.

"Miz Ireland, tell us first. When did you know he was at the window?"

"Well, the way I know the time is that Brother Ireland was late getting home from the Deacons and I looked at the clock. It was ten thirty-five. He's generally home by then."

"I stopped by Appleby's for some emergency formalde-hyde," Brother Ireland said. "I usually order my own direct, but I've had three expirations this week. Helen Jewell Appleby waited on me."

"Could you just tell us the circumstance, please, ma'am?"

"I'd taken a bath and was getting ready for bed. I heard a tap like someone hitting wood."

"You heard a tap?" Freight Train said. The councilmen were being highly attentive with all witnesses. Now they seemed to come to extra attention.

"Yes, and I went to the window. I could make out some-one sitting in my treehouse right outside. In the hackberry tree."

"So he wanted you to know he was there."

"I guess he did."

"Mighty bold fellow," Freight Train said.

A distinct astonishment went around the table. Council-man Hooper spoke up. "Likely he was going to feel his way to see if he could get something more than just a look."

Esau Ireland turned and gave the banker a withering look. "Bert, I'm sure we'd all be much obliged if you could keep your interesting speculations to yourself. And let our chief of police get on with the facts. Follow?"

"I follow," Hooper said meekly. "No offense, Esau."

"Proceed, Freight Train."

"Could you tell anything about him, ma'am? Age, size, clothes, anything like that?"

"No, it was real dark. The moon wasn't up. I could just see some kind of shape perched there. Like a big bird. A big bird with a mask."

"What kind of mask?"

"I couldn't tell. You couldn't see anything through it."

"What did you do?"

"Well, the first thing, I decided I was going to keep calm."

"You wasn't scared?"

"Not really. I'd heard about the present he left Sally, and I guess I figured a man who would do that couldn't be dangerous. I was curious. I can't remember when I've been this curious about anything. Mr. Baxter here had been over one night, and he and Brother Ireland discussed whether anything should go in the paper after Sally's peeping. While he was there the phone call came in from you about Betty Oakes being peeped. We got to talking about the Peeper, what kind of person he was. So I looked out and I just asked him, 'Why are you doing this?'"

Freight Train reflected a moment. "Well, all things considered, that wasn't a bad thing to ask. I might of asked him that myself if I'd been given the opportunity. I compliment you on being so calm."

"I don't know whether I was or not. Maybe I knew Brother Ireland would be home any minute and we might have a chance to catch him. I don't know. I had a lot going through my mind."

"Yes, ma'am. I reckon you did. What happened then?"

"Nothing. He didn't say anything. So I decided I would try a little teasing. I guess I was trying to stall, to keep the Peeper there for Esau to catch. And I guess to be honest it was a challenge to try to get him to say something. It was like a game. I said something like, 'Sir, it's not very flattering to be the third one in Martha peeped.' Fourth, I found out later. Well, he laughed."

"Fellow must have a sense of humor. Anyhow, you got the first sound out of him."

"I said something like, 'Well, at least I'm the first married one.' Then I said, 'If you like what you see, do you come back for seconds or is it just one per woman?' I was trying to tease and stall him. But also I was actually having some . . . fun, I guess you'd call it."

"You wasn't afraid of him?"

Holly Ireland shook her head slowly, frowning pensively. "No. No, I wasn't afraid of him."

Freight Train looked carefully at her. "Any answer to your question?"

"No. Then I said, 'How long is this going to go on? Do you plan to look at every woman in Martha?'"

"Did he reply to that question?"

"No."

"By the way, Miz Ireland, what was you wearing all this time? Begging your pardon, Esau."

"Not at all, Freight. You're acting officially."

"I had on my negligee. After my bath."

"Yes, ma'am. After your bath." The chief paused a moment. "Ah-h, Miz Ireland, excuse me for asking a personal question and don't answer if you'd prefer not. When Esau is at the Deacons', while he's gone and before he gets back, do you always take a bath and put on your neglijay like that?"

"Why, yes, I do. That's my custom. Brother Ireland is generally a little tense after presiding over the Board of Deacons."

"I see," the chief said discreetly. "Begging your pardon for this line of questioning, Mayor."

"Not at all, Chief," Brother Ireland said, somewhat stiffly. "This is all in official capacity. But might I inquire its purpose?"

"I was just wondering if the Peeper knowed of that habit of Miz Ireland's. I mean about taking a bath and putting on a neglijay about that same time on Deacons' meeting night." The chief sighed. "He seems to know everything else that goes on in town. Go ahead, Miz Ireland. You was having this talk with this man perched in the hackberry tree."

"Yes, and I said, 'Where's my present?' No answer. Then I said straight out, 'Who are you?' Brother Ireland and Mr. Baxter and I had talked about how it could be anybody, so I said, 'Are you Baxter?' No answer. 'Are you Freight Flowers?' No answer. Then I said, 'Are you Esau?'"

One of the councilmen laughed, and Esau looked at him sharply. It was Bert Hooper. He stopped laughing. Holly Ireland continued.

"Because, you know, for a moment the foolish thought

crossed my mind that it *was* Brother Ireland. It would be just like him to play a joke like that. He has a wonderful sense of humor. I said, 'Well, sir, two can play this game, Esau. I'm going to let you have a look at me.' "

Holly Ireland paused, and a profound silence hung over the Town Council room. I could hear the whir of the ceiling fan over the table, hear the minute fluttering of the American and Texas flags from the table's center. It was as if she were on a stage and had an enthralled audience here, in addition to the man in the treehouse. Freight Train cleared his throat. He glanced at the mayor, a look of apology, then back to his witness.

"And then?" he said.

"I think two things were going through my mind," she said quietly. I thought I detected the faintest tremor in her voice. "One was that it *was* Esau and if he was playing this practical joke, I would just *show* him. I'd outdo him. If it wasn't Esau, well, this would keep the man in that tree there for just a little longer and Esau would come home and catch him. Either way it seemed like a good thing."

"What seemed like a good thing, Miz Ireland?"

"To open my negligee."

I looked around at the men, and all of them were just sitting staring at her. Jesus God almighty, I thought. Women do the damnedest things. Only Freight Train kept his composure. He waited just the exact space of time before repeating his question.

"And then?"

"So I opened it. And then he finally said something."

Freight Train waited. He knew when not to ask. Suddenly she turned to her husband.

"Do I have to say, Esau?"

The chief himself gave the answer immediately. It was a moment of pure gallantry.

"Of course you don't, ma'am."

"Not unless you think you should, Sugar," Brother Ireland said. "Freight's just trying to find out all he can about this fellow, and this was the first time he spoke to anybody."

Then Esau said a gallant thing himself. "All you were trying to do was catch him. Remember, Sugar, you thought all along it was me," he said, giving her two outs.

"Yes, I did," Holly Ireland said firmly. "All right, then. He said, 'Freckles all over.' In a real low voice. Then I could hear him climbing down the hackberry tree. Fifteen minutes later, Brother Ireland came in."

I had not thought the silence could be more complete. All waited. It was clear as clear could be that every man in that room was having a look at Holly Ireland's freckles. Including, no doubt, Esau. Henry Milam broke the silence.

"Speaking for one member of the Town Council, Holly, I think you showed great courage."

"You made a real effort to capture the Peeper, all right." Sherm Embers joined the praise. I looked at him. His face was impassive.

"That was my idea," Holly Ireland said. "But it didn't work, did it?"

"But not for lack of trying."

"I'll say amen to that," Councilman Jenkins said. Even Saint Orville was compassionate. "It took moral fiber to stand up to that scoundrel."

"Really, gentlemen," Brother Ireland said dryly. "I'm sure all this is unnecessary. Next thing you know we'll be passing a formal vote of thanks to Sister Ireland."

I looked at the chief of police. I thought I saw a rather quizzical look cross his face. Then it was gone and he was all gallantry again.

"We *all* thank you, ma'am." He laughed shortly. "You given me an idea. Maybe we can set a trap for him. Get one of you ladies to stand at her window and take things off with all the lights on, and some of us'll be waiting in the bushes. Sounds like a winner."

She blurted it. It was as if she had been holding emotion back and now it came out. "I don't know what all this fuss is about. He didn't do any harm."

Brother Ireland, alarmed, turned to her. "Sugar, what's come over you?"

I looked at Holly Ireland with a suddenly accelerated

interest. She seemed awakened. She recovered herself quickly.

"I'm sorry. I guess I wasn't so calm and collected after all."

"Miz Ireland," Freight Train said, "you the first of the ones peeped to hear his voice like the mayor said. Could you describe it?"

She waited a moment. "Why, there wasn't anything special about it," she said carefully. "I didn't recognize it as any particular voice. He only spoke that once, about the freckles. And that was real soft."

"Anyhow, it wasn't a kid's voice?" I felt Freight Train was pressing her a little. I felt that he suspected something. I didn't know what.

"Oh, no. It was a grown man, all right. And then that present. The little book of poetry. It was a man."

"Would you tell the Council what the poetry was?"

"I'd be happy to." She spoke almost proudly. "It was *Sonnets from the Portuguese.*"

"From the Portuguese?" Bert Hooper said.

"They're love sonnets," Henry Milam said.

Hooper gave a short whistle. Esau looked sharply at him.

"Thank you, Miz Ireland," Freight Train said then. "You been helpful. Real helpful."

She left. There was silence for a bit, with wonder and respect in it.

Now that the ladies had gone, Freight Train put his hat back on. "Well, that concludes the witnesses, Councilmen," he said. "I'll add a couple points from the Betty Oakes deposition. First, she got a quick look at him before she yelled to the rooftops and he took off. All ladies don't take these peepings the same way. She said the mask he was wearing looked like it was made from ladies' pantyhose."

"Did you say pantyhose?" Bert Hooper said.

"They're cool, I reckon," Freight Train said. "Second, the way she knowed someone was there, she heard him humming 'Amazing Grace.'"

"My God, you mean he's a churchgoing man?" Saint Orville said slowly. "I can't imagine a church member doing anything like this."

"In my experience," Sherm Embers said, "church members like it like everybody else."

"Now for the hard part," Brother Ireland said. He sat very straight in his chair. "The meeting is open to ideas for dealing with this situation. What do you have in mind, Freight Train?"

"Several things, Mayor. One, I'd like to call a meeting of the women of the town. We got defensive driving. No reason we can't have a little defensive dressing."

"How do you mean, Freight?"

"Well, the first thing is, the women are going to have to stop dressing—and undressing—with their shades up. I'm going to instruct—or ask—all of them to keep them shades down. Now if all the women comply, that'll leave the Peeper with nothing to look at. But my experience where women is concerned is, you never get a hundred percent compliance on anything. So I reckon we need a few other measures."

The chief's voice proceeded, rhythmic and purposeful. "What do you councilmen think about deputizing the basketball team for night patrol? All them boys is fleet of foot. They'd have two duties. One'd be to go up and down the alleys making sure all the shades is drawn—at least the bathroom and bedroom shades. The other'd be, if they happen to spot the Peeper, to run him down. They's twelve boys on the full squad, so they could cover a lot of alleys. We might want to consider putting up a hunnert-dollar reward or so for the boy that catches him."

"Well, I tell you, Chief," Sherm Embers said. "I don't know if the women will appreciate having a bunch of boys going up and down the alleys looking in their windows. I have an idea some of them would rather deal with one grown Peeper than with a dozen slobbering high school boys."

"You have a point," Brother Ireland said. "Freight, why don't we hold off for the present on deputizing the boys? It may come to that, but let's see if we can make headway without them."

"I'm not sure you being fair to these boys," the chief of police said. "I think they'd realize it was a job to do. However,

I'll hold off if you councilmen says so. I'll take on personally trying to do the shade patrol."

He looked pointedly around the table.

"I hope you councilmen can trust *me* to keep my eyes on the job."

No one said anything.

"If it's just going to be me patrolling, I'll be stretched kinda thin. That's for double sure. But I'll work out some sorta plan and let you councilmen know. Anyhow, north side's all I got to worry about. He ain't touched the south end."

"There's one other possibility," Bert Hooper said. "We could bring in the Rangers."

"Might not be a bad idea," Orville Jenkins said. "The Texas Rangers have a pretty good record."

"Are you people out of your mind?" Freight Train said. "Hailfire, here you been talking about keeping it quiet, and now you talking about calling in the Texas Rangers! Gawd amighty, why not just notify the newspapers and the tee-vee networks and we'll have ourselves a carnival in Martha!"

For a moment it was as if he were a lieutenant back in the Corps, dressing down a platoon of enlisted men.

"Freight Train is right," the mayor ruled. "Nothing is so important as keeping this hushed up. No Texas Rangers. Besides, it would indicate we weren't smart enough to handle our own problems. If there's one thing Martha has always prided itself on, it's self-reliance. This town has never been one to suck on the outside tit."

The mayor sat up a little more. "That meeting of the women to get them to pull their shades down is the right idea. Freight can reassure them that we're doing something about this matter, and that'll help set their minds at ease. We don't want the women of the town panicking."

He looked sternly around the table. "Now, one final word. I hope I don't need to tell you councilmen that nothing said here tonight is to leave this room. Follow? You too, Baxter."

"Correct," Freight Train said. "The Peeper seems to know an awful lot about what goes on in Martha. Let's don't help him out, troops, by tipping our hand."

Esau Ireland tapped on the table. "Speaking of hands," he said. "Gentlemen, shall we play cards?"

The game was stud, either five- or seven-card, or draw, dealer's choice. Sometimes "hold 'em," a variation of seven-card stud. Nothing else. No wild cards, no high-low or other aberrations. A dollar ante and ten-dollar limit. The limit was taken off for the last hand of the night.

I felt I knew the games of the six other players pretty well by now. I better.

Orville Jenkins is a below-average poker player. A shade too eager when he has the cards, a touch too downcast when he hasn't. Over a given year he will be a net loser, but not enough so that another shipment of broccoli or carrots won't make up. The game poses no conflict with his religious principles. He says he can find nothing against poker in the Bible. Besides, he tithes his winnings, when he has winnings.

Sherman Embers is a better-than-average poker player and could be outstanding if he concentrated on it. Over the long haul he ends up with respectable if not spectacular winnings. He sometimes wins big or loses big because he is a reckless high roller.

Henry Milam is a careful, meticulous player, too methodical to be very good. He usually wins or loses small, plays slowly, weighing odds and consequences. Almost never bluffs and therefore can be bluffed out more than most. Never shows his cards when he doesn't have to. Month in and month out he comes out about even, maybe losing a little more than he wins.

Bert Hooper is often the big loser. But then he's got lots to lose, and poor poker players with money to lose never learn how poor they are. An occasional lucky streak only makes him think he is better than he is. He hates to sit out hands, which makes him lose more. All are glad to have him in the game. To keep him there, everyone always campaigns hard for his reelection.

Esau Ireland is the finest. He has the best poker face in town; one of the best in Texas, some say. He is impassive at cards. If he has an ace showing, it is close to impossible to read from his face whether he has another one or a deuce in the hole. He runs bluffs, some outrageous, and wins more of them than otherwise. Each year he puts in the bank a tidy sum, most of it won from the owner of the bank, an irony which delights him.

The chief of police has a winning edge. Aggies make better-than-your-average poker player. His winnings keep him in peanuts and Lone Star, which is saying considerable. Like me, he does not have the bankroll to take the necessary risks, though I take more than Freight does. Not having it, both of us can be driven out of hands. Both of us often win small and occasionally big because both of us know how to ride a streak and to play more strongly when we have the money to do so. Sometimes we have to drop out of a game when we have lost all we can afford.

Myself: Well, I am not in Esau's class. But were it not for the poker game I might have to give up the paper and my life in Martha, Texas. For sure I would have to give up my boat and all those trips to Padre. With my limited bankroll, I know I take more risks than I should. But it has to be that way. My real edge in life is my boat and those days on the island. I'll take risks to keep them, so long as I have anything to risk.

This evening was pretty much like any other Town Council poker game. There had been several trips to the refrigerator, and the supply of Lone Star was running pretty low. There was never much gossip over the hands. This was a serious game. The only difference tonight was that for the first time in my memory there was a fair amount of non-poker talk, all of it to do with the one subject. Even poker could not entirely take the men's minds off the Peeping Tom loose somewhere in the town. I could not have imagined anything that would so have defined the seriousness with which they were taking the matter.

The game always adjourns right at midnight. The rules state that the hand in progress when the First Baptist Church chimes begin to peal out their last hymn of the day is the last hand. I had found it a satisfying evening. I had about a hundred and ten dollars on my person that had not been there when I entered the room, most of it a transfer from Bert Hooper's pocket to mine. I think I was overdrawn in my account at his bank and reminded myself to deposit the hundred and ten there tomorrow.

Brother Ireland was expertly dealing the final card of a stud hand, calling out what was showing at each place as he flicked out the fourth up card.

"Pair of sixes," he said, dealing Councilman Hooper.

"Busted heart flush," dealing Councilman Milam.

"King high," dealing Councilman Embers.

"Pair of tens," dealing Councilman Jenkins.

"Jack high," dealing the chief of police.

"Pair of sevens," dealing me.

"Queen high," dealing himself.

"Pair of tens bets," he said.

Councilman Jenkins turned up just the tiniest corner of his hole card as if someone might get a peek.

At this moment the strains of "Onward, Christian Soldiers" broke down Cavalry Street and surged across the parade ground and through the piazza doors. We all stopped over our hands and listened to its swelling chords. Then Councilman Jenkins sat back and began to sing the lines. The councilman was a marvelous hymn singer, more so with a couple of Lone Stars in him, with a rich deep rolling bass voice. It mounted now with the pealings of the First Baptist Church chimes far away.

> *Onward, Christian soldiers,*
> *Marching as to war,*
> *With the cross of Jesus*
> *Going on before.*
> *Christ, the royal Master,*
> *Leads against the foe;*
> *Forward into battle*
> *See His banner go!*

"Pair of tens," Orville said. He looked at his hole card again. "Showing, that is."

I was certain he didn't have the third one. I looked at my

hole card to confirm my third seven. The phone rang. Freight Train picked it up.

"Martha Police," he said. "Chief Flowers speaking."

The chief listened for a moment. He brought himself straighter in his chair so that his big belly bulged over the tabletop. He shoved his Resistol farther back on his head.

"Yes, ma'am, I'll tell him. . . . Would you like to speak to him? . . . All right, I'll tell him right now."

He hung up. "Troops," he said to the table, "they's been another."

We all looked up from our hands at the chief of police. In the silence, the whir of the ceiling fan over us sounded like an airplane propeller. The chief's eyes went to one of us.

"Orville," the chief said, "Miz Jenkins was peeped this evening."

Councilman Jenkins just looked at the chief. "I am shocked. The scoundrel. She okay?" he asked.

"She sounded perfectly calm," the chief said.

"Gentlemen," Councilman Jenkins said, "I believe the rules state that a hand in progress when the Baptist chimes mark midnight shall be completed."

Damn, I thought, he has that third ten.

My weekend on the boat was utterly shot, and besides, Saturday opened with heavy rains. I checked the marine weather and found the Gulf was running eight-foot seas. There was nothing for it but to park in Martha at least for Saturday and see about Sunday. I went down to the paper with the idea of doing some work ahead to make up for this lost weekend by an unusually fat one next. I put in a phone call to the Reverend Billy Holmes, the young minister of the First Baptist Church, to gather some material for the *Clarion*'s regular story about Sunday services and other church activities. Yes, the following Sunday's program was set. Sister Ireland, he said, would render the solo. Her selection would be "O Perfect Love" and she would be accompanied by Sally Carruthers on the harp. His own sermon topic would be "Love Divine, All Loves Excelling." The theme of the morning service was becoming clear. For the night sermon his topic would be "Where the Lights Go Out on the Road to Hell." The solo, "Will You Be Found Wanting?" would be rendered by the choir bass, Orville Jenkins, Jr. We chatted a bit and I inquired politely after his wife. He has a very nice little wife.

"Any news from the Deacons' meeting?" I asked.

"Very little," he said. "The Deacons voted an appropriation for repairs to the pipe organ. At last. That was about it. The meeting broke up early. Brother Ireland said he had a dressing to do."

"Congratulations on the repairs to the pipe organ, Reverend."

"It needs them," he said with a sigh. He laughed. "Now I know how you newspapermen are, but I hope you'll join us some Sunday. If you're in town, that is. I know you usually go to the island for the weekends. And of course I know you always attend church services there," he said jestingly.

"Always, Reverend," I said. "In the great Cathedral of the Outdoors. If I'm in town I may make your morning service. Both for your sermon and for Holly Ireland's solo. I always enjoy hearing about love."

"It's what makes the world go round," he said brightly. "Sacred and profane." He laughed again. "Oh, I've got one piece of news. I'm going to be conducting missions one night a week in San Pablo. Starting Monday."

"Monday? I'll make sure there's an item in the paper."

"See you in church."

I hung up. I sat back in my chair. I liked him. He is one of the good-natured religious people, all too rare. I sometimes think the Reverend Holmes doesn't even take hell all that seriously, much less things like fornication, adultery, drinking, and gambling, and it makes him comfortable to be with. You don't have the feeling he is always trying to improve you. I had a sneaking suspicion that these were all peccadilloes in Reverend Holmes' List of Sins and that he considered the really serious transgressions to be activities like avarice, envy, pride, unkindness, smugness, vanity, and piousness, the whole litany of pharisaism. The Reverend Holmes certainly kept busy ministering to his Martha flock. And now he was reaching out to take on San Pablo.

I looked at the two sermon topics on my notes. Morning, "Love Divine, All Loves Excelling." Night, "Where the Lights Go Out on the Road to Hell." The morning sermon was customarily gentle, the night one fiery. It was as though if they didn't get you with the carrot they would with the stick. Or the poker.

PEEPER 3
All of Them

She was sitting in an armchair reading a book, a picture of nighttime peace. She wore a skirt of blue denim and a white overblouse. He had once heard her say she read a half hour every night before bed. Maybe she was reading more tonight, her husband being out of town preaching at a mission up the river in San Pablo. He looked at his illuminated-dial watch. This must be an unusually good book. He would like to have seen its title. Or maybe she was just not sleepy and he wished she were. Was she restless in her husband's absence or glad for the chance to read? Snug in the parsonage bushes, he passed the time thinking of her a few feet away through the window.

It was said that Priscilla Holmes had had the ambition to be a ballerina and had given all that up for service to the Lord and Billy Holmes's handsome looks and ways. Even now she had the figure of a fourteen-year-old. She was small-boned, and her thin body, and a kind of pallor about it, her rather childlike mouth, tilted nostrils, and angular cheekbones gave a sense of frail refinement. Yet there was a dauntless quality about her. Her huge green eyes were grave and intent. They looked out on the world like a small animal in the forest looking on the odd behavior of larger ones. Her hair was drawn back from a wide forehead and knotted at the back of her head. Her fingers seemed much too long for the rest of her. They were slender and beautiful. She had a tranquil air and a thin, sweet voice with almost a lisp to it. How she survived as a minister's wife he didn't know. Maybe her secret was that intrepid thing that you felt lay inside her.

He heard a sound and parted the bushes and peered through. She was laying the book aside. She stood up, waited a moment as if undecided about something, then began unbuttoning her blouse. She removed it and laid it on the back of the chair. She reached to the side of her skirt and pulled a zipper down—he could hear its welcome *burr!* through the open window. With both hands she pushed the skirt down around her hips with an amusing wriggling movement and stepped out of it, all with the skillful nonchalance of an act performed ten thousand times. She folded the skirt once vertically and placed it neatly alongside the blouse. She was wearing a light blue slip, and she pulled it over her head and spread it over the back of the chair and stood in pantyhose and bra. Girls were so marvelous, he thought, with their panties, their slips and their half-slips, their stockings and their pantyhose, their girdles and their panty girdles and their bras, all that wondrous forest of undergarments to be got through. Where he crouched, a wild honeysuckle bush grew right next to him, and as he watched he breathed in its scent.

She reached back, unfastened the bra, came out of it, and placed it on top of the slip. How differing were the breasts of women! In what a remarkable variety of sizes, shapes, textures, even attitudes they came. These were of a charming disposition, just enough of them to prove it was a woman you were looking at, the pale violet nipples disproportionately large, like saucy little obelisks. For all this, or perhaps because of it, they seemed oddly more bold than retiring, as of a young girl saying, *I've got them, all right.* She slipped the pantyhose down, then sat, pushed them carefully on down her legs to her shoes, stopped and removed these, and then pushed the pantyhose off. She stood, shook the pantyhose briskly out, and placed them atop the bra, full length so that they spilled over the chair's seat, then bent down and picked up the shoes and arranged them in neat order beside the chair.

It was a marvelous toothpick of a body. Almost waistless, with angular contours. You could see her hipbones sticking out from an indented tummy. She stood there a moment in her panties as though thinking of something—of a scene in the book she had just laid down? Of her husband? Of some forever missed career? The panties were bikini and, like the bra, of light blue. What weapons were these particles called lingerie, so insignificant, so puissant. Almost before he knew it, the hand quicker than the eye, she had flicked them down and stepped out of them, presenting for his viewing a seraphic nosegay at the top of those matchstick legs and, as she turned to add the panties to the other garments, an appealing, almost nonexistent urchin behind. She marched over to a closet, entered it, and emerged carrying a wisp of a nightgown. Raising her arms—he could see her ribcage and the doll breasts arched out above it—she went into it head first, pulled it down, and straightened it around her body, the whispers of the material coming through to him in the silent, windless night. It reached only to her knees. It gave her a funny yet altogether endearing look. You wanted to take her to you. She reached back with both hands and unpinned her hair and shook it out to fall trailing over her back, where it seemed to go down forever, her body seeming the more frugal for that huge dark backdrop. The ritual was concluded.

She went over to the bed, hit the pillow a couple of times with a solid *smack!* that popped in the night, sat, and swung her legs into bed and under the sheet. She reached for the vacant pillow, held it to her body as one might a child—or a missing husband—and reached over and snapped off the nightstand light. The room went into darkness. Now that his night operations had turned into a regular thing, there was hardly time to shop individually, so he had decided to standardize his present. He placed the gift on the windowsill, a silver butterfly with enameled wings. They were lovely, and he had bought two dozen of them across the border in Las Bocas.

He walked down the alley, taking off his pantyhose mask and stuffing it in his pocket, and into Pecan Street. He felt borne upward. He had never had such a sense of well-being as of late, he thought, as he went down the dark street. What it was about looking at women undressing and undressed that was so therapeutic and ennobling he did not know. Certainly it went far beyond anything so simple as physical excitation. There was something else. It was remarkably soothing. It enlarged both the spirit and the mind. Petty things became less important, trivia lost their sway, the dross of life fell away. One dwelt on loftier themes. He knew he was on to some great secret. He didn't know why it was, only what it was. Or rather where it was. He felt he had found the source.

It would be an experiment. He had been restricting himself to the town's proved "lookers." Bloomer Girls like Sally Carruthers and Betty Oakes. Figures which held high promise, like Holly Ireland and Kathryn Shields. Now he had decided to branch out, to look at a different kind of woman. If it turned out to be a mistake, there was only one night's loss.

Going down Iris Street he thought of her. It seemed that, elected to no political office, holding no official position, she had run so much of the town for so long. She ran the Woman's Missionary Union, the Daughters of the Republic of Texas, the Garden Club, all very important and influential, and so many other things in general. Martha had never really had a "matriarch" before Mrs. August Tefenteller, and it was hard to imagine anyone ever replacing her after she was gone. Not that that would be anytime soon. She kept herself, as the saying went.

Sister Tefenteller was rather portly, but she was well corseted and handsome in her way. He had a feeling that she had realized at an early age that she was going to be large and had had the good sense to choose the right hair style and clothes for her size. She had changed these styles little over the years. There was something immediately imposing about her. In her presence one would not have dreamed of committing the most trifling indiscretion. There was a Mr. Tefenteller, and she dominated him as she did anything with which she was associated. August appeared small beside her and somewhat undernourished. He seemed hardly to be present. But apparently he didn't mind, and she was always courteous to him. Anyone slighting him would have had Mrs. Tefenteller to contend with on the spot. He had an idea that August took a secret delight in the magisterial aspect his wife presented to the world. He seemed always to have a cigar in his mouth; surprisingly, she appeared to tolerate that habit almost fondly. It was as if it was the one thing in her environment she couldn't control and so, being intelligent, had resigned herself to it. "I think August had cigars as an infant instead of mother's milk," she had once said. She wasn't so bad.

He began to wonder what she was like behind that commanding front. Unlike the two Bloomer Girls, of whose bodies he had already seen a considerable amount in their public appearances even before the windows, he had seen virtually nothing of this selection. He had seen her a thousand times and all thousand fully clothed. He had seen her face and her calves and that was it. The more of a woman's territory you had not seen, the more exhilarating the idea of seeing it: It was probably this truth more than anything that had always made monogamy so difficult to achieve. His curiosity grew with each step. He turned into the alley and walked down it to the latch gate, checked for a clear coast, and went through the gate.

It was one of the largest houses in Martha. It was from her side of the family. Her people sold farm machinery, and there are few things more lucrative than that. He crossed the yard, treading gingerly, putting on his pantyhose mask as he went and straightening it. He crouched in the poinciana bushes, raised his chin until it was over the windowsill.

She was sitting up in bed in a half slip drawn up to display her stolid thighs. Her breasts were aimed across the room. In all his life he had never seen anything like them. They were illustrious. Eloquent, intemperate. A twin *magnificat*. Young bodies were fine; there was a special delight and charm in them. But the older body had a great deal to say for it, and who would have missed this one: this superb bulk, this gorgeous plumpness, the stately hummock of the belly, the fleecy flesh—these revelations of breasts. Commanding, lactescent, they cried out for attention, for employment. He wondered why she was sitting there like that, as if deliberately to exhibit them. They and she were looking across the room at something. He followed the line of her gaze.

The room's only light was over the bed, and in the half darkness across from it he had to focus to make out anything. He could not at first believe it. A woman stood there in the shadows, a small woman, wearing the classic uniform: black panties, black garter belt supporting black stockings, black high-heeled shoes, black brassiere. An unmistakable dyke! Her head was turned so that, crouching there in shock and confusion, he could not ascertain her features. His eyes sped back across the room to the lady on the bed. As he watched, hypnotized, her hands, in a beneficent gesture, came around and seized and cupped those heroic breasts, offering them to the gartered creature. This one actually pirouetted in a light fey movement, then emerged from the darkness and started across the room toward the bed, turning as she did, so that he found himself looking straight at her. She stopped, reached toward a chest of drawers, picked up a live cigar from an ashtray, took a long pull on it, blew out a gust of smoke, replaced the cigar, and continued across the room into the light and toward the lady in bed and the niveous Himalayas.

He looked one moment more, then turned and bolted out of the poincianas, staggering across the yard and out the gate, forgetting even to close it softly, so that it made a slight bang in the night. He had barely escaped when the laughter building up inside him exploded. He could hardly stop. As he started down the alley he realized he was still holding the intended present. In his haste to get out of there he had forgotten to leave it. He chuckled and thought, Probably just as well. The Tefentellers would not consider it a tribute. Let them keep their secret.

And though he had left Sister Tefenteller no gift, she had certainly given him one. On the spot he reached a great conclusion.

"Let's face it," he said magnanimously to the starry night "I love them all."

5.
The Women

I wrote a two-paragraph story stating that the chief of police had called a meeting of Martha women in the high school auditorium for 8:00 P.M. Monday. "The meeting," I wrote, "is in connection with certain nocturnal activities in Martha." I had a mean motive. If Mayor Ireland and the town councilmen wanted to "keep it quiet," I would show them what quiet was. I meant to make the stories on the matter so discreet and so mysterious—and so ludicrous—that my readers would wonder what in the world was going on. Maybe then Esau and the others would realize it was simpler to call a Peeping Tom a Peeping Tom. I wrote a headline, "Important Meeting of Martha Women," and put it under an 18-point Cheltenham bold head in a box just above the fold on page one.

I stopped by the chief of police's office before the meeting. There was a new fixture in the room. A huge detail map of the town had been mounted on an easel next to the chief's desk, and he was sticking yellow-headed pins in it.

"Come on in, Ace," he said. "Take a look at my battle map."

MARTHA, the map said in large block letters at the top. I looked at the Rio Grande angling both ways from the town, northwest to the distant Colorado mountains where it began, southeast to the Gulf where it finished. Across from it was the word MEXICO. I came closer. Each pin represented a household the Peeping Tom had honored with a visit. Slung

92

around the neck of each was a small tag with a number on it
to show that house's order in the sequence of peepings. The
tag also supplied the date and estimated hour of the visit and
the name and age of the lady.

The chief sat back and regarded the map thoughtfully. I
think he was back in the Corps in Aggieland. He was
beginning to regard it as a military campaign, and he was the
commanding officer chosen to repel the invader.

"He got to have a pattern. He just can't be doing all this
catch-as-catch-can. He's working outa some overall plan. I
been sitting here trying to figure out what it is. Mostly,
though, I been sitting here with one finger in my mouth and
two up my ass like the fellow in the poem."

"What poem is that?" I said.

He leaned closer to the map and squinted. "One, Daffodil
Street—Sally Carruthers, age eighteen"—he started calling
them off as though he were taking muster—"and that pretty
red hair. Two, Camellia Street: Betty Oakes, age seventeen.
Three, Goldenrod: Kathryn Shields, age twenty-five, taking
a bath. Four, Hibiscus: Holly Ireland, age twenty-eight, and
all them freckles. Fifth, Daffodil again: Mrs. Orville Jenkins,
age forty-five. Sixth, Jonquil: Priscilla Holmes, age thirty.
Seventh, Aster: Nancy Torrance, age thirty-eight."

"All on the north side," I said.

"Naturally. That's the best part of town. He don't go
economy class. The youngest, age seventeen," the chief said
reflectively, "the oldest forty-five. You see any pattern there,
Ace?"

"Yes," I said. "He likes women."

"They's got to be more to it than that. Got to be some
reason he's picking the women he's picking. Some reason
he's doing all this peeping in the first place. Something more
than just trying to become the greatest authority in Texas on
females undressing."

The chief sat back. "I think it's pretty well agreed by all the
troops that he's somebody upstanding in this town. So he's
risking it all. A man don't risk everything just to *look* at it, 'less
he's got a pretty good reason."

The chief shoved his Resistol forward on his head, leaned

back in his chair, and parked his Justin cowboy boots on the desk. He gave me a shrewd look.

"I got this call from Saint Orville. He said he got to wondering if maybe the Peeper was punishing these particular ladies."

"Punishing them? What in the world did he mean by that?"

"He said it was just an idea. But suppose, he said, the Peeper was some sorta Passover Angel—he said that was an angel in the Bible that hands out the punishment—and that each of these women had done something kinda underneath the poker table and the Peeper had taken it onto hisself to punish them for what they done."

"Done what, for God's sake?"

"Sinned in some way, Orville said. Like committing adultery."

"You mean the preacher's wife, the English teacher, the undertaker's wife, the Bloomer Girls, and the rest of them have all committed adultery? Hell, the Bloomer Girls aren't even married."

"Orville said he meant that about adultery just as a for instance. What do you think?"

"To use the favorite word of my new girl reporter," I said, "I think Saint Orville is full of bullshit. My God, his own wife has been peeped."

"So she claims," Freight Train said.

"What do you mean, 'So she claims'?" I said.

A glazed look came over the chief's eyes. "I ain't sure. But I got a feeling they's some mighty mysterious things going on, Ace. Do you know of any of them Passover Angels in town?"

"I could probably come up with a few. Orville Jenkins, for starters. How is the Peeper supposed to have found out about all these sins? Is he someone the ladies confessed to? A preacher? Reverend Billy Holmes? They'd talk to him."

"Yeah, I'm told ladies talk a lot to their preachers." The chief swung his legs off the desk and sat up. "I don't buy that adultery or nothing like that. All the same, I think the councilman may be on the right track. That is, they's some connection between the ladies he's peeping. *How* he picks the ones he picks. If I could figure out what it was, why, I might know who the next one'd be. And if I could do that, I could be waiting for him some night, bright-eyed and bushy-tailed, in the right alley. They's a lot of alleys in this town, and me chasing up and down them at night like a rooster on peyote ain't ever gonna turn him up. I gotta *outwit* him somehow."

He pushed the Resistol back and looked at the map. "All seven're pretty active in church matters. Sing in the choir, play the harp, teach in the Sunday school, do things in the Woman's Missionary Union or the Ladies' Aid Society. One's even the preacher's wife. So maybe he's after the church ladies. Maybe he's one of them ag-nostics. Hail, that don't make any sense. Betty Oakes heard him humming a church hymn hisself." He sighed. "It wouldn't help even if he was. I don't know any ladies in Martha that don't do one kind of danged church thing or another."

The chief regarded the array of pins studiously. "I even tried figuring, and two're blondes, four're brunettes, one's a redhead. So he spreads *that* around. They's no pattern there."

He leaned forward and twirled one of the tags.

"You'd think at least he'd go after our finest-looking ones, wouldn't you? When he first commenced operations the fellow did that. The Bloomer Girls. Kathryn Shields. Holly Ireland. Not a man in town, starting with old Freight Train, but what wouldn't relish seeing all of them for just as long as possible. Yes sirree." The chief got a far-off look in his eyes. "But you take Orville's wife or Nancy Torrance. Nice ladies, sweet and all, but nobody'd ever think of entering them in a beauty contest. We got dozens in this town'd leave them behind chewing spit. He's not even confining his activities to the good-looking ones no more, and I ain't never heard of a Peeping Tom like that."

The chief gave a small belch. A ripple went across the big belly. He sighed heavily.

"It's a puzzle."

"Maybe he takes potluck," I said. "Maybe he just walks down Cavalry Street looking them over, sees one that catches his fancy, and makes a date with her for that night. Only she doesn't know she's got a date."

"Naw, I don't think so. I think it's more thought out than that. He picks them for a reason. He just too smart for me to figure it out. Well, I knowed all along I was dealing with a clever fellow."

The chief looked up at the sign on the wall, ONE AGGIE EQUALS TWO ORDINARY MEN. He laughed. "Don't look like it so far, does it? But the war, it ain't over yet. Just a few skirmishes. Mr. Peeper, you gonna find out the meaning of them immortal words."

He sighed. "In the meantime, is the motherfucker not gonna stop until he's seen every woman in Martha over fifteen in their drawers?"

"Freight?"

"Yeah?"

"You got any guess? On the level. Even a hunch?"

The chief looked at me thoughtfully. "About who it is? Hail, Ace, I been running just about all the men in Martha through my mind. Including you. I even begun to suspect myself. I don't have a shot, and that's a fact. You and me could sit here and take every man in town and prove why he just couldn't do it. And why he just might do it."

"Every man? How about some of the boys?"

"Jobs is too clever done. A boy'd messed up by now. Anyhow, Holly Ireland said it was a grown man's voice."

"Yes. Well, Orville Jenkins, Jr., sings bass in the Baptist choir."

"Hailfire, man. That would have the Jenkins boy looking at his own mother."

"I meant Orville Junior just as a for instance. However, we've all heard of the Oedipus complex."

"What's that?" The chief gave me his shrewd look. "That new shopping center in Houston?"

I could hear the low whir of the ceiling fan. The chief sighed again. He stood up and looked out across the piazza over the parade ground. Dusk was coming on.

"I wish I had the Cavary here to help out," he said. "I could sure use 'em. He probably cranking up right now for another one. You know something, Ace? I almost envy the motherfucker. Yes, sir. We got a lot of good-looking women in this town. Hail, if he keeps on he'll have seen more of it in a month than I have altogether."

He turned back. "Hey, I got a new Aggie joke." He sat back down and crossed his cowboy boots on the desk. "This Aggie hitchhiker was picked up by a fellow in a big Rolls-Royce. The Aggie saw this bunch of golf tees on the front seat and he asked, 'What are those things for, sir?'

" 'They're to hold my balls when I drive,' the man said.

" 'Boy,' the Aggie said, 'these Rolls got everything, don't they?' "

The roar of laughter crashed across the room and set the chief's belly going like a giant bellows. He swung his boots off the desk, stood up, shoved his big hat forward, and hit me on the shoulder.

"Come on, Ace. Rise and shine. Let's go over and face the ladies."

He filled his moisture-proof tobacco pouch with peanuts from his peanut drawer, and we left and rode over in his pickup. It was equipped with a police interceptor system, a siren, a twirling red light on top of the cab, and a telephone. Its license plates read AGGIE-1.

It was the most women I had ever seen in one place in Martha. By the time the chief arose to address the gathering, every seat in the high school auditorium was taken and some of the younger of the menaced gender stood along the walls, having given up their places to older ones in the courtesy habitual to our part of the country. From the looks and ages of some of those present, I felt not everyone was there because she felt personally in danger. Even though I was there as a reporter, it felt odd to be in a hall where I was one of only two men among so many women, especially when they were gathered there to contemplate the uninvited intrusions of my sex on theirs. I say I was there as a reporter. Actually my staff, Jamie, was somewhere in the auditorium handling that herself, her first assignment. I was there really out of curiosity. I couldn't print the story, but for some reason I had to be there and have Jamie there. The story was beginning to get to me.

The chief opened the proceedings. He looked very big behind that lectern, his huge belly nuzzling it.

"Ladies and little ladies, I appreciate this splendid turnout. Shows you care what happens to your town. Martha is a peaceful town. But right now the peace, it's being disturbed by something we never been bothered with before. It's what's called a Peeping Tom."

The chief paused and regarded his listeners carefully.

"First off, I appreciate what you ladies are going through. What it must be like to be a woman and be in your own house undressing and never knowing who's looking at you. I reckon that would keep almost any woman on edge."

To me, his audience looked more interested than on edge and more curious than fearful. The chief took a deep breath.

"When a person can't even take off her clothes in peace, I call that a serious situation. I want you ladies to know we doing everything I can think of to find out who this fellow is. Some of those things I can't even talk about. This Peeper, he seems to have big ears as well as big eyes. But I been working on this matter twenty-five hours a day, as the man said. I and the mayor and the town councilmen, we doing things to catch this fellow. So they's no reason for you ladies to panic."

The chief looked out at his hearers. I looked too. The exclusively female audience was sitting in perfect calm. The chief continued in his slow-motion voice.

"But while some of these things is under security, I can tell you what we know about how he works and what we know about *him*. That might help you ladies to be on the lookout for this individual. First off, he's able-bodied for sure and certain. He don't just crouch down in bushes, he stays in that position for quite a spell. In the case of Miz Ireland's peeping he climbed up in a tree—one of them big hackberry trees —to get a look at Miz Ireland in her second-story bedroom. No weakling could climb that hackberry. So if you suspect someone who gets winded from walking three blocks down Cavary, forget it."

Some of the ladies turned and looked at Holly Ireland.

"So our man is in good health—even vigorous, I would

_____

say. Beyond that I'm sorry to say we don't have one blooming clue about him in a physical way: age, height, weight, color of hair, any of that.

"Other than the physical side of him, what kind of man might he be? For one thing, he's a clever, intelligent fellow. I base that on how careful he's planned the peepings and how hard we finding it to catch him or even know much about him. Another thing, I guess you could say he's considerate and thoughtful, to give the devil his due. Never fails to leave some kinda present after looking at one of you ladies. His way of saying thank you, ma'am, I reckon. The one time he talked, to Miz Ireland, he appeared to be a real polite fellow, fine manners and all. So he seems to know a thing or two about women."

Someone in the audience let out a laugh. The chief looked in her direction and continued.

"Next, he knows the town real good. He knowed Betty Oakes's family was visiting in San Antone. He knowed the Baptist Board of Deacons meets once a month on a Thursday and that Brother Ireland is chairman, so that would be a good night to peep Miz Ireland, which he did. He knows the personal habits of this town down to a T. He knowed that Nancy Torrance here takes a bath at nine o'clock every other night and so does Jim Torrance, reason being the hot-water tank at the Torrance place don't provide enough water for more'n one bath a night. A man that knows what night certain of you ladies takes your bath, I'd say he knows the town inside out."

The chief waited. "Everything we got says it's someone you all know. Someone you see every day. Someone, and I reckon this is the heart of it, you'd never suspect."

The chief waited longer this time, as though to let the exceptional nature of such a state of affairs register fully.

"Now in a moment I'm going to open this meeting to questions from the floor. But first I want to ask a favor of you ladies. The best protection you got against the Peeping Tom is to give him nothing to look at. If all you girls and ladies could do one simple thing, which is to lower the shades on

your bathrooms and bedrooms every night around eight
o'clock, we'd be halfway home. If we can dry up his sources,
so to speak, maybe we can dry him up."

"These pretty April nights, I don't like to use the shades,"
someone said from about the twentieth row. "I like to leave
them up and get the night air."

"Miz Boynton," the chief said briskly, "would you rather be
cool and let a stranger see you in your birthdays, or sweat a
little and keep it for Mr. Boynton?"

The chief reached into his pocket, got out his tobacco
pouch, unzipped it, dug into it, threw his head back and the
peanuts in. *Crunch-crunch.*

"Now I'll take questions, of which you ladies might have
one or two. Or even suggestions."

A dozen hands shot up. The chief of police recognized one
in the first row.

"Yes, Sister Tefenteller." Freight Train seemed to brace
himself. Mrs. August Tefenteller, the town matriarch, was a
formidable woman. Her voice now carried a clear note of
accusation.

"I just want you to realize that a number of us are
apprehensive at the aspect of a strange man outside our
window. And you men seem powerless to do anything about
it."

"Yes, ma'am. I can't say as I blame you," the chief said in
placatory tones. "But like I said, I don't think he's a *strange*
man. I think it's someone you know."

That defense was a mistake. "That makes it worse," Mrs.
Tefenteller said. "Don't you get smart with me, Claude
Flowers."

"I'm sorry, ma'am. I sure weren't trying to be smart." The
chief went into his tobacco pouch for more peanuts. *Crunch-
crunch.* "We all on the same side. Shall we move along? Yes,
Miz Mitchell?"

It was a voice from around the tenth row. "If we call you,
do we get to keep the present?"

"Yes, ma'am," the chief said patiently. "You can keep
anything the fellow gives you. You won't mind if I have a
look at it, will you? That reminds me. Some of you ladies

that's been peeped ain't called me soon as you found out. One instance, it was two days after the fellow visited you. Everybody check that windowsill last thing at night, first thing in the morning. If they's a little present there, call me double quick and I'll be right over and have a look at the evidence and take down your testimony while the experience is still fresh in your minds. Call me no matter how late or how early. Midnight, three in the morning."

The chief threw in more peanuts. "Speaking about when we catch him. I looked up the law on this matter, and you can get ten years for each offense for what he's doing. That's how serious the state of Texas takes this sort of activity. One of the most serious crimes under our system. A man's home is his castle. A woman's castle is her bedroom and bathroom. Leastways it is in Texas. Yes, ma'am, ten years per peep. So far he's seventy years in the hole. Yes, Miz Appleby?"

A rather bawdy-sounding voice came from midway back. "Freight, what do you think he goes on when he picks someone to peep at?" It was Helen Jewell Appleby, the druggist's wife. She hadn't been peeped. "She have to be good-looking? Or is he peeping at those he thinks might give him a present in return?"

There was a titter of giggles over the hall. Amid it came a shout, "Who asked that question?"

"I resent that!" came another. It was Mrs. Torrance, erupting from the eighth row. She had been peeped.

"Why, what did I say?" Helen Jewell said innocently.

"You know damn well what you said!"

"Chief," said another voice, "if he's all that clever, intelligent, thoughtful, and considerate, would you tell him I take my bath at nine-fifteen—every night?"

A lively eruption of laughter greeted this information.

"All right, ladies," the chief said wearily. "Let's get on with it. Next question."

A hand shot up way back. "I was interested in your statement that some of the women are waiting awhile to report that they've been peeped. Do you have any proof that every woman who is being peeped is reporting that fact to you at all? Or is it possible a number of them are simply keeping their presents and saying 'Thank you, sir'—and keeping their mouths shut?"

The chief peered out over the audience. "I can't see you, ma'am. Who are you?"

"I'm the new reporter for the Martha *Clarion,*" the voice sang out proudly.

"I see," the chief said. "Well, Miss New Reporter, when you not so new, maybe you'll learn that the women of Martha surely wouldn't do a thing like that."

It was a damn good question, I thought.

The chief let his gaze move carefully, cannily over his audience.

"Now, girls and ladies, we got the warmer weather coming on—the best possible season for our Peeper when a lot of you tend to go cavorting around a little birthdayish and frisky anyhow. Normal times, that's all right, no harm done. We all kinda family in Martha anyhow. But these not normal times, so let's try to keep that particular practice down until we catch this fellow, shall we, ladies? I be much obliged. Then you can go back to running around like you please. And *lower them shades.* Now if they's no further questions . . ."

I went back with the chief in the pickup. He seemed weary.

"Gawd amighty. I don't know why I should find that so exhausting. I've spent all night in the field with the Corps and not been this bushed." The chief sighed. "What we need is a Lone Star, Ace. Let's stop by the Cavary."

The Bon Ton has no regular closing hour. It closes when people stop coming. It can be nine, ten, midnight, and I have known it to be open at three in the morning. Down Cavalry Street I was glad to see it was still lighted. I had had a few Lone Stars—I noticed I was carrying one in my hand—and I could use a cup of coffee. Then down the dark street I noticed another light. It was the paper. I walked on down and stood across from it, looking through the window with its sign "The Martha Clarion" in a large, elaborately serifed typeface. It might not be much but it was mine. Mine and the bank's. Councilman Bert Hooper's bank.

The beat-up MG was parked in front. The paper's window was always dirty, but through it I could see her small figure hunched over the typewriter, batting away. I could make out even the hunt-and-peck system she used. It looked somehow comical. The classic reporter. I went in.

She didn't even look up. I walked around and stood behind her. She kept pecking away.

"Please go away," she said. She stopped typing and put her hand over her copy. "I'm busy. Besides, I don't like anyone to read something until I'm satisfied with it. And I certainly don't like people looking over my shoulder *anytime.*"

"That's an editor's privilege," I said. "You don't have to do this tonight. My God, it's after midnight. You're not writing for a morning paper. We don't come out until Friday."

Not, I thought, that I was anywhere near to deciding to print it anyhow. We were just going through the motions. A new game called "playing newspaper." It went against every instinct I had. I was beginning to feel uncomfortable with it, almost tarnished.

"I wanted to do it while it's still fresh in my mind," she said. "You've got beer all over your breath. I think you're *drunk.*"

"I am *not* drunk."

"What do you think of my map?"

I hadn't noticed. It was posted on the wall above her desk.

"There seems to be a big run on maps of Martha, Texas," I said.

This one was considerably smaller than the chief's. But like his it had pins in it, and for the same purpose. Where the Peeper had peeped. It even had tags with writing on them. I looked closer. Unlike the chief's, these tags had days of the week, nothing else.

"You notice something?" she said. "No Fridays, no Saturdays, no Sundays."

"So?"

"It means I've got weekends free. I can go to the island on weekends."

"Now listen to me. Your assignment is not to catch him. It's to report about it. Is that clear?"

"I just thought of something," she said. "He doesn't peep weekends. That's when you're out of town. Well?"

"Yeah," I said, "I guess you've found me out. I'm going home."

She pulled her copy out of the roller. It made a *whish*ing sound.

"I'll drop you. You've ruined my concentration."

She turned off the lights. Even the Bon Ton was shut now, the street all dark.

"You still haven't fixed that fender," I said.

"I can't afford it on what you pay me. I have to spend every cent just on survival. It isn't too beat-up for you to accept a lift, is it?"

She gunned the top-down MG through the silent dark streets of the town, skillfully, with the determination of someone to whom a car is not just wheels. The MG may have had a dented fender but there was nothing wrong with its carburetor.

"The speed limit is thirty in Martha, Texas," I said.

"I've got speeding tickets all my life. It's my hobby."

We roared past Pecan, Quince, and Redwood streets, past Sycamore, Tamarack, and Umbrella, the trees flashing by in a blur. She pulled up in front of my place.

"It doesn't look like much," she said. "It's probably very messy and dirty."

"Would you care to inspect it?"

"Not when you're drunk like this. Anyhow, our entire relationship is me sitting at your feet, remember?"

"Don't get any fancy notions, young lady," I said. "Nothing could be further from my mind. I can promise you that you're not in the slightest danger from me. Not in that direction anyhow, my dear."

"I don't like being called things like young lady and my dear. Do you need help getting out?"

"I am *not* drunk."

I got out, swaying just a little, and stood with my hand on the car. There was something different about her.

"Good God," I said. "You're wearing a dress."

"So you finally noticed. And they all said you're such a great reporter. It must be in the past tense."

She gunned off in her MG. I watched its red taillight fly down the dark street until it disappeared between the rows of trees.

PEEPER 4

Twin Glories

It wasn't really all that difficult. The defensive measures taken by the households themselves were decidedly lax and haphazard. There were more drawn shades now, but a lot were not drawn. Some shades would be down a few nights, then suddenly go up. On the whole, the shade patrol was a bust. This didn't surprise him. That every household could be persuaded to lower its shades every night was too much to expect in a town like Martha. People had pretty lawns to look out on. People liked the night breeze. It was not the kind of town that was going to shut up its houses simply because a man was going around looking in some of the windows. Nobody had got hurt, and besides, look at the odds. If he had peeped thirteen women in town, there were hundreds he had not peeped. People didn't scare easily in Martha. They were of an independent nature and did not like to be told what to do. This country had gone through Comanche Indians, Santa Ana and his march to his rendezvous with history at the Alamo, Pancho Villa and his raids, and the frontier in general for over a hundred years. It was not in the character of the town to panic and change its way of life and become a concentration camp because there was a man, harmless when you got down to it, who liked to have a look at women undressing and undressed. It was not the Texas way. A household which lowered its shades ran the risk of being thought timid, even cowardly.

Another factor had come into play that he had not suspected when he commenced his activities. It was subtle, full of nuances, much misunderstood, even possessing certain Byzantine overtones. It had given him considerable food for thought and he had never fully digested it. But so far as he could make out, there could not be men who liked to look unless there were women who liked to or at least were willing to be looked at. To function he had to have accomplices. This did not mean that women stationed themselves at their windows of a night and started taking their clothes off. Women did not operate in such a coarse, vulgar, forthright manner as that. Men might but women didn't. If they did, what man would ever get a glimpse of a stockinged inner thigh beneath a dress? It was much more subtle, sophisticated, primeval, contriving, Machiavellian—much more *womanly*—than that. It meant perhaps that a feminine hand which might otherwise have reached for a shade to lower it did not in every instance do so, though not even then by conscious act, admitted to oneself, refraining. After all, what law said you had to admit something to yourself? He would not by any means place the whole race of women in this category. He wouldn't place the whole race of women in any category. But he would place there a good many. He encountered plenty of windows with shades drawn. But he also encountered more than enough with shades up to keep him in business. Supply hadn't really been a problem of any serious dimensions. He was forced to the conclusion that there could not be voyeurs without voyees.

Heavy clouds hid the firmament, and he knew they held rain. The wetness of the air seemed to bring forth even more redolently than usual the scents from the yards. How grateful he now was for the chats he had had with Mary Armbruster when he passed her desk on business, taking time out for the social niceties, knowing that they, not the business itself, were the really important thing in life. She was so proper, but always with that amiable smile, that air of being unhurried, of always having time to stop and talk. A perfect secretary, to be sure. She had a quick wit, and there was a certain verve about her. She listened carefully, her surprising brown eyes watching you. Her piquant face showed character, intellect. It was not that he knew with any explicitness what she would be doing tonight. What he did know was that Monday was her "free" night, the night for "catching up on odds and ends," as she once had put it to him with her marvelous throwaway laugh.

He heard a frog croak somewhere, eager for the rain to come. Far off, now and then a low rumble of thunder moved down over the tucked-in town. He passed quickly through the gate, slipped on his mask, and stepped directly across the yard to the small house and the light in the window. He disappeared in the esperanza bushes and looked through.

She was doing her toenails. She sat on a bench at her dressing table, clad only in gossamer panties, left leg jack-knifed across the right with the heel resting on the knee. One thigh straight but the other in a cocked position, giving a perspective of the bunched underflesh of the thigh. Her long taffy hair—she must just have brushed it before turning to her nails—sweeping down until it touched over the bench, gathered itself around her buttocks, and now and then came around and brushed her breasts. The oval mirror assisted in the view, reflecting the curve of her body, the back bent in her task so that her burgundy-nippled breasts faced down toward her thighs. It was a picture of delight. Feminine refinement! he thought. These bodies with nature's sweetest perfume, these greatest treasures available to man, this first source of ecstasy. What a surge of adoration for them he felt as he watched. He always pictured her sitting so bright and proper before her typewriter and her secretarial pads. Now she sat before, in marshaled array, that arsenal with which women prepare their bodies. The creams, the lotions, the powders. The blushes, the enamels, the colorings, the scents. The rouges, the lipsticks, the lip glosses. The eye shadows, the eye liners, the mascaras. The perfumes, the colognes, the toilet waters. The shampoos, the sprays. The moisturizers, the cleansers, the nail polishes. He approved: Great goods should be appropriately packaged. Peering through the bushes, he watched in fascination as she proceeded with yet another task of adornment.

She dipped daintily into a small red bottle, took out the tiny wetted brush, and began meticulously and with absorbed attention to paint her big toe. The task of one toe alone took considerably longer than he would have imagined, but the cupped position of the body, the intentness of the task, made it an entrancing thing to see. He heard the ring of a phone and started momentarily in his bushes, then steadied and watched her walk to the bed. It was a slapstick progress. She walked gingerly, on her heels, toes up and spread, in order to keep from smearing the wet polish. She sat and picked up the phone from the nightstand. This change of venue gave him a new and stunning view of her breasts. All confidence, they were looking straight at him. From overhead he heard a clap of thunder. As she talked he became as interested in her conversation as her body. He couldn't believe what he was hearing, any of it, then finally: "Well, don't blame *me*," she said with a light girlish laugh. "I've just been sitting here waiting for you. Fifteen minutes, okay?"

She hung up, returned, quickly finished the toilette of her toenails, and turned her hair dryer on her feet. Then she went into her dressing-table arsenal and commenced to spray, paint, and touch up various parts of herself in a businesslike fashion. She stood and removed the fragment that was her panties, presenting a medium-growth blossom, heart-shaped and also taffy, went to her closet and came back with a peignoir, put it on, and sat again at the dressing table. She swept her hair out and back over the garment, so that it flowed down in a wonder of incontinence. Then just sat there and looked at herself in the mirror in final inspection. Her back was to him, but he could see reflected in the oval mirror a study in narcissism: a touch of smile, soft, smug, knowing. She liked what she saw. So did he. Beneath the pantyhose mask he felt the smile on his own face. She got up and headed toward his window. He had no fear. He felt it was merely the final act of preparation and hung tough. Right above him, she lowered the shade and he could hear her walk away. He sighed, stuck her silver butterfly on the windowsill, and left.

The rain began to come down as he reached the alley, and he took off his mask and headed for home. He would never have dreamed. Sitting there so bright and proper, with her typewriter, her secretarial pads. My God, that man was twice her age. And they said you couldn't hide anything in Martha. Well, to every rule there must be an exception. But Mary Armbruster and *him*? And a town councilman! As a matter of fact, parenthetical to his mission, he was discovering through the windows of the town a number of exceptions to the rule. He came out of the alley into Redwood Street, pondering all the way, oblivious to the fact he was getting soaked. All around him happy frogs were coming to life, croaking enthusiastically through the wet night. The conversation certainly indicated it was a regular arrangement. Every Monday night apparently. Odds-and-ends night indeed!

Under the ceaseless stars, strung in jeweled swatches across a windless Texas sky, he strode to his car, climbed in, and drove three miles to the south side, passing Queen Anne's Lace, Rhododendron, and Snapdragon streets. It would be his first selection in that part of town. He drove around for a bit to kill a few minutes' time, his thoughts dwelling pleasantly on the pedicure of two nights ago and looking forward to further delights this night, then parked his car on Xanthisma two blocks away.

Here was a different part of town. The lots were fifty or at the most seventy-five feet instead of the hundred-and-fifty-foot frontage characteristic of the north side. The houses too were considerably smaller. All frame, all one-story. But they were embraced by the same rich thick bushes and shrubbery whose mission was to give privacy. They had the same caliche alleys and the same oleander hedges further protecting that privacy and, set in the hedges, the same latch gates. He found the appropriate gate, entered it, and stood looking across the grass at the little frame structure of four rooms with its simple, clean lines. All he wanted was a glimpse of them.

He had been close to them often enough. They had near-brushed him now and then as she served him the cuisine for which the Bon Ton Cafe was justly famous up and down the Rio Grande. She had put in front of him the beef stew, steaming and succulent, the hot biscuits and the home-made cornbread, the country butter and the raw country honey, the baked potatoes and the home fries; along with, depending on which of the three growing seasons it was, the fresh collards and the fresh zucchini, the okra, the corn, the cucumbers, the string beans, the tomatoes, the turnips, the green cabbage and the purple cabbage, the kale, cauliflower, parsley and eggplant, the yellow squash and the crookneck squash, the red, yellow, and white Granex onions, all plucked, picked, or uprooted just a few hours before within twenty miles of the restaurant; also the pan-fried chicken with the cream gravy and the roast pork with the brown gravy; the fresh redfish and the red snapper and kingfish which, as the Bon Ton accurately boasted, had been swimming last night in the Gulf; not to forget the Bon Ton's celebrated chicken-fried steak.

She had served him countless wonderful meals and he had been close to them times without number when she leaned over him in the performance of her waitressly duties. At the counter and at the table, he had eaten at her hands. Each locale had something to say for it. At the counter the view was better, as she leaned across. At the table, tactile proximity was more possible. He chose his eating place for the day according to which sense, sight or touch, was predominant in him at the moment. He was principally a counter man.

And talked. They always talked. He found out that she had grown up on a farm down the river near Santiago, pop. 600, one of nine children, that she had liked the farm but it was nice to be on her own, that—she was proud of this—she was even paying off her own house on Martha's south side, that she went to bed in that house at nine o'clock every workday night. "You could set your watch by when I go to bed," she had told him more than once. "Talk about creature of habit! Mercy! I do appreciate my sleep. Try getting up at four o'clock every morning to open up the Bawn Tawn at five-thirty, and you'll appreciate yours. Of course weekends I *never* go to bed. Weekends you can generally find me at the

Here-Tis. Sattiday night's when I put on my fancy duds and shake and strut," she said, throwing her hip out a little, a gesture which sweetly accentuated them, and speaking with an exaggerated accent on top of her regular one. It was like a Texan imitating a Texan, and she would giggle herself at this rendition. "God, how I love to dance."

She had a lively and loving face and eyes blue as a Rio Grande sky. Just being around her lessened whatever anguish you might be undergoing about the unremitting vicissitudes of life. Life wasn't so bad, you felt. She was a good old Texas girl—at age twenty-nine. He was quite fond of her.

Only the one light showed. He must be on schedule. He looked at his watch and slipped into his pantyhose mask. The mask was getting slack, losing its taut, stretched feel. Also, he had apparently snagged it on a bush during the Armbruster visit, starting a run right above the eyes, and he knew what women meant by runs in their stockings. It was an irritant. He made a mental note to purchase a new pair at Carruthers Mercantile. He moved across the grass and went into his bushes—the bushes of Martha were home to him now. These he recognized as the *Hibiscus mutabilis,* the Confederate rose—a marvelous thing producing clusters of flowers which were white when they opened in the morning, turned pink by noon, and were red by night. He crouched in them and raised his chin to the windowsill.

He had arrived in the nick of time, not a moment too soon. She was in the very act of removing her waitress's white uniform, stained a bit with the Bon Ton's famous cuisine, perhaps here a bit of cream gravy, there a touch of the fresh broccoli she had served him at noontime dinner that day. Neck to hemline, the uniform buttoned all the way down the front, as he had frequently observed, the buttons large and pearl. As the buttons now became unbuttoned under her agile fingers and the uniform peeled back both ways from her body, he was astonished to see that she wore but a single garment beneath it. No stockings, no pantyhose, no girdle, no slip, no panties.

Only a brassiere. But an exceptional one, lavender satin

and garnished with lace, as if—never mind the white waitress uniform—what they sheltered deserved the best and the brightest. As she unfastened it—it was one of the nifty variety that disengages in front—he saw why, however she loved the freedom of dispensing with underthings, this garment was absolutely essential. She had a nice figure, even by the standards to which he had recently become accustomed, but the breasts . . . the breasts! My God, she was in the right profession but the wrong place. She should have been one of those topless waitresses they had in places like Dallas and Houston. Instead of serving chicken-fried steak, she should be serving *them,* which he understood was approximately what happened in those places.

Far and away the two most important structures in Martha were the Cavalry Post and the Bon Ton Cafe. The Cavalry Post, housing the Town Council meetings and police headquarters, regulated the lives of the citizens of the town. But a case could be made that what happened at the Bon Ton determined their lives even more. The Bon Ton was the gathering place. In its confines not only was the best food in town eaten, but the important gossip exchanged and not a few of the most important deals, of both a private and public character, struck. It was an honest place, with a low ceiling, Formica-topped tables, straight-back chairs, an unremarkable decor, and no stuffed animal heads on the walls.

The news of who had been peeped the night before was always over town by noontime next day, being so eagerly awaited. He first noticed it in the way the men who regularly ate at the Bon Ton looked at her. Over his chicken and dumplings he could see them sneaking glances, not just of curiosity but of admiration.

It was obvious that Flory sensed this. She carried herself with a new air of confidence, a fresh pride. When she caught people stealing looks at her, she looked back, at first shyly, then boldly. There was something about her now that had not been there before. An unmistakable glow. Also a new animation that was altogether becoming. When he watched her walking away toward the kitchen, she seemed to move with an extra little swish. She had on a glistening new white uniform and she had done her hair somewhat differently. There was a color in her cheeks, and her eyes sparkled.

It was plain that it had really set her up. After all, she was the first from the south side to make the list. Not one of the men mentioned her experience, of course. They were far too courteous to do that. But it was obvious that they were looking at her with new eyes. Some of the men were asking her for an extra cup of coffee beyond their usual quota. Men who never ate dessert were today ordering fresh peach shortcake or dewberry cobbler. Their glances spoke of respect. What had happened was unmistakable. If the Peeper had picked her, she must have something.

6.

The Green Sea

Far and away it went, a sea of green stretching to the hill-less horizon, a great wash of blue coming down to meet it. The red MG slipped down the Old Military Highway that crossed the fields.

"When I arrived in the city room of the Washington *Post* as a cub reporter," I said across to her behind the wheel, "all ready to start covering the White House or at least the U.S. Senate, the city editor said to me, 'Welcome aboard, Baxter. I have something nice for you. I am going to start you out at the zoo. Once you have demonstrated an ability to cover the activities of animals, I'll consider letting you cover those of human beings. And don't forget how fortunate you are. After all, this is the *National* Zoo.'"

"That city editor," Jamie said, "must have been a very witty person."

"Oh, he was. I learned a great deal from him. Unfortunately we don't have a zoo here. But in place of it I want you to cover the vegetables. To paraphrase my city editor, 'Once you learn to cover inanimate objects such as vegetables, we'll see about your covering animate objects such as human beings.'"

"You're just as witty as he was."

I did not let her lack of enthusiasm deter me. After all, I was the editor now.

"The vegetable beat is more important than you think. If it weren't for the vegetables, none of us would be here."

We had put the paper to bed, without the Peeper story. I had decided to put off one more week whether to go with it. I wanted to hear what she had found out. Then I had to make a decision. She had been out most of the week, interviewing the women who had been peeped and digging up whatever else she could. Meantime the peepings continued, three more in eight days—including two in one night. I suppose by cosmic measurements it wasn't an earth-shaking decision, but it was earth-shaking for me and Martha was my cosmos. I liked my three days on the island. I liked Martha, Texas. I wasn't eager to lose them. I told her also that if she was going to cover the valley, maybe I should show her some of it and take her around to meet some of the town councilmen. I told her to bring notebook and pencil.

I had got the Bon Ton to prepare a takeout lunch—ham sandwiches—which I told her we would consume on a big rock I knew by the Rio Grande while trying to reach a decision on the Peeping Tom story.

"It'll be a business lunch," I said. "Just like in Washington at Duke Zeibert's or in New York at Pearl's."

"Big deal," she said and then weakened for a second from the defiant posture which was her strategy for confronting the world. "That sounds fun."

When she arrived at the paper this morning I felt I was looking at someone I had never seen. She was wearing a putty-colored paisley cotton dress that fluttered over her bare legs. Somehow that change into the customary raiments of her sex made me, practically for the first time, conscious of her as a female. Pretty bones. A tilted nose. A fine modeling of the cheeks and temples, the kind of looks that would survive when youth was gone. Large brown eyes that danced with a kind of impudence, a secret mirth. Her hair was shot through with light. I had to remind myself what a little bitch she could be.

I had guided her and her red MG out of town to the Old Military Highway. The land was a jeweler's case of greens, each vegetable with its own distinctive shade. Together they spread out before us, their homologous squares fashioning an immense green quilt.

For once, caught up in the wonder of the fields, she drove slowly. The sun came down pleasantly hot in the convertible from a sky windless in the unbroken blue.

"What's that out there?"

"Carrots."

I explained to her about the colors, emerald for bell peppers, malachite for okra, jade for carrots. You couldn't see the vegetables, but if you knew the color code you knew what you were looking at.

"I want you to teach me everything you know," she said with a bright air. "I want to be a newspaperman. It's the only thing I've ever wanted."

"It's a good thing to be," I said. "It is really the very best of the professions. I can't think of anything else that isn't dull by comparison. You know what the best part about it is?"

"No."

"Being a newspaper reporter is the one profession where you don't have to kiss ass."

"Never? I think you have to kiss a few right here in Martha."

"I was speaking of reporters. I'm an editor now. Editors do sometimes have to kiss ass. Another reason to stay a reporter. Never become an editor."

"I'll remember that. I'm glad I'm a reporter. Or trying to be. I don't want you to hesitate to tell me whenever I do something wrong."

"I'll tell you. You have my word."

She giggled and I could feel her looking over at me. "You know something, Baxter? The only thing I like about you is that you don't take yourself too seriously."

As many times as I'd seen it, I was enjoying the country. I never get tired of it. I knew cities and loved a couple. But one thing here, you can breathe. Another, you're not so up against people, physically, mentally, or emotionally. I wanted to stay around it. I wouldn't like to have to give it up. Off to our right some Santa Gertrudis cattle with their lovely deep shade of burnished red stood in a green pasture.

"Do women make good newspapermen?" she said in her abrupt way. She looked at me and gave that derisive little laugh. She used it to take the edge off a serious question.

"Actually of the three best newspapermen I've known, two were women. But you have to pay a price."

"What price?"

A field of chalcedony passed by.

"What's that one?" I said.

"Cabbages."

"You cheated. You saw that truck over there full of them. It's hard to be a woman newspaperman and still hold on to some other things."

"Hold on to what?"

"I blame men for it. They make women become like men in that world. That's the price men make women pay."

"And naturally you don't think the price is worth paying."

"I don't think *any* price is worth paying for a woman if she has to give up very much of being a woman."

"Well. *Well.*" From behind the wheel of the MG she looked across at me. Her hair bounced. "What chauvinism."

"God, how I hate that word."

She took a deep breath and expelled it. "All I can say is, you're in the right place. With the vegetables and the sea—whatever it is you do down on that island."

"Having said all that, I hope you make it in the world of journalism and keep both the femininity and the reporter part. I'll do what I can to help you with the second."

"Good. I can take care of the first myself."

Up ahead I could see another stand of cattle. These were the big Charolais, the long-bodied "silver cattle" which had been brought over from France because they gave so much beef. Then I saw a field of emerald. "What's that?"

"Bell peppers."

"Correct," I said. "Turn there."

We turned down a caliche road, then onto a dirt road until we came to a grove of retama and I told her to pull in under the trees. We got out and looked across the field. Thousands upon thousands of plants, about two feet high, stretched away in emerald files. I twisted off a bell pepper from one of them, with a quick clean jerk so as not to damage it. It was firm and glistening, regal in its color and shape, the prince of vegetables. I broke it in two and gave her a half and we stood and looked out over the field and chewed our halves. It had a good green taste I liked. I knew the field and the man it belonged to.

"I want you to learn how the whole thing about vegetables works," I said. "We'll start right here. The first job of a reporter is to know what you're reporting as well as the people doing it. Then they can't fool you. Now. Here are four hundred acres of bell peppers. They have been growing here for a hundred and twenty days. They are ready to sell and harvest. Get out your pad and pencil. The grower has put about four hundred dollars an acre into them. For four hundred acres—"

"That's one hundred and sixty thousand dollars."

"What the grower gets for them depends on how bell peppers are doing elsewhere. I checked the USDA market reports this morning—and I want you to do that daily with the regional office in Melville—and he's sitting very nice. Man by the name of Rust Breckinridge."

I chewed some bell pepper.

"Here's why. There are three other places bell peppers come from this time of year. Florida. California. The state of Sinaloa on the west coast of Mexico. Well, Florida has been hit by very heavy rains, and the bell pepper crop there is pretty much rotted. Earlier this year frost killed off most of the crop in California. And Sinaloa has had a long heat wave which sunburned most of its bell peppers. So what you're looking at in these four hundred acres is a good part of the available, in-first-class-condition bell pepper supply right now for the United States and Canada. If there were bell pepper competition from those other places, these would go out of the valley at six or eight dollars for a box of forty pounds. But now they should bring fifteen or sixteen dollars. If everything goes well."

I chewed my bell pepper.

"He'll get about five hundred boxes to the acre. At sixteen

dollars, that's eight thousand dollars an acre. So for four hundred acres. . . ."

She did some multiplying. "Why, we're looking at three million two hundred thousand dollars' worth of bell peppers. Is that right?"

"Yep."

"That Rust, the owner of the field. He gets that?" she said in an astounded voice.

"Not quite. It works like this. Pay close attention. You'll be dealing with all this on the vegetable beat. The owner of this field has two routes he can go. He can sell the field on a commission basis, hoping to get the sixteen dollars at, for instance, the Great Atlantic and Pacific warehouse in Edison, New Jersey, where a lot of these vegetables go to feed New York City. If he gets the sixteen dollars, he gets to keep thirteen dollars and twenty-five cents of it. The other two seventy-five goes to the shipper, who sells it for him—people like Orville Jenkins. The harvesting, packing, and shipping all come out of the two dollars and seventy-five cents. But doing it that way, the owner of the field takes a risk. The buyer in New Jersey always reserves the right to refuse the shipment at the destination point—there could be decay in the vegetables, they could have been damaged en route, the market could have changed. A whole list of imponderables, things only God can predict. Rust could end up getting not sixteen dollars a box but four. And since the shipper gets his two dollars and seventy-five cents whatever the price is, Rust would keep only one twenty-five a box instead of thirteen twenty-five. Follow all this?"

"Yes. I think so." She was very intent. "What's the other way Rust can do it?"

"He can sell the field outright to someone like Orville. It's called a 'field buy.' In that case, the rule of thumb is that the shipper should have at least a chance to double his money if all goes well. So if the shipper thinks the bell peppers might fetch sixteen dollars per box at Edison, he pays Rust half of the thirteen twenty-five—they split it after taking off the shipper's two seventy-five. But once the deal is made, that money is Rust's. Orville pays Rust on the spot, before a single pepper is pulled. After that it's the shipper who takes the responsibility and the risk. He's the one who gets stuck if the market changes or those people in Edison, New Jersey, don't like the bell peppers or whatever. So for a field buy, in the case of this field we're looking at, multiply five hundred boxes per acre by half of thirteen twenty-five dollars, then by four hundred acres."

Her pencil moved over the pad, quite fast. "One million three hundred and twenty-five thousand."

"And that's sure and certain money for the grower if he sells it that way. From the moment he shakes hands with the shipper, that money is in his pocket. The shipper harvests the field, packs the peppers, ships them. Whatever happens to the field after that handshake, the grower is home free."

"I'll say he is."

I took another bite of bell pepper and threw the rest away. "But let's say the grower is a gambler and, instead of the field buy, he decides on the commission route. Then he gets exactly twice that."

She did some figuring on her reporter's pad. "That comes out to two million six hundred and fifty thousand. *Dollars.*"

She looked out over the lovely emerald field as though she were seeing dollar signs just above the stalks of peppers.

"That would be the grower's take if everything came off," I said. "So. The grower is betting one million three hundred and twenty-five as a sure thing against two million six hundred and fifty possible."

"Jesus."

"And if Orville buys the field outright, he's betting that he will get the sixteen dollars per box. But if one of those imponderables known only to God pops up and he doesn't get the price, he can lose his shirt and Rust still gets his money. So which way he buys the field makes a big difference to Orville, too. Going the commission route he'd make about fifty cents a box out of the two seventy-five after expenses. Two hundred and fifty dollars per acre. A hundred thousand dollars for the field. But if he buys it outright he could make one and a third million extra on this field—assuming all goes well."

"My God. Reminds me of blackjack."

"More like high-stakes poker. There's a saying in the fields that in that particular deck, God is the joker. Only He can say what will happen to the crop."

"Which way do you think the grower'll go?"

"I have no idea. Most growers prefer the field buy. The sure thing. They've been bit too often going the other way. But you never know. I know this field is up for sale today, and the grower usually sells it one way or the other to Orville Jenkins. So let's go see Orville."

"Oh, yes. I want to find out. You know something, Baxter? I think I might like the vegetable beat."

She was looking up at me, those huge brown eyes in that small face. If I had held my arm straight out, she would have been standing under it. We stood there in the fields, in all the green, and I thought how I had come more and more to like them, even to love them. Their shapes, their colors, the way they smelled. The vegetables. Becoming involved almost emotionally in that genesis, not just every year, but down here by the Rio Grande, in this riotous three-crops-a-year land, this alluvial womb, every few months. Seeing them grow into strength and maturity. Just like people, though sometimes, like them, stunted, marred, emasculated. It would be nice to pass some of this on to her. I bent down and snapped off another bell pepper and gave it to her to take along.

We climbed in the MG and drove back up the dirt road and onto the caliche road. "Orville, whom you're about to meet, is a town councilman, of course," I said. "He's both a shipper and a grower. The biggest in the valley. He's even got a canning factory. He wouldn't be my first choice to spend a month alone with, but there's no con in him. He likes his way, but he'll give you the straight dope every time. But what's really important is that our job contract for overprinting his canning labels pays a lot of the *Clarion*'s bills. In fact, we might just go under without it."

"But I don't have to kiss his?"

"Remember what I said about reporters? Only editors have to do that. Just be your natural polite self."

"Yes, sir, boss."

We drove back onto the Old Military Highway and a couple miles down it until we could see an immense concrete-and-aluminum building rising out of the fields.

"What's that?" she said. "The Strategic Air Command?"

"That," I said, "is a packing shed."

Huge semi-trailers were drawn up with their backs to the shed. We parked, the MG looking like a red bug alongside.

Inside the shed I stopped to let her take in its cavernous dimensions. It was five hundred feet long and two hundred feet wide and forty feet high. The height was to accommodate the packing lines at the tops of chutes. There were several lines going, one for onions, another for carrots, another for bell peppers. We went over to the bell pepper line. Through a large opening in the side of the building we could see an open-bed truck five feet deep in bell peppers pulled up beside a chute into the shed. The peppers flowed onto the chute gradually from an opening in the side of the truck. As the peppers started up the chute, three men and women on each side separated the red peppers from the green ones.

"Why are some of the peppers red?" she said. "Are they from different plants?"

I thought possibly she was going to make a reporter.

"No. Same plants. They turn red because of age or stress—lack of water, a touch of cold."

The red peppers were put in big pallet bins on rollers to be sold separately to freezing plants which would add them to food for color. I explained this to her. The green peppers climbed to the top of the chute and entered the building high up on other rollers. We climbed a stairway toward the roof and she followed the peppers intently as they passed through a bath which washed them, then crossed a grading table where three women on each side, their hands moving swiftly as the rollers took them by, plucked out the culls and dropped them in a slot between the rollers and themselves, down a hopper to a dump truck underneath.

"What do they do with the rejects?"

"They're sold separately for frozen foods."

She studied how the peppers continued through a sizing "expander" roller which separated them into small, medium and large. Then they dropped into their correspondingly stamped boxes beneath the rollers. The boxes were on automatic weighers which kicked them out when full. From there lift trucks carried them into the big mouths of the semis. At night they would head north on their long journey to market: to Edison, New Jersey, for the dinner tables of Manhattan and the Bronx; to Chicago; to somewhere north. We looked down at the boxes. "Orville Jenkins—Martha, Texas" was printed in large red letters on their sides.

We climbed back down and walked through the huge building to the offices in front. The doors to all the offices were open, and we walked in one. It was a very simple office, sparse in all respects, not at all large.

"Orville, I've doubled my staff," I said. "This is the *Clarion*'s new reporter, Jamie Scarborough. Orville Jenkins."

He stood up and gave her a careful, somewhat surprised look, as if he hadn't know reporters came in this gender. They shook hands and he sat down and leaned back, his head cupped in his intertwined fingers. He was without hurry. He gave the impression of a man in control of everything around him, and of an authority that was not dependent on troops of secretaries or banks of telephones. He looked in mint condition, vigorous, a man who would no more permit his body to go to seed than he would his business. No flab anywhere. He was close-shaven and neat, and his trimmed steel-gray hair went back in waves. You felt there was steel too behind his gracious manner. He had a strong nose, a long line of a mouth, and a prominent chin. He had the bronzed complexion of someone who spends more time in the fields than behind a desk. He wore an open-neck short-sleeved plaid shirt. His arms were muscular and covered with blond hair.

"What's new?" He laughed. "Isn't that what you ask a newspaperman?" He looked at Jamie. "Or do I say newspapergirl?"

"Newspaperman will do fine," Jamie said crisply.

The phone rang. "Excuse me," Orville said.

He listened for a bit. "Yeah, Rust, I know what the market is. . . . Rust, the market goes down as well as up. We both know that. . . . That's right, you could get sixteen—or you could get twelve, or five. Now I'm willing to give you thirty-three hundred dollars per acre. . . . No, Rust, I couldn't go five thousand. . . . It's very simple. Rust Breckinridge takes the risks. Or Orville Jenkins takes them. . . . No, Rust, not one and a half. One and a third. . . . Rust, nobody's ever been insulted by an offer of one and a third million dollars for a field of peppers. . . . You've got it. . . . We don't have to shake hands on it, do we? If you want it, come on over. Otherwise I'll just send you a check. . . . Give my best to Edwina."

He hung up and sat back.

"Mr. Jenkins," Jamie said, "did you just buy four hundred acres of bell peppers?"

"I did."

She looked down at her pad. "Five hundred boxes times six sixty-two equals about thirty-three hundred times four hundred acres equals one million three. That's what you paid, and that's what you hope to make out of it."

She said this as a statement of fact, not a question. Orville's eyes went wide in surprise and admiration.

"Say, you're pretty good. Someone's been teaching you well. Real well."

"You mean it's done as easy as that?" she said. "Like you did just now?"

"Why, sure, little lady. All it takes is money. Excuse me. Anson!" he yelled.

A man wearing chinos and a denim shirt appeared.

"Rust Breckinridge's field," Orville Jenkins said. "I just bought it. We're going for the ride."

A nice expression crossed Anson's face. "Good. That's good."

"Let's start tomorrow. Big a crew as you can get. I want it out of there fast."

"I'll get right on it, Orville," Anson said and left.

"I'd like to bring Jamie by tomorrow to watch the harvest," I said.

"Fine. Do that. We're going in at sunup."

"She's going to be covering vegetables for the *Clarion*."

He looked at her again. "I'm delighted to hear it."

Now that the Breckinridge field was bought and the harvest set for tomorrow, and now that he had been told Jamie's job, he seemed to want to talk.

"Don't ever hesitate to drop in and ask me anything about vegetables, Miss. Of course I'm as biased as a man can be about them. My father taught me to look at crops as if they were your children and God's, and nobody has ugly children. I still think there's something holy about working with the soil. Maybe because it's all in His hands. Only God grows the produce. It's laying out there for whatever God wants to do with it."

Probably because his belief was sincere, these things came out and could be received without embarrassment. They were stated in a tone as matter-of-fact as though he had been discussing the best chemical fertilizer to use in the fields. It was as if, now that he knew what Jamie would be covering, he wanted to get his beliefs, his essence, out on the table.

Orville's eyes lit up mischievously.

"Right now the particular God's children the market is hungry for is bell peppers. Good bell peppers are very scarce right now. And worth a lot. And that's all right. I have to assume that's what God wants to happen to His children."

He asked Jamie polite questions about where she was from and how she came to Martha. He seemed honestly interested in this newcomer. I thought we should move on to a better subject.

"Orville, what's new with the Peeper situation?" I asked.

I knew he felt strongly about it, but I was surprised to see his mood change so abruptly. But then Orville Jenkins looked upon Martha rather as he did his produce company, with a sense of proprietorship. It was his produce company, and it was his town. Things were supposed to go well with both. It was his job to see that they did. Right now things weren't going at all well with his town. He took a hard, rather sudden breath.

"Another Bloomer Girl last night. Rebecca Wilder. I have Freight call me when there's a new one. That makes sixteen." He shook his head. "What an outrage this is. To happen to a decent town like Martha. We've been contaminated, like the vegetables when they're attacked by a blight. We're going to ring his bell. He won't be looking at women or much of anything else when we get finished with him."

In his grimness I felt emanations of the Old Testament prophets of my childhood. I wouldn't want to be the Peeper and in Orville's hands. I stood up and then Jamie did. Orville rose politely.

"Come in any time, Miss," he said. He was all graciousness again. I fancied I saw an appraising keenness in his eyes as he looked at her. "Any time you want to talk about vegetables. It doesn't take much to get me started on vegetables."

"I'd like that," Jamie said. "I'm sure I can learn a lot from you."

My goodness, I thought. Who would have imagined?

Orville Jenkins beamed. "And I'm sure as a pupil you'd be at the head of the class."

We were driving away. I turned, and back of us I could see the huge packing shed sitting in the fields. Above it I saw the first clouds of the day, some billowing altocumulus, floating across the blue.

"It's hot. Why don't we drop by Henry Milam's and get some of that complimentary Lone Star. He's someone else you have to know if you're to be a reporter here. People like Henry and Esau Ireland are the backbone of Martha. Besides, everybody likes Henry."

It was true, and not just because of the free Lone Star.

"Henry Milam is the only man I have never seen even slightly upset," I said. "Henry looks upon the world with tolerant amusement. His reaction to anything out of the ordinary is just to be curious about it. He even reads books.

More important, that big Lone Star ad we get every week pays part of your salary."

"Such as it is," she said.

"How are you feeling today, Henry?" I said.

"If I felt any better I'd be dangerous."

"Henry, I'd like you to meet my new reporter. Jamie Scarborough. Henry Milam."

"Call me Henry. Here, let's all rest easy. It's a pleasure, little lady. Scarborough is a very old Texas name."

Henry had the manners of a squire. We settled into the comfortable leather armchairs Henry's office provided, under wall pictures of several generations of Milams who had held the Lone Star distributorship. Next to the picture of Henry's grandfather was the stuffed head of a bear taken by the patriarch. The bear was snarling and looked ready to eat the next human being it saw. Henry didn't hunt himself. He was one of the few men in Martha who didn't. Instead, he jogged and played dominoes. But he left the bear's head there because it had looked down on his grandfather. Henry was big on tradition. Five generations of Milams had been members of the Town Council, like an inherited seat in the House of Lords.

From behind his desk Henry leaned back and looked cheerfully at Jamie with his bright blue merry eyes. He had lean features, reddish hair, furry reddish eyebrows, and unusually white teeth. His body was narrow and sinewy, to the point of being bony. It suggested he didn't indulge too much in his own product. Actually he enjoyed Lone Star as much as any of us but worked it off with his daily dawn jogging. Everything about Henry Milam was relaxed and low-key. He cast a soft smile on you, as if to say, Everything is all right between you and me. He was very comfortable to be with and he never interrupted. The personal interchange, he seemed to be saying, should always be pleasant, if possible interesting, and in any case a nice moment in the day. Otherwise why have it?

"Baxter here doesn't treat you right," he said, "you come

around and see me and I'll put him in jail. Don't forget, I'm a member of the Town Council."

Jamie looked threateningly at me and then pleasantly at Henry, to whom she said sweetly, "Why, as a matter of fact he's about to give me a raise. But in case he doesn't treat me *very* well, I'll remember what you said—about jail, I mean."

"Don't get me wrong. We're glad to have him in town. Good man, Baxter here."

He pushed his buzzer, which chimed instead of buzzing. A very good-looking object materialized. She had shimmering hair the color of pulled taffy candy, the promise of charitable breasts pushing against a brassiere just visible beneath her white blouse, and a sharply turned-out air. We had passed her coming in and I had introduced Jamie to Mary Armbruster, Henry's much-admired secretary. She had been peeped a week ago.

"Mary," he said, "would you bring in three, please. The new draft."

"Three of the new draft coming up," she said with an indulgent smile, as if she liked doing this and liked her work. Presently three of Henry's Lone Stars in elegant intaglioed seidels were sitting in front of us. We sipped.

"Fine beer," I said.

"So good and cold," Jamie said.

"An excellent shipment," Henry said professionally, like Baron Philippe de Rothschild passing judgment on his most recent *premier cru*. "Too bad you arrived when the town is so upset about this Peeper situation, Miss Jamie. You'll get the wrong impression."

He looked up at the wall—whether at the bear or at his ancestors I couldn't tell. He seemed uncommonly solemn, for Henry.

"A curious business," he said. "Going into people's yards and looking at our womenfolk through windows. Imagine! I don't mind telling you I've been giving it a lot of time and thought."

"What have you come up with, Mr. Milam?" Jamie said, prodding.

"Call me Henry."

He sipped his beer. He always sipped, never guzzled, as if indeed Lone Star were a fine Bordeaux or a rare Burgundy. He spoke in tones of reflection.

"I've been trying to back off and see what we've got on our hands here. I have this peculiar feeling there's some key that will unlock the whole mystery and lead us straight to him. Strange business! Oh, I don't find the voyeurism strange. Most men do it every day, all the time. Trying to see as much as possible. Why, that's the biggest men's sport, indoors and outdoors. But he seems to have a case of *acute* voyeurism."

"Galloping," I said.

He tipped his seidel. His voice was measured, careful. "There has to be something else. Motive's what I'm talking about. He has to have another reason. Given the risk. Assuming he's someone we all know. Someone 'upstanding' in the community, as Freight puts it. Find out what that reason is, and we've found our man."

"Another reason?" I said. "You mean like Orville's theory that he's punishing the women for sins they've committed?"

Henry shook his head impatiently. "No, nothing infantile like that. More along the line that the Peeper is trying to do something *to* the town. But do *what*? Who would want to change this perfectly lovely town?" He looked suddenly at me. "Baxter, do you find yourself making a list of everyone you know, going down it and asking yourself, 'Could it be him? Could it just be him?' "

"Why, yes, I do," I said.

I felt Henry was looking at me in a manner unusually intense for Henry Milam. Then I wondered if I just imagined that.

"So do I," he said. Then he shrugged. "Of course I may be a mile off. Perhaps it's just the power."

"The power?" Jamie said, prodding again.

Henry ruminated a moment. "The power of watching someone without their knowing it. You could look at it just the opposite way: voyeurism as the supreme tribute to a woman and incarnating *her* power over the voyeur. Slave syndrome would be more like it."

He spoke in sober, rather professorial tones, but I thought

I detected a special merriment in his eyes. He sighed and sipped his draft.

"Well! It's a mystery. But it certainly exercises the mind, having him around."

"Henry," I said in a moment, "I'm thinking about starting to cover the Peeper story in the *Clarion*. Like you would a regular story." I tried to put it in their terms. "Nothing sensational. Just telling the people about it. Straight reporting."

Henry sampled his Lone Star and looked at me carefully. He put his seidel down. "I wonder if it's a good idea," he said. "This town takes itself pretty seriously. And it takes this Peeper seriously."

"So do I, Henry. That's why I want to print it."

Henry shook his head and rubbed his arms. He was thinking over what he was going to say. That was why he was a good councilman, a thoughtful man whose advice was worth listening to because it was never impetuous.

"Everybody's talking about it anyhow," I said.

"It's different when it's in print. When it's just talk, people can pretend to themselves and their friends—see it the way they want to. But when it's in the paper, then that's how it is. There's no getting away from it."

I had heard worse definitions of the purpose of journalism.

"I'm not sure they should get away from it," I said.

"Well, maybe not. But they won't like it, and it will be your fault, not the Peeper's. Think it over. Carefully."

We sat a moment in silence. Then I stood up. "Thanks for the beer, Henry. How's Emily?"

"She's still up in Idalou, with that sick sister of hers. I've thought about telling her to stay put until we catch him. But that house of mine is surely lonely without her. Especially the nights. Who are you reading these days, Baxter?"

"Turgenev."

"Good man. I'm especially fond of 'A Sportsman's Sketches.' Drop in any time, little lady. For a Lone Star. Or a chat. With or without Baxter." His blue eyes danced.

"Why, I will," Jamie said sweetly. "Thank you very much."

I was seeing a new side of her. She could surely lay down the scent when she wanted.

Henry got a six-pack out of a refrigerator in the corner for us to take along.

"Stay mellow," he said. "Meantime, little lady, be careful you're not peeped. You look like a right good candidate to me."

His eyes were shining merrily.

"Why, Mr. Milam—Henry."

Jesus God, I thought. We left and drove away in the MG.

"I had no idea you could turn it on like that," I said. "With just anybody, isn't it? Orville, Henry . . . both twice your age."

"Just like you. That business about the Peeper's motive. Thinking if he can figure that out, he can identify him. He may have something."

"He's reaching for something that isn't there. It's very simple. The Peeper just likes to see naked women. Like any man."

"You too?"

"Like any man."

Right ahead of us was a pickup with a red Irish setter in the back. It started wagging its tail and looking at us in the open MG. When the tail-wagging produced no results, the setter barked at us a couple of times, then gave up and stuck its head over the side of the pickup to catch some breeze.

"I like him. He's nice. Like being concerned that I was being treated fairly. I found that rather sweet and protective."

"He should mind his own business. Isn't that one hell of a good-looking secretary he's got? You can sure understand how she made the list."

"I suppose, if you like the type. That hair like an unmowed wheat field and those Guernsey boobs."

"I like the type."

"You would."

"There's talk about her and Henry. Of course it has to be just talk. Can you imagine Henry Milam carrying on with a woman?"

"Why, yes, I can," she said. "He's so courtly. So genteel. He's just the sort of man who really likes women and knows how to please them so that they will like him. You know what it is? There's a tenderness about him. That's one of the first things a woman looks for in a man."

"Good God," I said. "Let's go see Sherm Embers before I throw up. I want to go over some legal points, just in case. Anyway, you should meet Sherman too. He's a member of the Town Council, he's unmarried at the moment, and he likes girls. He screws anything that walks and has tits."

"And you talk about my language. Incidentally, the operable word these days is not girls. It's *women*."

"All right, he likes women," I said. "But he also likes girls."

Her hair bounced. "But isn't he even older than you?"

"That's hardly possible," I said.

The lawyer's office was on the second and top floor of the Carruthers building, overlooking Cavalry Street. You could see the women shoppers go by, their spring dresses rippling over bare legs. As they lingered at windows your gaze could linger on them. Cavalry Street had a sleepy look in the warm April morning. Take away the cars and you could be a century back in time. It looked pretty and comfortable, with the trees and potted green plants in front of the old red-brick stores, and everything looked well ordered and tended. Life is rather pleasant, it seemed to say, if you will just let it go its own way at its own pace.

"Nice town or I wouldn't be here," Sherm Embers said, turning back from the window. "But everybody knows what everybody does and exactly when they do it, Miss Scarborough. You should know that if you're going to be a reporter in this town. Or even live in it. It's the first of two basic facts about Martha, Texas." He looked at her with a sort of wolfish glee. "Bear that in mind if you're thinking about kicking up your heels."

"I wouldn't know where to kick them up."

"Oh, there are places. We may be comatose but we're not buried. There are ways and means. Check it out with me sometime if you're interested."

"That seems to be the secret of the Peeper's success: knowing what everyone does when. What do you think of the way he's kicking up his heels?"

She was pretty good, I thought. Embers looked at her more carefully.

"You may quote me as a town councilman as saying I am upset, concerned, and dismayed by the vile depredations of this intruder. Off the record . . . can we trust this young lady, Baxter?"

"We better be able to."

"Off the record I love it. Of course, I'm from 'outside.' I've only been here twenty-six years. It takes forty to be accepted, and even then it's probationary." He looked down over Cavalry Street. "But in those twenty-six years I've never seen anything like this. It's all people are talking about. To get the latest, all you have to do is eat lunch at the Bon Ton."

"Wouldn't it be simpler to follow the Peeper in print?" I said.

He turned back, looked sharply at me, and gave a low whistle. "You're not really thinking about doing that?"

"Let's talk a moment. If I decide to start printing the story," I said, "I wouldn't have any legal problem, would I—so long as I was accurate?"

Now he became a lawyer. "Accuracy's not the only thing you have to worry about these days. But who are you going to libel?"

"I'm not worried about libel. I'm not going to libel anybody except maybe the Peeper, and he's libel-proof."

"Yes, I would think so. Anyhow, I doubt he'd sue. What kind of stories do you have in mind?"

"Well, for one thing I'd be printing the names of the women who've been peeped. And interviews. Jamie here's been talking with them. I'd run their pictures and say the Peeper saw them nude or thereabouts. The pictures wouldn't be nude, of course."

"I'm sorry to hear that," he said with that wolfish grin. He looked out the window down over the street. "There goes one of them. Holly Ireland. Handsome woman. Freckles all over, as we now learn. I've known her for years and never knew that. We owe the Peeper something." He turned back. "Your problem is going to be invasion of privacy."

"I didn't invade it. The Peeper did. Therefore, they're legitimate news."

"A court might say both of you invaded it. Courts are getting extremely surly these days about privacy and the all-powerful press. I suppose if the women permitted you to take their pictures, you'd have something in your corner. But I'd make mighty sure they know how those pictures are going to be used: that is, as a woman who was peeped. I wouldn't tell them I was running a gallery of the leading ladies of the town. Though they do seem to be almost one and the same. Also I think I'd get signed releases."

"Now, Sherm, you know I can't go around asking people in Martha to sign releases. They'd wonder what kind of big-city trick I was trying to pull."

"Yes, I guess so. If you do this, I don't have to tell you to stay a hundred miles away from any kind of speculation about who the Peeper is, do I? Even though everybody's making guesses. Are you seriously thinking about running stories on the Peeper?"

"Not that kind, of course. Not even hinting at who it might be. But yes, the rest of it. I'm thinking about it."

He waited, looking at me. He had oddly soft but shrewd brown eyes. He was a handsome man. His mouth seemed permanently set in a cynical grin. It said that he expected the worst out of human beings so was never surprised or disillusioned. He lived as he pleased. He could get away with his manner of life because he was held to be the best lawyer in three hundred miles. He had a sharp tongue when crossed. He wore half-glasses, had a lean patrician nose, a strong chin, thick black hair graying only at the temples, and a clipped black mustache. He was fifty but there were no bags, no hint of jowls, and few lines. He looked well kept, very alert, and beautifully fit, not an excess ounce. There was a faint scent of limewater about him. The tie and sports jacket he always wore were a bit too flashy for Martha. He went against all the rules, since he was known to drink as he pleased and to take to bed anyone who was attractive and willing. He had once told me, "God, I do love them. I love the way they look, the way they feel, the way they smell. I can't get along with them but I love them."

He gave a heavy sigh. "Questions of libel and privacy aside, I just don't think this town is ready for something like that." He had spoken seriously for a moment. Then the old cynical grin returned. "Of course it might be good for the town. But I'd have to advise you not to do it. And I'd have to sort of hope that you would do it. Just to see people's faces. Except for one thing."

"What's that?"

"Well, as disagreeable as you are, I rather like personally having you around. Makes a second person who at least got out of this part of the country for a while. Not that I don't *love* Texas. But I find the most lovable Texans are those who have spent some time somewhere else. At least long enough to find out there *is* somewhere else."

"Come on, Sherm. You're not saying the *Clarion* and I wouldn't survive running those stories?"

"It'd be like betting on Bowie and Travis at the Alamo." He looked out the window. "There goes another of them. Kathryn Shields. You know, the Peeper's got me committing a sin, as I'm sure Saint Orville would point out. Every time I see one of them. Do you know what I'm talking about, Miss Scarborough?"

"Why, yes, Mr. Embers, I believe I do," she said, not thrown for a second. Then she called him. "You're undressing the Peeper's victims to see what he saw."

He burst out laughing. "Quick on the draw, isn't she, Baxter? As Lord Byron said:

> *"What men call gallantry, and gods adultery*
> *Is much more common where the climate's sultry."*

He sighed. "I'm not sure they're 'victims,' though. I almost envy the son of a bitch. Seeing all that. Maybe he's the smart one. What do you think, Miss Scarborough?"

"You mean you wish you were the Peeper, Mr. Embers?"

The lawyer looked at her. "Yes, by God, I do. I wish I had

his guts." He laughed shortly. "Not that I don't expect to be on a lot of lists. We're going to be way up there, you and me both, Baxter. No wives."

"I expect so," I said.

"Me, I've got the iron-clad alibi already. That Bloomer Girl Betty Oakes heard him humming a hymn. I don't even go to church." He gave me a straight look. "Preacher's son. You must know all the hymns, Baxter."

"I'm glad you brought this subject up, Sherman," I said, looking back at him. "Freight Train thought the Peeper had to be an agnostic. All these church ladies he's peeping."

"Yeah. Nothing I enjoy more than seeing Christians naked."

"You haven't told me the second basic fact about Martha," Jamie said.

"So I haven't. It's this. The town likes its peace and quiet. Its p's and q's. In fact, that's its stock-in-trade. Its principal asset. It takes most unkindly to anyone who stirs things up." And he looked at me.

"Like the Peeper is doing?" I said.

"And like you will be doing if you print it. With this difference. They can't seem to get at him. They can get at you. This town has methods for handling those who try to wake it up."

"I wouldn't be trying to do that. I'd just be trying to put out a newspaper."

"It'd come to the same thing in their eyes."

I stood up. "I'll think it over."

"I strongly advise it. But if you go ahead, I'll look foward to defending you," Embers said wickedly. "I'd relish, as they say down here, conducting the defense of the first freedom-of-the-press case with a Peeping Tom. We'd lose here for sure. Old Judge R. A. Graves would have made up his mind before I say, 'May it please the court.' But we'd take it all the way. The Supreme Court would love it. I'd be distinctly eloquent arguing that the peeping of Texas women is an indisputable news event. We'd get that Civil Liberties crowd to foot the bill. I'm expensive if there's money around."

"I appreciate your enthusiasm, Sherman," I said.

We went back out to the MG and headed down Cavalry Street. The town gave off a sense of contentment in the pretty spring day, with no sign now of the strange thing that was happening to it when night fell.

"I just don't know," I said. "I like this place. I came down here myself for some of that peace and quiet he was talking about."

"How many wives did you say he'd had?"

"Three. Why?"

"Nothing. There's something a little nasty about him."

"I'm hungry. Let's go down to the river and eat and talk."

"Are we through seeing the town royalty?"

"For today."

"Then I want to get out of this dress."

"A good idea. You do look a little freakish in it."

"You must have really knocked the ladies over, Baxter," she said. "When you were young enough to date."

She turned into Camellia Street, pulled up in front of the small white-clapboard bungalow she had rented, bounced out of the car without a word, and left me waiting. Eventually she emerged in her uniform of jeans, shirt, and sneakers. She slid in behind the wheel of the MG, and we zoomed off.

"That was a long time just to put on jeans," I said. "I thought you were dressing for the ball."

"How would you know what time these things take?"

I laughed. I guided her out of town and back into the fields. The fields were never very far away from the town, wherever you were. I guided her to a place near the Rio Grande and to a stand of mesquite I knew. I saw some clouds standing far off, high up in the wash of blue. They were beginning to darken.

"Pull in there, little lady," I said.

"Jesus," she said. "Don't you little-lady me."

7.
The River and the Sky

We parked the MG under the mesquite trees and started across the fields. Pretty soon we were circling the Rust Breckinridge—now Orville Jenkins—bell pepper field. She carried the sack of Bon Ton sandwiches and I followed with the Lone Star. She went over the country like some sure-footed young animal off a leash, her boy's body moving lithely, shirttail flapping, looking and almost sniffing around, comical as a beagle. There was brush between the fields and little rises. When the brush got thick, I went ahead to hold it back and make a way through for her. From the rises we could see the crops spread out before us until they met the long sky.

We cut along a tomato field and could see a couple of inches of water standing between the rows where the irrigation had been let in from the river. We picked a couple and she put them in the sandwich sack. We came up a flowing rise, then down again along plantings of sugarcane. I broke off a stalk and cut it into sections. I put one in my pocket for later, then cut the other in two, peeled back the pieces, and gave her one. We sucked them as we went along.

We came up out of a field onto a little rise and into the chaparral, the dense brush that guarded the river lands. I led her through and we looked down onto a small oval pond, perfectly hidden, where we could see nutrias intently work-ing it and rearranging it to suit their architectural taste. The

nutrias were unfrightened by us, more annoyed than anything, some of them looking up reproachfully from their
labors, as if asking how anyone could get by in this world
without doing some work. We went around the pond and
through more brush, where I picked up a fallen branch,
broke it over my knee to stick size, and used it to move the
brush back as we pushed along and down the rise on the
other side.

The thicker the brush got, the nearer I knew we were to
the river. Along this stretch the high brush and woods
shielded the river like a green wall. Soon we were in a world
of half darkness where great branches of the Mexican ash
and the Rio Grande elm and the alamo tree hung down, and
now and then foaming splotches of Spanish moss. It was
damp and dark in there, and sweetly cool, almost no sun
getting through. We could hear the river before we saw it.
The earth was pungent with the smell of damp, river-fed
soil. Then we stopped. We were in a small clearing of weird
loveliness, all greenness, beauty, and silence, dark as dusk.
We looked up. Far overhead the upmost branches of trees
met to form a green roof.

We moved softly in the clearing, as though not to disturb
something, necks craned, looking up into that vaulted cupola
of greenness where now and then a streak of sunlight sent a
shimmer of white tumbling down the highest branches, white
in the encircling green.

"It's spooky, all right," she said. "It is *spooky*."

We pushed on through the river forest, hearing it very
close now. Then suddenly we were through and there, three
or four steps away, glistening with sunlight, laden with heat,
was the river. It was a strange and sudden river. We stood
and watched it and said nothing. The river was up, way up,
heavy with the rains, and ran fast here, spilling around the
naked branches of an upstuck mesquite and hurrying on to
the Gulf, sixty miles away, on its mighty nineteen-hundred-
mile run from the Colorado mountains.

We were on a smooth rock shelf, not too high above the
river. Below the shelf lay a deep pool. Trees hugged the shelf
on both sides, and branches sheltered it from above so that it

was almost like a green cave. It was a place of great serenity, all quietness, only the river making sounds from the rains that had come into it in the last few days. The river bent each way, folding back into the other country to form a U. We were at the bottom of the U, the green coming down to the river on both sides and enfolding it in circlets of emerald. It was my favorite stretch of the river. But it was a hard place to get to, all right.

We sat down on the rock ledge and looked at the river both ways and across into the other country, that mythic land, dark and bright, blood-violent. Only the thin river separated the countries, and yet the river was as wide as all creation, for the two are as different as two countries can be. The cumulus had been gathering in the east sky toward the Gulf. Now, high and away to the west, we could see one cloud like a single unescorted ship that had come over the horizon of the sea to stand alone in the blue wash. It just floated there, white all around and dark in the center, elegant and serene.

I opened two cans of beer and she opened up the bag and got out the sandwiches and we ate.

"Good sandwiches," she said. "Good old Bon Ton."

A noise came from above us. She jumped a little. Then looked up.

A large bird was cawking and fussing, and we watched it swooping around. It went high over the river, swerved toward the U.S. side, then the Mexican side, then back again as if undecided which country to land in. Finally it glided in straight for our rock, like a plane toward a landing field, and touched down no more than six feet from us. It flapped its feathers until they were all tucked in and stood there looking at us.

"What a funny bird," she said. "What is it?"

"A chachalaca. If you say it slowly in syllables it'll say it back to you."

It was a funny, waddling, bizarre bird, with a long, green-glossed tail, large as a farm hen, swift and silent in flight, noisy and awkward on the ground. This land along the river was the only place anywhere in our country that the bird was to be found, so it was forbidden to hunt it. It stood looking at us. They were very friendly birds and seemingly almost untutored in fear.

"Here cha-cha-la-ca," she said.

The chachalaca cawked back the syllables, then waddled a little closer to us with its comical rolling gait. We sat by the river and ate the sandwiches and shared pieces with the bird. She took the tomatoes out of the sack and polished them on her shirttail and gave me one. It was almost better than the sandwiches. Then for dessert I got out the section of sugarcane, cut it in two, and gave her one. She lay back on the rock like a lizard sunning, propped herself on her elbows, and chewed on her sugarcane. I lay back too and we looked at Mexico across the river. The river, I thought. What one people called Rio Grande and the other Río Bravo. I had grown up along it, only about a hundred miles upriver from here, and knew it and the land along it as only a boy can. Then I had gone away and now I had come back. The river, and all that had happened here. All the names it has had. Río de las Palmas, Río de la Concepción, River of May, and the one I liked best of all, Río de Nuestra Señora. Sweet river, bloody river, mother river. The river was all. Without it there was no irrigation, no valley, no crops of any shade of green.

"It's so narrow," she said. "You could almost spit into Mexico. It doesn't look Grande at all."

"The Grande is for the length, not the width."

"It must be so easy getting it across."

"What?"

"The grass. The heroin. The cocaine."

"It is. Eight hundred and eighty-nine miles of easiness."

"That man I talked with at the TDS said more of it crosses here than any place in the world. He said you only heard about the two percent they caught. Not about the ninety-eight percent that gets through. The 'big busts' the papers are always talking about. It's a big joke, he said."

"Yes. It really is easy. That goes for people too."

"That boat of yours. Have you ever taken it up the river?"

"No."

"Could a boat come up the river?"

"One time, back around the Civil War, big boats came up here. Paddle-wheelers. They loaded cotton for the Confederacy—that was before the irrigation. Today we've got vegetables and Orville Jenkins's semi-trailers. Also, the river's gone down in that hundred years. In those days it was navigable. It isn't any more. Not by paddle-wheelers."

"But it could take a boat?"

"With a shallow enough draft. Five feet, maybe. Even so, you'd have to be pretty good at boats if you didn't want to go aground."

"Are you going to let me see your boat sometime?"

"Sure. Sometime."

"Some Time Baxter," she said. "What's the boat called?"

"*My Last Duchess.*"

"God, how'd you come up with a name like that?"

"The previous owner. He ran heroin."

I finished my sugarcane, tossed the pulp in the river, and watched it float across the pool to be gathered in and swept down toward the Gulf. I looked up at the sky. The cloud-ship to the west had been joined by a whole fleet, gathering while we talked, no longer serene but dark and menacing, maneuvering across the sky. Straight above was clear blue, but the two cloud formations of the east and west were moving slowly toward each other. We had better get on with it. It could come up so fast down here. I sat up.

"All right," I said. "Let's have it. Let's see what kind of reporter you've been. Tell me everything you've found out about this peeping business."

She sat cross-legged and very straight on the rocky ledge and began to talk to me like a reporter to an editor.

"I got interviews with all but three of the women," she said. "Three wouldn't talk to me. Also, I've talked with a lot of women in town who haven't been peeped. What I get is this. Some of the women of the town are upset. Some are frightened. And some are angry. At the idea of a Peeping Tom going around helter-skelter, looking in their windows. But the more he peeps, the less frightened, angry, and upset they are. Now that they see he isn't out to do any physical harm to them, they've started to relax. And more."

"What's the more?"

"There are some peculiar things going on. At least I *feel* there are. One of the women peeped—Mrs. Booth: I don't think she was peeped at all. Her story didn't sound right. And I have an even stronger feeling the same thing is true of Mrs. Orville Jenkins. I think both of them just pretended to be peeped."

"Why would they do that?"

"You know what I think? I think it's beginning to be a status symbol. The women who have been peeped, I get the feeling they look down on those who haven't. They feel superior. Quite smug, some of them. The women who haven't been are beginning to feel there's something wrong with them. So some of them are faking it. At least that's what I feel. I'll bet some of those reports of peepings that fat chief of police is getting didn't happen at all."

I smiled. If this was true, I rather liked it.

"I tell you how I just about know this. You remember Monday night when two women said they were peeped? Mrs. Kilgore and Mrs. Lang. They both reported it happened in the same thirty-minute period. Both said that when they went in to take their bath there was no present on the window ledge and when they came out there was. Well, their houses are fourteen blocks apart. I walked it off, and it took me twenty minutes at a good brisk clip. So unless the Peeper is not stopping to look, but just to leave presents, one of them had to have faked it."

I looked at her. It was good and clever work. I wondered why Freight hadn't told me this.

"Or there's more than one Peeper," I said.

"Holy cow. I hadn't thought of that."

"It could be catching."

"Anyhow, about Mrs. Jenkins. I found out there's a rivalry between her and Holly Ireland, at least on Mrs. Jenkins's part. If Holly Ireland could be peeped, Mrs. Jenkins was going to show her; she could be peeped too. For proof she showed me a volume of Lord Byron she claimed the Peeper left her. Even that made me suspicious—you remember he left Mrs. Ireland the Elizabeth Browning. I think Mrs.

Jenkins bought a copy of Lord Byron. Or maybe she already had one. I don't know all this, of course, but I think you'd feel the same way if you'd heard her talk."

"Fascinating if true. The chief had his doubts about her too. Go on."

"Incidentally, there's something about Mrs. Ireland's peeping. Something I found rather marvelous. I think she's in love with the Peeper."

"Come on. Come *on*. For God's sake. She didn't even really see him."

"That's the whole point. She lives in a dream world."

"That's true."

"What would be more of a dream world than falling in love with someone you haven't even seen?"

"I think you've gone off the deep end. This isn't the woman's page or the Dear Abby column. But go on."

"We talked about knights on white chargers. You wouldn't understand it."

"Why don't you educate me?"

"This part isn't for publication. But I suppose I can tell you. She said she loved her husband, but she had always wanted a knight on a white charger to carry her off."

"Well, whatever Esau Ireland is, he's not that."

She screwed up her face. "He was there at the start of the interview and he was encouraging her to tell me everything. He's kind of different. I can't quite figure him out."

"He's probably the sharpest man in town. The most intelligent. But he has a motto, 'Don't mess with me.'"

"Anyhow, her knight's the Peeper, I'd say. But here's the important part."

She took a deep breath, brought her yoga-crossed legs tighter, and scooted closer to me. She was eager and earnest.

"I think there's some kind of change taking place in this town. The town seems a lot more alive than when I first came here. I get this feeling the women are beginning to like having the Peeper around."

"Oh, come on."

"I know what I'm talking about. I've interviewed these women. It *does* something for the town. There's something happening! Every woman in town, every time she walks down Cavalry Street and sees a man or a boy tall enough to look through a window, she looks at him and asks herself, 'Are you the Peeper?' I do it myself."

She took a breath and went on with a considerable zeal.

"One woman told me she suspected that banker, Hooper —he's a notorious lecher. Another said it could be Brother Ireland, as they call him. She thought he was too much of a dandy. Another said Orville Jenkins Junior, because he's girl-crazy. Another woman said she suspected Horace Appleby, the druggist—she said he's mad about fannies. Even tries to pat them when you're in his drugstore. One woman told me she even suspected that young Reverend Billy Holmes."

"I can't print any of that," I said. "That's instant libel." Even to myself I sounded rather wistful.

"You know who I've thought it might be," she said. "The chief of police."

"You're kidding."

"I'm not. He has the best opportunities in the world. He can just say he's out patrolling."

"Ridiculous. Freight Train peeping in windows? He's too big to fit in the bushes. Besides, he'd belch and give himself away."

"I also think after today that lawyer, Embers, is a pretty hot suspect. Did you notice how he kept looking out his window and down at those women in the street?"

"For God's sake. He's been doing that for twenty years. Anyhow, didn't you hear what he said about the Peeper being a hymn-humming man?"

"*That's* exactly what makes me think it might be him. Great ploy to lead us all astray. What a neat idea. You never go to church, so you make sure to hum hymns while you're peeping."

"I begin to see what you mean by everybody suspecting everybody. One of the chief suspectors seems to be a very young lady I know who's sitting on a rock. Next thing we know you'll be suspecting Saint Orville Jenkins."

"No, I don't think so. But two women thought it was you.

Some people find it pretty peculiar that the Peeper never peeps on the weekend. When you're out of town. You're obviously in great shape. You could climb trees and hide for hours in bushes. Also you're an outsider. Also you're *unmarried.*"

She took a deep breath. She went on in exhilaration.

"Every day everybody's wondering, Will he peep tonight? and if so, who? It's something to look foward to. I wouldn't be surprised if some of them are even thinking, Maybe I'll be next. I tell you, the Peeping Tom is the best thing that ever happened to this town."

I looked at her. Her face was aglow with eagerness. She obviously felt she was on to something, and she liked what it was. And suddenly I began to feel, Maybe she is. Maybe she is on to something.

"All this talking and thinking about women and their bodies. Everybody imagining what the Peeper's seeing. Gets people worked up. You know what I bet?" Her brown eyes were big in the small face. "I bet there's a lot more and a lot better sex going on these days behind all those windows. I think the Peeping Tom does something for the women of Martha. And that makes the men want to do something *with* the women."

I looked at her. "What makes you believe that? Direct observation?"

"No, but it's almost as good. The women I've interviewed have told me so—in so many words. You see how I can get things you can't? They'd never tell you things like that."

She sat back, anchoring herself on the palms of her hands. She seemed quite prim and proud of herself. She sat up very straight.

"The women feel better these days," she said, as if trying to explain a difficult thing to me. "When a woman feels good, when she's appreciated, she's much more likely to come across."

I looked at her. She was beginning to amaze me sometimes.

"The Peeper sure seems to appreciate them."

"Yes, sir, things are better for everybody. The women,

PEEPER

especially. As the president of Southern Methodist University told us in his freshman orientation address, any woman can be soft and sweet if she's screwed regularly."

I burst out laughing. "Occasionally you do amuse me."

Part of the amusement was in her air of being so sophisticated, so worldly—and having seen nothing of life. Or maybe that wasn't true. I realized I really knew nothing about her.

She smiled in delight. "I'm glad. If you can amuse someone, that's the best bond there is between two persons. A lot more important than if you can just screw good. Don't you agree?"

"Shall we get on from the screwing?"

She smoothed her shirt out over her jeans.

"Oh. A little note. I understand there's a new game at the high school. It's called Peeping Tom. It's very popular among the students."

"I imagine it is." I threw a pebble in the river. "Let's assume that what you say about the women is true. About rather enjoying what the Peeper's doing to the town. The men certainly have not come around to such a benign point of view. The men have this strange idea that he's after what belongs to them."

"They ought to be grateful to him," she said firmly. "He's doing them a big favor. The men ought to hire him to stay on permanently."

"The men don't quite see it that way. Did I tell you? The Town Council has voted a reward for catching the Peeping Tom. They're getting desperate."

"A reward? It's just like the Old West. Did they say either dead or alive? How much?"

"Five hundred dollars."

"Hey, I'd like to get that. I'd hate to see it end, but maybe I could arrange it so he peeps me. Then I could make a citizen's arrest."

I looked across the river at Mexico and tried to balance things in my mind. On one scale: No one who called himself a newspaperman could pass up this story. Not with all she had told me. And one thing above all: how the Peeper was changing the town. Indeed, I had felt a good deal of that myself. It was becoming very hard to publish a newspaper here and just pretend this thing wasn't happening. There might be one thing harder: going under, having to leave. That was on the other scale, and it weighed a lot. I thought of what Sherm Embers had said. He had been sure of it. But I thought he exaggerated.

"Look at those clouds," she said.

I watched them for a moment. The formations of the east and the west had joined up. The blue and the sun were gone. I looked back at her.

"Well, you've done a good job. You may be a reporter yet. We'll see." If she could write it as well as she told it, I thought.

"Then can I get on with it? I've got a lot more reporting in mind on this story. I've just begun. And can we start running my interviews next Friday?"

"I don't know." I sighed. "They're damn serious when they say the businessmen wouldn't like it. Whatever we did, they'd say we were giving the town a bad name. Martha, Texas, has been here a long time and they wouldn't relish it. No, ma'am. They wouldn't relish it at all. Sherm Embers was right about that. And Henry Milam said the same."

"What could they do?"

"They could run me out of town. If not physically, at least economically. It's the same thing."

"Well, the hell with them."

"That's easy for you to say. We weren't all born Big Rich in Odessa, Texas."

"Do you really think they would try to shut you down?"

I thought a moment, hard, and gave my honest opinion.

"No, I really don't. I can't believe it would come to that."

We both waited. "Well," she said, "do we go with it? Or do we kiss ass?"

I looked at her. "That's what I mean by women in journalism."

"You say it."

I looked up at the sky. Far off I heard the first faint roll of thunder.

"We'll see," I said. "We'd better get along. I don't like the look of those clouds."

I stood up. Across the Rio Grande large dark clouds were assembling over Mexico, over the green treetops. Suddenly a series of thunderclaps broke, hammering against the forests on both sides of the river. Then a raging stroke of white opened up the darkening sky and one great sounding crashed down on us.

"Let's move," I said. "Right now."

We went back into the woods. A fresh array of thunderclaps rolled violently overhead. The forest seemed to vibrate with each one, and I wondered if I had pushed it too close. It was very dark now. I went ahead to make a way through for us, reaching a hand back for her, with the thunder following us all the way, moving fast as I could through the thickness of it, scampering, almost diving through the chaparral. The birds were making fussy, agitated noises, and there were quick, jerky sounds of animals moving for protection. All around, the thunder came down from the unseen sky, a low, continuous rumble, and wind stirred in the trees. Then we were through the woods into the open and on a little rise.

Now with the sky vast and unimpeded, I could see the dimensions of the storm. A vast armada of black and white cumulonimbus was building over the land, the anvil masts thrusting into the highest heavens. Blackness was closing in upon the green sea of the fields as if night were coming on, though it could not have yet been four o'clock, and only the horizons held light. I knew the storm would be on us quickly and hard. Just beyond us lay the Breckinridge field of bell peppers, stretching far away and banked at the end by a solid mass of high black cloud. Alongside the pepper field stood a field of sugarcane well up, ten feet or more.

"We're better now," I said. "Let's get away from these trees."

As we moved out, a tower of lightning extending from earth to zenith slashed whitely across the darkness. The thunderclap seemed to shake the fields. Lightning like this was frightening, but from the age of about three we all knew how to deal with it when it came. We moved forward into the clear. Now the rain came on.

"Let's run a little," I said, and took her hand.

We came down off the rise as the rain began to lash at us. Now it was flat and treeless, with the bell pepper field directly ahead and the long sprawling expanse of sugarcane to the left. I looked up at the sky and saw the huge dark thunderheads rearing over us. Then I saw something I had not seen earlier: a faint crown of red at the top of some of them. They were the red thunderheads of hail. Then, before our eyes, that scary transfiguration I had known before in my life occurred in the western sky. It turned a stunning emerald green.

"Look at that!" she said.

Between the fields of bell pepper and sugarcane stood a large corrugated metal standpipe for the irrigation. They hit it with a noise I knew, so that even before I saw any of it, I knew what it was. I looked back. We had come a hundred yards or so from the trees. Then, suddenly, the rain whipping into sheets of water, I could see nothing, not even the standpipe. By choice, I would have taken the woods instead of this, the mathematical chance of lightning against the certainty of what was upon us. But there was no choice to be had now. We would never get back across that hundred yards.

"Come on!" I said. "Run!"

Nothing was more feared in this country than to be caught in the open by large hail. It carried harm—to the crops, to field animals, to people. As a boy I had seen hail kill goats, and a goat is a very tough animal. The accelerating sound of big hail is itself terrifying. First the light *pop-pop*, just like popcorn, hitting the ground as it begins, then the noise beginning to swell until it is like a host of oncoming chariots, then the main wall of it hitting with a roar that is overwhelming. The field of sugarcane was just off to the side. It was not very good cover, but it was all there was.

"Get into the cane!" I yelled.

I put my arm around her and pulled her forward. I could

feel it pounding my back, crashing into my head, and I knew it was big hail. I pulled her into the first rows, ripping across the cane and tearing it, and when we were about six rows in, I pushed her to the ground.

"Get on your knees!" I yelled. "Put your hands over your head."

I began to pull down the canes to make a makeshift lean-to over her, then crawled under it myself and covered her with my body. Now the white curtains of hail came at us with an unearthly roar, the hail rocks slamming into the cane, wild and screaming. I could feel it getting through and smashing into me. I scrunched down, digging us both into the earth. My God, I thought, it does hurt. My back felt as though it were being stomped on, and now and then one hit my ear with a stinging pain. I felt my body becoming numb to the battering, dazed, half-conscious. I stretched out over her. She seemed quite small, something to be protected from anything that would do harm to her. And the hail came on.

It seemed a long time until it was over; it was probably only eight or nine minutes. It was enough. I rolled off her. For a while we just lay there, beat up and exhausted. Then I stood and pulled her up. We were covered with dirt and mud.

"Are you all right?" I said.

"Good God, that was big hail."

It was dark, almost like night. "Are you all right?" I repeated.

Her hand felt over her face and head. "All right."

She was looking at me. "You've got these welts. Big red *welts*."

She felt very gingerly over my face and head. "You've got *bumps*. One, two . . . three *big* bumps. More! They're big."

She took my hand, squeezed it for a moment, then let it go.

"Let's get along," I said. "Let's get along home."

We came out of the sugarcane and walked along the side of the bell pepper field. In those nine minutes the hail had destroyed that field and the tomato field up ahead and laid waste everything it could find. The bell pepper plants lay shredded from the bombardment, just stalks. Hail was piled up in the rows like white cairns, and the broken green peppers lay around them.

We came up over the rise and stopped. We could see the light returning to the horizon and beginning to work its way back up the sky. Stretching away into the distance, the many greens of the fields lay flattened and crumpled, glistening in the wetness.

"I could cry," she said. "For the bell peppers."

"Yes."

"God was the joker in the deck?"

"Yes. An expensive hail for Orville."

"But Rust got his?" she said.

"Yes. Rust got his. Just in time."

We went on back to the MG. It sat under the mesquite trees, untouched. A characteristic of this land is that you can have one kind of weather in one field and another in the next. Rain one place, hail another, sun a third—all close together.

We got in the MG and drove back into town. We were just on the outskirts, driving up Quince Street, when I made up my mind. I don't know why. Maybe because I had never learned to kiss them.

"Well, they're all against it," I said. "So let's go with it."

PEEPER 5
Surprise Party

It was a spur-of-the-moment thing. Actually he hadn't planned anything for the evening until he picked up the Martha *Clarion* and turned to the Social Notes column. It was the best-read part of the paper. You knew everybody in it, and it told you what they were up to. If the postmistress was down with a cold, this fact could be found in Social Notes. If Esau Ireland was celebrating his wedding anniversary by taking Holly on a trip to Padre Island, it would be noted. One might discover in its lines the birth of puppies to a

---

well-known Martha dog, the fact that the Appleby twins were going to the Hill Country for summer camp, the news that Bert Hooper was traveling to Colorado for three days to shoot mountain sheep. No meeting could take place without the column noting it—in advance. There were a lot of nighttime meetings of men in Martha—church deacons, American Legion, VFW, Gun Club, Domino Club—and it was important to him to know about them. The column gave saturation coverage to trips. A citizen of Martha could hardly step outside the town limits without the column's reporting the fact—ahead of time. Not that this required any great investigative reporting. It was the habit of the people of the town when planning a trip to phone the *Clarion* and inform it, almost as if they were dutifully telling Mother they would be gone for a few days. He was grateful for the custom. Social Notes missed nothing, and he never missed Social Notes.

The column had a light, pleasing touch. He came to a notation which read:

Dr. George Bradshaw, Jr., will be in Dallas May 2–4 to attend the annual meeting of the Texas Dental Association. Good drilling in Dallas, Dr. Bradshaw! Unfortunately George will miss his wife's birthday on May 3. "It can't be helped," Mildred Bradshaw said philosophically. "George needs to keep up on the latest in filling cavities. Martha must not fall behind Dallas."

People would smile, he knew, reading that, recognizing Mildred's gentle humor.

He had really planned to take the night off. But there it was. Dr. Bradshaw was out of town, and Dr. Bradshaw was almost never out of town. There were too many cavities to be filled, too many silver amalgams, gold inlays, and porcelain caps, too many extractions, bite repairs, and dentures, too much plaque and tartar. At twenty-eight, Dr. Bradshaw was one of the busiest men in Martha. The annual Texas Dental Association was virtually the only time he ever left his chair. Mildred Bradshaw would not be this available again for another year. Given Mildred's possibilities, it was too rich an opportunity to pass up. Besides, a woman deserved some attention from a man on her birthday. Her husband being gone, it appeared to fall on him. He would give her a surprise party.

He had always been enamored of Mildred Bradshaw, even with her clothes on. One could meet her and know in a minute that she was a person of breeding, of inner aristocracy. She had about her an air of splendid carelessness. She was tall, almost statuesque, but she carried herself easily, as if her body never gave her any problem. Her hair was lambent chestnut, and her teeth were so white one felt sure there was not a filling in her mouth. She had fine, chiseled features, high-boned cheeks, and her creamy complexion was unblemished. In another woman these aspects of perfection might have turned people off. But Mildred Bradshaw was pleasant to one and all. It was a pleasure to go to the library, where she did volunteer duty, just to check out a book from her. She had a nice sense of humor, and the white teeth and the brown eyes sparkled if you told her a funny story. She taught a Sunday school class of fifteen-year-old girls who looked at her soulfully as if she was what they dreamed of being. She was active in the good works of the Ladies' Aid Society. But these things were done quietly. She did not smell of her Christianity.

If she had a vice, it was horses. She could be seen every late afternoon on her Arabian gray, posting along the irrigation-canal banks, which made excellent riding paths. Where others rode in jeans and cowboy boots, Mildred Bradshaw rode in jodhpur breeches and polished riding boots. She was the only rider in Martha to use an English saddle. The rear view was of her exceptional behind rising metronomically from it. The front view was of her sitting straight up in that marvelous posture, her scarf flying from her neck, her gallant breasts, outlined through the riding shirt, leading the way, her jodhpured thighs pressing firmly against the animal's flanks. He had enjoyed both views numerous times.

He was a decisive man. He put down the paper and went to check out his equipment. He got out a fresh dark shirt and a pair of dark, newly pressed trousers and inspected his Keds. These had a few caliche smears. He took his bottle of India ink and touched them up. He checked his pantyhose mask and snipped off a couple of dangling threads with his manicure scissors. One should dress smartly for a date with Mildred Bradshaw.

The thing to do in life, it occurred to him as he walked by the front of the splendid Corsicana-brick Bradshaw place on Iris Street, was to enlist in one of the essential professions, and of these the best were those having to do with the upkeep of the human body. Doctors, who kept the various parts of the body in order; pharmacists, who supplied the ingredients necessary for the same purpose; dentists, who filled the holes in one's mouth; undertakers, who finally sent the body on its way. For such as these, the pangs of recessions, the heartbreaks of depressions, the dislocation of economic cycles did not exist. Most people would spend their last hundred dollars to have a broken arm set and their last twenty-five to get a cavity filled. The fine lines of the Bradshaw house, set back on its deep Saint Augustine lawn, reminded him of this elementary fact.

Under the starry darkness he continued on his constitutional, passing the house a couple of times. It was all dark, a fact which did not surprise him. She would be riding later than usual tonight with her dentist husband gone, and the Bar-M Stables were five miles away across town. He strolled the neighborhood, never letting the Bradshaw place far out of sight, moving down Sycamore Street, passing the alley in back of the house. Then from down the way he saw the lights of a car turning into the alley. He strode crisply toward it and watched the car's taillight go down the alley, stop midway, and turn into the garage. He waited a few moments, then moseyed down the caliche and along the oleander hedges, stopped at the Bradshaw latch gate, and looked around. No one was about.

Quickly he passed through the gate, squatted on his haunches in the shadow of the hedge, and looked at the house. Only the kitchen light was on. Perhaps she was having a tall glass of milk after her ride. He was familiar with the house and with the huge chinaberry tree, a few steps away, which served as the backyard's centerpiece. Old Dr. Bradshaw himself, who liked to eat outdoors, had built the picnic table which entirely surrounded its trunk and the bench which surrounded the table. He stepped swiftly across the yard, entered the tree's huge black shadow, took a pew on the bench, and waited for her to finish her milk. In a few moments the light in a corner bedroom flicked on. He put on his pantyhose mask and with rapid steps hunched across the yard and crouched in the yellow jasmine bushes outside the window, then slowly brought his eyes up to just above the vegetation line.

She was standing by the bed in her riding habit of black boots, brown jodhpurs, and pongee riding shirt, just standing there, with a soft thoughtful smile on her face. Some fond thought of George in Dallas? Or simply a feeling of well-being from the horseback ride? He could hear a tub being drawn in the adjoining bathroom and he looked along the bush to the higher bathroom window to calculate whether he could join her there momentarily. Yes, but first he would see what she offered prior to bathing. He peered through the window. She moved her hand back over her chestnut hair in a languid gesture and began absently to unbutton her riding shirt.

She undid the last button and tossed the shirt carelessly on the bed. Then she undid her bra and let it join the shirt. She stood there wearing jodhpurs and riding boots, naked from the navel up. He felt his mouth fall open. He hardly knew they came that perfect. Neither too large nor too small, but exactly the right size for her sculptural figure, they stood straight out in creamy arrogance from her flat-tummied body, without the slightest droop. Indeed, they curved upward, capped by two of the choicest apricot nipples it had been his pleasure to observe. Riding must be truly wonderful for a woman's breasts! He was not at all surprised to see her stand there for a moment, the same languid smile on her face, look down, and run her hands lightly and lovingly over them so that he could see the nipples come pleasingly erect.

The gesture was as of a ritual she performed habitually at this point in her toilette, as though to remind herself how pleasant it was to possess them. It seemed entirely natural, and he could imagine anyone wanting to do the same.

She brought her hands down from her breasts and began to unbutton the side buttons of the jodhpurs. Completing this procedure, she sat on the bed, jackknifed an ankle across a thigh, and pulled off one boot, then the other. They were beautiful boots, but he had no time to linger on inanimate niceties. For she had arisen and was beginning to lower the jodhpurs. She was bent a little in this task so that the melodious substance of her breasts bowed over her thighs, holding as assured and intact from this position as when she stood erect. She pushed the jodhpurs down from her hips until apricot panties began to appear, the very hue of her nipples. As she brought the jodhpurs to mid-thigh she sat again and pulled them off. She stood and added them to the growing heap on the bed, then lowered the panties and stepped out of them. With a flip of her fingers, a gesture which admitted they were really nothing, she added this apricot wisp to the pile, turning so that her behind was offered full view to him. Mother of God! High-slung, tight and pert, rounded yet firm, richly candescent, its symmetry challenged that of her breasts. Lucky horse! His heart leaped, his very being seemed to pulse in contemplation of the imminent bathing of it all.

From the vicinity of the back gate a commotion and a low murmur of voices! Jolted from intense concentration, he disappeared like a diving submarine into the jasmine bushes. He felt his heart now truly pounding. He closed his eyes a moment to regain some modicum of calm and to tell himself he must not panic. He opened them, slowly brought them to bush height, and looked through the window. Apparently she had heard nothing, for she still stood there, immobile, the nakedness of her body resting on one leg. She seemed once more to be in thought, to be momentarily somewhere else. She turned a little and he saw the butterscotch bouquet sitting atop her long honey thighs like some exquisite frond shielding a rare flower. It was a sight normally to rivet all attention, but in his rising anxiety he found it difficult to concentrate even on it.

He looked toward the gate. What the activity there was he could not see, the large trunk of the chinaberry tree blocking his line of sight. He knew above all he must not cut and run. There was nothing for it but to sit tight. He peeked through and saw her start toward the bathroom. It was out of the question now for him to join her for her bath. He hunched in the jasmines, hoping that whatever it was back there would go away. The noise again! This time there was no doubt of its identity. It was the unmistakable chattering of many women.

In the room she stopped, head cocked in her nakedness. She stepped to a closet, brought forth a robe, and slipped into it. He disappeared again into the bushes. He heard something and slowly brought his eyes up and squinted toward the gate. There was some sort of action around the chinaberry tree! Then he saw the shape of a woman emerge from the tree's black shadow and walk across the yard. He held his breath as the shape proceeded straightaway to the back door and without knocking or ceremony entered it. Suddenly he was startled to see the back yard flooded with light—the intruder had apparently turned on the light from inside. As he peered over the bushes in horror, he saw revealed in the lights a covey of perhaps a dozen women standing around the chinaberry tree and heard them abruptly sing out as in one voice, "Surprise!" They thereupon burst into song, squawking the words into the night:

> *Happy birthday to you!*
> *Happy birthday to you!*
> *Happy birthday, dear Mil-l-l-dred!*
> *Happy birthday to you!*

There was a pause, then a shrill chorused cry: "Ladies' Aid Society! Ladies' Aid Society!"

Under the floods he could make out a large cake and what would surely be cartons of Appleby's Drugstore ice cream set up on old Dr. Bradshaw's picnic table around the chinaberry tree. They had come to cheer her up on her husbandless birthday. Exactly like him! His pantyhosed head jerked back to the room. She was looking straight at him and she was no more than two feet away. She had obviously come to the window to see what the backyard ruckus was, seen over and beyond him her well-wishers, and also seen him. The words which came from her were not in panic or alarm, hardly even an ejaculation, but more as if the sight of him was a surprise itself. They came like a statement of fact, almost as if she were speaking to him but loud enough, he was certain, to carry to other present hearers.

"Why, it's the Peeper!" she said.

Like a dash runner from his starting blocks he erupted from the bushes and took off, heading at flank speed around the corner of the Corsicana-brick house for the front yard. He had barely made it there when he heard from behind him a medley of sounds, a night-piercing pastiche composed of the rapid movement of running women across Saint Augustine grass, screams, yelps, and shrill throaty outcries, and then above these an assortment of shouted injunctions, of which he heard, distinctly, "Get him!" and "There he goes!" He fled across the spacious front yard in high acceleration and took off down the sidewalk of Iris Street to the accompaniment of fading cries. At the corner of the block, never breaking stride, he looked back. Through the night he could make out that only two, possibly three, of his pursuers were still in chase, two or three athletic enough to fancy they could give him a run. He heard the word "Peeper!" twice. He turned on the gas and took a left turn, racing down Tamarack Street, his tennis shoes hammering the sidewalk. He fled flat-out down the block, turned the corner at Jonquil Street, poured on the coal, and turned into the alley between Jonquil and Cavalry. He kept running hard until he was certain he had ditched them. He slowed to a trot and then a walk.

He took off the pantyhose mask, stuffed it in his pocket, and continued to walk for several more blocks. He could feel his heart still pounding, both from the running and the near miss, and he continued to walk until this organ had quieted. After a bit, he went so far as no longer to feel alarm over the experience but only irritation at the Ladies' Aid Society and their interfering ways. The worst part of it was that it would be his last chance to see Mildred Bradshaw, and he had had such little time with her. There had been her bath still to come. She would be on the alert after this. But wait! Maybe she would reason that he wouldn't dare come around again after tonight. Maybe he should strike again while she was still thinking in this fashion. Very soon. Like tomorrow night. Dr. Bradshaw would still be out of town tomorrow night. It would take boldness, but what if not that was required for all he was doing? Boldness was his shield.

8.
The Martha Clarion

I t's always nice in the newspaper business if you're sitting on what you think might turn into a pretty good story to have a spot news peg for it fall in your lap. The surprise party provided it for us. Jamie and I spent every minute of the next three days putting the big story together. Every minute, that is, we could squeeze out of the normal processes, the infinity of things to be done, of getting the paper ready for its weekly run—the classified ads, the display ads, the Social Notes, the Church Notes, and the rest of it. The story, heretofore suppressed, would tell the town what it already knew, that there was a permanent Peeping Tom in its midst, but also would give people for the first time the complete picture of the situation. Which is what a newspaper is for.

I put Jamie to work interviewing the remaining peeping victims and collecting piano-top pictures of all of them or setting it up for me to take their pictures. I talked with the chief of police about the surprise party and the state of his investigations to date, then made an appointment with Mildred Bradshaw and went out to her place on Iris Street and interviewed her. On a paper like the Martha *Clarion* you have to know how to do everything. I had been a good reporter, and I knew how to edit copy. I knew from my teens how to operate the Mergenthaler Linotype and had brushed up on that, just in case Beto got sick or quit. I had learned how to take pictures with an old Speed Graphic that came with the paper, and I took it along and used my charms to persuade Mildred Bradshaw to pose in her yard. I even persuaded her to put on the jodhpurs and the rest of her riding gear she was wearing that night, to help give the reader an idea. Actually it didn't take all that much charm or persuasion. Mildred Bradshaw was a Texas woman, and I think she was rather amused by the whole idea. I planned to run the picture on page one above the fold. It was a wonderfully old-fashioned, fully "posed" photograph. It showed Mildred pointing to the window where the Peeper had looked in at her, the jasmine bush from which he had done it, and, in the foreground, the chinaberry tree with the circular table where the Ladies' Aid Society had placed the birthday cake and Appleby's Drugstore ice cream and raised their voices in song. It was a good picture, with Mildred smiling a curious smile. I enjoyed the interview with her. She was a classy lady and a hell of a good-looking woman with her creamy skin, flowing chestnut hair, and statuesque figure, various aspects of which came through the riding habit in a nicely etched fashion. Maybe the Peeper was the bright one and the rest of the men poor earthbound slugs.

I divided the members of the Ladies' Aid Society into two groups of half a dozen each and had Jamie do phone interviews with one batch. I did the other half by phone myself, all except Kathryn Shields, the athletic schoolteacher who had given the Peeper a chase down Iris Street. I interviewed her also in person. Jamie and I went out together to the site of each of the seventeen peepings so far and did a thorough grounds inspection—the yard, the gate the Peeper had come through, the alley in back. I can't say that we added any clues to the short list already in the hands of the chief of police, but when covering a story I believe in a first-hand, grounds-on familiarity with what I'm going to report. I want an overflow of knowledge of the situation to write from. With all the other chores concerned with getting out an issue, this took up Tuesday and Wednesday, dark to dark.

Thursday morning I came down early to start putting it all together for the press run that night. Cavalry Street was still dark, as it had been when I left the night before, and not a sound came from the sleeping town. A dew lay across the green lawns like heavenly tears, and the stars were beginning to fade. I thought about the town and its world, as apart and different as any world could be from the great cities of Washington and New York. Maybe it was the sense of compulsion that life had there, of being hurtled from one thing that had to be done to another that had to be done. Many of them were things you liked and wanted to do, a lot of them fun, but there was no time to stop and decide, did you really want the time you had to rush by that way, and wasn't there maybe something else? At least the compulsion was off here, and if I hadn't discovered anything much, at least I was beginning to think, instead of just going from one thing to the next.

All I could hear was my own footsteps. I wondered how the town would take the story, and most especially how the men who ruled the town and on whose dollars I depended for survival would take it. On the top, the story didn't seem all that much, hardly the thing one would go to bat on. But then you had to go to bat sometime. Besides, I had a feeling there was more to the story than simply a man looking through windows at girls and women undressing.

In the first light down Quince Street I saw a lean silhouette in movement and I squinted. For some reason the combination suddenly flashed my mind back to a ship's bridge and myself standing there with the conn, knowing that last light and first light are the submarine's favorite time to strike, when the visibility of opposing eyes is at its lowest. I smiled and shook my head. I was looking at no submarine but at Henry Milam on his early morning jog. He came toward me and pulled up. He was wearing navy blue shorts, dark gray T-shirt, and dark sneakers. He always reminded me of a tall, lean, wise bird: the secretary bird, maybe, with its tall toothpick legs.

"Good morning, Henry. For a moment I thought you were a submarine."

He was panting a little as he looked at me. "You all right? You haven't gone around that famous bend?"

I smiled. "That remains to be seen."

"What are you doing up so early? You better be careful. People will think you're the Peeper coming in from a night's work."

"And yourself?"

Henry gave his little laugh. "Well, I have a good alibi. I jogged at this hour long before there was a Peeping Tom. What's your alibi?"

"Press day."

"Ah, yes, the big Peeper issue. I've heard. Everyone is talking about it. They say you're running pictures of every woman that was peeped. I don't think Martha has ever had anything quite like that." He waited a moment.

"Go ahead, Henry. We've still got free speech. I'm hoping we have a free press."

He was a little uncomfortable. He did not really like confrontation or disagreement. He liked peace and harmony. Maybe that went with being a distributor of Lone Star beer.

"I understand," he said. "I can see both sides but . . . well, the Town Council won't like it, and your advertisers won't like it."

I thought of that Lone Star beer ad I got every week. "Including you, Henry?" I said.

He gave an embarrassed smile. "I like Martha to be peaceful. I'm not one of your radicals. I go along with community opinion, whenever I can. I think that's best for the town. Well, I mustn't keep you from your work, and I have another mile to run before I wake up. To turn Robert Frost around."

I watched him jog off down the street, a thin figure in dark shorts and dark T-shirt. He had never answered my question. He had a point about keeping Martha peaceful. I liked it that way too. It was one reason I had come here.

I sighed and went on my way.

Down the street I was surprised to see a light burning behind the inscription that said "The Martha Clarion" across the big glass window. For the first time, I think, a certain pride coursed through me, seeing that sign, and I thought, That is me. I might as well try to make it mean something.

She was there before me. I could see her through the window, bent over her typewriter, her small figure in those everlasting jeans and shirt. Her interviews were over, and she wouldn't have to wear a dress today. She looked as if she had been there awhile, working on her story.

It was going to be a long hot day. The sun was just announcing itself from beyond the big flat horizon down Cavalry Street. Then from squarely in the middle of the street the great red ball appeared and began to move upward between the rows of one-story and two-story buildings. Next to watching it emerge from the sea, this was my favorite sunrise. I stood and looked at it a moment, then entered the premises of the *Clarion.*

I switched on the ceiling fan and said good morning to my employee. She looked up, said "Hi," and went right back to it. Her first real story. I thought of years back and knew what she was going through. I went into the tiny darkroom I had rigged in a closet off the composing room and developed the rest of the pictures to have ready for the engraver when he dropped by at eight o'clock. Engraving was done as a sideline by Michael's Printers, just around the corner on Laurel. Then I worked awhile on some classifieds to have ready for Beto when he arrived. The sun was flooding the quarters of the Martha *Clarion* when I sat down at the old L. C. Smith and called Jamie over. With her sitting beside me to feed in quotes from the Ladies' Aid women, and to learn, though I didn't say this, I started in on the lead story. I used the moment of Mildred Bradshaw's epiphany for the lead paragraph, the first words appearing on the paper through the machine reading:

"I was just removing my jodhpurs," Mildred Bradshaw said, "when I heard the surprise party of the Ladies' Aid Society shouting and singing 'Happy Birthday' around the chinaberry tree in the back yard. Little did I know that I was to get two surprises that night."

I explained to Jamie that the purpose of a lead was to get the reader to read the second paragraph, and I thought this lead fulfilled that purpose.

"I see what you mean," she said intently. "They want to see those jodhpurs lowered the rest of the way."

"Something like that," I said. "Speaking symbolically."

"Lowering jodhpurs is pretty symbolic," she said. "Especially if someone is watching. You were out there an awful long time on that interview."

"Well, it's our lead story," I said.

"She has quite an ass," she said. "I've seen her on the irrigation canals on that horse."

I turned my head and looked at her. "Yes," I said. "The charming thing about her is that she hasn't the faintest idea of it. Or of the other aspects of her considerable beauty."

"What a fool you are, Baxter," she said. "You may be a hell of a newspaperman, but you don't know women from third base."

"Shall we get on with it?" I said, rather curtly. "Will you let me do the writing and the talking?"

"Yes, sir," she said, not at all sarcastically. "I'm sorry. I'll shut up."

I wrote the second paragraph:

Mrs. Bradshaw, the wife of the well-known local dentist, was about to become the seventeenth female to be looked at by a Peeping Tom. He has been operating in Martha since the night of March 10, when he peeped Sally Carruthers, daughter of the mercantile family, while she was dressing for the annual Bloomer Girl Ball. The other victims in order of their peeping are:

I listed them all by name, age, address, and date of peeping and continued with my story, punching it out:

In his visitations the Peeping Tom has concealed his identity by wearing a face mask constructed from ladies' pantyhose. The Pantyhose Peeper has shown every sign that he is here to stay.

"Hey, that's good," Jamie said. " 'The Pantyhose Peeper.' "

"Yeah. Don't interrupt. . . ."

I brought the story back to the Bradshaw peeping and fed in the observations of the visiting surprise party of the Ladies' Aid Society. Among the women who had got a glimpse of the Peeper, one said that he was tall, another that he was of medium height, a third had him practically the size of a midget. "I'm certain after seeing him he's a high school boy," Mrs. Torrance had said. "And about a tenth-grader at that." They could agree on hardly anything. I pointed out to Jamie, as a journalistic lesson, that this proved the unreliability even of first-hand witnesses and that eternal skepticism was the first principle of a good reporter. Some of them were women who had been peeped themselves and thus had a special interest in the Peeper. I fitted in quotes from these ladies. I worked in my interview with Kathryn Shields:

> "When you were chasing the Peeper down Iris Street," Miss Shields was asked, "were you thinking of revenge for being looked at in your bath?"
>
> "Well, not exactly," she said. "To tell the truth, I was thinking of the reward. I could use five hundred dollars. You know what teachers' salaries are."

Having disposed of the spot news peg in the form of the latest peeping, I wrote about the emergency Town Council meetings held to consider the Peeper crisis. I described the meetings as deadly determined on ways and means of combating the menace and reported that the men of Martha were much upset by the presence of the intruder. I wrote of the various proposals offered for dealing with him, including the importation of Texas Rangers. I concluded my story with the interview with the chief of police:

> "We're working on a number of leads," Freight Train Flowers told the *Clarion* with an air of mystery. "I can't say any more at this time."
>
> "Can you say anything about your list of suspects?" the chief of police was asked.

"Yes, I can answer that question," the chief said. "My list of suspects consists of the male population of Martha, Texas, above the age of fourteen."

"Do you have anything to say to the women of Martha?" the chief was asked.

"Yes. Lower your shades."

I finished the story and then edited it. One of the pleasures of owning the *Clarion* was that I got to edit my own copy. Then, with Jamie sitting by me to learn how it was done, I wrote a head for it. The *Clarion* had never carried anything larger than a one-column head, and I used to speculate whether at the Second Coming I should go to three columns or settle for two. Now I decided not to wait for that event but to make this the first two-column head the paper had ever run. I thought about 36-point type, which would be 12 points bigger than anything I had ever used. Then I decided to go whole hog and make it 48-point Cheltenham, double our previous record. There are 72 points in an inch, and our body type is 8-point on a 9-point slug. I explained to Jamie that a two-column 48-point Cheltenham bold allowed you thirteen characters maximum, including spaces, and that you shouldn't go under eleven because it would leave too much white space. I fooled around and finally came up with:

Peeping Tom
Nearly Caught

"Let's do a twenty-four-point subhead," I said. "On one-column Cheltenham light indented, you're allowed seventeen characters. If it's lower case you count *i*'s and *l*'s as half, *m*'s and *w*'s as one and a half, and three *t*'s as two characters. Got that?"

"Got it."

I made some stabs and came up with:

He Is Surprised
At Surprise Party

"And we'll do an overline for the whole thing," I said. "Eighteen-point Cheltenham italic. How about something simple?" and I wrote:

Seventeen So Far

We went through the swinging door into the composing room, and I gave the story to Beto to set on the Mergenthaler. I got a pica stick and went over to the headline-type cabinet and pulled out the 48-point Cheltenham bold font. "It's a two-column head," I told her, "so you allow eleven picas for each column, add a half pica for the column rule, and set the stick for twenty-two and a half picas." I set the head and took it over to the makeup stone. I took the type carefully out of the stick, showing her how to hold it tightly between thumb and forefinger, squeezing it in to keep the individual letters from collapsing and the whole thing pieing, and fitted it in the page-one chase, columns seven and eight, top of the page, just below the flag. I pulled out the font, set the 24-point Cheltenham light subhead while she watched closely, and fitted it in below the main head. Then I pulled out the 18-point Cheltenham italic font, gave her the pica stick, and told her to set it.

"See how the font is in three parts?" I said. "The right-hand side has the capital letters. The middle part has some punctuation marks at the top, then the numerals, then ten of the lower-case letters: a, r, o, y, p, w, i, s, f, g." I ticked them off, running my fingers over the compartments. "You don't have to memorize them now. You'll learn them quick enough. The left-hand side has the rest of the punctuation marks at the top, then below all the other lower-case letters. Okay?"

"Okay."

"See these narrow compartments? They have the less-used letters, like y and w. The bigger compartments have the most-used letters, for instance, i, o, and e"—and I ran my fingers over them—"which as we all know is the most-used letter of all."

I watched a moment while she studied the font. Then, her

fingers searching over the letter slots, she pulled out an upper-case S.

"The main thing to remember is to get the type right side up. It's awkward if you have an upside-down letter in a headline. Here's how you make sure. See this groove on the type? Keep that *away* from you. Then you know the letter is right side up. Okay?"

"Okay."

It took a while but she caught on fast, her small fingers moving with dexterity over the slots for the letters, plucking them out and notching them into the stick. I showed her how to justify it. We took it back to the stone and she took it very warily out of the pica stick and fitted it in the page form. She seemed pleased at setting her first headline without spilling type. We stood at the stone and looked at the headlines.

"One thing you'll learn is to read type upside down," I said. "Well, we're on our way."

The words Peeping Tom right at the top jumped out at us, even upside down. It was such an event seeing type of that size in a *Clarion* page form that Beto came over from his Mergenthaler to have a look at it.

"Hey, that is some head," he said. "Isn't that Cheltenham pretty, boss?"

"Especially that size," I said.

"I never thought we'd use it," Beto said.

It sounded as if he simply disliked seeing handsome type wasted.

"That's a very big head for the Martha *Clarion*," I said. "You don't think it's too big, Beto?"

"It looks just right to me," he said. "I like it."

"It's a big story," Jamie said. "It'll hit them right between the eyes."

"That's what I'm afraid of," I said.

"Don't get chicken now," she said.

"*Amárrate los huevos*, boss," Beto said. I turned and looked at him for a moment in the gloom of the composing room. Jamie doesn't understand Spanish but I do, and Beto has a mastery of the language not to be found in Cervantes.

I gingerly touched the head in the page form.

"Oh, no," I said. "Not now. I'm a very brave person. I won't get chicken and I'll keep tight *los huevos*. Oh, by the way." I addressed them both. "Bravery will be required of all hands, not just me. Let us not forget that all three of us have a stake in the outcome." I think that sobered them. "Well, let's stop admiring our head type, you enlisted men. We've got work to do."

Beto returned to the Mergenthaler. I could hear the old crate beginning to chatter away in the *clack-clack* tenor-pitched bird's singsong as the first of the Peeper copy went into hot type. Jamie and I returned to the *Clarion*'s other room. The sunlight was almost blinding.

"Oh, by the way," I said to Jamie. "You got that story on the interviews with the ladies with their clothes off?"

"Yes, I've got it." Her voice was a little tight.

"Well, let's have it."

While she worked on Social Notes—and, I could tell, once or twice stole a glance at me across the room—I sat down with a pencil and started in on it. I had to edit it pretty heavily. When I got about a quarter of the way through, I decided it needed more than that. It had some good things but it needed something else, and I thought it was better for her to try it. It was better to find out. I called her over to my desk. She seemed very small and alone standing there. She could see the heavy editing. I sat back and talked with her, keeping my voice even and not hard.

"It just isn't right," I said carefully. "I'd like for you to start over." I waited a moment. "What you want to do—well, it's approximately like this. After you gather the facts on a story and before you write it, back off and look at the story and ask yourself, 'What is it all about?' The difference in reporters is between those who can do that and those who just list facts."

So there it was. She would either get it or she wouldn't. If she couldn't get that, I didn't think she would ever really make it. I mean be a good one. I didn't like being an editor—I was always on the other side—and I liked even less being a teacher. But there she was, and it was my paper.

"Would you like to try that?" I said quietly.

She hiccuped. Her voice was very small. "Sure," she said. "Why don't I back off and try it."

She took it away and I worked on the issue and handled the people who came to the counter with classified ads and dealt with the nonstop phone: Social Notes, club meetings, who was suing whom, who was going to Dallas for the weekend. What the Reverend Holmes was preaching about Sunday, the midweek prayer-meeting topic, the bake sale of the Ladies' Aid Society. Engagements, marriages, births, deaths. They all had to tell the paper about it. It was almost as if it hadn't happened or wouldn't happen if it wasn't in print. I took it all down and wrote it all up. Across the room I could see her, bent over that typewriter again, intent, the machine clattering away, then stopping in a long silence, then clattering again.

About an hour later there she was, standing at my desk and holding it patiently until I looked up. I took it from her and began to go through it. There was still considerable editing to do, but she had got it. She had backed off. She had got what the story on the women's interviews was really all about, in the way she had told me on the river, which was that, unlike the men, the women were not all that upset at the Peeper's descent upon the town. There was a subtle underlying motif in the interviews, even though they didn't say it outright: The Peeper was bringing a certain excitement to the town. He had awakened their lives. The women could go around town doing their shopping, attending social gatherings, even at church, and look at the men of the town and ask themselves, "Is it you?" To think that someone they all knew, someone they saw every day, was doing that at night! An air of mystery! Where will he strike tonight and who will be next? It was thrilling, and it was fearful in a thrilling sort of way. As I read I felt a kind of excitement myself that was new to me: the dawning of a possible bright talent in another person, in someone young. I called her over and she stood by my desk. I looked at her for a moment. She seemed quite still, subdued.

"This is better," I said. I was trying to keep any emotion out of my voice, though I felt some.

"Thanks." I think she did too.

"It could be still better, you understand." She was looking across me at the editing. "But you catch on. Hell, it's even faintly possible you'll be a newspaperman some day."

"I want to." She was shy, her voice small but firm.

I took a while to explain my editing. I had had editors who had done that and editors who hadn't, and I always liked the first kind a lot better. I learned from the first kind. Of course she resented any changes in her prose. All writers do, starting with me. But I knew now that she had what makes the difference in people. The capacity to learn. It is surprising how few people do. Most people just want to be right.

"I see what you're doing," she said, her excitement beginning to show a little.

"Yes."

"I'm depending on you to teach me," she said, almost fiercely. She looked straight at me with those huge, remarkable eyes, with the pupil-iris brownness that forced you to look at them. "Don't you ever try to be nice to me, Baxter."

"I'll make a special effort."

She waited a moment. "I'm talking about in the office. When you're teaching me how to be a newspaperman. You can be nice to me outside if you want."

And she flounced away across the room, her hair bouncing. I read it through one more time. The quotes from the women were good. I have no idea what gives some people an ear for language while others have almost none. She had the gift, or at least the seeds of it. I sighed. Even bright seeds have to have a chance to grow. We would see.

I wrote a headline, "What We Know About the Peeper," and a story that told just that. Its brevity made me realize just how much he had the town chasing itself in circles. Only a few hard facts. Keds tennis shoe tracks. Camel cigarette butts found at the sites of the peepings. A fit constitution: he had climbed into the Ireland treehouse to get a look at the mayor's wife and had rather easily outdistanced the members of the Ladies' Aid Society in the chase after the surprise party. He struck only during the week—never on weekends.

He had hit both north and south side, with a favoritism to the north side. It appeared obvious, I wrote, that he was a longtime resident of Martha, familiar with the town and its ways, since he knew precisely when to peep whom, based on the schedules, activities, and habits of the townspeople.

I concluded the piece:

> As our chief of police has himself stated, he must be an unusually intelligent and clever fellow to prevail in his nighttime forays, to impose his chosen ways on the town. And finally, he has a certain style. When he peeps a lady, he never fails to leave a present.
>
> Beyond that, nothing is known that would shed light on the identity of our fellow citizen who continues, unabated, unrestrained, and uncaught, on almost any given night, to practice his curious hobby.

I fed this copy and Jamie's story to Beto and kept feeding him Social Notes and classifieds and the rest of it. All through the day I could hear the Mergenthaler chirping its birdsong through the swinging door. Then there he would be, coming through the door with the fresh proof for Jamie and me to read. If you ever ran out of anything to do, there was always proof to read. He would turn back from the sunlight as if anxious to get out of such harshness and back into his cave, and soon I could hear the Mergenthaler begin to take up its *clack-clack* again.

I finally made up page one and took it to the composing room and gave it to Beto. As I came back I could hear from down the street the chimes of the Baptist church strike up "How Firm a Foundation, Ye Saints of the Lord" and the bells peal out over the town two resounding dongs. We had been at it eight hours.

"I'm going to order something from the Bon Ton," I said across the room. "Would you like the chicken-fried steak with cream gravy and mashed potatoes or the roast pork with the brown gravy?"

She turned and looked at me. "Ugh. Do you suppose

they'd run me out of town if I ordered a peanut butter and jelly sandwich?"

"I'll use my influence with Flory. I'll tell her we won't run her picture unless she fixes it."

"And a tall glass of milk."

I phoned over, and in about twenty minutes I could see through the window Flory in her white waitress uniform crossing the street with a tray. She was a fleshed-out girl but she had quick moves and she stepped deftly behind a pickup and came on across Cavalry. She brought it through the swinging gate and lowered it onto my desk. Not a drop of the milk had been spilled. She was a handsome girl, a good figure in that uniform with the pearl buttons down the front. You'd have to be queer to look at Flory's front and not wish to unbutton them.

"Thank you, Flory," I said. "You're rescuing the perishing."

"It's all here, I think." She looked it over, and I knew she wanted to linger. "The ham sand with tomatoes. The ice tea. The milk. The PBJ."

Flory looked around.

"Everybody cain't hardly wait for it," she said. "How you doin'?"

One thing I wouldn't have in the issue was surprise. The whole town knew I was coming out with it. They seemed almost as interested in that fact as in the story itself.

"You really gonna run all our pictures?" Flory said.

"That's it, Flory. You and sixteen other women are going to be famous."

She cocked her considerable hip and put her hand behind her head in a comic pose. The pose threw out her breasts most distinctly.

"I expect people will be asking for my autograph. Who are the others?"

She already knew, but I think she wanted to hear the list of the company she was in.

"Mrs. Orville Jenkins, Sally Carruthers, the Reverend Mrs. Billy Holmes . . ." I rattled some of them off.

". . . and Flory Henderson," she said. "Well, all I can say, he's picked the class of this town." She giggled. Then she was serious. "I want to buy ten extra issues. My folks'll want one. I got a lot of relatives down the river. And one up the river: Huntsville, two years for cattle rustling. Dumb bastard got caught."

"I'll save them," I said. It occurred to me that there would be a demand for extra issues. I reminded myself to tell Beto to increase the press run.

"Whereabouts you running them?"

"The front page."

Flory's eyes got big. "You mean you're running all our pictures on the front page? Lord amighty. I think you better run off extra copies for everyone. It's going to be, like they say, a collector's item."

I watched her behind pass through the swinging gate and hoped the collector's item wasn't going to be me. She had nice moves from that direction too. Then we fell on our food. The bread was homemade, the tomatoes were fresh, the ham country.

"You've got a friend in court in that Flory. You do like to lay on the charm with them, Baxter."

"She brings the food."

She bit into her peanut butter and jelly. "It's good. Do you like them big like that?"

For a moment I didn't know what she was talking about. "Like what big?"

"Tits. Do you like big tits like Flory's got?"

I shook my head. I would never get used to it. "Tell me something," I said. "Honestly, I mean. Does everyone your age speak like that these days, or are you something special?"

"I asked you a question first."

"The answer is yes."

She sighed. "Well, I'm glad all men don't like big tits and big asses. I'd have to cut my throat."

I know when I am having needles stuck in me.

"A man likes something he can get hold of," I said. "Button tits and dime-sized butts . . . hell, you might as well do it with a boy."

"I know some *refined* men whose preference is *not* for

Hereford cows. They prefer something else. Something fine and elegant—and classy."

I laughed. "Is that a self-description? Well, I'm not surprised. I picture you as attracting only refined men. The question is, can they do it?"

Pay back is pay back.

"Who's being vulgar and obscene now? You like to be so superior. You're really so stuck on yourself. I mean where brains are concerned. You think you're the smartest person in any room. I'm *not* talking about the newspaper part. You're okay there. I mean the rest of it."

"Speaking of Herefords," I said, "you've got milk on your mouth."

She licked it off. "Do you like the Peeper?" she said suddenly, in that quicksilver way she had.

"What?"

"Do you find yourself liking the Peeper?"

I swallowed some iced tea. "As a matter of fact I do."

"Why is that?"

"I don't know. At first I thought it was because he was doing what every man would like to do. But it's more than that. I don't know what it is. But I like him. Yes, I do."

"So do I," she said.

"Why?"

"Maybe it's that I think he'd be good with women. Something about those presents or something." She looked thoughtful as she bit into her sandwich. "I adore peanut butter and jelly sandwiches. I eat them for breakfast. Do you remember an actor named Leslie Howard?"

"Sure. *Petrified Forest, Intermezzo, Pygmalion.* . . . How can you remember him?"

"I've seen every picture he ever did. And, well, I have never known a woman who wasn't in love with Leslie Howard. If you ask them why, they always answer with one of two things. Gentleness. Acceptance." She swallowed some milk. "It may be a fantasy and the Peeper may not have it at all, and probably it isn't important whether he has or hasn't. But I think that's what these women see in him. I've backed off like you said and that's what I've come up with. You're always talking about how crucial it is to be able to learn. I just thought you might like me to educate you a little in these matters."

"I'm very grateful. How do you explain the fact that the men are so upset?"

"The men own the women. That's why."

I sighed. "It's too hot for this kind of talk. Let's get to work."

The afternoon was brightened by the visit of Sally Carruthers, who had been the first and, I felt, was rather proud of it. At the phoned request for a picture, she had said she would go through her collection and drop one by. I imagine the collection was considerable. She came bouncing in on the hot day, smartly turned out as always. She was wearing an ice-green dress which set off her strawberry hair. She looked like a wood nymph stopping by a coal mine.

"Hi there," she said in her breathless way. "Well! You're going to think I'm horridly vain. I finally chose not one but two. I want you to make the final selection."

She brought them out from a manila envelope and laid them on the counter. I saw at once that I had a choice of two delights. It was an important choice, because Sally's picture would lead off the gallery of peeped ladies. One showed her at the harp wearing a white evening dress, demure and maidenly. The other showed her in her Bloomer Girl uniform with the black bloomers, her hair tossing wantonly, performing one of the thigh-displaying kicks for which the Bloomer Girls were famous.

"What do you think?" she said.

"How is one to choose between two such beautiful young ladies?"

"Why, Mr. Baxter."

"The Bloomer Girl picture might be more pertinent to the story. The chief of police believes that watching you Bloomer Girls is what got the Peeper started in the first place."

"Isn't that thrilling?" She laughed that gay, what-a-lark laugh. "We must be even better than we think."

She was putting me on a little. "Well, that's hardly possible," I said.

She burst into laughter.

"I'd like to keep the harp one too," I said. "To run sometime with Church Notes when you're doing a solo on Sunday."

"Well! Don't you know how to set a girl up. I'll be on my way. I can hardly wait to see the story."

"None of us can, Sally."

" 'Bye now."

I took the Bloomer Girl picture around the corner to Michael's for the rush engraving job which would cost me double. When I got back to my desk there was a note in my typewriter. "Why, Mr. Baxter. You do know how to set a girl up. I'd love it if you would get in my bloomers and play on my harp."

I looked across the room, where she was working at her desk. I crumpled it in the wastebasket and went back to work.

It was late afternoon, as we slogged on, when I looked up to see Mayor Esau Ireland standing over me. Barely, with his five feet five and one hundred and thirty-five pounds. Even on this hot May day he was dressed like something out of a men's fashion catalog, possibly for a cruise. White Palm Beach suit with vest and paisley tie, his straw boater in his hand. He looked dapper and sharp, and his small polished bald head gleamed.

"My God, it's hot in here, Baxter." He fanned himself with the boater. "Don't you believe in air conditioning?"

"My account books don't."

"I'll bring you over some Ireland's Funeral Home cardboard fans."

"Have a seat, Mayor."

"Haven't the time," he said. "I just dropped by to leave my column."

That's how Brother Ireland always refers to his image ad. He handed it over.

The mayor is usually in fairly good humor when he brings his copy by, like any writer delivering prose he knows is certain of publication, but he looked now as if he were attending my wake.

"You've got your neck out from here to the Red River. They aren't going to be happy. They're going to chop it off at the collarbone. Why stick it out on something like this? My God, man. A little thing like a man looking in a window at women undressing. A little thing like a Peeping Tom. Why make a crusade out of something as ridiculous as that?"

"I'm not making a crusade. I just want to report things. I didn't realize you thought it a little thing, Mayor. Personally, I think it may be quite a bit more than just a man looking into bedroom windows."

"Oh? What's the rest of it?"

"Who knows, Mayor? We'll have to see."

"It makes the town look foolish, what you're doing," he said in his reedy, imperious voice. "Bad for our image. Bad for business if it gets around that Martha is a town where this sort of thing goes on. Especially since we haven't caught the fellow."

"Hell, Esau, it might even help business. Anyhow, half of it's already in type."

"Can I see some of it?"

"No."

"I didn't think so." He sighed. "I thought I owed it to you to give it one last try."

He put his boater on. On his way out he stopped at Jamie's desk and took it off again with a little bow.

"How are you liking your work, Miss Scarborough? It's nice we're getting a feminine touch in a hard-nosed business like newspapers seem to be."

This reference to me came through loud and clear from just a few feet away. Jamie took him on instantly.

"Well, if it weren't for newspapers," she said, "I'd hate to think how many more crooks and bullies we'd have than there already are. Especially in high places."

"Say! You've got a firebrand here, Baxter. I like your spirit, little lady." He replaced his boater. "I'll have Sister Ireland drop you by some cardboard fans," he said to me. "You're going to need them."

* * *

The sun had left for this day, and gray shadows had taken over Cavalry Street when we finished up. We were done. Then I had an impulse. I went out to the composing room and sat at the Mergenthaler and punched out the one-line slug myself, took it over to the makeup stone, went down the type and took out five leads, and plugged it in the page-one form at the beginning of the story on the women interviews. Then Beto stood on one side of the stone and I stood on the upside-down side and we looked at it once more under the glare of the overhead shade light, the darkened composing room around us.

"What do you think, Beto?"

"It looks good to me, boss."

The lead headline still looked big in its 48 points, and words like "Peeping Tom," "Peeper," and "Gallery of Martha Girls and Women" seemed to jump up at me from all over the page, larger than life. Well, it was too late now.

"All right," I said. "Let's lock up."

To the word, it was what we always said, on any issue of the Martha *Clarion,* on any Thursday night.

He began to justify the page with two-point leads and now and then a six-point slug, his hands moving over the type, skillful as a concert pianist's over keys. He got the columns snug, then tightened the four quoins with a key, tightening each a little at a time so that the page would not end up lopsided, then taking his mallet and planer and going over the type to make it smooth, hammering it with quick, clean *plop-plop!* strokes, then going back with his key and tightening the quoins some more until finally they were all the way in. It was ready for printing and he looked up at me.

"I think there'll be some requests for extra copies," I said. "Why don't we double the run."

Beto looked across at me under the light's glare.

"Double, boss?"

"Double," I said.

I went back to the front. She was still at her desk, working away.

"What are you doing? It's finished. It's all in."

"I'm just getting some things ready for next week's issue," she said.

"Oh, of course." I appreciated her confidence.

I was tired and wound up, and I knew that combination called for something besides sleep. I looked at my watch.

"Beto's starting the inside pages. It'll be a few hours until the outside. How would you like to go across the river?"

She looked up at me. "To Mexico?"

"I think it's time for a margarita. Maybe two."

"Why, I'd like that."

"Then let's shove off."

She stood up. "I'll just go and wash this ink off my hands."

"You've got some on your face too."

9.
Boys'Town

I know of no drink easier to botch up than a margarita, and you get some pretty terrible ones in some places. Made properly, with the right tequila, the right liqueur, fresh Mexican limes (above all), the drink shaken with ice cubes in a cocktail shaker and strained (lest the ice cubes make it too watery) into a chilled stemmed (lest the heat from your hand warm the drink) glass (not a wineglass with its inward curving rim), the rim rubbed with a cut lime and pressed just the right way into a plate of salt so that it is coated (not caked), no drink dissolves tribulations and sets you up better. In Las Bocas, Tamaulipas, Mexico, an excellent margarita is to be had at the Alhambra.

We sat in lounge chairs in the bar with the Don Quixote painting and surveyed the scenery, which includes a patio of that lovely old pockmarked stone, green plants, and a waterfall. There must be more bars in Mexico with waterfalls than any other place in the world. The scenery also included the uncertain clientele who inhabit the place. In the Alhambra you can cut the machismo with a knife. When I'm there, I look around and wonder how many of them are involved in taking it across the border. Maybe if I were a Mexican and trying to live on twenty-five dollars a month, I might consider a job offer to take it across at five thousand a trip, which works out to something like seventeen years' wages for one trip. Certainly you'd have to think it over. I like looking at these men and trying to figure out which one does that and which one barbers hair around the corner. Sometimes it's one and the same.

Since it is against the law to have only one margarita, we had another, then stopped by the shop which forms the front part of the bar. They have nice things, not the usual cheap tourist curios. We looked at the huge and whimsical papier-mâché animals, the giraffes and the lions and the Russian wolfhounds, which Mexican craftsmen do with such a gift of humor; at the alabaster vegetables which look almost like the real thing; at the silver from Taxco and the tapestries from Oaxaca and the sisal rugs from the Yucatán. She wandered down the counter looking in the glass jewelry cases.

"Baxter, look at this," she said. "Look at those butterflies."

"I see them."

"Señorita," she said to a sales clerk lolling nearby. "May I see one of these?"

The clerk unlocked the case and brought one out. Anything that costs over five dollars is locked up at the Alhambra. It was pretty, the body of silver, the wings enameled in bright colors, made into a brooch.

"It's exactly like the ones the Peeper's been leaving," she said.

"Yep."

"Well?" she said.

"Everybody comes to Las Bocas," I said.

"How much are they?" she asked the señorita.

"Ten dollars U.S."

We went on out and down the walk, attended by a cluster of small brown barefooted boys sidling up to us and hissing, "Cigarettes! American cigarettes!" We went down to Sam's on the corner.

Sam's is a big, barny, low-ceilinged place. If you want waiters in dinner jackets and something brought out on a flaming sword, there's another place nearby. If you want good Mexican food, you go to Sam's. We ordered beef enchiladas, refried beans, rice, tostadas, and *pico de gallo,* which is smashed avocado with pieces of fresh tomato and cilantro, and Negra Modelo, the great Mexican beer. We were hungry. We really put the food away.

"What a novelty to see you eat something besides peanut butter and jelly sandwiches," I said.

"It's nice to have all that about food worked out in your life. Then you can concentrate on other matters of more importance."

I swallowed some beer. "What are these other matters of more importance," I said, "in your case?"

"That is a personal question," she said, "not lying in the proper purview of employer-employee relations."

"I withdraw it."

"In a properly run company I could probably take you to court for asking a question like that. Just like I could if you made a pass at me and said I couldn't have a raise unless I came through. There was a case the other day on that, and the judge ruled for the woman and ordered considerable restitution. About fifty thousand dollars, I think."

I sighed heavily. "She must have been a pretty good piece at those prices. I'd just as soon not speak to you at all."

"Oh, I think talk's all right. So long as it isn't followed up by action."

"Don't get your hopes up."

"Hopes!"

She certainly didn't call me boss outside the office. It was as if I were two people. At the paper, someone whose every word in matters of the newspaper business, of covering stories and writing them and copy editing and setting head type and all of it, was to be listened to as if I were journalism's oracle at Delphi. Outside, as if . . . well, as if I were simply one more of that species against which a woman must forever be on her guard not to be pushed around, put down, ignored, looked down upon, mistreated, taken advantage of. One felt her openness, eagerness, for whatever gave promise of something good, a fierce determination not to miss anything, but with it a keen and immediate defense against anything she judged not to be in her own direct interest. That yes-and-no combination—that was what made her formidable. Not much more than a girl, she knew by instinct every tool and weapon in that awesome arsenal of female strategy and was prepared to use the last one of them in her own behalf. She was some tough little package. She wanted it all. So had I.

"What would you do if things didn't work out in the town?" she said.

"I like the delicate way you put it: 'Didn't work out.' You mean if they really froze me out, stopped advertising?"

"Yes, that's what I mean."

"Then say so. Well, I suppose I'd ask for my job back in Washington. I think they'd take me back. I hope."

"But you want to stay? I mean forever?"

"I never think about things like forever. But it's a good life. I like what I do."

"I want to do what you did. I want to cover the Senate or the White House. Afghanistan and China. I think you really like this business about the Social Notes and the Domino Club and the Town Council. Why is that?"

"They relax me. They're self-respecting activities, and they don't harm anybody. Well, maybe the Town Council does sometimes. And having three days out of seven absolutely your own—that's pretty good."

"That boat, you mean. I don't suppose it'd do any good to ask to go down with you sometime. Like this weekend."

"Why in the world would you want to do that? The idea of time off is to get away from the people you have to be with to earn a living. Anyhow, the boat's in dry dock getting the barnacles scraped off. I'm not going down until Sunday to take her out—wouldn't be worth your time."

"You always have an answer, Baxter."

"What would you do?"

"What? Oh, I see. You want to change the subject. You mean what do I do if the Martha *Clarion* goes on the reef. Hey! Not bad when we've been talking about boats."

"It's terrible."

"I don't think about it."

"Go back to college?"

"I'd streetwalk first."

"No, you wouldn't. You're not built right."

Her eyes were lighting up, and I took warning.

"Personally," she said, "I think it's your problem. I think you're responsible for me. You got me down here at the end of the world. A really responsible man would see that I was taken care of if it came to that."

"I suppose he would. Well, I've never claimed to be a responsible man. If anything happens to the paper, you're on your own, kid."

"I don't believe you. I think that's a big put-on. I think you'd take care of me. Some way. Don't call me kid."

"Take care of you? Good God. I don't take care of anybody but myself."

It was pretty hard for me to worry about someone whose family had the kind of money hers did. Then I knew that was a cop-out. She had never talked about her family, but I thought I had a pretty accurate idea. If I was right, all that money didn't solve anything in her life. A number of Texas rich people are as nice as you and me, but a number aren't. That business about my being responsible for her. She had to be light about it, but there was something deadly serious that the lightness was intended to cover up. Still, she really wasn't asking me or anybody to take on her problems. She would have far too much pride to do that. But I think she was sending out some sort of signal. Well, that part of her was none of my business. Mixing that stuff up with your work—I couldn't have imagined anything more messy, more stupid. People who played volunteer guardian angel usually got their wings chopped off. Deservedly so. It was not for me.

"Let's talk about how I'm doing as a reporter," she said brightly.

"You're doing okay. You're intelligent. You got the mood of the town, the women, very accurately, I thought. You're skeptical. You figured out that some of the women were probably only pretending to be peeped. Persistent—God knows you're that. You're doing okay."

She preened a little. "You mean it?"

I decided I was building her up too much. "You're off to a pretty fair start. I wouldn't want you to think you don't have a long way to go."

"Oh, I won't forget that. That's why I'm sticking around you. You'll find it won't be easy to shake me off. Not until I've learned everything you have to teach me."

"At which point I suppose you'll take the next plane out."

"Of course. I get a good teacher in you; you get me at these slave wages. I know I'm a good worker. So we'll just use each other until it's all used up. It will be interesting to see who stops being useful first."

"We better get on back and run the papers off."

"I'd like to see Boys' Town."

"What? No, you wouldn't. Anyhow, they don't let girls in. Not unless you're a working girl."

"Just like the Town Council. They don't let girls in anywhere down here. I could pass."

"What?"

"With a cap."

"You don't want to go there."

"I've got a cap in the car. For when it's windy. It's a regular driver's cap. Come on, take me. I want to see it. It's good for my experience as a reporter."

I sighed. "What a pain you are. And what a liar. Okay. But just to drive through. We're not getting out of the car."

We went out and she got a suede cap from the glove compartment and put it on.

"How's this?"

She could pass. She was a funny-looking little thing in that cap and that oversize man's shirt. She looked like a waif out of Dickens, Oliver Twist screwing up courage to ask for a second bowl of soup, and I thought, God, what a fraud. We drove across the city and then down a little dirt hill and across a small bridge over a muddy little creek. At the end of the bridge was a guardhouse and a couple of policemen standing outside it.

"What are the policemen for?"

"To check the girls when they cross the bridge. Their cards. To see that their VD cards are reasonably up to date."

"How thoughtful for the men."

We entered it. The streets were dirt, with the biggest potholes you ever saw. The walks were dirt too, and the one-story buildings all in a row were stucco. They had that end-of-civilization look that dirty stucco gets. All this seediness was lighted up by obscene-looking fiery red neon lights giving the names of the different bars. It was a corner of Gehenna. All the bars had fast-service rooms in the back and some had what were called "stage shows." I had been in a couple of them, and they were great if you liked to sit at one of the tables surrounding a patch of floor and see what a girl could do to herself with a banana. We took a right turn at the end of the main street and started down another extremely narrow street, no more than four steps across, also heavily potholed and lined on both sides with cubicles, little bigger than large closets. A girl stood in front of each cubicle and as we passed by she made her pitch and suggested we come in and let her pull the curtain. The closets were without doors. The street was dirt and filth and disease and poverty, and what made it far worse was that so many of the girls were astonishingly pretty. They began at about sixteen and were much more heavily rouged, lipsticked, and mascaraed than girls that age need to be. Some had even dyed that lovely long licorice-black hair they have that is the silkiest in the world a shocking, curling, and whorish white-blond. They were all wearing very short skirts which showed much of their pretty young thighs and blouses which showed most of their pretty young breasts. The MG had to go at a crawl to keep from being disabled by the potholes, and this gave the girls an opportunity to step forth from their positions in front of the cubicles to push their wares. They came at us from both sides of the car. They had learned all the essential English words, and from both sides they told us what they would do to us. They leaned into the slow-moving, open-top little car and rubbed themselves against Jamie and against me and enumerated the acts they were ready and eager to perform, for only ten dollars U.S.

We drove to the end of the street and there was nowhere to go but a U-turn. We came back and went through the defile again, with more breasts and hands thrusting and clutching at us now over the sides of the car. Then back up the main street with the red neon lights.

"My God," I said.

"What?"

"Over there. Going down that walk there. It's Orville Jenkins."

She turned and looked. "Well, what do you know."

He was just walking along. There was no way of telling whether he had been in one of the bars or was thinking about going in one.

"That's about the last man I'd ever have expected to see in Boys' Town," I said. "Perhaps he's converting all the child Mary Magdalens."

She bumped the MG through the gate, past the guard-house and the two policemen, across the bridge and up the little dirt hill, and then onto pavement and back through the town. Pretty soon we could see the International Bridge up ahead and beyond it in the night the American flag flying over the Immigration and Customs pass-through. We passed back over the Rio Grande. Exactly in the middle of the bridge was a trash disposal hamper with a push-in drop and a sign, DEPOSIT YOUR DRUGS HERE. We stopped at the pass-through, and the Immigration man leaned down and asked us if we were U.S. citizens and if we were bringing anything back, and we answered yes and no. He waved us through. We came onto the broad American highway and she accelerated. I looked across. She took off her suede cap and her short hair went flying in the wind.

"Well, now you've seen it," I said.

She raced the car, a good twenty miles above the 55 mph limit that we all observe to conserve energy. The clean breeze felt good. Soon up ahead we could see the town. She slowed, and we came into it and down between the rows of trees and behind them all the green lawns and neat houses. We turned into Cavalry. Everything down it was dark and locked up save for one light burning. The Martha *Clarion*. Let the newspapers light up the world, I thought, including all dark places. Including Martha, Texas.

She parked the MG, and we went back into the composing room and the old comfortable printer's-ink smell. Beto was just turning the big wheel which rolled out the flatbed. He carried the four page forms for the outside run over to the bed. Pretty soon he pulled the switch, and the old Miehle began to lumber and grind, then settled into a loud *clank-clank* sound. We watched the papers come off, and I pulled two out and gave her one and looked at mine. I thought it looked okay, even handsome. We had put out a newspaper.

Then I could see she was looking quite quickly past the rest of it and at one particular story.

"Well, what do you know? 'By Jamie Scarborough,'" she said. In the composing-room gloom I could see her eyes big. "Doesn't it look wonderful? I'm like Flory. I want to order a hundred extra copies. My first byline. Oh, Baxter. What a nice thing to do. Why would anybody ever be anything but a newspaperman?"

"I've often wondered," I said.

PEEPER 6
Count Your Many Blessings

It seemed that everybody turned up on Cavalry Street on Saturday. Even people who had little or nothing to buy walked up and down the street in a *paseo*, looking into store windows and at each other and stopping to chat. This "visiting," as it was called, repeatedly halted sidewalk traffic. No one minded. People were patient in Martha. Marthans would have been shocked to their bones to hear someone behind them say, "Move! You're blocking the sidewalk!" After all, those blocked would probably be doing the blocking presently when they ran into friends. "Going to Cavary" went back to farmers' shopping day, when everybody came to town. The townspeople too. If you wanted to see people you knew, you went down to Cavalry Street on Saturday. They'd be there, many of them just walking up and down.

It was a hot May day, and he wanted to see certain people.

He also had some valid shopping to do. He needed a new pair of pantyhose. He would begin at the Bon Ton, since he wanted to make sure of a place at the counter. The restaurant was always crowded on Saturday.

He was there none too soon. He spoke to a few fellow diners and made his way to one of three remaining counter stools. She came over, and though he hardly needed to study the menu, which he could recite backwards, he did so as she waited for his selection, standing there pleasantly and in no hurry. He reviewed the choices ranging from the beef stew with hot biscuits to the chicken-fried steak to the broiled redfish, which had been "swimming last night in the Gulf," as the menu noted. His eyes moved in a vertical rhythm and, on the upswing, edged over the top of the menu to where, at his seated level, he was looking directly at them. She wore a freshly laundered white cotton waitress uniform, with the big pearl buttons down the front. It sparkled, clean and starched, as yet undisfigured by specks of crookneck squash or fresh zucchini. As he looked the uniform dissolved and he saw them naked and magnificent, exactly as when she stood by her bed, having shed her high-toned satin-and-lace brassiere.

"Flory Henderson," he said, "you have the most glorious breasts in Martha, Texas."

This was spoken to himself. He looked at her. Her blue eyes shimmered. Only a farm girl could have eyes that clear and honest, that blue. He spoke aloud.

"I am torn between the redfish and the roast pork with the brown gravy. Flory, your eyes are even more ravishing than usual today. Could it be that this is Saturday and your thoughts are on the dancing tonight at the Here-Tis?"

"Sattiday night," she said. "Lawd, how could I go on if there wasn't Sattiday night."

He would like to have brought up the subject of that other night and of its effect on her. Of course it would be bad form to mention such a matter. But unless it was his imagination, she seemed more alive, more confident, more feminine. A kind of radiance that was new. No, it certainly hadn't hurt her. And if there had been any doubt, there was one other thing. He leaned forward. It was pinned at the top button of the uniform.

"What a pretty butterfly," he said.

She leaned forward and held it for him to inspect. He leaned very close. He felt almost as if he were resting his head right between them.

"A beautiful piece of work," he said. "You've got good taste, Flory."

She looked around her and leaned even closer and spoke in a whisper. "*He* has good taste."

"Well, what do you know," he said. He looked at it again. "Yes, I agree. He has exquisite taste." He looked at the menu. "What would you advise?"

"Hot day for roast pork, ain't it? Unless you really relish roast pork."

"You're right. I'll have that redfish that was swimming sometime in the Gulf."

"Ice tea?"

"Please, ma'am." He looked over the menu's top. He wanted to keep them there a little longer. "It's going to be a warm day," he said.

She lingered. "They don't keep the air conditioning up enough in here. This uniform is sticking to me already."

She brought her hands up and shook the uniform a little. They moved behind it. Only fractionally, but it was very pleasant. Firm ones never moved much, whatever the size. He wondered if she would have executed that particular gesture before the peeping. She leaned to take his menu and they came closer and through the waitress uniform he saw them, lavish and unfettered. How sumptuous they were, how oyster-white, capped by what noble nipples.

"God, but they are gorgeous. Fit for a king." To himself.

He walked out onto Cavalry Street. The shopping district was six blocks long and nothing was over two stories. Most of the buildings had been there a half century and some a full one, but they were well kept. Most were brick, often topped off by patterned cornices. Flower pots and potted trees stood in front of a number of them. The sidewalks were crowded, people flowed across the narrow street as they pleased, and the cars drove slowly and watched out for them. Every fourth or fifth car was a pickup. Many had a dog in back. Sometimes people crossing the street spotted someone they knew in a car and the car stopped while pedestrian and car rider "visited" and the cars behind waited. He swung down the walk, speaking to people as he went, lifting his hat to the ladies. He would never understand cities or why people lived in them. Here you could get close to people, know them. And what was life all about if not that?

Coming toward him with a shopping bag in one hand and a purse slung over her shoulder was the high school English teacher, Kathryn Shields. She walked with that saucy, confident, I-know-what-I've-got air. Her licorice-black hair made a striking contrast against her milk complexion.

"Well now, Miss Kathryn. Aren't you doing your hair a new way? It becomes you."

"Why, thank you, I am. How nice to run across an observant man for a change. I just cut it a little. This weather." She flounced it and tossed her head impudently. "Now I'll let it grow to Christmas. Santa Claus will just have to bring me some new hair."

Nothing wrong with the old hair, he thought, and looked at her. As he did, all the pretty clothes she was wearing came off and there she was, in the middle of Cavalry Street, in her bath. Soaping that soft, smooth body, lovingly lathering her breasts and all of it until she was covered with white froth, and through it the raspberry nipples now and then. He saw the froth fall away under the hand shower until there came in view, wet and glistening, between her milky thighs, that other burst of licorice hair, silky and thick.

"Something nice must have happened to you recently," she said. "You look like the cat that swallowed the little bird."

"It must be the pleasure of seeing you."

Her eyes and whole face brightened. "Well, aren't you the *galante* one."

"Good day," he said and continued his *paseo* up Cavalry. He did it twice, from Gumwood Street to Maple Street, up one side and back the other, strolling. He ran into five of them. With three he managed to stop and chat. One and all, they seemed bright-eyed and much alive. Women dressed well for the Cavalry Street coursing. It was a kind of fashion parade. They were all in their flowing hot-weather dresses, pastels and chiffons, floral patterns and geometric designs, delicate slips visible beneath. He saw through them all.

"Mildred! How nice to see you." To himself: "It's nicer to see you on that Arabian gray of yours. It's nicest of all to see you lower your jodhpurs."

As he chatted amiably she did just that, boots came off, bra and panties flew to the bed, and he looked at her standing naked on Cavalry. Upswept breasts adorned with apricot nipples and, as she turned, a high lustrous behind, curved and pert.

"Give George my best. Tell him I'll call about the appointment for the inlay."

He walked a half block. "Why, Mary Armbruster!" He stopped and chatted with the secretary and, as he looked, her garments evanesced and he saw her seated at her dressing table, her body, clad only in wispy panties, reflected in the oval mirror. I never imagined I'd enjoy so much seeing someone do her toenails, he thought. The way your breasts arched downward, and your heel cocked on your knee to give a view of those inner thighs, so satiny. "Good shopping, Mary!"

He crossed the street and stopped on the curb. "Good afternoon, Mrs. Tefenteller." He bowed slightly to the town matriarch. "What a lovely hat." He looked, and her dress and all she must have under it dissolved. Those bosoms of yours are like the Baptist church bells, and you have a behind like a heavy cruiser. And those eiderdown rolls in between. But seen all together, it does make a certain effect, all that fleecy rippling flesh. Quite touching and charming in its special way. Impressive, certainly. Everybody's different. Especially you women. But that's what I like about you. "So pleasant running into you, ma'am."

He threaded his way slowly, feeling all gentle, on down the jammed sidewalks. What a pleasure it was to see through their pretty dresses! How much more delightful their company, now that he had this double vision. What a tang and a spice it gave to the most ordinary conversation. How much more he would appreciate them every time he saw them.

Which brought him to a problem.

He could not expect to get around to every woman in town. Martha was small but not that small. He must ration himself. There was a certain number of women whom he saw regularly. Surely the thing was to make certain he got through these. Not waste time on women he scarcely knew and hardly ever saw. The true pleasure, continuing down the years, would be to see in their customary clothes, again and again, women he had seen otherwise. He should make a checklist of the women he knew, saw often, and determine how many remained to be done. He should go about it systematically. He had been really too hit-and-miss so far. The list should place them in order of importance, and he should work down it. Probably there weren't more than a dozen or two left to do.

He remembered that he had important shopping to do. The old pair was becoming worn and full of runs and hung loose and ungainly on his head. At first he hesitated about purchasing them at Carruthers. It might be reported to the Town Council. But then the very act seemed a kind of protection. The real Peeper would never do it. He went back down Cavalry and dropped into the store. The place was jammed, the clerks busy. Mrs. Carruthers attempted to wait on him. He thanked her and said he was still looking. He had to wait awhile, counter shopping, until he caught her.

"Well, Miss Sally! Next stop, the University. We'll all miss my favorite Bloomer Girl."

She gave that isn't-it-all-a-lark laugh. "I'll bet you say that to all the Bloomer Girls," she said pertly. "Yes, sir. Austin, here I come."

"Hook 'em horns!"

He felt a special fondness toward her. She had been his first. She was wearing natural-linen slacks and a clay blouse. Her pale red hair hung in a shimmering fall down her back.

"Well, I'm an errand boy again today. One pair of panty-hose."

She smiled in understanding. "What color this time?"

"Black again. Oh, Sally?"

"Yes?"

"I don't think I got the right kind last time. I hear murmurings of runs, I believe you ladies call them."

"Well, the fact is, you bought the best quality, I believe. The more expensive, the sheerer, the quicker to run."

She stepped purposefully to a counter and produced a cellophane package.

"These are not quite as sheer but they last a lot longer. I call them bullet hose."

"Why, what a witty way to describe them."

"Just the thing if you're looking for wear rather than" —she giggled mischievously—"see-through."

"I think wear is what's called for in this instance. Based on her experience with the other, I mean."

"And they're only ninety-nine cents." She stepped to the cash register. "Here you are—one black long-lasting panty-hose. And your change."

"Thank you for your help." He looked and everything came off. The natural-linen slacks fell away, the clay blouse disappeared, the brassiere and the panties vanished. She stood there in Carruthers Mercantile sweetly naked: the young breasts surprisingly full, the nipples pink as rosebuds, the thighs soft and pearl, the strawberry crown planted between them like a flower, a sunrise matching almost perfectly that other pale soft hair above. He sighed.

"Was there something else?"

"No, that'll be all. For today."

On his way out of the store he noticed a card table set up to the side with the sign, "Please contribute to Foreign Missions." It was annual collection time for the Woman's Missionary Union. The wife of the minister was manning the card table.

"Good afternoon, Sister Holmes. May I make a contribution?"

She smiled. "We haven't turned anyone away yet."

She looked up at him with those huge green eyes, grave and intent. Her blouse and skirt evaporated, and he saw the marvelous toothpick of a body, that of a fourteen-year-old, adorned only in a fragment of light-blue panties, saw the saucy little breasts with their obelisk nipples, turned her around to see the doll-like behind, bare and charming. He got out his billfold and extracted a ten-dollar bill.

"Why, what a generous offering."

"It was worth it. Size isn't everything. Small is beautiful." He spoke aloud: " 'Lay not up for yourselves treasures upon earth.' Good day, Sister Holmes."

As he walked back down Cavalry Street, looking at the people, at the men and the women, a moment of philosophy, of reflection, came upon him on the summer day. The afternoon was getting on, the sun beginning to head toward its horizon home.

If he had upset the men of the town, well, he was not too sorry. The men needed to be upset. As far as he could see, they seldom bothered about the women, seldom bothered really to please them, to nurture them. And women were what mattered. He wasn't even thinking about women's bodies at the moment. He was thinking of something else.

Not, he told himself, that he had started out on any such high mission of learning. He had started out very simply because he loved looking at women's bodies. He had moved on to an appreciation of all women's bodies and still further to an appreciation of . . . yes, their souls. He boldly used that word. These havens of all gentleness. These embodiments of the sublime. Their ever-changing moods were the very essence of their delight, the imprimatur of their glory. He would go so far as to characterize whatever aspects of craft and guile, of deceit and dissimulation, they might from time to time employ as necessary defensive weapons against the treatment they had received, across long harsh centuries, at the hands of men, and still so today. The hell with the men. They could take care of themselves in this world. In fact, that was what men did best—took care of themselves. How much men took and how little they gave! But God is not mocked. Men's very selfishness made them lose out in life on what was the most important thing of all for them, even from their own selfish point of view. It made them lose out on women.

If he was upsetting the men of the town, he was not, on the whole, upsetting the women. Specifically, the women he had peeped did not, on today's reading, seem any the worse for wear. Indeed, in addition to *seeing* them, that was another reason he wanted to confront them today, to determine how they were making out. If he had found them in trauma, he would simply have stopped his activities. But they seemed perfectly splendid. They appeared healthy—physically, mentally, emotionally. Some were even wearing the presents he had left them. He would not have liked to do them any harm, and he was convinced he hadn't. There was no reason not to continue.

The sun was beginning to soften, the first intimations of evening hung upon the air. The night's work lay ahead. He would be stepping out in his new bullet pantyhose and he needed to make the essential alterations in them. It would be his first Saturday-night peep.

He turned off Cavalry and headed for home. It had been a nice day but night, after all, was his favorite time.

10.
Hip and Thigh

I got back from the beach Monday morning, feeling pretty good, even though I'd had only Sunday. I always do after the time out on my Grand Banks and the blue Gulf. I can recommend this sort of activity to anyone bedeviled by the ills the world casts on us and who doesn't get seasick in six-foot seas. It fortifies one to handle the vicissitudes that come on almost any Monday morning anywhere. *Duchess* seemed to kick along even better with her clean hull.

"Christ, I'm glad you're back" were the cheery words with which Jamie greeted me when I sailed in around nine o'clock. "I hope you got good and rested down on that island, because the shit has really hit the fan. This is going to be one hell of a week, I promise you."

I felt my eyes roll, more at the language than the substance. The phone rang and she picked it up. I listened to her end of it while she made notes.

"Yes. . . . Yes, Mrs. Torrance. Yes, I understand. . . . Yes, Mrs. Torrance. . . . Well, I don't think that happened, but I'll tell him. . . . Yes, Mrs. Torrance. . . . Yes, you have my *word.* I'll tell him *exactly* what you said the *moment* he comes in."

She hung up with a big sigh. "That's what I mean." She consulted her notes. "She says ordinarily when the *Clarion* runs a group of pictures like that together, it's for girls getting engaged or women being elected to the Daughters of the Republic of Texas. She said she had no idea they were going to be lined up on page one like"—she read from her notes—"prize call girls. She says she feels she was tricked into letting us have her picture."

"Tricked? Hell, she was the first to give us one. Has there been a lot of this?"

"A lot! I've got them all written down for you."

"Well, we're getting a reaction anyhow."

"I got into a big argument with some people at the Bon Ton I don't even know. Flory helped me out. When they started talking about the paper invading people's privacy, Flory said her privacy had been invaded one night a lot more than this."

"Good old Flory. That reminds me. I'll take her those ten issues I promised I'd save for her."

The phone kept ringing. After several more calls I decided, as a news judgment, to do a story on what people felt about our issue on the Peeper. Favorable as well as unfavorable calls came in, and it seemed that just about everyone in town was going to have a decided view one way or the other. I intended to make this an open paper, in which anyone could express an opinion on almost anything, and this seemed a good place to begin. Of course Voltaire thought of that before I did, but then Voltaire wasn't from Martha, Texas.

"We'll both be taking the calls," I told Jamie. "This involves the whole town, so I think it's enough of a news story to put on page one. What we'll do is run them in two columns alongside. The pro and the con. I want just the direct quotes, with the name below it. You're not to argue with the callers even if there's vituperation on the other end of the line. Just be polite and get the quotes down word for word. Got that?"

"Yes, boss. I'll get the vituperation word for word. And I won't argue."

I looked at her. The appellative was neither sarcastic nor self-conscious. I don't think she was even aware of it.

These new Martha *Clarion* columns were well on their way by late morning as the phone kept jangling. The "Martha Says No" column, it was soon clear, was going to be considerably longer than the "Martha Says Yes" column, but that was all right. I was finding even the unfavorable reactions amusing, and this was not a plebiscite to determine whether the paper would continue to report the news. That decision had already been made by the editor. It was only around eleven o'clock that I began to get some news myself, an intimation that the same thing could just possibly happen to me that happened to Mr. Voltaire.

"Orville Jenkins here," the voice said. "Baxter, we're getting down to basics: what's good for a community and what isn't. We're dealing with a fundamental matter. I think what you did makes a hero out of the Peeper. You're glorifying this felon."

"Oh, I disagree with that, Orville. I didn't endorse what he's doing. All I did was report it."

"Why did you do it?"

"It was a news story."

"Well, I'll give you another news story. I don't see why I have to give business to a newspaper that prints things I don't think should be printed."

Something went hollow in the pit of my stomach. I made a stab.

"I don't see the connection, Orville. I don't print the newspaper on the canning labels."

"I think I'd just be encouraging you. Now I don't like doing this, but you were warned. I think I have to stand up and be counted. I'm taking my business elsewhere. I do this more in sorrow than in anger."

Jamie came over and stood at my desk.

"That was Saint Orville, wasn't it?" she said.

"Himself."

"Well?"

"He canceled his overprinting contract. He wanted to stand up and be counted."

She took a deep breath. "Well, the pious son of a bitch. And to think that we saw him in Boys' Town."

"Everybody goes to Boys' Town. Even you."

About noon I got word that the Town Council was meeting that night—a night earlier than usual. Sherm Embers called and mentioned it casually in the course of talking about the

Peeper issue. Normally when the Council meets I get an official call, either from Esau Ireland or from Freight Train, so that I can be present. No such invitation was forthcoming this time. I was to be excluded.

"Now you know how a woman feels," Jamie said when I told her. "What are you going to do?"

"My father is a preacher, and he always said, 'Worry is a sin.' He's seventy-seven and he doesn't have a wrinkle on his face and only about six gray hairs."

By that time Monday, the week's ads for Carruthers Mercantile, Bradley's Variety Store, the bank, and some others have usually been delivered to me. None had come in.

"Those piss-ants," she said. "What *are* we going to do?"

"We're going to keep putting out a newspaper."

"A real newspaper?"

"I always hate it when someone uses that adjective that way. When I say a newspaper, I mean what the word says."

I looked through the window with its backward-running letters that said "The Martha Clarion." That, I thought, and the Grand Banks were absolutely the only things I had to show for life, for forty-one years of it. Even so, Bert Hooper's bank held huge mortgages on both.

"What are you thinking?" she said.

"I was just wondering which they'd repossess first, my boat or my paper. I speak more in anger than in sorrow."

The phone calls headed for the yes and no columns kept coming in that afternoon, but the ads didn't. Oh, a few small ones, but none of my big accounts. I phoned some of them and got a curiously similar pattern: the "boss" was out and would phone me when he got back.

I walked home in the twilight. The yards were empty. People would be sitting down to their supper. It had always been a strange time of day for me, a lonely time. In some distant tree I heard a grackle give out its raucous *yak-yak* and a mockingbird clownishly give it back a moment later. I felt the town orbiting about me. It is amazing how much a newspaper stands at the center of its town. The town revolving around it, feeding into it, and the editor deciding which of those feed-ins, of those thousand same yet ever-changing aspects that constitute the small town, to put into print. No vetoes, no "superiors" to overrule. There is nothing like it, and it is this that makes some damn good newspapermen, who could make it anywhere, choose very deliberately to run a small-town newspaper. *People telling you what to do.* That's what you could get away from here. A small-town newspaper is one of the last refuges for bringing to life whatever it is that you may have inside you. Instead of having it filtered, altered, mutilated, castrated by fifty other people.

Of course, you have to get people to pay for supporting you in this fashion. That's the tight line, the high-wire act. If you're not good on the high wire, my advice is to forget it and head for one of those hierarchies.

All I knew now was that somehow this whole thing had got beyond the matter of a Peeping Tom in the town. It had got down to whether or not I could put out a newspaper. I mean a real newspaper, I thought, using that redundant adjective myself, just so there would be no misunderstanding.

The phone call from Freight Train came in about ten o'clock next morning. I was sure he hadn't approved of what I'd done, but he hadn't called to gloat. He wasn't the kind. First he told me that there had been a couple more peepings last night and I took down their names. Then:

"They was so worked up at the meeting that they just broke early without even having the poker game afterwards."

"God, I didn't know there was a crisis that extreme."

"It's double-bad, Ace," he said. "You in it up to here. I reckoned I'd let you know."

"I appreciate that," I said. I waited for him to let me know.

"Mainly it was a matter of degree, as we used to say at the old Aggie school when we was trying to get them girls from Texas Women's U to put out."

"I understand."

"Saint Orville was in something like terminal apoplexy. He called down curses from above. Bert Hooper only a little less so. Milam, he never says too much, but he thought it didn't do anything to help the town. Sherm Embers was the only one who thought it was fine, but he didn't persuade nobody."

"And Esau?"

"Well, you know Esau. The mayor don't like to agree with nobody about nothing. He said he'd have to think it over some more. For the time being he was keeping his counsel."

For the first time I felt some hope shine through. If Esau Ireland was holding back, I had a chance. He had a way of making his views prevail, even over people like Jenkins and Hooper, once he made up his mind. It was as if they were afraid of his cantankerousness, his pugnacity. If the mayor kept his advertising, so would the rest of the merchants. But he was his own man, and no one could talk Esau Ireland into anything. It was better not even to try.

"They didn't vote to burn down the paper or anything like that, did they?" I said.

"Naw, that's not the way they do it. They got other ways. You'll know when it starts to happen. That's for sure and certain."

"It already has." I told him about Orville Jenkins canceling his overprinting contract Monday morning.

"That's Saint Orville, all right. He always believes in getting there first on the kill. Drop over for one of the Town Council's Lone Stars tonight, why don't you, Ace? I reckon you won't be getting much else from them."

The calls, pro and con, kept coming in during the day. Also there were blind calls supplying us with the identity of the Peeper. One said it was Horace Appleby. Another that it was the Reverend Billy Holmes. Two said it was Freight Train Flowers. Another said it was me. Some people called and in the same conversation chewed me out and gave me an item for Social Notes. Free speech was in good shape in Martha, Texas, and all we had to do now was give it company in the form of a free press. I didn't exactly feel I was fighting on the ramparts, but I did feel I had staked out a position I would like to hold. Speaking of standing up and being counted. Of course, I had motives about as selfish as a man could have. Freedom of the press was getting pretty tangled up with holding on to my boat and my paper. I kept at it, and the rest of the paper went on as always, with Jamie and myself on the phone and at the counter and from beyond the swinging door the Mergenthaler singsonging away the hot day long as Beto put the activities of the town into type.

Just before lunch I put in a few phone calls about when ads were going to be delivered. The boss, like Mr. Carruthers of Carruthers Mercantile, was still out and would get back to me. Even though she was across the room working on Social Notes, classifieds, and other such matters, I had the feeling Jamie was monitoring these efforts of mine. Indeed, I had the feeling all during the week that she was monitoring me.

"Those pricks," she said after a no-show series of calls. "You're not going to back down, are you?"

"Listen, let's just get the paper out, okay?" I felt a little edge in my voice.

"Well, what are you going to do about it? You can't just sit here and let them *do* this."

"I'm thinking."

"It's terrible to have to depend on pricks like that to put out a newspaper."

"Yes. Well, that's the way the system is set up. The pricks have a built-in edge."

After lunch the Reverend Billy Holmes dropped by with his announcements. Sometimes he brings them by, sometimes we do it over the phone.

"Well," he said jocularly, "here I am once again with the makings for your famous column Church Notes, which the citizenry of Martha awaits so breathlessly each week. As they do my sermons. I'm preaching Sunday morning on the topic 'A Little More Love All Around.' "

"That sounds appropriate," I said.

"Appropriate?" He laughed. "You mean that's the message the Peeping Tom is spreading?"

"Well, that's not quite what I was thinking," I said. "It hadn't really occurred to me that was his message. Does he have one?"

"The Lord moves in mysterious ways," he said.

There was a glint in his eye. The Reverend Holmes's own

wife had been peeped. He was one of the few men in town this didn't seem to bother.

"Oh, by the way." He looked straight at me. "Don't let them get you down. There's only one way to deal with the Philistines."

"What way is that, Reverend?"

"Smite them hip and thigh."

And he was gone. I stood looking after him for a moment. The phone rang and Jamie picked it up, then put her hand over the speaker.

"One of the pricks," she said.

It was Bert Hooper. I took a deep breath and settled in.

"You shouldn't have done it, Baxter. People around town didn't like it." I could almost see his guardsman's mustache quivering.

"I've had a lot of calls. Some like it. Some don't."

"I think you should face some facts and make an important distinction. The people that *do* like it are not the people who buy ads."

"Yes, I've begun to have a few hints of that."

"They may be willing to give you a second chance."

"A second chance? What in the world is a second chance, Bert?"

"If you just stopped it right here, they might let bygones be bygones. After all, these aren't vindictive people."

"Stop it right here? You mean not report the peeping story anymore?"

"And stories like it."

I think that phrase did it. For the first time it brought something like a fury up in me. " 'Stories like it'?" I repeated. "What does that cover, Bert?"

"They don't like certain things in their newspaper. You know what I'm talking about."

"You bet your ass I do," I said. "Would you care to deliver my answer to whoever it is you're speaking for besides yourself? Tell them for me that the answer is no. Tell them I won't try to run their mercantile company, their produce company, their drugstore, or their bank, and I don't cxpect them to tell me how to run this newspaper. Got that?"

"Now look here—"

"And tell them one thing more. Tell them it is not their newspaper. It is *my* newspaper."

And I hung up.

"I got it too," Jamie said from across the room. "Hooray."

"Talk's cheap," I said.

All afternoon, while I was going through the motions of putting out the paper, motions that were as much a part of me as my skin and bones, I kept running through my options. I could sell my boat and put the money into the paper. With that I might be able to hold out long enough to hustle some other outside printing jobs. I might get them or I might not. There weren't many accounts around like Orville Jenkins's overprinting. There was always the deal Hooper had offered, which was to put out the kind of newspaper a lot of them seemed honestly to want. If you were in business you were supposed to give your customers what they wanted. I could just follow this normal sound business practice and everything would go on as usual: the paper, the boat, the good living.

Looking up, I was surprised to see night beginning to come to Cavalry Street. Jamie was standing at my desk. I had had a curious feeling about her during the week. She was both a help, a pillar of sorts, and an unwelcome conscience.

"You're not going to let those buggering bastards run you out of town, are you?" she said. "You can't just sit back and let them fold this paper."

I almost envied her, able as she was to put it all in black and white. It was simple. All you had to do was make the correct moral choice. At least the language in which she fashioned these choices helped clear the air.

"Well, I've never liked being buggered," I said. "I've always been a straight man."

"See that you keep it that way. Get a good night's sleep. 'Bye."

I watched her go through the swinging gate, her hair

bouncing, the tail of that man's white shirt hanging down over her jeans. Some conscience, I thought.

I needed a few Lone Stars. So just after dark I went over to the old Cavalry Post. Freight got a couple out of the Town Council refrigerator, and we sat on the piazza with our feet parked on the railing and looked out over the parade ground where once bugles had sounded and the old blue line of the Second Cavalry had stood in to ranks before riding out where peril lay. For a while we didn't talk much about the Peeper or the paper's issue on him but about the vegetable crops and about fishing. Mostly we just sat and looked at the stars decorating the huge sky above the quadrangle rim of the clean white buildings and listened to the cicadas making their song. He was comfortable just to sit and be with, and when he talked, those slow rhythms of his somehow soothed. So did the Lone Star, and we had one, then another. He shoved his big Resistol hat back.

"You liked the Navy, Ace?"

"As a matter of fact, I did."

"Me too. The Army, I mean. Things was simpler. What was you in?"

"PTs."

"PTs?"

"Patrol torpedo boats."

We sat for a while.

"Can I speak off the record, Ace?"

"Of course."

He swallowed some of his Lone Star. "Personally I approve of what you done. Going up against the motherfuckers."

"But I didn't do it for that."

"I know that. I know what you done it for."

"This stupid town," I said. The whole thing seemed of a sudden to well and surge up in me in a fountain of fury and frustration. "God, this town exasperates me. I just want to give them a good newspaper. This stupid motherfucking town."

"What all's happened, Ace?"

I told him about the phone calls and some people liking

the issue but most of them not. I quoted some of the more vehement calls.

"Yeah, every town has its crazies," he said. "Takes something like this to flush 'em out."

"It's not the crazies I'm worried about," I said. "It's the sane people: Jenkins, Hooper, people like that."

"The motherfuckers, you mean, as opposed to the crazies? Hail, they's more of them in this world than they is crazies. That's for sure and certain. And you right. It's always the motherfuckers that's the real problem. Fact, that's the one problem it seems a man keeps running into over and over again: How do you deal with the motherfuckers?"

"How do you?"

The chief recrossed his cowboy boots on the railing. "Well, in the case of the chief of police office, the way I do it is to let them *think* they's running things. They ain't, of course. Freight Train Flowers runs the chief of police office."

"I don't think that would work with a newspaper."

"I reckon not. Difference is, they can see what you do and they can't see what I do. Everything you do is out front, ain't it? What *are* you going to do?"

It seemed everybody was asking that question all week, including myself. I laughed, abruptly, mirthlessly.

"The first amendment says Congress shall make no law abridging the freedom of the press. It doesn't say anything about advertisers. I don't know what I'm going to do. I haven't decided."

I told him then how the ads weren't coming in and about the deal Hooper had offered: Let bygones be bygones. Just don't let it happen again. Shape up.

The chief gave a small belch. "I guess a man's got to run his own shop in this world or else let the motherfuckers run it for him. When you get down to it, maybe that's all the choice they is. They's always motherfuckers around wanting to run your shop if you let 'em."

He swallowed some Lone Star.

"Yeah, you can always just go along. Thing is, you don't seem like a man who's good at kissing ass. The trouble with that, you got to get down on your knees."

He went in and brought back another pair of Lone Stars, nestling them against that stomach which stuck out beyond him like fourteen-inch armorplate, his belt with its big silver Quetzalcoatl buckle cinched far below it. Cupped in his free hand, the size of a bear's paw, he brought some peanuts which he had scooped up out of his peanut drawer and offered me some. We sat and chewed them and drank the beer, nice and cold.

"How's the Shade Patrol going?" I asked. I was sick of thinking and talking about my problems.

"It's one big washout, that's how it's going. Hailfire, I can't get them to keep their shades down. Hard to get people to change the habits of a lifetime. Especially if the people happens to be women, who never like to change any habits, far as I been able to judge. Also, people here just naturally resent being told what to do. About *anything*." He belched a little. "Especially if them people's women."

He recrossed his Justins on the piazza railing.

"Every time I know for certain who it is, something happens to prove it can't be that one. Like him being out of town on a peeping night."

"I know what you mean," I said. "Other day Horace Appleby down at the drugstore and I caught ourselves looking straight at each other. I was wondering if he was doing it and he was wondering if I was doing it."

"Yeah. I been getting so many phone calls telling me who it is, it's getting hard to come up with anyone that ain't made the list. You be happy to know you about third on it and coming up fast."

I looked at him sideways. "I can't imagine why."

"I reckon everybody knows you crazy for it. And don't have none of it at home."

"Just like you." I waited a moment. "I've been getting quite a few calls myself," I said carefully. "As I recollect, about six picked you for the honor."

He waited too. "It's nice to know a chief of police has at least a half-dozen admirers."

He tipped his Lone Star, sipped, belched a little, and looked into the night.

"Well, unless it's you or me, he's out there somewhere. Strange the lengths a man will go to, even to just look at it. Putting life and limb, position and reputation, in peril. Just imagine. He's seen seventeen already. Ace, how many would you say the average man sees in his lifetime that way?"

"Not counting pros? Well, that's speculation, of course." We spoke in weighty tones, befitting such an important subject. "Men talk a lot. But discounting that, if I had to come up with a figure, I'd say your average man doesn't see more than six women that way in his entire lifetime. Tops."

"Gawd amighty," Freight Train said, "it's like he's lived three lifetimes already. And far as I know, he's only just begun."

We were silent a moment, reflecting on the mathematics of men's lifetimes.

"Yeah, they got us where it counts," the chief said. "When you shake out the trivial stuff and get down to what counts, that's where it's at. That's the double truth. Wouldn't you agree, Ace?"

"They've got a monopoly on their product all right."

We were on the far side of the third Lone Star and it was beginning to lighten me. He tipped his beer up, then down, and gave a medium belch.

"Being a bachelor. It's a lonely state, Ace."

"You think so? I like it."

"They say marriage is terrible. But I think bachelor is worse. I reckon marriage is the worst thing they is except that they's not anything as good."

The line inside clanged. The chief had it rigged for what must have been the loudest decibel available from the phone company. It sounded like general quarters. He swung his Justins off the railing and went inside to take it.

"Miss Kathryn?" I heard him say through the doorway. "Sit tight. Be there in two minutes."

I followed him down the corridor and the stairway, marveling at how fast he could move that huge body along when he had to. We cut down the parade ground walk and into his pickup. He spun it out of the Cavalry Post, kicking up caliche, and down Cavalry Street, the siren wailing its pulsating beat through the night. I could see the whir of red made on the sidewalk by the light revolving on the pickup's top.

"Kathryn Shields," he said in a flat tone. "She's caught the Peeper."

At Gardenia Street the pickup took the turn at an acute angle left, flying and screaming, and roared down it, the headlights splaying the green lawns on either side. We went six blocks before Freight braked the pickup to a screeching stop at the curb in front of 612, where Kathryn Shields lived alone in her little bungalow. The porch light was on. He jumped out and ran up the walkway and I ran after him. As we crossed the porch Kathryn was standing at the door in the boxer running shorts she often wore with the slits up the thighs. She had a pleased smile on her face.

"Gentlemen, come in," she said, holding the screen door open as sweetly as if she were welcoming us to a party. "I have the Peeper for you."

We stepped into the small living room. Sitting on the couch was Orville Jenkins, Jr. His head was down, almost to his knees. He looked forlorn and godforsaken.

"Gawd amighty," Freight Train said. "Not you, son."

He was a somewhat overweight boy with moon cheeks. He looked up at us with his scared eyes.

"This was the first time, Chief. I swear."

"Don't start swearing yet, boy," the chief said. "They be plenty of swearing to do later. Miss Kathryn?"

She looked cute as a peach standing there in those white shorts showing those sweet thighs and that blue bandanna blouse. It was one of those blouses that tie at the center and leave the navel showing. It was absolutely clear that if you put your hand on her solar plexus and moved it either way, you would encounter nothing but naked breast. I felt sympathy for Orville Junior.

"I'd been out jogging," she said. "I'd just started to undress when I heard this noise at the window. There wasn't any-thing to it. I popped through the door, and Orville Junior started to take off. Poor Orville Junior. I caught him before he reached the alley. I must say he stopped immediately when I grabbed him and said his name."

"Why, that was nice of him," the chief said. "Real nice. Now, boy, listen to me. How many others of them peepings have you committed? I want a straight answer and a quick one."

"I swear this was the first time, Chief. Miss Shields here, she was my very first one. And I didn't even see anything. That's the honest truth, Chief. I never did it before."

I don't think any of us believed for one instant that Orville Jenkins, Jr., was *the* Peeper. He wasn't that bright or imaginative. But it was by no means as clear that this was only his first one.

"Boy," the chief said, "you going to have to prove that like you was Jack the Ripper. I hope you got plenty iron-clad alibis."

The lad seemed to whine. "I was just researching one of them theme papers Miss Shields assigned us. . . ."

"One of *those* theme papers, Orville Junior," Kathryn Shields corrected him.

". . . I thought some first-hand experience would help. She assigned us to write a theme on the Peeper in English class."

"Don't be smart with me, boy," the chief said. "I got several methods for handling smart-ass kids. And don't insult my intelligence. I'll have your ass up to Huntsville before you can say Peeping Tom, and you can research some first-hand experience at your leisure. Excuse me, Miss Kathryn."

Orville Junior's eyes popped and bulged. Freight sighed. "All right, boy, come along. I hope for your sake it *is* the first time. That way you'll only get ten years. But you going to have to prove to me exactly where you was during all those other peepings. Otherwise I'll send you up ten years for each of them."

The lad looked up. "Chief," he said, "do you have to tell everybody?"

Freight looked slightly disgusted. "You got to take the consequences, boy. Peeping is peeping."

"I don't mean the peeping. I mean about Miss Shields catching me. The guys on the basketball team . . . I mean, a woman, and a woman *teacher* outrunning me."

There was more to Orville Junior than I had thought.

"I think we continue this at the Cavary," Freight said. "Let's make tracks, Junior."

The Orville Jenkins, Jr., peeping had taken my mind off my own problems for a bit. Wednesday morning they were all back again. Jamie stood at my desk.

"You aren't going to chicken out, are you?" she said. "You're not actually considering making that deal Hooper was talking about? That sellout."

That angered me. I sat back and looked at her.

"It's really easy for you, isn't it? First you tell me I can't let them fold this paper. Then you mount the stairs to the pedestal, hold up a skinny arm with that torch in your hand and that slogan doubtless coming out of your mouth, 'Not one cent for tribute.' Yeah, you've got it real easy. Especially with that fifty million bucks your old man's got. Or is it a hundred million? This paper is my rice bowl. Can you get that through all this flaming, fucking, moralizing idealism of yours?"

She just looked at me for a moment, and I could see the fury in her.

"I'm going to work on the Social Notes," she said and stomped away across the room.

I rang up Freight Train to see how he was proceeding with the latest Peeper case. "What are you going to do with Orville Junior? Try for two hundred years in Huntsville? Or settle for ten?"

"Naw, him and I just had a little talk. I doubt he'll be able to look at any of it for ten years. Anyhow, I reckon we can count on Orville Junior's father to provide the necessary discipline. Oh, Ace."

There was something in his voice.

"They's another little development that clears Orville Junior. The real Peeper hit us again last night."

"Who this time?"

"And you know what was peculiar about it? He peeped real late. Eleanor Lou Mackenzie. *Two hours* later than he's ever peeped."

"How do you know that?"

"Well, Eleanor Lou had been setting up with her sick ma and didn't get home till midnight. Later on she checked the windowsill like I instructed them women to do. Another of them silver butterflies."

"I see you've whipped them into line."

"I don't know about that. Don't you find it interesting him peeping that late?"

"He must have his reasons."

"I'm sure he does." He waited a moment. "How's it going with the paper, Ace?"

"We're still here."

"Hey, I got a new Aggie joke. This Aggie factory owner was looking over a government questionnaire. It asked, 'How many employees do you have, broken down by sex?' He answered, 'None that I know of. Our main problem is alcohol.'"

I laughed with him. I knew he was trying to cheer me up.

"Keep checked in, you hear?"

Just before lunch, a three-member delegation from the Daughters of the Republic of Texas entered, led by Mrs. August Tefenteller. She was an imperious woman, as broad almost as she was tall, solid as the U.S.S. *Missouri*. The two women flanking her looked like PT boats alongside. All three wore broad-brimmed hats and carried parasols, like a man wearing both belt and braces. It was a hot day. I got up and greeted them across the counter.

"We felt it our duty," Mrs. Tefenteller said, "to express in person our dismay and disapproval. It's bad enough having him without having to read about him."

"I understand, ladies," I said. "I appreciate your coming all the way down here to tell me that on a day like this. They say the thermometer will break through the ninety mark today."

"We just finished our weekly meeting of the Daughters," Mrs. Tefenteller said in stern tones, "and we were discussing what would Davy Crockett do? Or Sam Houston or Colonel Travis. So we decided to come straight here."

"Well, I don't know about Travis," I said, "but if I know

Crockett or Houston, they would have asked, 'Where's the nearest whorehouse?'"

The three gasped like a chorus. "Ladies," Mrs. Tefenteller said, "it's time to leave."

And she marched out, the other two in lockstep with her. I was operating close to the edge. Maybe I needed nourishment.

"Let's go eat," I said to Jamie.

"Okay," she said pleasantly. "I think I'll have something else besides peanut butter and jelly today." She never kept her irritation long. She said just one thing now. "I don't have *skinny* arms."

We went across to the Bon Ton and both ordered the Wednesday special of pan-fried chicken, black-eyed peas, and homemade cornbread.

Not long after lunch I got a phone call from Orville Jenkins, Sr. One thing at least about Saint Orville, he didn't beat around the bush. He said it in plain English, which I always appreciate a person speaking in, especially if he's trying to buy me. If I would keep any mention of Orville Junior out of the paper, he would restore his contract on overprinting his canning labels and otherwise do nothing to try to affect the paper's advertising revenues. Having eaten, I felt considerably better and reinforced.

"I can't make a deal like that," I said.

"You put the idea in that poor boy's head with that issue of yours."

"Horseshit, Orville."

I hung up.

It seemed such a nice place to be as I walked down the dark and empty streets that Thursday morning, getting to work early as I always do on press day. Even in hot weather the irrigation from the Rio Grande kept the town green and preserved its sweet and lovely scents, and I felt about me a susurrus of comfort, as from the town itself.

Down Cavalry Street I could hear the train which ran twice a week from the valley leave the station. Soon the line of freight cars began to clatter across the street between me and the business section, starting its journey over the long lands of the republic with the vegetables that fed all those city people and sustained the town. As I came near I could make out in the first light just beginning to appear from beyond the horizon the haunting names on the sides of the cars. Louisville and Nashville, Baltimore and Ohio, Chesapeake and Ohio, Missouri Pacific. Suddenly there struck the air that long, moaning whistle which has always been to me the most poignant sound in all America. Then the caboose came by, and I waved to the brakeman, just as I had as a boy. I walked across the tracks and entered the business part of town.

I opened up and went straight to work on that long roll call of things to be done on press day. One thing I didn't have to work on was my main-line ads, none of which came in. As the morning marched on, I seemed to be functioning as if I were two persons, both operating full out: one person putting out the paper, the other thinking through the whole thing once more. The different options kept parading through my head. A very short parade, but over and over again.

Then the phone rang and it was Mrs. Lawrence Wharton wanting to announce the engagement of her daughter Francine. A little later it rang again. Mrs. Robert Cantu had given birth to a baby boy weighing seven pounds seven ounces, to be christened Robert Junior. Someone came to the counter with a classified ad about six beagle puppies for sale. The weather report came in, and I sat down and wrote the forecast. A family friend called to say that Will Ford had died after his long illness. There were calls about the new post office regulations and the calendar of events for the summer youth program and the library's new acquisitions. The county farm agent called with the weekly report of production of various crops. Mrs. Edward Miller phoned to announce a bridal shower for her daughter Linda Mae. Legal notices and court records came in. The phone rang. It was Mrs. Gilbert Mosley with an item for Social Notes. Her daughter Clara Beth had been admitted to North Texas State University at Denton.

"It's the only school ever to have two Miss Americas," she said proudly. "Could you say that?"

"I'd be happy to say that, Mrs. Mosley," I said.

The town was still revolving around the paper. It did so far more than any of them realized.

And then I had the idea.

It sounded wild and outlandish, but I knew the moment I thought of it that it was the right answer. And besides, I was tired of being pushed around.

I began to dig out the filler copy I use to plug holes in the paper when they occur and took the stories out to Beto to set and put in where the ads would normally have gone. One was a feature story Jamie had written a while back about the lady who gave Martha, Texas, her name. I gave her a byline. Finally, late afternoon, I got a call from Esau.

"I'm sorry," he said. "I don't relish doing this. But you were warned."

"That's true, Mayor. I've been told that before."

"You understand, this is a temporary action I'm taking. Or such is my devout desire. While I wait and see."

The meaning of that was not lost on me. "Esau, why don't I save you some trouble? The policy of the *Clarion* about covering the news is not going to change. So why don't we knock off this 'temporary' nonsense. Why don't you just make it permanent?"

"Now don't be hasty. People change. Reasonable men can always reach a compromise."

"Not this time, Esau. There'll be no compromise. Not on this."

I heard him sigh. "You're a stubborn man, Baxter. I'll miss writing my column."

"Yes. Well, I'm sorry you won't have a forum anymore for those thoughts of yours, Mayor. I'm sure the town will miss them. I know you don't relish that part of it."

There was a silence on the line. "That's a bit odd, putting it just that way," he said. His voice suddenly had a touch of true worry. "How do you mean, I won't have a forum?"

"Why, just that, Mayor. No audience. No readers. No following."

He seemed genuinely concerned. "There's something here that disturbs me. I wouldn't want you to do anything foolish."

"But I've already done that, Mayor. Now if you'll excuse me, I've got a paper to put out."

I hung up. From across the room Jamie turned and looked at me. I could see the first wrinkles I had ever seen in her forehead. One end of the conversation was enough to let her know.

"That bald-headed, blue-balled *embalmer*," she said. "The pompous old fart."

"Enough," I said. "Go get Beto."

He came in in his inky striped apron. They sat at my desk and I told them what I was going to do and explained why. I told them that we would talk more about it later.

"Right now," I said, "let's get the paper to bed."

They looked stunned.

"You're sure you want to do this, boss?" Beto said.

"I'm sure. It'll happen sooner or later anyhow. It's better to do something before we're down and out. This isn't some harebrained scheme. It's the most practical thing we could do. We've got a fighting chance this way."

I made up page one, leaving a prominent hole for the announcement. I took it out to Beto, and he began making up the page. Jamie and I stood on the upside-down side of the makeup stone. The light glared down on the page form and cast in looming shadows the stalagmite shapes of the composing room: the Mergenthaler and the Miehle press and the cabinet containing the fonts of headline type, the lovely weaponry for putting out a newspaper. Both of them seemed numb. I didn't blame them. But I thought I knew what I was doing. I sure as hell hoped so. Jamie was leaning down and looking over the page-one form.

"Where's the story on Orville Junior?" she asked.

"There'll be no story on Orville Junior."

She looked at me. "Oh. You mean freedom of the press doesn't include fucking up a kid's life? Well, now, that's very admirable. Never mind that the bloody son of a bitch his father doesn't deserve it. But why didn't you tell him? Oh. Okay. I know why."

I went to my typewriter and wrote the item. You only needed one paragraph to say it. There was no point in giving reasons. I wrote an 18-point Cheltenham head and took it and the copy back to the composing room. I gave the copy to Beto and set the head myself. I took it over and plugged it in the space. Beto brought over the type. He began tightening the quoins on the page form. I went back to the front.

Night was coming on down Cavalry Street. I switched on the light and looked through the window. A pickup with a bunch of kids in the back went by. In a while Jamie came in.

"You have ink on your face," I said. "Left cheek."

"What are you going to do?" she said.

It seemed that I had been asked that question all week. Well, this time I had an answer.

"I'm going down to my boat."

"For how long?"

"I don't know."

She waited a moment. "Can I go with you?"

"I don't think so. No."

"What am I supposed to do?"

"Take a vacation. It's almost summertime."

"Are you sure you want to do it this way? There isn't anything else we could do?"

"Yes to the first. No to the second."

Suddenly she grinned at me.

"Who's holding up that torch now?"

Beto brought in the page-one proof and we all looked at it. It wasn't very large, only 18 point, but it leaped from the page:

THE MARTHA CLARION
SUSPENDS PUBLICATION

"Let them see what this town is like without a newspaper," I said.

11.

The Lower Latitudes

It's a 36-foot Grand Banks that I got a couple of years ago, putting down the eight thousand dollars I had left from my life savings after buying the paper and getting a boat mortgage for the remainder of the thirty-two-thousand price tag. A bargain. I got her in a Coast Guard auction after the owner was intercepted one night off Port Aransas running cocaine and Mexican brown up from the Bay of Campeche. So they do catch some of them. I don't know what federal institution the former captain is now residing in or how long a lease he has. I have sometimes wondered about a man who would name a boat *My Last Duchess*. She was built in Hong Kong, where all the Grand Banks used to be built. Now they're built in Singapore.

There's no better trawler than a Grand Banks. It's not one of those fancy fiberglass yacht-looking things that men from Indiana who want to play captain put down two hundred thousand dollars for, but I wouldn't trade. I like the full-displacement hull, the mahogany planking over the yacal frame, and the teak decks. The ten-knot speed is good enough for me. I'm not in a hurry, and I'm not out here to race or have my picture taken with a fish twice as high as I am. How I would hate to lose *Duchess*.

Actually it didn't cost all that much. A Grand Banks is a good ticket for a man who has to count his money. Ninety-five dollars a month berth rental at the Harbor Inn marina and another $24 for electricity. Every two hundred hours I have to change oil, twelve quarts, $30 for the case. Once a year I put her on the ways at the Port Isabel boatyard and have them scrape the barnacles and oysters from the hull and propellers and paint everything below the waterline —$250 for the whole job. Above the waterline I do the painting myself and otherwise take care of her. Oh, yes, $700 a year for insurance. And there's the mortgage payment. Still, it wasn't all that much.

Who was I kidding? For a man who suddenly didn't have any money at all coming in, it was God's own fortune.

Sheets of white came off the water where the sun hit it. I took off my shirt. Whenever I get out here I wish I could stay forever. I wish I had some sort of permanent nuclear fuel and some sort of permanent nuclear food so that I never had to set foot on shore again. Especially now. All my problems were on land. I listened to the sound of the sea and the sound of the boat. They are the two nicest sounds I know. Though I like also the other sounds I have on land, the bird singsong of the Mergenthaler Linotype and the *clank-clank* of the Miehle flatbed. Between the one set of sounds at sea and the other set on land, at the newspaper, there's nothing else I want. How I would hate to lose *both* of them.

Sometimes I think I'd like to have some sort of permanent nuclear woman too, but I think I could do without that as a price for the other. The hell I could. The boat slid down into a trough and rode through it. When I get to thinking like this, I know it is time to turn *Duchess* around. I headed back in to Port Isabel, planning to pick one of them up and head out again with her.

Nowadays I get it mainly from the boat hitchhikers. There are always girls and women around the marina. They have great tans and they always wear shorts, usually white, and above them blouses or shirts and, lots of times, halters that show off their belly buttons. Some of them work as waitresses or cocktail waitresses on the island, and some don't appear to work at all. Some have large ideas about making it big in real estate or some get-rich-quick tourist-attraction scheme, and some of them are quite bright. A lot of them have that lean, tippy-toe look and lithe bodies. They come from everywhere: Kansas, Minnesota, now and then all the way from Canada.

On the inner side of the back cover of a random journal I keep that passes for a log, though it's quite unnautical in some ways, there is a list of states. I don't believe I'm trying to prove anything. It's not a gun-notch sort of thing. It just amuses me to keep the list. So far there are six states on it.

But then, suddenly, as I came near the inlet I decided I didn't want it. One-night stands. They had never been all that good, and lately they were just nothing at all. I don't know why. Not their fault. They were really nice girls. I looked off to starboard where sat Texas and then dead ahead to the south where lay Mexico. I have a latitudinal theory of history. My notion is that the upper latitudes work harder and invent more gadgets. The automobile, the airplane, air conditioning, and the atomic bomb were all thought up on the higher parallels. But the lower latitudes have more fun, enjoy life more.

If this was to be my last trip I wanted to make it a good one. But most of all I suddenly realized that I had to get away. I mean *away*. There's no better place for that than Mexico. Instead of turning in, I headed into the lower latitudes.

I felt like eating fish, I speak fluent Spanish, and the diesel is a lot cheaper down there, only 19 cents versus $1.25. In addition to getting away, these were three good reasons for aiming my boat south. From Matamoros to the Yucatán, that scimitar of shore that is the Mexican Gulf, if you follow the coast you will dine every night on the best seafood you have ever had. Every night I put into a different Mexican town and in every one I did at least three things: I strolled around the plaza, found a *restaurante* and ate the fish the fishermen of the town had caught that day, and visited the *iglesia*. Every town has one, and it is always bigger than anything else. Even in a small town, coming in from the sea, before you can see any of the town itself you can see the bell tower rising out of the fields. I like to go into those buildings of pockmarked stone and stand there and look at the paintings high up on the ceiling telling of annunciations, resurrections, and trans-figurations and at the statues of assorted saints arranged around the walls, each saint with its own niche. I like to look down the long damp aisle and see far away the candles burning in the darkness and around me women kneeling on the cold stone, old brown faces, black shawls over their heads, clutching rosaries and imploring the Virgin of Guada-lupe or one of the saints for some favor. Sometimes I feel I might find the answer there, in religion, if I worked at it. Sometimes I feel I go into those places thinking I might see God. Now and then I go down the aisle and light a candle myself.

At Tampico I threaded through the tankers standing high above me and went ashore and ate crab claws. At Tuxpan I ate sea bass and took a walk along the pretty river they have there. At Vera Cruz I ate marvelous clams and visited the old fort on Gallega reef where the prison cells flooded at high tide. At San Andrés Tuxtla I ate black bass from Lake Catemaco. All the towns have plazas, and all the plazas have sidewalk cafés. At night I'd sat at one of them drinking Negra Modelo, watching life go by. But what a hoax all this amigo stuff is—what a dangerous country it is for Ameri-cans. And yet I like going there. Because, I think, no country is so different from ours. A country looking backward into history while we look forward. That's the big difference. I started counting the number of barefoot people who came by. I watched the Indian faces, which were here so long before any of us were, and entertained myself by trying to figure out which were Olmec, which Toltec or Mixtec. Sometimes one would turn as he walked by and look at me suddenly out of those ancient, distant eyes.

It was a relaxing time. I found myself revving down and down. Out at sea I'd take off my clothes down to my skivvies and watch the boat move over the sun-blanched water at my sensational cruising speed of eight knots. My PT could do forty-five. But I was in absolutely no hurry. Things were easy. I did about a hundred miles a day and got brown as a

Zapotec. I worked down the coast and looked across the mirror sea at the blue mountains strung out against the sky of Mexico. The mountains were never very far away, and you could understand how when Cortés was asked by Charles V to describe the topography of Mexico he crumpled up a piece of paper. Now and then there would be a few thatched huts set back from the sand, and I'd move inshore. There'd be some Indians sitting on a porch and naked Indian children swimming in the clear green water, and I'd stop the boat and talk with them. The Spaniards gave them their language and their Catholic religion, but the country is still Indian a lot more than it is Spanish. Approaching Papantla, I'd smelled across the water the vanilla from the orchid forest that has given the Totonac Indians such a profitable life. Then, in the pineapple country around Nautla, I brought the boat in close and traded a tin of cheese for some fresh pineapples which the children swam out with. Farther down I got some wonderful mangoes the same way. Sometimes in a town after my walk around the plaza and my visit to the church, I'd drop by the open market all the towns have and pick up some fresh vegetables. At sea I would set drags on the rod holders at *My Last Duchess*'s stern, bait up with the mullet, and run the lines out at a hundred and fifty feet and cruise along. When I heard a *ping* I'd set the boat on automatic pilot and go back to play the fish. Sometimes I'd get one. Then I'd stop the boat, just parking it out in the middle of the sea, and broil the fish in the oven in the wheelhouse. Once I had red snapper, and another time I caught a fine pompano and had it with slices of mangoes and fresh tomatoes. In Vera Cruz I'd picked up a box of H. Upmanns, the big seven-inch Corona Imperiales that Winston Churchill used to smoke, straight from Castro's Cuba and not admissible to the U.S.A. The real article. I'd light one up and taste it, the next best thing in life to having a woman, and get *Duchess* underway over the shimmering sea, whitened by the sun, peaceful, everlasting. St. John Perse was right: the plebeian land, the patrician sea. Why go ashore where dwelt all the hassles? By the time I'd smoked through the seven inches, I'd see in the distance across the water the bell tower of another *iglesia* rising out of the fields and I'd head in.

This fine life cleared the mind and set it to thinking what was the best way to spend your time. I had one of my Larger Thoughts. The best way of all to spend it, I finally decided, was to fuck off. Fucking off. That's what it's really all about.

I was heading down toward the Yucatán, which is the best part of Mexico. There live the Maya, who are by far the nicest of the Mexicans, as contrasted, let us say, with the Aztecs, whose unceasing machismo can get pretty wearying. From San Andrés Tuxtla I worked across to Ciudad del Carmen, then up to Campeche, where, near shore, I saw fishermen in dories throwing nets to catch their fish, just as in the days of Galilee. I took a bus over to the ruins at Uxmal, climbed a pyramid, and had a look at the glorious temples the Maya built a thousand years ago before that civilization just dropped from sight, with no one having the remotest idea of what happened to them. I filled myself with profound notions about the mortality of men, and about how most people just threw away their one shot at it. It occurred to me that I wanted to take her back something, so I bought a nice little Chac. Chac is the rain god.

Suddenly I began to get rather lonely. I didn't know why or for what, but I revised my previous opinion and decided that even fucking off has its limits. For the first time since I could remember, it seemed that something was missing. Things were too peaceful. I couldn't imagine what it was. Then I knew. It was beginning to seem dull without her. Dull and lonely. I missed the hair-bouncing. Then I thought, My God. Then I laughed.

And now I had about run out of Mexico. There was nowhere to go but back. The whole trip I had managed fairly well not to think about it. Now, suddenly, it was all over me. What a stupid thing it had been to put it all on the line for something as insignificant as that, for a Peeping Tom, for God's sake. And for what? For people who didn't want it anyhow. Maybe in a big city it meant something. But in

Martha, Texas? What difference did it make? Life was damn good in Martha just as it was. Why mess around with it? It did have one result. It threw everything that constituted my life out the window. The paper and the boat. What a stupid goddamn fool I had been.

I headed back, moving a little more quickly this time. When I crossed the invisible line to American waters, I really didn't know how long I had been gone, but I checked the calendar and it was seventeen days. I didn't turn in immediately to Port Isabel but for some reason, possibly just a reluctance to go ashore and face it, kept moving up the coast, looking now at Texas across the blue water. Then the sea began to chop up. I listened to the marine radio, which said an early tropical storm named Alma was about three hundred miles to the southeast. The wind was freshening, the seas were starting to come at me, and *Duchess* was bucking, busting into them. As I worked north, whitecaps frothed up everywhere, and serious waves began to break over the bow, sending water slashing across the windshield of the wheelhouse. I could hear the hull slapping hard into the sea. The wind had come up to around a Force 6, and the sky was all heavy dark moving clouds. We were running five-foot seas and then seven before I knew it. I decided, Grand Banks or no, to take her into Port Mansfield for the night.

It was there, lying awake in a seedy little motel called Shore Leave and hearing the skirts of Alma flapping overhead, that I had my final Larger Thought of the trip. Age forty-one and age twenty-one. They were different worlds. No one age forty-one looked at things the same way anyone age twenty-one did. People should stick to their own ages. There would be enough problems without adding that one. I was thinking about any lasting arrangement. Passing ones might be different. But that assumed not being around the other person afterwards. It certainly assumed not working in the same room with her, day after day. I had tried that once and had sworn never again. Certainly not in the newspaper business. It was the Second Commandment of Journalism: Thou shalt not screw thy fellow reporter. At least not on the same paper. The opposition, that's okay.

Besides, sleeping with a woman changed everything. It gave her a claim on you. If you don't think she thinks that, you're out of your mind.

Perhaps it was to Alma, howling over me, that I owed this last Larger Thought. If so, I figured it was another lady I could be grateful to. For I hadn't realized how close I was to it.

Sometime during the night, Alma changed course and headed northeast for Louisiana. Still, even in her wake she left a white-capped sea, though nothing the Grand Banks couldn't handle. I had decided I couldn't put off facing it any longer and had set a course for Port Isabel when I got a message over the ship-to-shore. I took it down. YOU ARE URGENTLY NEEDED CONCERNS PAPER PLEASE COME ASHORE REPEAT URGENT JAMIE.

I came through the Laguna Madre and between the posts that mark the dredged channel and slowly into the marina. Then I saw her. She was standing by the Texaco pump. She was wearing her jeans and the oversized man's shirt hanging down over them. She raised her hand and waved.

"The town just about came to a standstill," Jamie said eagerly. "You should hear the fuss."

We were headed back up the valley. She was revved up, exuberant, and so was the red MG. The top was down and she was passing everything on the highway.

"You better slow this rocket down," I said. "This is TDS country."

"Everybody has been complaining and whining," she said, not just disobeying my driving advice but ignoring it. "They're very cross about it. They are *surly*."

She was on a high excitement.

"They've been *lost* without their paper. The mothers think it's awful that there's no place to announce their daughters' engagements and run their pictures. The women feel it's terrible that there can't be notices on when the Ladies' Aid Society and the Garden Club are meeting. Attendance at everything has been off. The church people are furious. The

Woman's Missionary Union, the Youth Fellowship, and the Daily Vacation Bible School can't print their schedules. . . . It's been wonderful."

She was in high gear in more ways than one. She zipped around a long open-bin truck carrying green cabbages.

"Three people died. Esau Ireland complained it wasn't proper, it wasn't *fitting*, not to have their write-ups and pictures in the paper. He said a person *always* gets a write-up and picture when they cross over Jordan."

"Two more people are going to cross over Jordan if you don't slow this thing down."

"Don't be so bossy." We shot past a Winnebago. "That's just the beginning. The Town Council was considering some rezoning, but Sherm Embers gave them a legal opinion that they couldn't do it without a public hearing notice in the *Clarion*. Also they want to paint the school building and they can't proceed on that without a notice in the paper putting the job up for bids. Orville Jenkins said that it looked like they couldn't do *anything* without the *Clarion* there. Isn't it lovely?"

She flashed around two pickups, one semi, and a white Mark V. The fields hurtled by. Workers were hacking off cabbages and crating them.

"Even the advertisers are sore. Carruthers didn't have any place to run his ad for his semi-annual white sale, so he's stuck with a lot of towels, sheets, and pillowcases. Isn't that sad?"

She gunned around a long carryall of new cars.

"And Social Notes! They miss that most of all. Somebody said it wasn't Martha unless you knew what everybody was doing. Even the Daughters of the Republic of Texas missed you. Mrs. Tefenteller bitched to me that she didn't know who was being married, who was being divorced, and who was suing who—whom—without the court records being printed. It's been a trying time for everybody. Isn't it heavenly?"

She told me that Mayor Ireland had demanded that she do everything she could to find me and haul me before a meeting of the Town Council. She had found me through the Coast Guard and had phoned him from Port Isabel of her success. The meeting would be tonight.

"So it worked," she said. She was bouncing with exhilaration. "Your idea of letting them see what it was like without a newspaper *worked.*" She slowed the car and looked across at me. "Isn't that gorgeous?"

"I don't know whether it worked or not," I said. "Let's wait for the meeting before we start canonizing me. It's not over yet. I know those men. They don't give in just like that. Give this thing a little gas, will you? I've got things to do. What have you been up to?"

"I've been *working.* Keeping piles of Social Notes and other things that happened while you were gone. We can't all flake off. In the newspaper business somebody has to stay around and keep a record of what goes on."

"Let's hope there's some place to print it," I said.

She pushed the accelerator down. We roared around a Mercedes.

"While you were gone, all the councilmen dropped by the paper. Freight Train too. It seemed one or more of them came in every day, to see if there was any news of you. And to see that I was doing all right. I must say, they were all very solicitous of me. Wanting to know if I needed anything."

"I imagine you enjoyed playing queen of the newspaper office."

"Hooper kept eyeing the place like he was ready to foreclose the widow's house any moment. He even went out to the composing room and took a look at the Mergenthaler and the presses."

"I'd like to stuff him into the Mergenthaler. Preferably when the hot lead was being poured."

"All of them kept asking me questions about you. Not in the sense of a cross-examination but just casually. Like what kind of person you were."

"With what you must have told them, it's a wonder I'm being allowed back in town."

"As a matter of fact, I told them you were very thoughtful and considerate. I'm a good liar when I want to be."

"I believe that."

"And I told them one or two truthful things. I told them you were a very good newspaperman and they were lucky to have you and they ought to appreciate you and get off your back."

I was rather touched.

"The mayor especially kept coming by. Wanting to know if I'd heard anything from you. I think he missed writing his column."

"You mean that paid ad."

"He's quite vain about it. I found that rather dear. He asked me for my suggestions," she said primly. "He told me advice from a professional writer like me would be very helpful. I've changed my mind about him. I think I really like him."

"I wonder why," I said. "God, he really knows how to give the song and dance with women. If you're going to be a reporter you've got to stop being so gullible. As if Esau Ireland would ever ask anybody's advice about anything."

"Yes, if I do say it, he took quite a shine to me."

"They all do," I said. "You're the honey bear. Pretty soon that old geezer will be bouncing you on his knee. One thing, you're about the only woman in town he's taller than."

"Also Esau and I had some interesting discussions—"

"You call him Esau?"

"He asked me to. We had some interesting discussions as to the Peeper's identity. He was very anxious to get my views on that subject too."

"Well, have you decided who it is?"

From behind the wheel she turned and looked at me.

"I didn't tell him anything."

"God, you sound as if you knew."

She turned back to her driving. "I did mention that I had thought at one time it was the chief of police."

"What did he say to that?"

"He just laughed."

"Speaking of the Peeper, how many women has he conferred honors on during my absence?"

"None," she said.

"You mean *nobody* has been peeped?"

"Nobody."

"He must be taking a rest. Or maybe he's quit."

She looked across at me again, a rather probing look, I felt. This time I felt uneasy.

"Maybe," she said. "We'll see."

"Keep your eyes on the road," I said.

I reached into the duffel bag at my feet, pulled it out, and placed it on the dash between us.

"I brought you something."

She looked down and her face, so set and concerned, turned all bright and pleased.

"Why, you *can* be nice if you just try. What is it?"

"Chac. He's the rain god."

"I like him. Where have *you* been?" she said. "What have you been doing?"

"Fucking off."

"Why, Baxter. Watch your language. You're in the presence of a young lady."

"Yes. Well, how has the young lady been?"

"I really missed the paper too." I looked across and saw her hair bounce. "Of course, it was nice to get away from you."

"What do you mean, going off and leaving this town without a newspaper?" Mayor Esau Ireland said. "You should be ashamed of yourself."

"You left us high and dry," Henry Milam said.

"You really put it to us," Sherm Embers said.

"Unworthy," Orville Jenkins said. "Not at all civic-minded."

"Just taking off like that without a word," Bert Hooper said, "and leaving the town stuck."

I saw what the approach was to be. It was all my fault. They all spoke approximately at once, and they sounded as though they hadn't had anything to do with it. I felt the old exasperation return but tried to hold my peace until I found out what they had to offer.

We were gathered in the Town Council room. The Longhorn was there on the wall. Colonel Robert E. Lee's horse's neck collar was there on the wall. Black Jack Pershing's spurs were there. The noisy old Town Council refrigerator full of Henry Milam's Lone Star beer was in the corner. The big round oak table, dented, scratched, and burned, and the overhead poker shade light and the tiny flags of the United States and Texas in the center all were there. The five councilmen and Freight Train Flowers were there. And I was there. I decided they might as well have it straight.

"Well, I may have done it a little abruptly. But I didn't have any choice. I know of only one way a good newspaper works in this country. That is for the advertisers to pay the bills and not have a thing in the world to say about what goes in the newspaper."

That immediately heated up Bert Hooper. "Brother," he said, "that sure goes up against the way it's done in any other business in this country. Any other business, the man who pays the bills has one hell of a lot to say about what goes into the product."

"That's where newspapers are different," I said.

"It's a very peculiar idea," Orville Jenkins said. "I run a big operation, and when I put up my money I expect to be heard. Anyhow, I'm not sure you're right. From what I hear, the advertisers have a good deal to say about what the newspapers print, all over the country."

"They do on some," I said. "But you won't ever get a good newspaper that way. Anyhow, I've decided I don't want to run that kind of newspaper."

It was big talk. I wondered if I was bluffing. More important, I wondered if they thought I was.

"So what you're saying," Bert Hooper said, "is that you want us to keep giving you the ads that make it possible for you to publish your newspaper and keep our mouths shut about what you print."

"You can have your say," I said. "And I'll listen. But the ads don't give you any special rights. Not to tell me what to print."

"Jesus," Bert said. "You don't ask for much, do you?"

We were at an impasse, all that quickly. They weren't about to give in. They never would. I should have known.

Esau Ireland had been listening carefully, saying not a word. That was his way: to let all have their say and then move in.

"I see your point, Baxter," he said. "You want us to let you run your business."

I took a breath. "I don't tell Bert how to run his bank, Orville how to run his produce company, Sherm how to practice law, Henry how to run Lone Star beer, or you, Mayor, how to embalm us all one day. Yes, I have to have that right. To run my newspaper."

"There's one little difference," Esau said. "Whatever we do in our various businesses, it's not there for everybody in town to see. It seems to me *that's* the difference. That's the reason a town has to have something to say about what kind of paper it gets."

It was a good point, and Bert Hooper jumped on it. "Well said, Mayor. Let's take a hypothetical case. Let's say somehow Baxter got a picture of my wife nude and decided to print it. What's to protect us? I'm not saying he would print it. But I am saying all the principles aren't on one side here, by God. We have a right to be protected too. And one way we have of protecting ourselves and keeping the paper in line is holding back our ads."

"Of course he'd have to get the picture first," Henry Milam said.

"And he'd better have Carolyn's signed permission in triplicate to run it," Sherm Embers said.

"Bert's talking about a principle," Orville Jenkins said. "What's to stop him from running a picture of Carolyn Hooper that way?"

"Gentlemen, we're never going to get anywhere if we get hung up on whether the *Clarion* has a right to carry a picture of Mrs. Bert Hooper with her clothes off," Esau said in that reedy, brisk voice of his. "What we're dealing with here is that the people of Martha are without a newspaper and they don't like it. Now, what are we going to do about it? We can worry about Carolyn Hooper being shown in the raw in the paper when that happens."

"I'll tell you another place that's going bonkers," Freight Train said. "The chief of police's office. My phone, it's ringing off the wall, people asking me what the news is, what's happening. People is downright edgy when they don't get their news."

Everyone waited. We appeared to be at the stone wall. Esau moved in. He was not a theorist. His object always was to get something done.

"How about this, gentlemen. Baxter will start up his newspaper. We will return our advertising. We won't tell him how to run his newspaper. He will exercise good taste. Well?"

"Good taste?" I said. "Who's going to rule on that?"

"Why, we are," the mayor said with a friendly smile. "You are. Everybody is. Just like always."

"Just like always?" I said. "You mean like with the Peeper issue?"

"Now, now. As Bert says, bygones are bygones. Don't you, Bert?"

"That's what I kept telling him," Bert said. "Before he up and flew the coop."

"Well, Councilmen?" Esau said. "Well, Baxter?"

A moment of glowering held the table. In the silence, only the whir of the ceiling fan was heard and the fluttering of the tiny flags under it. They all looked at me. I wasn't kidding myself. This wasn't a meeting in support of freedom of the press or the first amendment. It was a meeting in support of having their Social Notes, their crop news, their club meetings, their church news, and their classified ads. No matter. It all came to the same thing. Or was damn well going to come to the same thing. I didn't know what was next or what was expected of me. However, I knew what I expected of them.

"But it's to be a *news*paper," I said. "All the news. Or all the news that's fit to print."

Esau Ireland brightened as if he'd just seen a clear path through a minefield. He leaped on it.

"Why, what a beautiful way to put it," he said. "'All the news that's fit to print.' That protects us all the way. It solves everything. How did you ever think up a phrase like that, Baxter?"

"It just came to me," I said modestly.

"Don't you see, gentlemen?" Esau said. "Baxter will print the news that's fit to print. Surely that's what we want. We couldn't ask for any better protection than that."

"Yes, that's all we want," Henry Milam said. "That's what a newspaper is supposed to do. Let people know what's happening."

"It sounds all right in principle to me," Orville Jenkins said.

Esau turned to Bert Hooper and spoke in conciliatory tones.

"Doesn't that cover it, Bert? What's fit to print?"

"I guess so," Bert said. "I guess it'll have to cover it."

"Well, everybody!" Esau said brightly. "We seem to be in accord. Baxter, let's get this paper started up. Follow?"

I waited a moment. I knew they would be keeping an eye on me, would continue to monitor me. But I knew also that this was as far as they could go, and for them it was pretty far. It would always be their newspaper, but it was my newspaper. My problem would be somehow to make those opposing ideas both work.

"Yes, Mayor," I said. "I follow."

I started to go. "Oh, by the way, Baxter," Esau Ireland said. "You'll be interested in this."

His face had taken on a glow. Even his bald head seemed to shine more brightly.

"A number of people told me they missed my column," he said. "I'm speaking of 'The Quick and the Dead.' Seems it has quite a following."

"You might try running the back columns, Mayor," I said, thinking of all that ad space.

"Back columns?" the mayor said. "There *aren't* any back columns. My God, man, you can't expect a writer to write if there's no place to print what he's written. You don't know anything about writers."

"Yes, I understand, Mayor," I said with a sigh. Writers were always so difficult.

"But I'll have my new column over the first thing tomorrow," he said.

I stood up. "I'll be on my way, gentlemen," I said. "I've got a lot to do. I'm going to bring everything up to date. Everything that happened while I was away."

Bert Hooper gave that smile that showed only his lower teeth. "Speaking of while you were away," he said. "One thing you won't have to catch up on is what started all this. There weren't any peepings while you were away."

He was looking straight at me, a hard, sly look. And then so were the other councilmen—and Freight Train. Six pairs of eyes. Suddenly I remembered the odd look on Jamie's face. My God, I thought, *she* suspects me.

"I'm glad to hear it, Bert," I said. I decided I could play this game too. "Oh, by the way. Speaking of that hypothetical picture of your wife you mentioned. The nude one, I mean. Carolyn still hasn't been peeped, has she?"

There was a deadly silence.

"Why, so she hasn't," Esau said. "You've been real lucky, Bert. Unlike Orville and me. Of course Henry's wife hasn't been either. And Sherm, he doesn't have any."

"Emily's been out of town visiting her sick sister in Idalou." Henry Milam defended his wife and exonerated himself.

"Naturally it goes without saying that a man whose own wife has been peeped can't be a suspect," Esau Ireland said. "So it's just Carolyn that's gone scot-free."

Everyone stopped looking at me. Instead, we all looked at Bert Hooper.

It was good to have it all back. That old familiar ink smell of a newspaper like none other on earth. The clattering of the Mergenthaler, the irreversible disarray, even the people passing by on Cavalry Street and peering in. Most of all it was good to stand with Jamie and Beto in the gloom of the composing room and watch the *Clarion* come off the clanking Miehle flatbed. I had run a little box on page one:

We are happy to resume publication. We regret any inconvenience we may have caused our readers by not giving them the place to announce a wedding or the birth of a baby, to advertise for a lost dog, or to note that the Domino Club or the Ladies' Aid Society is about to convene. All these things we shall now continue to do.

We trust that in Martha most of the news, in the future as in the past, will be good news. We take comfort in the fact that the high function of deciding whether news is good or bad is amply served by the many worthy institutions we have in Martha devoted to that.purpose. But only one institution can make certain that the choice, as it must be, is presented to the citizens.

That institution is called a newspaper.

"Thanks for goading me," I said to Jamie.

"What an unpleasant word. I never goad."

"And my name is Colonel Robert E. Lee. Shall we celebrate? Let's go across the river and have a margarita."

"Let's have two."

PEEPER 7

The Goddess from Dallas

He had not ventured out at all for a number of nights: special circumstances had intervened. He took to the street in high anticipation. He wished to complete the peeping of the councilmen's wives, and a check of schedules had disclosed opportunities to do so tonight. Bert Hooper and Henry Milam had activities that would keep them occupied for the evening. Bert Hooper was president of the Gun Club, which had its monthly meeting tonight. This was principally a motion picture affair, consisting of two genres of that medium. An industrial film made by some manufacturer of weapons depicted hunting experiences in various part of the world—the conquest and shooting of mountain cats in Jalisco, greater and lesser kudu in Africa, or jaguar in Brazil—with formidable cannon ranging from the Remington 270 to the Weatherby 300 to the Winchester 375. At the conclusion of the gun movie came an "adult" movie obtained by Bert Hooper from sources of his, with such titles as "Two on One," "Balled in the Bathtub," and "Swallow My Load," all depicting the conquest of women by men. Taken together and in sequence, the gun and "adult" movies seemed to illustrate man's evolutionary upward progress on the conquest curve. Bert Hooper would be thus engaged tonight and Carolyn Hooper perhaps free. As for Henry Milam's wife, she had been out of town all spring attending to a sick sister in Idalou, Texas, but now she was back. Tonight was also the weekly meeting of the Martha Domino Club, of which Henry was president. It was a favorable night to do these two wives.

In addition, at the Bon Ton that day he had heard Freight Train Flowers himself, on his way out after eating, say something in conversation with a couple of men about the Peeper situation.

"I been on the north side lately, and it don't pay for a chief of police to show favoritism," Freight said in a clear voice. "So tonight I'm going to saturate the south side."

It was always helpful to know that he and the chief of police would be in opposite parts of the town on a given night.

Going over to the Hooper place that evening, he thought about her. He recalled the remark of Christian Dior after he returned to Paris from a visit to Texas. "The most beautiful women in the world," observed the great designer, "are to be found not on the streets of Paris but on the streets of Dallas." Of course Dior had never made it to Martha. But he had to admit that Dallas girls had style.

She was one of them. She had come here from Dallas and never forgotten it. Martha, Texas, would never be allowed to rub off on Carolyn Hooper, her manner seemed to say. Carruthers Mercantile was not for her. One could hardly imagine that she would wear even a pair of panties from anywhere but Neiman-Marcus. The Hoopers had a private plane, and Carolyn Hooper was known to fly to Dallas for the day just to have her hair done. The plane when it returned sometimes seemed like the mail cargo plane, bundles of packages from Neiman's tumbling out along with Carolyn Hooper herself. While in Dallas she would have lunch at the Zodiac or the Pyramid Room with one of her sorority sisters. After eighteen years "sorority" was still one of life's operable words to Carolyn Hooper. She had pledged Pi Phi, which everyone knew was *the* sorority at the University of Texas. It had been the biggest event in her thirty-seven years, and it was hard to imagine anything happening for the remainder that could surpass it. At the University she had also met Bert. Only someone with his money could have made her give up Dallas for Martha.

She wore elegance like makeup and hauteur like a raiment. She had perfect manners, and it was plain that she had been brought up to treat her many inferiors with kindness and condescension. There was a pleasing fullness to her figure. One caught oneself wondering about the size of her breasts beneath those lovely garments and the texture of her flesh at the top of her inner thighs. All these areas seemed unapproachable and forbidden. Her nice smile itself seemed an instrument for transmitting aloofness and keeping people at a distance. It seemed to say, Don't you dare even think about me in that fashion.

The Hoopers had the town's showplace, a large Spanish house with red hollow-tile roof, and its twin square towers stood out in handsome white silhouette in the starlight. He went through the back gate, his Keds taking him soundlessly toward the house by way of the shadows of a long line of Japanese privet hedges which led up a walkway, from where he hunched swiftly across an open space of Floratam lawn deep as pile carpet. Lights shone from several rooms, but he knew the house well and targeted his way to the arched window of the master bedroom. There he sank into his familiar bushes and peered into the room. Its appointments were all of carved wood, the work of San Miguel de Allende artisans. The chairs, the loveseat, the dressing table with its stained-glass panelings. A king-size bed, set on a pedestal, was encased in a fourposter of delicately sculpted wood overlaid with damask. From the posts, hovering cherubim and seraphim, joyously naked, gazed down with anticipation. It looked like a platform for making love. The room stood in expectant silence, as if waiting for someone to employ its sensual loveliness. He rested in his bushes, rising now and then for a squint. A door came open across the room.

She was wearing a white silk peignoir. He could hear the rustle of it as she moved across the room to the bed. There she removed the robe, laid it full out, and turned to where she was facing him.

She was wearing not panties but step-ins. *Step-ins.* He had almost forgotten there had ever been such a word. They were patently silk, the color of young peaches, came down near mid-thigh and ended in curlicues of delicate lace. How much more sexy they were than the crass bikini style. They were matched by a peach brassiere, which she removed almost before he had a chance to appreciate it. Then she lowered the step-ins and tossed them aside.

Lord above, she had a right to hauteur. A goddess. If he had ever had a bad thought about Dallas, he took it back. Her body was a rich, deep alabastrine white. One felt the sun had not to this day touched it. The flesh of a milkmaid, one would have thought, had she been of a lower state in society. It was surely the best-tended body he had seen in his weeks of beholding the assorted flesh of women. It must have been treasured and nurtured over the years by the most expensive creams and oils, the costliest lubricants. He searched in vain for a mole, a freckle. White curving hips, white marbly thighs, white full breasts of incitive generosity, adorned by crimson-blushed nipples of a special size. Sumptuous flesh! She seemed even more regal naked than clothed. An Athena, a body one would hardly dare touch, let alone violate, only behold and adore.

She took two steps toward the arched window. It was obvious that she had forgotten to lower the shade and was about to remedy this lapse. A sadness went through him: such a short glimpse. Then she stopped perhaps a dozen feet from him and stood there in her queenly white nakedness. She spoke, not with the Martha sound but in the refined accents she had brought with her to the Rio Grande.

"Are you out there?" she said. "I could not imagine that you wouldn't get around to me. I'm not that bad, do you think? And of course it's Gun Club night, isn't it? So I expected you. Well, why don't you and I play bang-bang?"

He froze in the bushes, shocked to his marrow. The words were said not as a goddess speaks, not even as a lady of hauteur, but in the tones of humor. Her face actually held a smile—and not the aloof smile he knew. She continued to speak.

"You see that marvelous bed? Do you know how long it's been since it had its proper use? I won't tell anyone. No one will ever know. But why trust me? Just keep your mask on. We've got two hours, maybe three. Depending on how long the 'adult' movie is."

Now, as he looked in disbelief, her hand held out to him one of those white breasts. Her fingers brushed the blossoming nipple.

"It's been so long."

He submerged into the bushes and held himself in a frozen ball. He began to tremble. A surge of conflicting emotions ran through him.

"I know you're out there." He heard her voice. "You don't have to talk. You don't have to say a word. That might be fun, don't you think? Not one word. Just doing it."

His head moved up through the bushes. Her body was arched back in offertory. Her hand reached down across her belly.

"Why don't you come in? Come in the back door. It's unlocked."

For one terrible moment he hesitated. He raised up more. He took one full look at the hour-glass hips, the longing breasts, the fiery nipples, the rich white thighs spread wide, the soft hair between them glistening with invitation.

With an explosive, reckless movement he slammed her present on the windowsill and erupted from the bushes. He ran across the lawn, down the walkway, under the shadow of the privet hedges, and burst through the gate, heedless of the loud clapping noise it made. Not until he emerged into Cedar Street did his step slow.

He jerked off his pantyhose mask, stuffing it in his pocket. He kept walking up one street and down another, his heart pounding, the sweat gathering on his body. Walked until he felt he had some measure of control. Then, suddenly, he began to retrace his steps. He went back to the Hooper alley, walked up it, and stood awhile just looking at its lines, at the twin square white Spanish towers rising against the black of the night, and thinking this: Beneath that hauteur was a woman.

Then he remembered Emily Milam. Of one thing he felt certain, no such scene would be witnessed in Emily Milam's bedroom. He looked at his watch with its illuminated dial. It was almost time for it. He felt he needed it to quiet him. He walked to the Milam house on Esperanza Street, into the alley in back of it. Through the latch gate. Squatted and put on his pantyhose mask. Saw a lighted bedroom and alongside it a lighted bathroom window. Looked at the darkened neighbors' houses and crossed the yard. Crouched in the lantana bushes outside the bathroom window, then stood up quickly.

He knew about her bath, every night at ten. She was a dear little thing, and as he watched, it began to soothe him after the tumult of Carolyn Hooper. He felt a smile beneath his mask. She seemed, remarkably, still to have her baby fat, like a fluff child. Skin as clear as a baby's, all buttery, a healthy baby-fat picture. He watched her soap and bathe, then emerge from the tub. Rounded butterball baby-fat breasts, baby-fat tummy, rounded baby-fat behind, wonderfully pudgy baby-fat legs. But moving around the bathroom with such a light step! Amazing how supple baby-fat women could be, whether dancing or in bed. He knew what a good dancer she was. Some of the nimblest dancers he had known had been fat girls. You could move them like a feather and they were as smooth and turned as easily as gazelles. It was as if their joints were lubricated with some special baby-fat grease. He smiled again, left his present, and slipped away. He breathed easily now. She had relaxed him. He looked up at the stars shining in their gentle majesty over the town.

He was just debarking through the latch gate when he saw the vehicle at the end of the alley. Its lights had been on and then flicked off. There was no mistaking who it was. No other pickup in town had that large light on top, a fiendish revolving lamp when it was on but the silo shape of it clearly outlined even in the starlight. The pickup was moving slowly down the alley toward him, a soft menacing hum. It didn't belong here! Freight Train had outfoxed him. But momentarily at least the chief had outfoxed himself. Had the pickup's lights been on, he would have been spotted. He felt his heartbeat accelerate. He slid into the oleander hedge next to the gate and went down on his haunches.

So here it was. It had been a strange and in some ways terrible night. Something in it appeared foreboding, calculated and intended. The chief's assurance in the Bon Ton about doing the south side tonight—a sly effort to mislead. Carolyn Hooper's astonishing performance. Were they tracking him all the way tonight, had they had him under observation from the beginning, at the Hooper place, at Milams'? Were they waiting to pounce on him in the act? Had they set him up?

He had thought about what would happen if he were ever caught. But it didn't do to think too much about it. It only interfered with his enjoyment. But he thought about it now and felt raw fear. For a moment he thought of ditching the pantyhose mask, stepping boldly out of the oleander hedge, and trying to bluff it out. Just amble out and say he was trying to do his bit, a spot of voluntary patrol. It would never work. For one thing, his shoes. People didn't blacken their Keds tennis shoes with India ink in Martha. Then he thought of giving himself up and telling anyone who cared to listen that it had been fun while it lasted and that after all a man only lived once. No, he wouldn't do that. He wouldn't go down easy. That was not in his character.

There was something else. He wanted to keep on peeping. He wanted to keep on seeing them. He wanted to live some more.

No, he would make a run for it. He could certainly outrun him. He had a weapon left, his speed. He had outrun the

Ladies' Aid Society women. He could certainly outrun this big fat-bellied hulk.

In back of the next house the pickup stopped, the motor went dead. He saw the huge figure emerge from it and stand for a moment looking around, big hat shoved back on his head. He was about to spring from the hedge and take off. Then he saw someone else get out from the passenger side and become a shadow. A very small shadow. It was wearing a white shirt with the tail hanging down.

In a rush the fear came at him again. He was not at all certain he could outrun her. With that body she looked as if she just might be able really to light out. He froze and listened to his heart. Then he listened to something else.

"You go that way," a hoarse whisper came. "I'll take this side."

The big shadow started in the opposite direction, toward the latch gate of the adjoining house. The small shadow was walking toward the Milam house. Walking straight toward him. He waited there, impotent, having no idea what he would do, trying to melt into the hedge. She stopped and peered down at where he was. A little gasp came from her. She jumped back.

"See something?" he heard the whisper from down the way.

Silence. Then he heard her hiccup. Through the eye holes in the pantyhose he could see her still looking down at him where he crouched in the hedge.

"No. Not a thing, Chief."

She turned and walked toward the pickup. The big figure of the chief of police came back from the other way. They met at the vehicle and climbed in.

As the pickup moved slowly down the alley, under the stars, he saw the silhouette of an arm, a very small arm, come out from the passenger side and flap, as if waving cheerio.

12.
The Trap

When the Peeper did not strike for two weeks, people began to think it was all over. He had at last got his fill of watching women undress; no man could do that forever. This made it all the greater shock when suddenly he did two women in one night. It made it even worse that they were councilmen's wives.

It was the angriest Town Council meeting I had ever attended, a tense and acrimonious affair, laden with emotion. Orville Jenkins led off.

"Twenty-six women and girls have now been looked at in various or complete stages of undress," Saint Orville said. He had the hard even tones of a commander announcing combat losses. "Including now four wives of present company. Are we going to allow this to go on until he's seen every woman and girl in Martha?"

The tension in the room hung like a weight in the air. Freight Train Flowers was plainly on the mat. The chief of police had not delivered up the Peeper. You could feel the smoldering, frustrated mood. Councilman Jenkins was wound up. He had come prepared to deliver a sermon and get, once and for all, some action. Not for nothing had he prepped at the same school, Texas Military Institute, that gave us Douglas MacArthur. As the owner of a large vegetable enterprise, he was accustomed to commanding men and getting results. His neat steel-gray hair seemed to bristle as he continued in a clear, caustic voice.

"Maybe the time has come to examine the quality of our police protection. It doesn't say much for it that one man can hold a whole town hostage. My God, how he must be laughing at us! He's got us on a string. He pulls it as he pleases. We jump. Even the women are making fun of us. As a citizen, as a businessman, as a church member, as a councilman, I've had about enough."

"I've had *more* than enough." It was Councilman Bert Hooper. The other councilmen turned and gave him an extra look as the latest husband with a peeped wife. He was even more on fire than Orville. "When I can't go to a Gun Club meeting without someone watching my wife take her clothes off, that does it. It makes me want to use some of those guns on somebody. I'm not asking for strong action, I'm *demanding* it. I'm speaking now not as a councilman but as a husband. I'm not leaving this room until I'm satisfied that he will be caught."

"Count me in on that," Henry Milam said. Thin-faced, a bit gaunt even normally, he now seemed strained, obviously from his wife's peeping, and, in his own reserved, courtly way, on the attack. "It surely hit home with me when he peeked in at Emily in her bath. And almost at the moment she gets back in town. Like he's just been waiting for her."

I was a little surprised by the uxorious vehemence of these two men. Hooper because everyone knew he played around so much: No one considered it a happenstance that Bert's bank had all those pretty tellers. Milam because he was such an equable man. A man's wife being peeped obviously could bring out the savage beast.

"All right, Esau," Bert Hooper said. "You're the mayor of this town. And you, Freight Train, are the chief of police. I insist you do something."

The chief shuffled in his chair, his huge figure bulging from it on all sides. He knew his office was on the line. His voice had a soothing, even defensive tone to it. He looked tired, and there were heavy shadows under his eyes—loss of sleep from the night patrols, I guess.

"This town is eight point eight square miles," he said. "This Peeper fellow, he got what we used to call in the Corps 'tactical surprise.' That's quite a edge in this case. He can *pick* where he wants to peep. You got one man, me, trying to guess where in all that territory that'll be. They's a lot of alleys in this town, and they's even more women than they is alleys. And them women, they just won't keep their shades down on any regular basis. Them shades'll be down one night and up the next, and when you get one down, six others go up. Considering what I got to do, it makes the Alamo look like it was defended by the Eighty-second Airborne backed up by a good part of the Marine Corps."

"That's no excuse! Those idiots who said he would go away!" Bert flared. "God almighty, men! We can't just live with this the rest of our lives like it was some sort of permanent institution in Martha. Either we do something or I'll go see the Governor myself."

Voices were rising.

"Councilmen, Councilmen," the mayor said. "Let's take an even strain. I've yet to see tempers solve a difficult situation. Though I agree the time has come for some new measures. That's why we're gathered here tonight. To figure out *what* measures."

A mild even voice spoke up. "It may be even worse than you think."

It was Sherm Embers. Everyone turned to look at him. That permanent cynical grin was there, the shrewdness in the soft eyes. I felt he took a certain satisfaction in the Council's travail.

"Has it occurred to you men that this Peeper could be seeing a lot of things in this town besides women with their clothes off?"

"What are you talking about?" the mayor said.

"Let me tell you a little experience I had the other evening," the lawyer said. "I stopped by a client's house to drop off some papers I'd drawn up for him. Man wanted to settle his bill. He went over and lowered the window shade. Then he came back and pulled out his desk drawer. It was full of green money. He always pays in cash, which is his business. Well, when he handed me my money he said, 'Those ladies may not pull their window shades, but I sure do. I don't want that Peeper to know how much I keep in this house.' That man's a lot smarter than we've been. Everybody's been concentrating so much on the ladies, it never occurred to us that this Peeper is probably seeing a lot of other things."

"What kind of things are you talking about?" Orville Jenkins asked.

"Oh, little things like adultery, sodomy, smuggling, who's screwing whose wife and whose secretary."

"Sweet Jesus," Saint Orville said.

"Lord amighty," Esau Ireland said.

"Christ up the creek, Sherm." Even the chief of police spoke up.

The lawyer looked pointedly around the table at his fellow councilmen. There was a long pause, a deep silence. I could hear the overhead fan whirring.

"Sherm's right," Esau Ireland said slowly. "Almost everyone has some sort of secret."

Everyone was silent for a bit, chewing over the gravity of this new thought. Perhaps chewing over, too, what secrets each had to hide from men at windows. The mayor looked at the somber faces around the great table.

"It just means we've got all that much more reason to grab him," Esau said. "Now let's shape up."

The mayor sat up even straighter in his chair. He looked fit and hard. His round, jowl-less face glowed pink and fresh as a baby's and his bald head gleamed immaculately under the overhead poker light. I think he wanted to let everyone get the steam off, and now the time had come to take charge. His tough, bottle-green eyes moved around the circle of councilmen as though bracing them.

"I don't want to hear any more complaining. Or any more talk about seeing the Governor. If anyone's going to see the Governor, it'll be the mayor of this town, and I haven't decided just yet that we want to announce to the whole state of Texas what's going on here. I want some *ideas*. We've got a lot of brains sitting around this table. We're agreed, this just can't go on. Now. I'm going to open this meeting to suggestions. I want them in an intelligent, reasoning, unemotional way. Follow, everybody?"

That settled the air a bit. "What about lie detector tests?" Henry Milam said. "I mean for every man in town. I'll go first."

"Wouldn't be legal," the chief of police said. He shoved his big Resistol hat back. "You got to have some reason to give a man a lie detector test."

"Sounds to me like if a person is a male and living in Martha, Texas, these days, that'd be reason enough," Milam said.

"Henry," the mayor said, "can you imagine asking Reverend Billy Holmes to take a lie detector test saying he wasn't running around town at night watching women undress?"

"We could exempt the clergy," Milam persisted.

"And the legal profession," Sherm Embers said. "I for one would refuse to take a lie detector test. On principle. Anyhow, Freight's right. As a lawyer, I'm telling you that you just can't line people up and give them lie detector tests simply because they live in Martha and aren't women. Highly unconstitutional."

"Besides," said the chief of police, "the town don't own a lie detector apparatus."

"Next suggestion," Esau Ireland said briskly.

Bert Hooper spoke. "You councilmen may remember that some time back I presented a proposal for handling this matter which you gentlemen saw fit to veto. I suggested calling in the Texas Rangers. They got a pretty good record."

"Freight Train?" the mayor said. "What do you think?"

"We all admire the Texas Rangers," the chief of police said. "But they's a funny thing. People got this idea they's lots of Texas Rangers, like a army division or something. You know how many they actually is? They's exactly ninety-four Texas Rangers altogether. They got all of Texas to cover. With all the murders, pistol-whippings, stabbings, cattle rustling, husbands shooting their women and the other way around, and drug smuggling across that nine-hundred-mile border we got in Texas, I reckon the Rangers'd figger they got better things to do than to keep one fellow from watching our women take off their clothes."

"Besides," Esau said, "as mayor I hate to call on outside help. We've always solved our own problems in our own way in Martha. That independent spirit of ours is our greatest pride."

"What if we formed the *Martha* Rangers?" Orville Jenkins said. "Right amongst the men of this town. Blanket those alleys. Fore and aft and in between."

"You're talking about a posse," Esau said. "Posses are awful dangerous. Posses are people taking the law into their own hands. You start something like that, and God knows where it will end."

"Well said, Mayor," Freight Train said.

"Besides, the Peeper would just take cover until the patrols stopped," Esau said. "Then pick up again."

"What if we armed the women?" Henry Milam said. I thought it an extreme suggestion from such a peaceful man.

"Armed the women?" Sherm Embers said. "How do you mean, Henry?"

"The way you usually arm someone," Milam said. "With guns. All the hunters we got in Martha, there's probably an average of four or five guns to a household. We have enough weaponry in this town to equip the entire Nicaraguan Army. We could let the women have some of it."

"You mean have the women open fire every time they hear something rustling in their back yard?" the chief of police said. "Hail, Henry, you'd have shellfire filling the skies of Martha like a nighttime guerrilla attack. Also, the way some of these women shoot I'd hate to be in the next house or across the alley."

"Henry, you jog in the dark," Esau said. "Some of us take walks at night. We could have a terrible accident."

"Course, you might get just the opposite," the chief said. "You might not hear a shot fired. I ain't getting what you would call the fullest cooperation from the women in catching this fellow anyhow. I'm not sure how many women would be prepared to cut him down with a Remington two-seventy if they was looking him right in the eye."

"Yes, that's curious about the women," the mayor said. "They don't seem as agitated as they ought to be. I doubt if my Holly, for one, would put a bullet in him."

"I don't see arming the women," Orville Jenkins said. "We'd be asking the women to do what is properly our job. This is man's work. You can't expect the women to protect themselves."

"You surely can't," the chief of police said forlornly. "That's my whole experience in this Peeper matter."

"The women do seem to be taking it in stride," Henry Milam said. "Emily wasn't near as upset as I'd expected. She just took an aspirin."

"A little more than in stride," Sherm Embers said. "One of my clients said it was kind of fun."

"That's almost shocking, Sherman," Esau said.

"Which woman said that?" Orville Jenkins snapped.

"Can't reveal her name," Sherm Embers said. "Professional confidence."

The councilmen sat in the pool of light from over the table, in a pool, too, of ill temper and frustration.

"God almighty, Freight, don't you have *any* clue?" Bert Hooper exploded. "Any clue at all as to who he is? You must have some idea, man."

The chief shoved his hat back. "Bert, I hate to say it but we in Zilch Gulch with the rain coming down. I don't have a blessed thing. I said from the beginning we dealing with one of the cleverest men that ever took the law in his own hands. He makes all them Ripper fellows they get over in England and never catch look like bumbling idiots."

"There's something real odd here I can't put my finger on," Bert said. "No paper. No peepings."

Bert glared at me a moment, and because he did, the others looked also, so that I felt all of their eyes on me. It was exactly what had happened at the last Council meeting. Only this time the looks seemed even harder, more suspicious. A chill sauntered down my spine. Ever since I had come back from my sea journey to the Yucatán, I had felt it. I knew what some of them, maybe all of them, were thinking: There hadn't been a single peeping in the seventeen days I was away. And now, hardly had I returned when suddenly there were two. Even before my trip I had felt that I was a pretty hot suspect on a number of lists. And now . . .

"By the way," Bert said, still looking at me, "Carolyn *has* been peeped now. I guess that clears me."

Bert sighed and turned away, and as he did, so did all the other eyes. I was grateful. All those eyes went back to looking at him.

"Well, what the hell do we do?" he said. "I'm surprised the chief of police has no real plan. That's what peace officers are for. Whoever holds that job ought to be coming up with something. Whoever does."

His voice held an unmistakable note of menace, as if talk of a replacement might be in order. The chief sat back a moment and seemed to be in reflection. Then he belched slightly. All at once I knew he had come prepared.

"Well, troops," he said in his slow, measured voice. "Now that everybody's had their say. I do have a plan."

We all looked at Freight. He brought that big barrel of flesh up in his chair and stuck his hat forward as though ready for serious business. It was as if he had wanted to let these amateurs expend themselves in unworkable ideas, then come down on them with a realistic, professional plan. He let the attention gather for a moment.

"Troops, they's something coming up where we'll know ahead of time that the Peeper will be peeping. Know one hundred percent, in my opinion."

"All right, Freight," the mayor said. "We're listening."

The chief looked carefully around the table.

"You councilmen know what tomorrow night is?"

No one seemed to know except Bert Hooper, who nodded.

"Tomorrow night is the Bloomer Girls' Slumber and Swimming Party," the chief said. "At Bert's place."

This was an annual event on the Bloomer Girls' calendar, rewarding themselves for their year of hard work with an all-night party at the Hooper place. The slumber part of the party had been held for fourscore years, since the founding of the Bloomer Girls, at various houses in the town. The swimming part was newer. It had been added seven years ago when Bert Hooper first offered the girls the use of his house with its skylighted pool, known to all as the Glasshouse. The pool was such a big attraction that the party had been held there ever since. Bert Hooper was very popular with the Bloomer Girls.

"If I know this Peeper fellow," the chief said, "the Bloomer Girls' Slumber and Swimming Party is one event he absolutely can't pass up. It'd be like a prospector passing up the mother lode. Now let me show you the plan. 'Scuse me a moment, troops."

The chief walked through the door into his office, came back with a rolled-up paper, and spread it out on the big round table. It was a rough sketch of the Hooper place including the grounds, the house, the skylighted pool attached to the house, and, stretching from the house through the back yard, a walkway flanked by high Japanese privet hedges.

"Everybody's familiar with the Hooper place. They's only two ways to get to that swimming pool." The chief had the manner of a CO briefing the brass on an assault operation. "From the house itself and from this here walkway. Walkway leads to the alley. I just got to feel our Peeper fella's gonna come up that walkway tomorrow night. I aim to stake it out."

The councilmen all leaned forward, studying the diagram.

"You mean you think he's going to climb up on that skylight and look down at the Bloomer Girls?" Orville Jenkins said.

"That's exactly what I mean," the chief said. He put his finger on the diagram. "You troops will notice that the Glasshouse is encircled by a six-foot stucco wall. *That* wall has another brick wall going around it. For aesthetic purposes, I reckon. Well, that brick wall, it's only three foot high. I took the liberty of going out and measuring it yesterday." The chief looked over with an apology to Bert Hooper. "Easiest thing in the world to hop on that wall and look down through that skylight. I done it myself. Beautiful view of the pool. I feel double sure he's gonna climb up there and keep his rendezvous with the Bloomer Girls."

The chief moved his finger.

"See them hedges by that walkway leading from the alley? I plan to station my men behind them hedges. Perfect cover."

"Your men?" Orville Jenkins said.

"The basketball team."

"The basketball team?" Henry Milam said.

"They's fleet of foot," Freight Train said. "Case the Peeper don't surrender immediately seeing he's surrounded but instead takes off running, he won't get away with one dozen basketball players chasing him down. I aim to use the whole squad. We'll have overpowering force, which is how you win wars. As we was taught in the Corps."

The chief paused to let this reflection on military tactics sink in.

Orville Jenkins was studying the diagram. "Why should he want to visit the Bloomer Girls at the swimming pool?" he said. "What's there for him to see anyhow? For him, looking at girls in swimsuits must be like looking at them in Mother Hubbards."

A cunning look filled the chief's face. "Well now, Orville, I tell you," he said gently. "I don't think we need to get into it, but take the word of one that knows, they's more goes on at that Slumber Party than slumbering and a fashion parade of girls' swimsuits. My understanding is they do a lot of *frolicking*." He looked down at the diagram. "Yes, sir, that's a mighty private swimming pool."

"I'm not positive I know what you're talking about, Chief," Saint Orville said archly. "But let us say that I get your drift and never mind."

Bert Hooper, the owner of the premises, spoke up.

"This is all a lot of bullshit," he said. He seemed angry even at the idea. "We've said all along that whoever the Peeper is, he's no moron. Even though it's in my house, I don't know what they do at Bloomer Girls' slumber parties, as the chief seems to. But I don't care if half of them stand at the windows twirling their tits and the other half turn around

and wiggle their asses, the Peeping Tom isn't going to show.
For God's sake. It would be too obvious for him to show. Too
dangerous. He knows that."

The chief of police spoke softly. "I taken all that into
account. I don't think he'll be able to resist attending that
party. Wouldn't have looked in twenty-six windows in this
town less he was a real daring fellow. But they's something
else that really cinches it in my mind."

The chief looked craftily around the table at the upturned
councilmen's faces.

"This is why I almost *know* he'll be there. He'll think we
think it's so sure he'd be there that we'll think he wouldn't do
it and therefore we won't stake it out and therefore he will do
it." The chief turned to Esau. "Follow, Mayor?"

Brother Ireland waited a moment. "I follow," he said.
"Chief, I think it's a very clever plan. I'm all for it. That
Peeper fellow just couldn't pass up a chance to see *all* the
Bloomer Girls frolicking."

"What a police officer's got to do is get inside his quarry's
mind," Freight Train said, with a faint touch of vanity at
having figured out the Peeper's thought processes. "Well,
Bert?"

Everyone waited. Freight Train really had to have Bert
Hooper's permission to stake out his house with himself and
a dozen high school boys.

Bert must have decided that with all his demand for
action, it would look peculiar if he put wraps on the chief of
police now. "All right—all right! But this is your last chance,"
he said. "If it doesn't work I've had it." He glared at the chief
of police. "And maybe some other people have too."

"Much obliged, Bert," Freight Train said, almost sweetly.
"I 'preciate it."

Bert seemed really changed, now that Carolyn Hooper
had been peeped. I have noticed a curious thing. The men
who play around the most are the very ones to scream
loudest and call up their machismo if their own wives take a
lone fling. Carolyn hadn't done that, but someone had *seen*
her, so maybe it came to the same thing for Bert.

"Now that that's settled," the chief said. He had a new

pleased and confident air. I had a feeling that there was more to the chief's plan than he'd said. I think he knew something we didn't or was up to something he wasn't sharing with the Town Council. "Mayor, I got two more little requests."

"Let's hear them."

"First, I want to recommend that the reward for catching the Peeping Tom be jumped. From five hunnert to a thousand. I aim to divide it amongst the boys if they catch this fellow tomorrow night. That'll make it close to a hunnert per boy. Give them some incentive."

"Any objection?" the mayor asked. "So ordered. Reward is now one thousand dollars. What's the other request?"

"Just this. Troops, this operation all depends on the kind of secrecy them of us with military background associates with D-Day. You all honorable men, I know. But I'd like to make a special request you say not a word about it. Not to your wives. Not to your hound dogs. Whoever that Peeper is, he got as big ears as he has eyes. So keep a tight lip, and after tomorrow night maybe we be home free."

There was a moment of silence. "I think you have our solemn word on that, Chief," the mayor said.

"I 'preciate it, troops. I knowed I could trust you. You all honorable men."

I felt certain then. The chief had a strain of slyness in him a yard wide. I knew there was more to this.

"Well, all us honorable men need to unwind," the mayor said. "Let's play cards."

"Amen," Saint Orville said. Of a sudden he brightened in anticipation, like the sun breaking through dark clouds. "I have a feeling I'm going to call somebody's roll up yonder tonight."

"And I feel amazing grace coming on," said Sherm Embers.

"Count your blessings, men," Henry Milam said, "and bet your cards."

There had been something strange about Bert Hooper all evening. And now that strangeness carried over to the poker game. He had never been a very good poker player. His game was too predictable, too lacking in those unchartable deviations and surprises that are the hallmark of the first-rate player. Well, he was full of surprises this evening. He played well, with a shrewd determination, changing up from hand to hand in a way you couldn't nail down, and the stacks of chips in front of him grew steadily. The game was "hold 'em," a variation of seven-card stud in which all players use the same five up cards in combination with their two hole cards to make the best five-card hand.

It was coming on to midnight and Esau was dealing, pitching the cards out in an expert, effortless manner. The first three "community" cards were the king of spades and the six and five of hearts. Hooper shoved in ten dollars. Milam called, Orville promptly raised, and it was twenty dollars to me, Freight, Sherm, and Esau. We all stayed. Hooper raised Orville's raise another ten. Apparently everyone was chasing a straight or a heart flush. Milam dropped out; the rest of us stayed.

"Sixth card," Esau said, and a king of clubs fell in the middle of the big round table. The chief of police whistled low.

"Two kings on the throne," Esau said. "And two little hearts hugging each other."

At that moment the strains of "Faith of Our Fathers" broke from the Baptist church tower down the street, floated across the parade ground, and entered the room through the tall piazza windows. We all waited and listened until it was finished.

"Last hand," Esau said. "Limit's off."

"Bet a hundred," Bert Hooper said immediately. He had not looked again at his hole cards.

"Good-bye, troops," Freight said, folding.

"Defense rests," Sherm Embers said, throwing in his cards.

Orville looked at Hooper. Then at the community cards.

"Which do you have, Bert, a flush? Some more kings? A full house? Well, I don't think you have a thing."

He looked at his hole cards, then shoved in a pile of chips.

"Call and raise two hundred."

"I'm gone," Esau said, folding.

"Take me with you," I said.

"That," Bert said, "and another two."

Orville looked a moment at Bert, who was looking down. "And three more."

Bert Hooper did not look up. "Three for the call," he said, starting to shove in chips. "And another five hundred for the raise."

I could feel men catch their breath around the table. The difference in limit and no-limit poker is this: In limit you're shooting at a target. In no-limit the target shoots back at you. Bert Hooper had shot back with a cannon. Orville looked up and over at the mournful big Longhorn on the wall. Then at Bert. Then he waited, and we waited to see what he would do.

"Five hundred to you, Orville." Esau nudged the game on a little. "In round figures."

Orville looked at his hole cards.

"Call," he said, and shoved in the chips.

"Last card coming out," Esau said.

A four of hearts fell from the mayor's hand.

"Bet one thousand dollars," Hooper said immediately.

An utter silence fell over the room. You could hear the flags of Texas and of the United States fluttering in the center of the table under the ceiling fan. It was the biggest bet I had ever seen made around that table. Under the pool of light, those of us who had dropped out leaned forward and looked at the community cards. Then at the pot. It must have held almost four thousand dollars. A fortune to me. Not all that much to Bert Hooper or Orville, except I had the feeling that more than money was riding on this hand.

Orville looked a while, a long while. He took a swallow of his Lone Star. He looked at Bert for some clue. So did I and could tell nothing from a man I always thought I could read. Orville looked at the kings and the three hearts and he looked at the backs of Bert's two hole cards as though his eyes might bore through them. The four, five, and six of hearts seemed to shine under the overhead light. They looked scary.

"One thousand dollars to you, Orville," Esau said softly.
Orville sighed.

"Well, Bert," he said. "I guess you've really got it. Flush or straight, either beats kings and tens."

And he threw in his hand.

Then Bert Hooper did something brutal. As he pulled in the pot, he flashed his hole cards toward Orville. They were the jack and seven of diamonds. Useless. He raked in the biggest pot I had ever seen in the Martha Town Council poker game. I could feel Orville steam.

I wondered what had happened to Bert Hooper. It seemed a strange change just because another man had seen your wife in those pretty hand-made step-ins it was rumored she wore. Someone has said that limit poker is a science but no-limit poker is an art. Maybe that explained it.

Anyhow, Saint Orville's roll really got called up yonder that night in the old Cavalry Post, around the big round table of the Martha Town Council, down by the Rio Grande. Suddenly I saw the chief of police looking square across the table at the banker with a look I had never seen on his face.

13.
The Stakeout

"**B**oys is all in place," the chief of police said in a hoarse whisper. "Behind them privet hedges inside. You and the little lady come with me. Let's move."

Night was coming on fast. Freight Train led us through the back gate and up the walkway between the hedges. He turned off the walkway and took us across the Floratam grass up a little knoll to a Texas ebony tree. Beneath the tree was the solid black shadow the ebony casts.

"Ain't this nice?" the chief said. "Ringside seat. Just like one of them press boxes. You can see everything that happens."

The ebony tree on the knoll commanded an excellent view. Straight ahead and on our level was the swimming pool, its skylight gleaming in the light of the first stars. The walkway was well down below us, but from the knoll we could see the hunched forms of the boys behind the privet hedges. We would be able to see the Peeper come through the gate and start up the walkway. After this his progress would be obscured by the hedges for a few moments until he emerged onto the open terrain between the hedges and the Glasshouse. We would be able to see him negotiate that space over the grass, mount the three-foot wall, and look down through the skylight. Finally we would be able to see the boys, led by Freight Train, charge across the grass and capture him. As a vantage point for observing an operation, it could not have been improved on.

"Don't I take care of the press all right, Ace?" the chief said. "Just like it says in the Constitution?"

"You certainly do, Chief."

"Up here you won't interfere with my operation but you can see the whole thing. I'm counting on you two to be double quiet, same as the boys. No noise, no smoking. Got all that loud and clear?"

"Loud and clear, Chief."

In the deepening twilight we could see the big shape of him and his Resistol hat walking down the little rise toward the Japanese privet hedges, then see it sink down like a beaching whale and disappear in the shadows among the boys.

Now full darkness settled over the Hooper landscape. Jamie and I sat and waited and now and then talked in whispers. I could see her only as a small dark shape sitting there in the deep shadow, legs folded yoga fashion, back straight, sitting close for the whispered talk. It was a pretty night to be outdoors. The scent of Confederate jasmine was around us. Beyond, the twin white square towers rose against the sky, a sky hung with stars. We sat and looked at the constellations. I know them for their beauty and as the objects you use to guide your way over the sea. I told her a little about them, pointing out where Cygnus and Draco and Hercules held dominion over the dark heavens. She was a good listener and seemed eager to learn what was where in the sky. You get great skies down here, whether on land or sea. The sky had it all to itself, the whole horizon. But nothing equals the sea for that. Only at sea do the stars seem truly to reign.

"I'll take you out on my boat sometime," I heard myself say. It slipped out before I realized it. Anyhow I meant it as one of those "sometime" things you never do.

"I'd like that," she said in an eager whisper.

"You don't get seasick, do you?" I said. I already regretted it. It must have been the night that made me do it. "It's a pretty small boat. I've seen as rough seas in the Gulf as anything I ever saw in the Pacific."

"It isn't *fair* to take back an invitation." She could read me so well, like some bright little animal. She scooted around a little. "You can either *promise* right now to take me down there, or I don't want you ever to mention that boat again in my presence. I mean it."

I laughed quietly. "All right," I said. "I'll take you. I promise."

"Then that's settled," she said.

I was coming almost to like that tone of triumph, that quick switch, when she had got her way. Sometimes I found it actually relaxing to be with her. Then she would suddenly jar me. Just taking off suddenly on something else, in that way she had. Usually something that was none of her business.

"Have you screwed a lot of women on that boat, Baxter?" she asked.

"Jesus," I said.

"Actually I don't mind at all that you have. I hope you've had dozens. I think it's nice for a man to be experienced."

"You don't know what a load off my mind it is to have your permission."

"It's probably what makes you so much better-natured on Mondays."

"That's about enough," I said.

She gave a big innocent sigh. "Yep, you're not nearly so impossible and difficult early in the week. Later on, as it wears off, you get pretty awful. So bossy and all. You're so afraid someone's going to move into your life. I can't imagine why anyone would want to."

"Good. I'm glad we've got that settled." I decided it was my turn. "I'll confess that I've been a little concerned about your ultimate intentions."

"Ultimate intentions! Don't flatter yourself. I'll tell you what my 'ultimate intentions' are. They're to get a job on a decent newspaper."

"This 'decent newspaper' you speak of. Have you decided which one? There's sure to be a bidding war for your

---

services: the *New York Times,* the *Washington Post,* the *L.A. Times.* It'll be fierce. I can hardly wait to see who lands the prize."

"You *promised* you would give me a good recommendation. Are you going to go back on *that* solemn word?"

"I said I'd give you that recommendation when you were ready." The Bloomer Girls had begun the occupation of the Hooper premises. "They sound like they're having a good time."

From the house and across the lawns came their shrill cries. Giggles, yelps, screams, and whoops.

"Of course. There are no men present."

All the noise came from inside the house. Outside, all was silence, nothing but the metronome of cicadas. The chief of police had really put the fear of God in the boys. Not a peep from behind the hedges and no sight of anyone. She kept her eyes on the gate.

"Do you really think he's going to come through that gate?" she said.

"He has twenty-six times. But no, I don't think so tonight. He's too smart."

"Poor thing, I'll be sorry in a way if he does. I hate to see him captured. I think I'll root for him to get away. He's probably a very nice man. He always brings a present."

She squirmed around, arranging herself.

"There's something about him. He's got style. And class. I'll bet he really likes women."

"What a deduction."

"No, I don't mean just that way. I bet he *likes* women. Do you know what I'm talking about? Not many men like women. They want something from them but they don't *like* them, and that's what women really want."

"From the mouths of babes."

"*You* could learn something from the mouths of some babes."

"Sh-h. Mustn't raise our voices."

"Be a shame in a way if he is caught," she said more quietly. "He's jazzed things up so. This town was about to fall asleep on its ass. Now it's alive and kicking."

I looked at the dark shape and sighed. I wished I could get used to it. Such a nice girl's voice coming to me through the dark.

"Yeah, he's done that. I kind of hate to see him captured too. He's helped circulation."

"You're so crass."

"You get that way when you're running a small-town newspaper. This job would make Saint Francis crass."

The black shape of her uncrossed its legs and sat up.

"Speaking of crass. I want a ten-dollar raise."

"Out of the question."

"Those stories of mine. Those interviews with the women. You said yourself they were good."

"They were okay," I said.

"So they must have *helped* the circulation. Ten dollars will only bring me to seventy-five dollars. Considering I work eighty hours a week, that's still less than a dollar an hour. Those government programs for high school brats pay more than that."

Her voice was beginning to come on small and hard in that determined way she had when she had decided she was being used or not treated with one-hundred-percent fairness. It said that no one was going to push her around just because she was a girl and weighed a hundred pounds and was barely five feet and was so defenseless and all that propaganda. I braced myself.

"Even with the seventy-five dollars," she said, "I'll still be making only one third what is required by the Minimum Wage and Hour Act."

"I've told you, if it's money you're after, you're in the wrong business. If you want money, the last thing you want is to be a newspaperman."

"Don't give me that bullshit, Baxter. You're violating enough federal statutes on me to send you up for twenty years. You're not withholding, for one thing. Ten dollars or I sing."

"Not withholding is doing you a favor," I said.

"That's true. If you withheld the government's part I couldn't eat. But I don't think that will do you much good in

---

court. You better come across with the ten. Don't forget, I can always quit."

She was an expert on blackmail. The hard fact was, I had reached the point where I couldn't imagine running that place without her, or someone like her. And I didn't have someone like her handy, and wasn't at all certain I could find one.

"All right, all *right*. But only on condition that no further raises or discussions of them will be entertained for a year."

"A *year*? What makes you think I'll be here a year from now?"

That sent a certain alarm through me.

"Two months," she said. "Ten dollars now and we'll discuss another raise in two months, depending on how the paper is doing. Don't forget I keep the books. In addition to all my other duties. You're *making* money on that paper."

"What a shock. You mean I'm not actually putting it out as a charitable enterprise?"

"One reason you're making money is that I've organized things so much better. You have no sense of order and you're a very poor administrator. But you really are sweet to give me that raise."

"It isn't sweetness," I muttered. "It's duress."

Now that she had her raise and her way, she was all sugar and spice. She was also ready to resume another favorite subject. She looked down toward the alley gate.

"Imagine just coming into people's yards like that and looking in their windows," she said. "He's bound to be caught. Sooner or later. Like tonight. He's someone upstanding, to use Martha's most flattering word, and he's got everything to lose. All to see a bunch of women in their underwear."

"Yeah. It's strange what a man will risk to see women in their underwear."

"He *is* a romantic figure. He *is* sort of that knight on a white charger every woman wants. Would you like to be looking at those Bloomer Girls in there right now?" she said in one of her quicksilver changes of direction.

We could hear borne across the grass and denting the

night air the giggles, screams, and cries from the Glasshouse. And music. I could make out the old Beatles song "Yesterday." It was a favorite of mine. The faint haunting strains fell sweetly on the night. I thought of the Bloomer Girls in there.

"They're a little young for me," I said. "I don't like green fruit."

"Green fruit? Oh, my. Oh, well, they *are* awfully young," she said with a superior air. "Seventeen and eighteen. When does the fruit ripen enough to suit your taste?"

"Thirty, minimum. Preferably thirty-five or forty. I don't find young girls hard to look at," I said grandly. "But I like to be able to talk before I do it. Nobody can talk to a girl under twenty-three."

"You're so full of wisdom. So profound. So bigoted. Do you like living alone?"

"I never think about it."

She churned around a little on the grass. "I'm trying to decide whether to live alone the rest of my life or get married," she said airily.

"Yes. Well, you don't have to reach a final decision on the matter tonight. How old are you? Eighteen?"

"How old are you? Eighty? You know very well how old I am. I'm almost twenty-two."

"Yes. Well, you've got a week or two to decide about marriage."

She twisted her body and sat up straighter. "I can see *immense* advantages to living alone. You never have someone telling you what to do. You're probably not aware that that's what girls have to put up with all the time and all their lives that boys never do. People bossing them around, telling them what to do. Personally, I hate for people to tell me what to do."

"In that case you don't have to wait a week to make up your mind. You can decide now never to get married."

"You're so the world-weary cynic, aren't you?"

"Has it ever occurred to you that having lived twice as long I might know four times as much?"

"That would be your kind of arithmetic. My own experience is that the older people get, the more stupid they are."

"It must be pleasant to realize that you're getting dumber every day."

"You think you know so much because you've read books and been places. You think that makes you so outstanding. So lordly. Well, let me tell you something. *I* could teach you a few things." She scooted her fanny and leaned toward me. "Baxter?"

"Yeah."

"There's one thing older men have going for them that you're probably not aware of."

"Are you going to tell me?"

"Well, as we all know, the physical aspect—the *looks*—are important to most men in women. With a woman they're not very important at all. A man can be old and broken down, almost *decrepit,* and downright homely on top of that, and if he has something else, even a quite young woman can really go for him."

"Are you sure? No matter how homely and decrepit?"

"Oh, I *am* sorry. Of course I didn't mean you."

"Of course you didn't. What's the something else?"

"A kind of spark. Something that makes her feel good around him. That's what a woman wants in a man."

"Fascinating."

"All you have to do is make a woman feel good and she'll do practically anything. How peculiar that so few men know that."

She gave a big sigh and fidgeted around.

"There's one other advantage an old man has."

I found myself actually beginning to resent this categorization. "I can hardly wait to hear it."

"Most young married couples I've known, the big deal is whether the husband is going to make it in his business or profession. That's what absorbs them both, and it's got to lead to a lot of tension. Well, I have one friend who married a man a lot older. She said it's great. He'd *already* made it, so that's all out of the way. So they just have fun and enjoy each other."

I looked at her with a certain astonishment and wished I could see her better in the dark. She gave that big sigh again.

"Anyhow, I don't find young men interesting enough to suit me. All they want to talk about is movies and records and *themselves*. All they want to *do* is screw."

I had to smile. Yes, she did amuse me sometimes.

"Maybe some nice older man will come along one day," she said in that airy, blithe way she had, "and find me witty and charming and fall at my feet and beg me to consider marrying him."

"Older man? You mean someone in his sixties?"

"Sixties! That's practically dead. My understanding is that men lose their ardor earlier than most women think." She spoke as if she were revealing a dark and fearful peril. "So a girl has to be careful. After all, I wouldn't want to wear somebody out with my *demands.*" She tossed her head. "I'd say thirty-five is the upper limit a smart young girl could even consider. Oh, I'm sorry. You're forty-seven, aren't you?"

"Forty-*one*," I said testily. "But only recently. You're right. A girl as hot-blooded and full of demands as you think you are has to be careful about these things."

"*Think* I am?"

She wriggled around and folded her legs again, yoga fashion, back straight.

"Personally, I think all this screwing business is overdone. Anybody can screw. Would you like me to tell you what I'm looking for in a man?"

"Be delighted."

"Humor. Curiosity. Sensitivity. Honesty. Old-fashioned care."

"If you find one, let me know. I'll marry him myself."

"Would you like to see me that way?"

She was a bundle of non sequiturs, or maybe they weren't to her. Maybe she had everything in exact order in her mind and all figured out. Maybe she knew exactly where she was going.

"What way?"

"*That* way, for pete's sake. What have we been talking about all this time? Like the Peeping Tom sees women."

"No."

"Well, I wouldn't let you. It was an entirely hypothetical question. I just thought I'd ask."

"All right, now you know."

She hiccuped.

I lay back on the grass. It was very dark under the ebony tree. Now and then dark clouds rode lazily across the sky. I knew there was an early morning forecast of rain, but for now it held off. I could see a single star in the lower part of the sky. It looked lonely sitting out there by itself. Suddenly it hit me. Loneliness. It didn't happen often, but it happened often enough. It came like a knife in you. I hadn't really chosen to be alone. Or had I? I could have made a bigger effort. What makes it work with a woman? Tenderness, surely, more than anything. It wasn't finesse really—that was a rather calculating word. It implied doing things to someone for your own purpose. Tenderness was something you did for the other person, not for yourself. I had never worked it out with a woman. I wasn't talking about shacking up. I had worked out my share of that. I meant really working it out with a woman to where there was no question but that you had to be together, that nothing else mattered. And if a man didn't get that with a woman, with one woman, hadn't life really passed him by?

There had been plenty of attractive women in places I'd been. Washington, New York, Texas: You couldn't ask for a better selection than you'd find in those three places. Then what had gone wrong? What had I done wrong? Because it was always the man's fault. You came to know that after a while. I didn't mean always a man's fault with a particular woman. A particular woman, *one* woman, could be the awfullest bitch, shrew, shrike that the devil ever put together. I meant that if a man didn't work it out with *some* woman, it was the man's fault. The chips, the control, were really all on the man's side. A man started out with an ace showing and a joker in the hole. If he couldn't win with that, it wasn't the fault of the cards and it wasn't the fault of the woman, who almost always held inferior cards if you really started looking into the hands. What had happened?

God, I had the ability to learn. My father, a great man

really—so much so that he had undertaken all my education rather than send me to schools where he felt you learned virtually nothing at all—had told me when I was about five that the most important single thing that could happen to you on a given day was to find out you were wrong about something. Because then you would have learned something, and learning things was what it was all about. That one lesson determined the rest of my life. No, I had had no problem about being wrong, about learning. But I hadn't learned about a woman. It was the most difficult thing in life for men to learn, and it never happened in one day. But I had had a lot of days, and nights, and I still hadn't learned. . . .

I awoke, startled. Someone was shaking my shoulder, quite—well, tenderly. I looked up and she was very close to me, leaning over me. Close enough to smell her skin. She had a wonderful smell about her. It wasn't perfume. It was herself, her skin. In my sleepiness I almost reached up to pull her down to me, just to hold her. She was so small and she would probably be something to hold. Then I was awake and stopped myself.

"The chief of police," she was saying. "The chief of police sends his Constitutional compliments to the sleeping press. The chief of police says he's shutting down."

"Shutting down?"

Then I was all awake. The stars were gone and there was a smell of rain. "What time is it?"

"Two o'clock. A.M."

"Two? My God. I fell asleep."

"You're kidding." She spoke softly. "I'd have waked you if there'd been anything."

"So he didn't show." I sat up. "Well, what do you know. What did Freight Train say?"

"He said he'd be pleased if we dropped by the Cavalry for a Lone Star."

"Good idea. Did I snore?"

"A little. If they'd been loud I'd have waked you. Mustn't scare off the Peeper."

"Something scared him off."

"You have soft little snores," she said. "They're nice."

We walked down over the knoll and across the yard to the walkway. The house and the Glasshouse were all dark, pretty unseen maidens presumably all tucked in, sleeping, perhaps snoring softly. We went out the latch gate to the alley and walked to her MG parked three blocks away to avoid suspicion and drove to the Cavalry Post. Everything was dark and quiet, the town gone to bed. A light sprinkle began. At the Cavalry Post I helped her put up the top of the MG. We walked across the parade ground in the rain. We could see one light shining from the old Post. We went in and up the stairs and down the wide hallway into the chief's office. He was sitting there with his crossed Justins on his desk and his big hat shoved back. Looking into space.

"Let's have some of the Town Council's Lone Stars," he said. "You drink beer, little lady?"

"Yes, I do."

"Kids start about fourteen these days."

"I celebrated my fourteenth birthday a while back, Chief."

The chief looked at her. "I reckon. I was just philosophizing aloud. Beer don't seem to hurt them."

He went through into the town council room and we could see him open the ancient refrigerator. He came back with three Lone Stars carried lightly against his huge belly with one hand. He opened the top drawer of his desk.

"Peanuts?"

Jamie took a handful and so did the chief, and we sat out on the piazza. A mist hung across the parade ground, giving a softness to the dark. We sipped our Lone Stars.

"Well, they's one consolation," the chief said after a while. "At least the sonofabitch—excuse me, ma'am—at least, he didn't get to see them Bloomer Girls. But it don't figger. Somebody musta tipped him off we was going to be there."

"It's hard to keep a secret if twelve boys know it," I said. "Some of the boys must have talked. He must have heard of it that way."

"Oh, I didn't tell the boys. Not ahead of time. I was born stupid but I've progressed. Some, anyhow."

"You didn't tell them?" I said. "How did you get them here?"

"Oh, I just set it up to tell them we wanted a group picture for the *Clarion*. Naw, the boys didn't know nothing about it till they got here and I told them."

The chief took a long pull on his Lone Star and moved his hat forward. "It don't figger. It just don't figger."

He parked his cowboy boots on the piazza railing. "Let's do a little of what if I ain't mistaken they call deductive reasoning. Of course it's just possible he never aimed to show, like Bert Hooper said. But I don't believe it. So if I'm right, he musta not showed because he knowed for sure I'd be there waiting for him. And if he knowed that, someone that knowed would of had to tell him. Follow so far, like the mayor says?"

"I follow."

The chief sipped his beer and went on in his slow-motion voice.

"Ace, you remember how I cautioned all them councilmen not to talk and, seeing as how they was honorable men, took their word they wouldn't? Well, they *is* honorable men. I'm not saying they ain't sly, vain, greedy, pompous, tricky, women chasers, and a few other things, but they's *honorable*. If they give their word they keep it. Every one of them. So I don't believe they talked, any of them."

The chief shoved his hat back. "So if they didn't talk and if only five people knowed I was going to stake it out, and . . ." The chief paused. "Actually they wasn't five people knowed. They was seven. They was the councilmen. They was me. And"—the chief paused and turned in his chair, and I could feel him looking at me in the half-dark—"they was you."

I looked at my hand holding the Lone Star beer and it was steady. The can felt light and I emptied it.

The chief gave a nice little belch. "Excuse me, little lady," he said. I'd never heard him ask to be excused for a trait he considered perfectly natural. "Oh, well. I took a course onct up at the old Aggie school that said deductive reasoning was a mighty fine tool if you knowed how to use it, but you ought to remember you could prove just about anything with it. Nice cold beer, ain't it? A pretty night with that mist and all."

"It's getting late," I said. "We better hit it, Jamie."

The chief brought that barrel of flesh to its feet.

"Here, I'll give you one to carry."

"Kind of you, Freight."

"Kind of Henry Milam, you mean."

He came back carrying the two Lone Stars. I took one and Jamie the other. We started to go.

"Oh, Ace," Freight said. "You gonna be around for a while, ain't you?"

"Around? What are you talking about? Of course I'll be around."

"I meant this weekend. You gonna be here or you planning to go down on the island?"

"I'll be going to my boat, I imagine. As usual."

"When do you generally go, Ace?"

He knew that. Why was he asking?

"Oh, sometimes Friday. Sometimes Saturday."

"Could I ask a favor of you? Would you mind checking in with me before you go? I'd be grateful."

"Of course. Any particular reason?"

"It's just that I might have something for you. Sleep tight, Ace. You too, little lady."

We went out across the parade ground and got in the MG and started down Cavalry Street. A thin rain was falling, and Jamie turned on the windshield wipers. We didn't say anything for a while.

"Well, I'll be damned," I said then. "I think he's finally got a suspect. Me. He thinks I'm the Peeper."

She drove slowly past the business buildings into the residential section, past the houses set behind their pretty lawns, these now receiving the always-welcome rain. She pulled up in front of my place. Instead of leaving the motor running as she always did, she shut it off.

"Baxter," she said softly. "Let's talk a minute. I have something I want to tell you."

We sat and sipped our beer. "I never told you, but I ran into the Peeper Monday night. The night he peeped the Hooper and Milam women. When I was out with the chief on his patrol."

I looked across at her. I could just see her shape in the dark.

"We'd stopped in the alley back of Esperanza Street to do some checking, and I went down it one way and the chief went the other. And—well, down my way I saw him hunched down in the bushes."

"You saw him?"

"He didn't say a word, but I could hear him pleading with me as much as if he'd spoken and said so, not to turn him in."

"So what did you do?"

"Do?" There was a surprise in her voice at the question. "Why, I went back and met the chief at the pickup. I told him I hadn't seen a thing."

"Why in the world did you do that? Why did you let him go?"

She turned and looked across at me. I could hear the rain falling on the MG canvas top.

"Oh, Baxter. Don't you know why? And don't you know you can trust me? If that didn't prove it, what would?"

PEEPER 8
The Mother Lode

Martha was not a town of locked doors. People would go off for the day, to shop, attend the Ladies' Aid Society, or drop by the library, and never turn a key. If there was a little more tendency to lock up at night, it was probably just a primeval reflex to the dark, though even at night many homes were never locked. Such towns still exist.

He arrived at the Hooper house a little before seven and went up the winding walkway, his musette bag slung over his shoulder. The family, he knew, would have departed for the night, leaving the house to the Bloomer Girls, whose custom it was to start showing up around eight for the annual Slumber Party. He was arriving a full hour before that. Nevertheless he pressed the doorbell. Some errant girl might have taken it in her head to turn up early. He heard the chimes sound through the house, waited, and pressed the bell again. He looked around at the beautifully landscaped grounds and pressed the bell a third time, waited. Then he opened the door and walked in.

He stepped through the foyer into the living room. He knew the house well. From the living room the view burst immediately upon you through large French doors. In a classic Spanish courtyard stretching the width of the house stood an exquisite garden, a luxuriance of plants and shrubbery, all under an arching skylight. Set in the middle of this green was a pool made entirely—bottom, sides, ledges—of blue and white San Guadalupe mosaic tile. If there was a lovelier tile on the planet, he did not know where you would find it. Around the pool corn poppies mingled with foxgloves, rain lilies thrived alongside horsemint, and Mexican shellflowers prospered with neighboring American cowslips.

He stepped through the French doors into the pool courtyard. The scent of many flowers fell sweetly over him, but he gave the vegetation less an aesthetic appraisal than a professional one. The bushes were thick all along the walls —any would do. He walked alongside the pool until he came to the far end. Then he stepped to the courtyard wall, turned right where a small gardener's passageway led alongside the bushes, proceeded to the far wall, turned right again, and made his way along that wall to midpoint. The bushes hit him at about the shoulder blades, and he looked straight out over the pool.

Unslinging his musette bag and shoving it in ahead of him, he entered the bushes. The bushes of Martha had never failed him, and the fact that these were indoors rather than outside diminished his sense of security only fractionally. They were *too* thick. He could see nothing through them. He moved around, grubbing, burrowing, until he found a place where a bush seemed slightly thinned out. He scrunched down and began a minor pruning job. He looked through again. It was just right. Through the small opening he could see the length of the pool. Then, anticipating a longer-than-usual visitation and aware that even a man in his superb condition could not squat forever, he cleared a space to allow for sitting. He settled in snugly in his nest and waited for his targets to appear. Soon he heard from beyond the pool, in the house, the first high-pitched cries that announced the arrival of young ladyhood.

The next hours went by in an astonishing flash. He felt as though a covey of excitable, shrill, giggling, and immensely talkative birds had taken up residence. Sudden screams that would have startled a tiger, high trilling shrieks, abrupt yelps, whoops of jollity—sounds that said young girls were at last in a haven of their own. Free from males, free from adults, about to begin something that was *theirs*. The whole horrid world of unceasing orders, restrictions, instructions, commands, advices, most of it unnecessary and three fourths of it stupid, all the world of vulgar adult authority and incomprehension shut out. The cries came from all around, principally from the living room, but also from the upstairs bedrooms over the courtyard. Teenage girls!

At one point two girls brought out a small table and placed it near the end of the pool. Another followed with a record player, and still another with a stack of records. Presently the sounds of music filled the Glasshouse. Between selections, he listened intently for other sounds from beyond the high walls of the courtyard. They must be out there, all in place behind their privet hedges, guarding the approaches to the Glasshouse. Yet he could hear nothing. He must try to find a way to congratulate the chief on his professionalism. Quite an accomplishment, inducing a dozen high school basketball players to be so quiet for so long. Of course the reward helped. Too bad the boys wouldn't get anything for their night's work. They were executing their plan to perfection, as silently as trained commandos. He smiled, remembering the chief casting the operation in military terms. The only thing was, the beachhead had already been secured, the invader dug in. He smiled again. He listened. Not a sound.

He relaxed in his bushes and waited.

Above, he had a view impeded only by the clear skylight. While waiting for the evening's main event, he entertained himself by watching night fall. He was not bored or impatient. He was a self-sustaining man, not given to panic if he found himself alone with himself. He saw the first star appear in the still undarkened sky. Then the darkness began to come on swiftly until that star was joined by an increasing host of its sisters. He loved stars and the constellations and, peace in his soul, he watched them assemble. The coming of night was surely the chief glory of the universe. He thought of the sky as the stage, the brighter stars as the soloists, and the constellations as chorus. Nightly they mounted a performance which provided both excitement and tranquillity. What better combination could one expect from any experience in life? Now the windless heavens began to come alive above the Spanish courtyard, and he watched as the performers appeared to take up their assigned positions. Bootes moving into place from the east, Libra crossing into the southern sky, and to the far north beginning to make her entrance Cassiopeia the queen. Soon the sky ablaze, its sweet serenity so contrasting with the decibels coming from the house, its galaxies shining down benevolently on the lovely white colonial walls, over the courtyard, over the garden, over the San Guadalupe pool. The shimmering blue and white tiles and the twinkling stars seemed to signal to each other. Ancient galaxies! which looked down upon the Greeks, which seemed to tell us, We are old and forever, you are transitory and have but now. Therefore while we live let us live, he thought, in one of those moments of reflection that are likely to come upon a man implanted in a bush with nothing to do.

So caught up in these contemplations was he, so soothed by the heavenly actors, that he was startled, and actually jumped a little in his bush nest, when from the pool environs he heard a familiar voice raise itself to make an announcement. He peeked through his foliage opening and saw the Bloomer Girls' president, the already viewed Sally Carruthers.

"B.G.s!" she sang out. "The hour has arrived. It's skinny-dipping time!"

With a shrill medley of whoops and hollers the girls disappeared into the dressing rooms beyond the pool.

And then they emerged.

They came flocking out, in loose pageant, in haphazard parade. A burst of young beauty, radiant in their new-found femaleness, the merest brush of shyness. To reassure himself that no one was missing he counted them as they came. One, two, three . . . four, five, six . . . seven, eight, nine . . . ten. All present and accounted for. Bringing their young unspoiled flesh they came, flesh of every vintage of white, from cream to snow to milk to pearl to ivory to alabaster to eggshell to fleece. Through the lilies and the cowslips they came, through the foxgloves and the horsemint. Soft and sweet they came, bringing gifts fairer even than the garden's and in greater variety. Bringing their chaste young breasts of every shape, weight, and size they came, some barely nectarines, some young pears, some full and rounded honeydews, some bold, some timid, bringing their nipples of every dimension and projection and of assorted colors. Bringing wondrous young thighs they came, some lean and some fuller. Bringing their sweet behinds like confections, some tiny, some larger, some high-pitched and saucy, some drooping endearingly. Brunettes and blondes and of licorice-black hair they came, and one true strawberry redhead, with pubic efflorescences of complementary hues and in densities from boutonniere to posy to nosegay to bouquet to a rich and luxuriant thicket. So they came. He squinted hard through his foliage opening. Even their belly buttons seemed to his eye objects of interest, altogether winsome and charming. With an air not cocky but entirely self-confident, of knowing what they had, they came, sassy, pert, stopping just short of brazen, yet curiously soft in their femininity, the young fragrant blossoms of bodies ready to bloom into full womanhood, in blissful ignorance of their vulnerability. Thus they came.

His eyes darted here and darted there, sampling the dreamlike feast, giving it quick once-overs, coming back to dwell at more length on Becky Thornton with her cantaloupe breasts astonishing for a seventeen-year-old, on Maria Cavazos with her tiny coquettish carbon spray between her thighs, on Daisy Appleby with her conical polished behind outshining the stars above. He had seen three of them previously, so he concentrated on the other seven as they made their way to the pool. Not that the three wouldn't deserve a second look on any ordinary night, but seconds could wait. They came to the pool and took up positions along the sides of it, sitting, their feet and calves dangling in the water, kicking lightly, making splashes and also making inner thighs rise and fill, their bodies surpassing in charm and glory the shimmering blue and white San Guadalupe tile.

An epiphany of young flesh. An Elysium of beholding, a sweet debauchery of viewing and reviewing. How fascinating they all were. How infinitely different! He settled in and looked and looked. He had no notion of time. When one is thus occupied, what could be more inaccurate than a watch? He gazed out on unceasing wonders, he beheld. Taking their laps of the pool, floating on their backs, diving, sitting yoga-fashion on the tile apron, chasing each other around the pool's edge, sprawled on their tummies. The views, the views! He inspected, surveyed, scrutinized, examined, gaped, gawked, perused, browsed, explored, studied, pored over, checked out, contemplated, gloated, appraised, gorged, exulted, devoured, examined, and reexamined. Time was not.

Only when they had begun to drift off, to fade into the reaches of the house, only when the pool was once more given back, with a seeming sigh, as though it had lost its fairest jewels, to the shimmering tiles, and he waited for the slumber part of the party to begin, only then did he begin to reflect. Yes, the chief of police had been right about one thing. He could not ordinarily have missed the Bloomer Girls' Slumber Party. But Freight had been wrong as could be about the other. Of course they would stake it out. Of course he would therefore not have shown. But then that clever operational plan of the chief's had changed all this.

Now the only sounds were those from the upstairs rooms —an occasional whoop, a random giggle—and these were beginning to fade. He waited yet a little while, feeling at peace, blessedly full both with having outwitted the enemy and with the infinite bounty of the Bloomer Girls. For the first time since he had started his long pilgrimage, he felt a happy satiation, a blissful surfeit. He had now come full circle. The Bloomer Girls had got him started and now he had seen them all—as well as a few others. The full circle represented something deep and abiding in man's experience. There was something altogether fitting and appropriate about it. Now that the circle had closed, it seemed a good time to quit.

He had brought a musette bag full of presents for each of the girls: ten of those pretty enameled butterflies from Las Bocas. He decided not to leave them. He decided on some sudden and true instinct that he didn't want anyone ever to know that he had peeped all the Bloomer Girls. It would be his secret.

This left a problem, a moral one. He well knew that the chief suspect in town was that newspaper fellow. Almost every grown man was suspected, but he led all others. The idea of an innocent man being suspected was not to his liking. Especially since he wasn't such a bad fellow. Of course there was something a little superior about him. He felt he was smarter than anyone else who happened to be present. But most newspaper people were like that. They were peculiar people. Oddballs. Not at all good solid community citizens like himself. But he wasn't a bad sort. He didn't like for him to be blamed for something he hadn't done. And yet, to be entirely truthful, part of his plan as he went along had been to make the fellow the prime suspect. To this end he had given up peeping on weekends when Baxter was generally out of town, down on that boat of his, except for one Saturday when he took advantage of his presence to do a couple of peeps. And then he had ceased operations entirely during the seventeen nights Baxter was gone after shutting down the newspaper so abruptly. That had been a considerable sacrifice on his part, to be deprived of peeping for so long. Yes, he had to admit, he had contributed to Baxter's suspect role and he felt a little guilty about it. But he didn't feel too badly. After all, Baxter hadn't thought of *him* when he shut down the paper: it had left him without the invaluable Social Notes to help tell him which women would be available. Of course he had never dreamed the fellow would actually stop the paper or he would have done more to back him up. He had certainly done his part to see that the paper was started up again. So they were quits, more or less. Still and all, he wasn't entirely comfortable with the idea of an innocent man being suspected. He just didn't know any way around this problem at the moment. Maybe he would think of something. And maybe he wouldn't. For the time being they would just have to go on thinking it was Baxter.

Through the skylight the stars went away and rain began to fall, thinly at first, then more lively, making a crisp tinkling noise on the glass. The pool with its glittering tiles stood empty. He looked up above the courtyard to the second floor where the bedrooms were and saw that all was dark. He heard a muffled giggle and then another and then silence again. Slumber Party. He stepped out and made his way softly around the pool, through the living room, and out the front door, closing it quietly behind him so as not to awaken any sleeping beauties. As he started down the walk, serious rain began to fall. He stepped out into Camellia Street, the rain now sweeping in sheets across it, flaying the trees and the lawns and the many bushes. As he sloshed homeward, soaked and euphoric with the bounty of the Bloomer Girls all naked and sportive, he heard the bells of the First Baptist Church strike three. What a nice town they had.

PEEPER 9
The Last Peep

It was a glorious night in June. The stars in the great sky shone down profusely over the town's winsome geometry, on its prosperous white-board and red-brick houses with their deep, self-confident lawns. The old reassuring scents fell over him, the honeysuckle and the gardenia, the Confederate jasmine and the yellow rose. The tenor call of the nighttime songbird was heard. Going down Hibiscus Street en route to his last peep, he felt a tender sadness now that it was all over, but also the sweet glow that comes with a worthy mission successfully accomplished. He was glad it was completed, yet sorry there would be no more of it. Assuredly he would continue the night walks he had taken for years, but they would not have that peculiar zest a walk has when there is an objective at the end of it. But the time had come. It is as important to know when to retire as when to begin. What sadder and more tragic figure than the man, be he politician, business executive, or sports figure, who, high mission already achieved, insists on going on forever. A man with class did not wait until the valleys came. He stepped down at the peak, on the high tide. In any endeavor of life, nothing is more fatal than greed.

Besides, his cup had runneth over. As he walked down these sweet streets, their assorted and diverse bodies passed in review through his mind's eye. He saw again the high-bred, chestnut-haired Mildred Bradshaw lowering her jodhpurs to reveal that high candescent behind, that nakedness kept marvelous by the daily ride on her Arabian gray. He saw Holly Ireland and her glorious tapestry of freckles. He saw Kathryn Shields and the soap froth of her bath falling away to display first the raspberry nipples on milky breasts, then the licorice corsage. He saw saucy Sally Carruthers, the strawberry crown there matching the soft waist-length hair above. They appeared in turn before him, front and back views in most instances, each offering something different from the one before. The charming tableau of Mary Armbruster, clad only in a fragment of panties, her licentious taffy hair hanging long and loose, her breasts dipping forward as she pursued the toilette of her toenails. The rich, regal flesh of Carolyn Hooper, the peach silk step-ins, the white hourglass hips. The dear baby-fat plumpness of Emily Milam. The sublime bosoms of Flory of the Bon Ton with their noble crests. And finally he beheld again that explosion of girl flesh: the ten Bloomer Girls frolicking in the Glasshouse swimming pool, their nude bodies diving, floating, sprawling, a celestium of darling breasts and bewitching behinds, of heartbreaking inner thighs. The real worth of supreme experiences in life seemed to him not so much the experience itself as the banking of memories for continuing replays through the years. As a lover of women and their bodies, he had in a short space of weeks amassed a store-house of replay materials.

By his own careful count he had seen twenty-eight of them, including the seven new Bloomer Girls in one peep. The chief of police had a different "official tally" of twenty-six, but this was wrong for various reasons. Not only did the chief not know about the seven, but he was carrying on his books nine others who didn't belong there: as he and he alone had good reason to know, they had never been peeped but had claimed they were. Still another category consisted of four women who had definitely been viewed and never reported it. He smiled, thinking of these things. Curious and past understanding are the ways of women! They are not as we are. Not just their bodies but their minds, too, operate on frequencies, dwell in regions entirely unknown to a man. They seem hardly to belong to the same species.

Reported or not reported, he had seen enough to beatify his future days and nights when he ran into them—at town meetings, at library committees, at church, at bazaars, just walking down Cavalry Street. Not to forget the weekly basketball games where the Bloomer Girls would appear, costumed to the rest but otherwise to him. Down time's road he saw something else. As the list began inevitably to dwindle —some moving away, some passing on—he might need to replenish his supply. For the time being he had a sufficient backlog. But when the time arrived, he would make a comeback. A man should retire at the peak, but it was acceptable and in the finest tradition to make a comeback after a decent interval. And by then there would be a whole new crop of Bloomer Girls coming along.

As he turned the corner into Cedar Street, he told himself with honest pride that he had done something for the town. Not that that had been his purpose. He smiled, remember-ing the intense colloquies in the Town Council, exchanges in which he had offered his own most interested commentary, on what his purpose could be. He actually laughed aloud, recalling one councilman's crass suggestion that he was punishing certain women of the town for their "sins." Pun-ishing them! He had had one purpose and one alone: to *adore* them. If there had been any doubts that women stood at the very summit of the good things of life available to man, or that anything else was more than a distant second, they were now resolved. And there was one thing more. He had come to a veneration for all women's bodies, of whatever shapes, dimensions, textures, weights, and contours. But then he had progressed beyond that, in a way he could not describe, to an enlightenment as to the true essence of women. And what was it? It was that tender, generous nature which the Creator had assigned to them alone. Surely it was due to that nature that women knew so much more certainly than did men what the really important things in life were. And no knowledge was as important as that.

But something else had happened that went beyond his own transfiguration. The real thing he had achieved, unintentionally to be sure, was to make the men of the town be aware of and value what they had. There had been a hundred signals to affirm this. The men treasured their women more now. This had been his gift to the women of the town, an exchange gift for what they had given him. And a gift also it was to the men. He deserved the credit for that, though he would never get it publicly. So much the better. Anonymous gifts were the only worthy ones.

As for the game itself, there had been some scary moments. But on the whole it had been splendid fun. He had enjoyed outwitting his pursuers. It had been an uneven contest from the start. They had never had a chance. Not only were there hundreds of alleys for him to choose from and several thousand women. He had also known where the opposition would be on a given night, known every plan and tactic, indeed had helped to father them. To be a member of your adversary's combat information center and thereby remove all element of surprise—to use some of the military terminology which Freight Train had applied to the operation, he thought, with another smile—well, to use a strictly nonmilitary phrase, it had been a piece of cake. And as a final assist, his vocation had helped him pursue his avocation. Because his hours of work were unpredictable, he had never had to explain an evening's absence, not even to those closest to him.

He gave a contented sigh and turned into Daffodil Street. Only two blocks more.

He had given considerable thought to the question of which woman in town should know his identity. He was resolute that someone must. It simply seemed to him the better part of courage and of daring. If there were two qualities he felt modestly that he possessed, it was these. Not to have anyone know would be a sneaky, skulking thing, unworthy, almost cowardly. It was fitting, as a final act, that one woman should know. It fitted his image of himself and his image of the proper way to do things.

He had narrowed the choice to two, Holly Ireland and the new girl in town. That girl reporter. They were the only two he had really considered. For though he wanted to do the correct and courageous thing, he was not foolhardy. He had no wish to reside behind bars. It was imperative that it be someone he felt confident would never talk. Never tell. On that score he felt certain of both of them. Holly Ireland—her very testimony before the Town Council certified that she was clearly taken with him. Besides, he knew her character quite well. She was no tattletale. As for the girl reporter, she had had an actual opportunity to capture him and had refused it. In the end he had decided upon her. He could not say exactly why. One reason surely was an artistic one: it seemed fitting to give himself up, in a manner of speaking, to someone he had not previously peeped. And to do so immediately after peeping her. That seemed a proper finale. The laurel had fallen to the girl reporter. He had thought then at some length about a suitable present. It should be something special. And then he knew.

So now he made his way toward the small bungalow she had rented on Camellia Street. Incidentally, it would be interesting to see what she had. On the outside it didn't seem much. In that get-up she wore—the jeans and the man's white shirt hanging over them—it was impossible to tell. But from what he knew of women, if she had had much to show, she would have shown it. In his experience women did not hide their salient features, provided they had salient features. So as he approached her place he did so without great expectations in that regard. He was just going through the proper ritual before revealing himself to her.

He turned into the alley, went down it a way, and stood at the gate in the oleander hedge. He gazed up a final time at the beautiful stars, gave a bittersweet sigh, and for the last time put on his pantyhose mask. He opened the gate. He made his way across the yard, halted in the shadow of a mesquite tree, and studied the house.

It was Wednesday night, her early-to-bed night before press day on Thursday. He realized the risk he was taking. If he had misjudged her, the timing would be perfect for her to score a scoop for Friday's *Clarion*. And newspaper people loved scoops. Headline: PEEPER CAUGHT. Beneath it, one of those vain first-person stories in the "participatory" style of journalism now so prevalent. Beginning, no doubt, "I captured the Peeper single-handed last night." But he was sanguine. However strong the professional temptation, he didn't believe she would do it.

Hunched under the mesquite, he watched the lighted window in the corner. He emerged from the tree's shadow and made his way in a crouch to the bushes outside the window, for the last time sank into them. He raised his head professionally and peeked through.

It was the smallest bedroom he had witnessed in the course of his peerings into the windows of the town. The bed itself took up much of the space, and most of what remained was commandeered by an unusual dresser: one of those dressers used on the western frontier, principally in bordellos, if he was not mistaken. Must have come with the house. It was a tall and massive thing. It consisted of a three-way full-length mirror with drawers and marble-top ledges at the bottom of the side mirrors. The space between was left free to provide ultimate viewing of the female figure. Standing there before it was one of these, though it was difficult to be sure in her attire and with her hair cut shorter than many a boy's. She looked at herself a bit, then retreated to the bed, plumped down, and took off the dirty sneakers she wore. He was surprised to see her return barefoot to the space within the mirrors.

Standing there she first removed the jeans, lowering and then almost jumping out of them in an agile hopscotch movement, kicking them aside. Then she reached under the shirt and performed the same down-and-out-of movement with gymnast skill. A pair of panties flew across the room toward the bed. She stood there in the all-encompassing mirror. A peculiar way to undress, but then one of the tidbits he had picked up of late was that women performed this ritual in astonishingly diverse, idiosyncratic ways. One could write a whole dissertation on the way women undress, starting with why some women shed their panties first and others their bras. The shirt covered her hips and even the top of her legs.

She began to unbutton the shirt from the top. The first button, a thoughtful pause, then the second. The third button, the same pause, then the fourth. Finally all the buttons stood unlatched. The shirt, however, remained hanging and unopened. For a moment he wondered if she slept in it, and if what he saw now would be all he got. But then, looking at herself all the time in the mirror, she began to peel the shirt back from her shoulders, coming slowly out of its sleeves. It was almost as if she were performing for a viewer. Maybe she was practicing for somebody. Then the shirt was off. It flew across the room. She reached up and, the hand quicker than the eye, a brassiere followed it through the air. She and the mirror stood looking at each other. And in his bushes he squinted. He had a circumferential view provided by the living flesh and the three-way reflection of it. There was no part of her he could not see.

It was a slim, boyish body. Rather coltish, with racehorse legs, fairly straight. Small, pleasant breasts above a flat tummy. As he had expected, nothing exceptional anywhere. A healthy, clean, nice, but rather ordinary slender young woman's body. Nevertheless, there was something special about hers. It had that same saucy air he had noted in her whole manner, in her very spirit.

He was surprised to see her begin to inspect these various aspects of herself. She turned around, so that what he had seen live he now saw in the mirror and what he had seen in the mirror he saw live. She looked over her shoulder and gave her small rump a critical appraisal in the glass. Then he thought he heard from her a sound rather like "Humpf!" which he somehow translated as "Not much!" She turned around and directed her attention to her breasts in the same analytical fashion. The same sound "Humpf" came out, and he gave it a similar translation, *They're* certainly not much." Her eyes traveled downward and looked studiously at her legs and the sound came again. Apparently finished with her inspection, her head turned, her hair bounced, and she gave an abrupt hiccup. Somehow it was like a final signature of disapproval.

He felt he knew now why she wore that get-up. It was because she didn't think much of her body and assumed no one else would. She dressed that way to pretend she didn't care, as though she were above all that. But of course she wasn't. No good woman could be.

Seeing her and hearing her negative registers, a wave of compassion moved through him. She was wrong, all wrong! He had to tell her that she was undervaluing herself, that every woman's body has its own loveliness, its own special delight. He had learned that in these last weeks.

For the last time he emerged from his bushes. He moved in a crouch around the house, stood up boldly, stepped onto the tiny porch, and pressed the doorbell.

It took a while for her to answer. Then the door opened and she stood there barefoot and wearing the shirt and jeans again. She stared at him, and he heard her gasp at the sight of the mask. He could see her hand go to her mouth and her eyes become very large. He reached up and took it off and, with a little bow, handed it over to her, his present.

For what seemed an inordinately long time, she simply looked at him. Then a marvelous expression came over her face. It was altogether conspiratorial—an avowal of comprehension, of utter understanding. He was entirely safe. Never would she tell.

"Won't you come in?" she said. "Do you know something? I was always disappointed that you never got around to me."

"Why, little lady, I just did."

"You did?"

"It was a great pleasure."

"It was?"

"Young lady, listen to me," he said in his reedy, commanding voice. "All those things you were looking at: nothing. Those various parts are not what make a woman beautiful. They have nothing to do with it. What makes a woman beautiful is one thing alone: the knowledge that she is a woman. Follow?"

Again she gazed at him for what seemed a long while. In her look there was a dawning revelation of something terribly important. After all, she had the ability to learn, and she was a Texas girl. It was as if he had brought as his present to her something greater by far than any of the presents he had brought the other peeped ladies.

"I follow, Mayor—Brother Ireland—Esau," she said.

PEEPER 10

One of Us

"Mayor"—the slow rhythmic voice of Frieght Train Flowers came over the telephone—"we got to have a emergency meeting of the Town Council. They's been a break in the Peeper case."

He looked across the big mahogany table at his wife. His heart skipped a beat.

"I'd prefer to save the details for the meeting if you don't mind, Mayor. It's kinda involved," the chief of police said. "But you can take my word for it. It rates a emergency if they ever was one. But they's one crucial thing."

"What is that, Chief?"

"I don't want Baxter invited."

He relaxed a little, though by no means completely.

"But we have to let the press in," he said.

"Keep him out of this one, Mayor." The chief's voice was a little more authoritative. "And call the emergency meeting. Take old Freight Train's word. You be glad you did both."

"The floor is yours, Chief," he said.

They were gathered around the big round Town Council table, dented with cowboy boots, scratched by poker chips, burned by cigarettes, stained by the rims of countless cans of Lone Star beer. The French doors to the piazza balcony stood open onto the old Cavalry parade ground. Night had just fallen, and the cicadas could be heard tuning up for their regular summertime concert. Their ancestors had buzzed at the stirring of horse troops setting forth on great deeds, returning from heroic feats of arms. The ceiling fan above the table stirred the warm air and fluttered the tiny flags of the United States and Texas in the center of the table. From the wall the old Longhorn with its enormous horns sticking out hazardously into the room looked down on the assemblage. In the corner the ancient refrigerator made its steady rasping sound. Their faces cast in light and shadow by the glow of the overhead poker light, the councilmen waited.

"Troops," Freight Train began, "let's all rest easy. I got a notion we gonna be here for a spell. I got a story to tell, and I want all you men to listen with both ears. Listen real good."

So sober was the chief's tone that the councilmen sat up a little from their customary slouched positions.

"As you troops know, when I set my trap for the Peeper at the Bloomer Girls' Slumber Party, I was sure and certain he would show. So certain that when he didn't I figured something peculiar was going on. I just knowed he had to be there. So late the next morning, while the girls was having their champagne breakfast, I went over to the Hooper place for a look-see. First I looked all around the outside just in case. Then I went inside to the swimming pool."

The chief's gaze went around the table, taking in the councilmen individually.

"Every one of you knows that place. That pretty shrubbery and vegetation that surrounds that swimming pool. All them bushes. Well, I looked around that shrubbery and in them bushes, and what did I see?"

The chief paused. No one knew what he had seen.

"I seen *tracks.* Tracks that I know better'n I know a buck deer's tracks."

The chief gave a minor belch and pushed his hat back a little.

"Troops, they was *tennis shoe tracks.* They was the same tracks I seen every place the Peeper's been."

The councilmen sat gloomy and silent at the news that the Peeper had so inventively succeeded where they had so diligently tried to stop him. Orville Jenkins said it.

"Then the fellow really did see the Bloomer Girls after all?"

"He seen them all right," Freight Train said. "Not a doubt in the world about that."

"Well, well," Bert Hooper said with a gloating air. "It looks like he outfoxed you again, Chief."

The chief's big head turned slowly and he cast a baleful look on the banker. His huge frame shifted a little in his chair, from which he lapped over on all sides.

"Yes, sir," Freight said. "He outfoxed me. And we have to see otherwise who outfoxed who and who the fox is going to bite."

"Are you positive the tracks were the Peeper's?" Henry Milam said. "Everybody wears tennis shoes today. It could have been one of the Bloomer Girls—or the gardener."

"Not them tennis shoes," Freight Train said. "His has got a busted place in the tread on the right shoe. It leaves a mark like a arrowhead."

"You never told us that," Bert Hooper said.

"I didn't tell you everything," the chief said. "Looks like I told you too much as it was."

"What do you mean by that?" Hooper said.

"You'll see. Also the tracks went right *into* the bushes. I could even tell which bush he hid in. Them bushes is thick, and he'd pruned one back so he could look through nice and cozy at them Bloomer Girls frolicking in the pool." The chief gave a slow look around the table. "And I guess we all knows how them Bloomer Girls frolic at that annual party of theirs."

"Shocking," Orville Jenkins said, turning to the mayor, "for him to see all that."

"That was a bold and daring thing, to go inside like that," he said.

"Mayor, he been bold and daring from the beginning," the chief said.

"That's true," he said. "He must have gone in there way ahead of time, before you even got there. Ingenious."

So caught up were they in the fact that the Peeper had actually viewed the Bloomer Girls in their entirety, in both meanings of that word, that for a while the councilmen did not grasp the larger significance of the successful peeping. Sherm Embers was the first to do so.

"Why, that means," the lawyer said slowly, "the Peeper must have found out you were going to stake out the grounds. So being the clever fellow he is, he just went inside. He knew you were coming."

"He found out," the chief of police said softly. "He knowed."

Freight Train looked around the table at the councilmen's faces. As he talked, he seemed to be studying each one consecutively.

"He knowed, all right," the chief repeated. "And that set my brain to working. I went over everything that's happened since the first night he looked in on Sally Carruthers. And I got to thinking how he been able to outfox me, as Bert puts it, every step of the way. I allowed for all the edges he had—element of tactical surprise, all them alleys, all them different women to choose from. Still and all, it seemed he had to have *extra* information. Information he could of got only one way. It just took the Bloomer Girls party to make this sure and certain."

The chief paused and regarded the faces again. He moved his eyes from one councilman to another, looking at each in turn. Now he sat back and his eyes took them all in.

"Troops, the Peeper has knowed our every move from the

very start. He has sat in on our most secret plans to catch him. He been in this room all along. Sitting at this table."

A shock wave caromed around the table. The faces of the five councilmen, caught in the poker lighting, were held in frozen, stunned expressions. The chief intently watched these. Then Bert Hooper spoke into the silence.

"Baxter." The word fell with an air of immense discovery. "He's been present at every meeting we ever had."

Recovering quickly from the shock, the others pounced on the solution to the crime.

"By heaven, you're right, Bert," Orville Jenkins said. "It's Baxter. I've kind of thought so from the beginning."

"Personally I think he's a pretty good sort," Henry Milam said. "But I have been sort of suspicious. He was always on my list."

Bert Hooper cinched his case in a burst of analysis. "He's an outsider. He's unmarried. They say he likes women very much. And do you recollect when he shut down the paper and took off? There wasn't a single peeping while he was away."

The banker sat back in triumph. The air of unanimity filled the Town Council room. They had their man. Freight Train gave a considerable belch.

"Troops," the chief said, "I hate to break up this victory celebration and disappoint all you councilmen, but they's just one little thing wrong with all that. Baxter was with me that night of the Bloomer Girls' Slumber Party. All during the stakeout. He come along to cover it for his paper."

"*All* night?" Bert Hooper said. "He was with you *all* night?"

"Up until about two A.M.," Freight said. "Him and I even come here after for some of Henry's Lone Star. Tell the truth, I first thought it was Baxter myself when the Peeper didn't show—I figured he knowed about the stakeout and held off. Until I found them footprints inside the next day. Then I knowed it couldn't be. I had him in my sights from dark till two A.M., and by that time the Peeper had done his work and the Bloomer Girls was all tucked in. So they ain't no way Baxter could have peeped them girls. The Peeper was inside while me and him was outside."

The chief looked around the table. "Also, that girl reporter of his was with us both the whole time. Case you need further confirmation of where Baxter *and* me was while the Bloomer Girls was being peeped. So him and I has to be eliminated from the seven individuals that knowed about that stakeout ahead of time."

A profound silence descended over the proceedings. Then the unthinkable meaning of it hit the councilmen simultaneously.

"Well, if Baxter's out and you're out," Sherm Embers said in wonderment, "then it leaves five who knew. That means—"

The lawyer stopped.

"Why, it means—" Henry Milam began.

"Two from seven equals five," Bert Hooper said. "Why, that means—"

"My God, it means—" Orville Jenkins began.

None was able to articulate the awful fact. Then he did it for them.

"It means," he said, "that it's one of us."

The chief looked slowly around the circle. "That's what it means, Mayor. Troops, we down to five suspects. And they all present and accounted for. Troops, one of you councilmen is the Peeper."

"My God," Orville Jenkins said. "It's one of *us?*"

In the deep silence only the sounds of the ceiling fan whirring overhead and the tiny flags of the United States and Texas fluttering gently beneath it could be heard, along with the whining of the cicadas stationed on the Cavalry parade ground. Then each councilman started looking around the table at the others. Keen, appraising looks, scrutinizing, inspecting each other, as though suddenly all were total strangers. Finally the voice of Orville Jenkins was heard.

"I guess I can say it now. I've been holding back on it, but I suspected something like this some time ago. It was such a horrible thought I just put it out of my mind." He looked in succession at his fellow councilmen. "Right now I wonder which one of you it is."

That reduced the list of suspects to four.

"To be perfectly honest, I've been thinking along those lines myself," Bert Hooper said. "I've been thinking quite a while that he had inside information. No man could be *that* clever to get away with it over and over again. It was a terrible thing even to think, and nobody wants to accuse a friend. Especially a fellow councilman. But I wish I'd had the courage to speak up."

That reduced the list of suspects to three.

"The chief has done a first-rate piece of detective work," Sherm Embers said. "I'm not going to ask him, but I expect that trap at the Bloomer Girls' Slumber Party was really a trap for us. Absolutely brilliant, Freight. You have an open-and-shut case. It all comes clear now. It has to be somebody in this room. I'd like to handle the case myself when it comes to trial. And since it's a public duty, the fee will be nominal."

That reduced the list of suspects to two.

"It isn't me," Henry Milam said.

That reduced the list of suspects to one. Everyone looked at him.

"Gentlemen," he said. He spoke as if he were dealing with the hopelessly naive. "I hardly think that whichever one of us five it is, a man as sly and covert as he has been is going to jump up and say, 'Look at me. I'm it.' Freight, you're absolutely certain it's one of us?"

"Not a doubt," the chief said. "This ain't been a easy thing for me to do, Mayor. After all, I work for you men." He paused a moment and added, "As well as for the town of Martha."

"I appreciate that, Freight," he said. "We all owe you our thanks. Or at least all but one of us do."

He looked the chief of police hard in the eye.

"Freight Train," he said, "I don't like to do this. But as the mayor of Martha, Texas, I have to put it to you, and I might as well do it in the open, fair and square. Do you know which of the five of us it is? I direct you to answer that question."

"I don't have a clue. God's truth. If I did, nothing would stand in the way of me doing my duty."

"Why don't we find a Bible," Orville Jenkins said, "and have everyone take an oath that he isn't the Peeper. There ought to be a Bible around here somewhere. I'll go first."

He regarded the vegetable king with a mixture of pity and contempt.

"Orville," he said, "do you seriously think that a man who broke the law twenty-six times would quibble at breaking it a twenty-seventh by swearing on every Gideon Bible in Texas that he didn't do it?"

"It's even worse," Freight said. "He picked up seven new ones in one swoop at the Slumber Party. All them Bloomer Girls but three was first-timers. So I make it thirty-three, Mayor. Altogether."

"All right, gentlemen," he said. "We've made a lot of progress. We've narrowed a considerable list of suspects —the male population of Martha—down to five. And we have them all in custody, so to speak. Where do we go from here?"

Another silence set in. Then suddenly things exploded.

"I don't like this!" Orville Jenkins burst out. "The more I think about it, the more I resent any suggestion whatsoever that a person with my background could be included in any list of suspects."

"So do I," Bert Hooper said. "Hoopers have been bankers here for a hundred years. Does anyone think for a moment I'd risk a background like that to go jumping in and out of bushes all over town?"

"If we're going to bring in background," Henry Milam said, "Milams have been distributing Lone Star beer here long before you were growing vegetables, Orville. And before your bank was even opened, Bert."

"I'm not all that strong on background," Sherm Embers said acerbically. "I've only been here twenty-six years. But personally I don't find it necessary to skulk in bushes to see naked women."

"Some defense," Bert Hooper said sarcastically. "Neither does anybody else. We've always got Boys' Town."

"Bert has a point," Orville Jenkins said, giving the lawyer a drilling look.

"You should know," Sherman Embers said, giving the look right back. "Someone told me they saw you in Boys' Town not long ago, Orville."

Jenkins spun on the lawyer. "I'd be careful with my mouth if I were you, Embers. I know a little law myself, and what you just said is viciously slanderous."

"You mean going to Boys' Town is slanderous?"

"There was a Hooper at the Alamo," Bert Hooper said.

"On which side?" Sherm Embers said.

"I resent *that*," Bert Hooper said hotly.

Tempers were pushing up, voices rising. The councilmen began to say things to each other that they had never said, only perhaps thought. In any society, even in families, even with one's best friends, there is hardly a more dangerous thing to do.

Bert Hooper's eyes moved around the table, glowering at his fellow councilmen in sequence.

"Obviously the Peeper is a man who has trouble seeing good-looking women any time he wants to," the banker said. "With someone like Carolyn at home I have no need to go peeping." His eyes came to rest on Orville Jenkins. "Incidentally, Orville. Carolyn told me Irene was joining Weight Watchers."

"Bert," Orville Jenkins said acidly, "I'd hoped I wouldn't have to bring this up, but you force my hand. The Peeper plainly has to be someone who plays around, who has some immature juvenile craving for a variety of women. People have talked for years about you and all those pretty bank tellers of yours. The whole town knows about *that* hanky-panky. They've said it everywhere except to your face."

Livid, the banker turned on the vegetable king. "Orville, you may need a lawyer yourself."

"I'm proud to say," Orville said serenely, "that I have not violated the Seventh Commandment since Irene and I were joined together twenty-five years ago."

"They don't call you Saint Orville for nothing, do they?" Bert Hooper said.

Jenkins wheeled on him. "Who calls me that?"

"Everybody. But only behind your back," Hooper said spitefully.

"One thing certain. No one will ever call you Saint anything, Hooper."

Jenkins looked around the table at the other suspects, glaring, examining. His eyes fixed on Sherman Embers.

"It's got to be someone who can get out any night he wants to. Very difficult for a family man. You're unmarried, Sherman. At the moment."

"Now see here, Orville."

"Orville may have a hot lead there," Bert Hooper said. "Yes, sir, someone who doesn't have the problem of telling a wife where he is every night. An unmarried man or"—he turned abruptly on Henry Milam—"someone whose wife has been away. Emily certainly spent a long time with that sick sister of hers in Idalou, didn't she, Henry?"

"Bert, if that means what I think it means," Henry Milam said, "you and I better step outside."

"I've always admired that Armbruster girl you've got for a secretary, Henry," Hooper went on confidently. "That good-looking one with the big headlights. Wasn't she peeped?"

"Bert," Henry Milam said, "I've wanted to ask you something for a long time. It concerns those filthy movies you get from somewhere and show at the Gun Club. Tell me, what kind of man is it who would enjoy looking at pictures of three men making it at the same time with a woman? I've always been curious about that. He has to be one of two things. Impotent or sadistic. Or both."

"Henry," Hooper said, enraged, "you'll do well to remember that Lone Star isn't the only beer people can drink. There's always Pearl and even Schlitz."

Henry Milam, ignoring this threat, spoke to the table at large. "I called Emily every night at nine. You can check the phone records. The phone company keeps records of all long-distance calls."

"How long did you talk?" Embers said, lighting a cigarette. "All night? There's plenty of dark after nine."

"There's not a man here works the hours I do," Orville

Jenkins said. "I'm up at six every morning inspecting my fields, and I'm lucky to be home by eight. I wouldn't have time for it. Even if I had the inclination."

"Horseshit," Embers said. "The world's busiest men find time for that."

Jenkins swung around. "Sherman, I take exception to your attitude of being a prosecutor. It sounds to me like you're trying to take attention off yourself."

"Second that," Bert Hooper said. "So far as I know, Sherman, you've not as yet been voted prosecuting attorney with the power to cross-examine the four of us. Pretty suspicious, I call it."

Hooper turned to the chief of police. "Freight Train, correct me if I'm wrong, but didn't you say you found cigarette butts some of the places he peeped?"

"That's right," the chief said. "Camels."

"Well," Bert said, looking around the table, "Esau doesn't smoke. Henry doesn't smoke. Orville certainly doesn't smoke. And *I* don't smoke."

The banker looked fixedly at the cigarette pack on the table in front of the lawyer.

"I see just one man smoking here. And it's the right brand."

"Why, that's so, isn't it?" Orville said, looking at the pack, then the lawyer.

"My goodness," Henry Milam said, looking.

Embers inhaled deeply and blew a long contrail of smoke in Hooper's face.

"Ignoramuses," the lawyer said. "Ignorant assholes. All of you. If they weighed all of your brains on a postal scale, an eighteen-cent stamp would cover it. Those butts mean the one thing the Peeper doesn't do is smoke. A six-year-old would know they were a red herring to throw the chief off. What those cigarettes do is clear one person here. Me. There are only four of you now."

"Not so fast, Embers," the banker said.

His voice was softer as if pleased that he was getting to the lawyer. He turned to the table.

"Aren't we forgetting the biggest thing of all? It goes without saying that a man whose own wife has been peeped can't be a suspect. Well, mine was."

"Mine, too," said Henry Milam. "As soon as she got back from Idalou."

"So was mine," said Orville Jenkins.

"And so was Esau's," Hooper said. "*All* our wives have been peeped." He turned on the lawyer. "Except Embers. He doesn't have a wife."

The lawyer was unfazed. "He obviously peeped his own wife. *Noblesse oblige.*"

"What?" Bert Hooper said.

Sherm Embers lighted another cigarette.

"Wait a minute. I just remembered something." Hooper's face lit up. "I was at the Gun Club the night my wife was peeped. That itself lets me out."

Henry Milam brightened too. "You all will remember that Emily got it that same night. I was at the Domino Club. So I'm in the clear."

The chief of police belched considerably. He looked at both men. "That's what you say. I decided to check that out. Henry, you said you had something to do and left the Domino Club early. Bert, you didn't even stay for the finish of that night's dirty movie. You left for some mysterious reason."

"Emily was feeling poorly," Henry Milam said. "I had to get back to her. She's exhausted from looking after her sick sister."

"Carolyn wanted to . . ." Bert Hooper said. He grinned lecherously and lowered his voice to a conspiratorial tone. "Gentlemen, this is rather embarrassing. But the fact was, Carolyn was *not* feeling poorly at all. Just the opposite. And after a little of that movie, I . . . well, you take my meaning. Yes, I certainly left the Gun Club early and went home as fast as I could."

"Jesus," Sherm Embers said disgustedly. "What a sod you are, Hooper. Is there nothing you won't keep sacred to get off the hook?"

The banker's face went scarlet. It was pointed right at the lawyer.

"I for one have made up my mind who it is," he said in fury, "if we want to call for a vote. And I might add this. It fills me with indignation to think I'm sitting at the same table with the snake and have been all this time. I feel contaminated."

"Just so," Sherm Embers said calmly. "Any trial lawyer will tell you that indignation is the first refuge of the guilty. No one contaminates quicker than a seasoned criminal."

Suddenly the mayor banged his fist on the table. Some of the councilmen jumped. All looked at him, startled. Even the flags of Texas and the United States jumped clean off the table before settling back.

"*Gentlemen,*" he said. "I've had about enough of this. For shame!"

He sat erect, immaculate in his white Palm Beach suit and polka-dot tie, the smallest man there and the most commanding and at sixty-three the most vigorous. The councilmen looked sheepish. Once more, he had taken charge.

"I've had about enough of this yelping and snarling and throwing accusations at each other. This *panicking.* Is this a meeting of the first grade or of the Martha Town Council? Now I want you men to keep your voices down, to stop accusing each other, and to start acting like the leading citizens of this town that you're supposed to be. We need cool heads here. Four men at this table are innocent and one is guilty. We have a crisis on our hands. Everybody *follow?*"

He barked the word. His bottle-green eyes burned the table.

"In your rush to exculpate yourselves you have overlooked the single most alarming implication of this matter. We have the Peeper cornered, in a manner of speaking. But our troubles have just begun. Do you men realize the significance when the town learns that it's a member of the Town Council but doesn't know *which* member?"

"My God, Esau," Orville Jenkins said. "I hadn't thought of that. Why, they'll suspect every one of us."

"Exactly, Orville," he said. "Who's innocent and who's guilty is beside the point. We're all going to be guilty. As it now stands, each and every one of us will be the Peeper as far as the town is concerned."

"Lord above," Henry Milam said. "That would be just terrible."

"Make no mistake, gentlemen," he said. "If the only thing the voters know is that it's one of us five, they're likely to throw us *all* out, just to make certain they get the right one. On top of that, they'll probably boycott all our businesses for the same reason. The disgrace will sweep us away. We're all going to be marked men, every man jack of us."

The council sat a moment in a kind of stupor, an almost impotent seizure of gloom and dismay.

"Gentlemen," he said, "I'd like to make a final appeal to all of you."

His eyes moved around the big table, resting a moment or two on each. He spoke almost compassionately.

"I want to give the guilty party one last chance to confess and save the rest of us. We'll go as easy on you as we can. I think any court would take into account the fact that one of you stepped forward of his own free will. I put it to you on a high principle. Not to let the innocent among us suffer."

He waited. Like trees planted by the water, all were unmoved by this lofty appeal.

A small belch was heard.

"Yes, Freight Train?"

"Mayor, I got a plan for keeping it from being a disgrace. At least to keep it from being a public disgrace."

All eyes turned to the chief of police.

"Troops," Freight Train said, "what I propose has nothing to do, frankly, with any consideration for you gentlemen. It has to do with the honor and welfare of Martha. I ain't exactly proud of you councilmen, even if you is my employers. The way you all been scurrying for cover. And especially I ain't proud of one of you. But I got a higher loyalty. I would do anything for Martha." The chief's voice came on like a sonorous bugle summoning the horse troops bunked below. "I love Martha, Texas."

"Yes, yes, Chief," he said impatiently. "We all do. What is the plan?"

"The plan is this. I ain't going to tell anybody it's one of you. And neither are you. I've studied and studied about this—I never figured the culprit would confess, and it seems I figured right. I don't know which of you it is and I may never know. But the people of this town, they ain't going to know that it's *any* of you. Because if they did know it was one of you and not know which one, it would do the town in. Considering you is their highest elected officials and that every one of you is also a leading and upstanding citizen. Or supposed to be. It'd take the town a long time to recover from the idea that its five top men, any of them could be the Peeper. It might never recover. This is a good town and they's good people here. This town deserves better than to have something terrible as that happen to it. The people of this town depends on you men. They counts on you. You their *leaders*."

At this bracing, the councilmen sat up a little straighter. The scared looks on their faces diminished slightly.

The chief's eyes glazed over. "And tell the truth, it wouldn't do your chief of police a world of good for people to find out what a jackass one of you has made of me. So, troops, I'm not going to say a word about it and you not going to say a word about it. We all just going to keep our mouths shut."

"You mean never let the town know that it's one of us?" Orville Jenkins said.

"You got it, Orville," Freight Train said. "That's exactly what I mean."

"The chief's got a point," Bert Hooper said. "If they thought the guilty party could be any of us . . . why, the town wouldn't trust anybody after that. Trust is every-thing. Every banker knows that. We've got to think of the town."

"Our good townspeople might even get cynical," Sherm Embers said.

"We can't let personal considerations sway us," Orville Jenkins said. "We've got to put the good of the town ahead of ourselves. That's what we're here for. The people would expect it."

They all looked to him for his leadership. He waited a few moments, deep in thought.

"An imaginative proposal, Chief. Gentlemen," he said then, "the more you think about it, it's the only course that makes any sense. Freight's right: The town comes first. We can't afford to have the people of Martha not trusting *any* of their leaders. Of course we'll be guilty to each other. But that's something we'll have to live with. It'll just be a private burden that we'll have to carry."

"But, Esau?"

"Yes, Henry?"

"That leaves just one thing. Who are the people of the town going to think it was?"

"Anybody. Just like they have all along." He thought a moment. "A lot of people think it's Baxter. He's been a top suspect. I don't like that part at all."

"I don't like it none either," Freight Train said. "But I don't know what we can do about it. Matter of fact, Mayor, this is why I didn't want Baxter here. I figured it might come to this."

"I hate to see an innocent man carry the load," he said.

"But after all," Orville Jenkins said, "he'll only be getting some of the same medicine the four of us who are innocent are getting—being suspected wrongly of being the Peeper."

"There's one little difference," Henry Milam said. "We'll just suspect each other. Half the town will suspect Baxter."

Bert Hooper shrugged. "He's never really been one of us. You remember when he wouldn't go along with us on the Peeper stories? And when he shut down the paper and ran away? Well, this should teach him a lesson."

"Now, Bert, that's rather harsh," he said. "He's not such a bad fellow. I don't know. It bothers my conscience some to have an innocent man take the blame all over town. For something he didn't do. I don't relish that."

"Esau," Bert Hooper said, "would you rather have one innocent man or four innocent men take the blame all over town?"

"That is a point." He wavered. "I suppose we do have to think about what hurts the least number."

"Anyhow, it probably won't bother him too much," Orville Jenkins said. "After all, he is a newspaperman."

"Of course," Bert Hooper said. He gave that smile that showed just his lower teeth. "No big deal. It won't hurt him. Newspapermen have broad backs. Everybody's always criticizing newspapermen. They're used to taking all kinds of flak."

He laughed heartily. "He might even like it. For people to think he's a big ladies' man."

"I guess," Sherm Embers said doubtfully. "But I was never present at this meeting."

"What meeting?" he said. "Well! We seem to have a consensus. That's quite an accomplishment for a meeting that never took place."

"Mayor, I got a final word," the chief said.

"Your floor, Chief."

"I just got two points. First, as of right now people don't know about him seeing the Bloomer Girls—the basketball team has told everybody he didn't show. Well, I think we should leave it that way. The Bloomer Girls is about the biggest thing they is in this town, and I got a notion it would upset people no end to find out we couldn't even protect them. In fact, it might put them in quite a uproar."

"A well-taken point," he said. "It would only exercise people needlessly to know all the Bloomer Girls had got it." He gave the chief a meaningful look. "Why, they might even lose their confidence in your department. Follow, Chief?"

Freight Train's eyes glazed. "I follow, Mayor. It wouldn't help."

"I believe we can all concur in the official line that the Bloomer Girls kept their purity," he said. "Except, of course, those that were peeped individually. What's your other point, Chief?"

"Just this. Whichever one of you men is the real Peeper," the chief said, "then it's time to stop. Right now. If they is as much as one more peeping, I'll figure out a way to tail *all* of you, to know where every one of you is every minute. And when I catch you, and I will, I won't keep quiet then. I'll tell the whole town. You have my sacred Aggie word on this. And that's the double truth."

He waited a moment to let these threatening words settle home.

"Chief," he said, "I think I can say with assurance that Martha's ordeal of peeping is over. The women can now raise their window shades."

"Hail, they never really lowered them," Freight Train said glumly.

"That's so," he said. He gave a sigh of contentment. "So. This meeting never took place. However, I don't see any reason to waste it. Now that everything's settled, you men have time for a little poker?"

With that, light flooded through and seemed to wash the room.

"Always time for poker," Henry Milam said with a sudden smile.

"A pretty night for the cards," Orville Jenkins said, brightening. "But what night isn't?"

"Gentlemen, draw your chips and bet your hands," Bert Hooper said with a glow.

"Poker would certainly relax me," Sherm Embers said. "If anything would."

"Wheel and deal," he said.

The prospect of a good poker game never fails to brighten the darkest corners, to lift men out of the continuing tribulations that are so much a part of life.

"Why don't we raise the stakes a little?" he said. "Say double. To celebrate having completed important town business with no one present. Besides, I feel I have a hot hand tonight."

He turned to Councilman Milam. "Henry, I think we could all do with a little refreshment. Would you care to fetch us six of your excellent Lone Stars?"

But Henry was still brooding. "When you stop to think about it," he said, "I don't guess he did any harm to the town, did he?"

"Harm?" Saint Orville said. "Why, no, I guess he didn't."

"He might even have helped it," Henry said. "For some reason I don't understand, the women seem a lot better."

"Why, so they do," he said. "Now that you mention it."

"And what's best for the women is always best for the men, isn't it?" Henry Milam said.

"Why, Henry," he said. "What you just said is so smart a man would almost think you were the Peeper."

The cards were broken out. Soon each councilman was sitting comfortably behind his own neat stacks of red, white, and blue chips and his own bottle of Lone Star. Under the overhead poker light, a warm aura of contentment and of self-congratulation and even self-esteem, of having acted in the best interests of the town, enveloped the scene. That marvelous sense of a difficult problem solved hung sweetly in the air. Now the men who had solved it deserved to relax. He felt a certain pride. Where they had been so divided and even rancorous, he had brought them together. Where had been rage and fury he had brought concord. Where had been hostility he had brought consensus. In short, he had shown the mark of the true leader.

He had always possessed the best poker face in town, one of the best in Texas, some said. He had always been a superb handler of cards. Now, under dealer's choice, he called for a stud hand and dealt off the first up cards in an exceptionally festive manner.

"A handsome jack to our able Councilman Milam."

He dealt another. "A double-digit ten to our redoubtable Councilman Jenkins."

He flicked off another. "A trey to our shrewd Councilman Embers."

Another card flashed out. "A deuce to our astute Council-man Hooper."

He flipped another. "A great big ace to our ingenious chief of police."

And the final one to himself. "Grateful dealer draws a pretty queen."

A sound was heard at the door. The councilmen looked up from their cards to an unfamiliar sight at a Town Council meeting. Standing there was a woman. She was wearing a belted linen dress of pale green which shaped her slim figure and rippled around her bare legs. These ended in good-looking thonged sandals. A string of chalk-white beads encircled her neck.

"Why, Miss Jamie," he said. "How fetching you look. I hardly recognized you."

"I'm sorry to interrupt your poker game, Mayor," the newspaperman said politely. "But I found this in my mailbox with a note to please deliver it to you tonight at ten o'clock."

"Nobody knowed we was meeting," Freight Train said. "Except us."

She stepped over and handed the envelope to him and was gone. He looked at the envelope.

"It's addressed 'Town Council,'" he said. "In block letters. To all of us, I presume."

"Then let's all of us hear it," Bert Hooper said.

He opened the envelope, unfolded the single sheet of paper, and spread it on the table. It, too, was in block letters. He read it aloud:

"DEAR FRIENDS: THIS IS TO INFORM YOU THAT HAVING DONE WHAT I SET OUT TO DO, I HAVE CEASED OPERATIONS. I WILL ENTER NO MORE ALLEYS, TRAVERSE NO MORE YARDS, LOOK THROUGH NO MORE WINDOWS. IN SHORT, I HAVE HUNG UP MY STOCKING. I HOPE THAT YOUR SPECULATIONS ABOUT MY IDENTITY WILL GIVE YOU AS MUCH PLEASURE OVER THE YEARS TO COME AS MY MEMORIES WILL GIVE ME."

He looked over the top of the letter at the others.

"It's signed, THE TEXAS PEEPER. Just like him to think of himself in that grandiose way."

"He outfoxed us again," Sherm Embers said. "Quitting before we forced him out."

"You may be right," he said.

He looked at the letter, then around the table. "Well, like we said all along, that was one smart son of a bitch. Ace bets."

14.

The New Girl

W e stopped at the supermarket in Port Isabel and loaded up with groceries. I bought coffee, tinned corned beef, cheeses, eggs, guava jelly, bread, crackers, bacon, sugar, B and M beans. We must have carried a half dozen of those large sacks out to the car.

"Isn't this a lot just to be going out for the day?" she said. "Or are you going around the world?"

"It's time to stock up. Do you mind?"

I stopped at a bait place and bought some mullet. We drove on across the new high bridge over the Laguna Madre. As we came to the top of the bridge we could see the strip of sand, thirty miles long and one mile wide, that is South Padre Island, and beyond it the Gulf. The sun was just up from the horizon. The light blue sky came down to meet the dark even blue of the water.

I took her below and showed her the forward cabin with its isosceles-triangle bunks, then led her into the aft cabin.

"This is the guest cabin," I said. "When I have a guest. It's a little less rough back here in heavy seas."

"It's very nice."

"I've got to check a few things. Do you want to wait or go along?"

"I think I'd rather go along."

"First the engine room. It's right here."

I opened up the bulkhead beyond the bunk.

"Down on all fours and follow me."

"Yes, sir."

I crawled into the engine space and she came after me. I checked the oil level. I took the cap off the fresh-water tank and stuck my finger in, and it was up to its four-gallon level.

"Now this is the stuffing box nut," I said. "Very important little piece. Regulates the amount of seawater coming in to cool the propeller shaft. If the nut's loose the bilge pump has to overwork. If the bilge pump goes, you get too much water in the hold. If the nut's too tight, the water isn't lubricating the propeller shaft and the shaft will get scarred. It should be slowly dripping water."

"It isn't. It's coming in steadily."

"So it is. Here's what you do."

I loosed the lock nut to get to the stuffing box nut. I tightened it until I was getting the right drip. Then tightened the lock nut.

"See?"

"Yes. It looks just right now."

"Back out."

We crawled back into the cabin and stood up. I replaced the bulkhead panel, and she followed me up to the wheelhouse.

"Before casting off you check all of these," I said. "Like this. Fathometer . . . ADF . . . VHF. . . ."

I could see her paying the close, concentrating attention to everything that she did when it was something she wanted to learn. Just like she had with the newspaper—the reporting, the writing, the typesetting, the Mergenthaler, all of it.

"All right. Outside."

I showed her how to unhook the electrical line that tied us to the shore. I brought in the lines that secured the boat to the dock. I stepped back into the wheelhouse and she followed.

"This is the generator button. Switches us from shore power to ship power."

"Shore power to ship power."

I flipped the starter. "Hear that buzzer? That means we

have oil pressure. Now you wait five minutes for the engine to warm up."

We went up to the flying bridge and I took *My Last Duchess* at a couple of knots through the marina, then out into the Laguna Madre and between the posts that mark the dredged channel. On nearly every piling sat a sea gull. Sometimes another gull would fly in and make the first sea gull give up its place and it would make a fussing noise and fly off. We passed the Coast Guard station. The flag was hanging almost limp against the pole. I showed her how to rev the boat and picked her up to sixteen hundred rpm's, about eight knots. We went on past some berthed shrimpers, all shrouded in nets hanging high from their masts and clear down to the decks to dry. A freighter was coming down the Browns-ville ship channel high in the water. I waited for her to pass through the Port Isabel inlet and stayed out of her wake.

"You don't want ever to get too close to those babies," I said. "That wake can mess up a boat like this."

She looked rusty and beat-in and we could see "*Belle Brummel*—Liverpool" on her stern as we followed her between the jetties. The current that always comes in through there even on a calm day hit the boat and pitched us. It caught her by surprise. She tottered for a moment and I grabbed her elbow.

"Steady as you go," I said.

She brushed off my arm. "I'm quite all right. Just you watch the boat."

I grinned. Then we were through the channel and into the open sea and the boat steadied. Before long we could see it.

"Look down there," I said. "That's the mouth of the Rio Grande. That's where it all ends after that nineteen-hundred-mile trip from the mountains of Colorado."

She looked. "Isn't this exciting!"

I headed out for the blue water. It was a pretty day, only three or four fat cumulus now high up trailed by strips of cirrus. We could feel the boat under us, taking the soft swells. I told her a little about the boat—mahogany and teak, full-displacement hull.

"She looks like a boat ought to look," she said. "She looks special."

"She is. See how she rides in the sea. Like a ship."

Today was the kind of sea I like best. Swells enough to know you are in blue water but not enough that you had to fight them. The Grand Banks went easily with the sea, moving down into the troughs and staying there when the swells came at her, riding up just enough to give a decent pitch under your feet.

"Would you like to take the helm?"

"Could I?"

The sea had been gentling all day. Now it was flat and pale, a looking glass, the only sound that of *Duchess* taking us across the hushed waters. No clouds hung in the great wash of blue, only the sun, starting down now. She had been as excited as a child getting some big and bright new toy for Christmas. She was wearing a pair of linen shorts and a shirt that tucked neatly into them, a pair of new Hush Puppies with brass buckles, Bermuda socks, and even a ribbon in her hair. Some kind of change had come over her recently. I didn't know what had brought it about, but there was no mistaking any more that she was a girl. She had begun to let her hair grow. The huge brown eyes shone when she turned to me, her hands moving over the helm spokes, where we stood on the flying bridge.

"Why did you wait so long to take me out?" she said. "Keeping this all to yourself. How could you be so selfish? I love it."

"Yeah. Nothing's very complicated out here."

"You see, I was right all along. I told you I'd make a good sailor. I don't get seasick. I'm good with boats too, just like I figured. I take orders real well. You were wrong all the time. Isn't it a lot better with me than just being all by yourself?"

I smiled. But it was true. I was surprised to find out how much I liked having her with me on the boat. She had been so eager, so happy. She learned fast. It had been good all the long day.

"I'll have to see you in a seven-foot sea," I said. "I'll have to see how you are if the engine breaks down."

"If I learned that Mergenthaler," she said, "I could learn this boat's engine."

She probably could. She had learned a lot since that first day she drove down from Dallas in that beat-up MG, with her shirttail hanging out.

"Let's eat," I said.

I showed her how to pull the throttle to idle and I went to the fo'c's'le and paid out the anchor. I broke out the Bon Ton sandwiches and opened a couple of Negra Modelos.

"Good old Bon Ton," she said. "I'll never forget the Bon Ton."

We finished the sandwiches and I opened two more beers. We sat looking out over the satin sea. It was hard even to make a horizon. Nothing was in sight anywhere.

"Baxter, I can see now why you like this boat. Like being on the sea. You're almost human out here. I see now what brought you way down here away from everywhere. That package of the newspaper and the boat. That's it, isn't it? The boat makes the difference."

"Well, with the Peeper shut down, I'll probably be spending a lot more time out here."

"It is pretty dull around town now with the Peeper gone. Everybody says so. You know, the town *misses* him. Yes, sir, pretty dull."

"Half the town thinks it was me. I resented that at first. Now I'm glad. I'm more popular than ever in Martha, if that's possible. With the ladies. I even drop hints that they might be talking with the McCoy."

"What an impostor you are, Baxter."

"But you were sure I was."

"That was before more information reached me."

"My God, you're beginning to talk like a Washington reporter. The next thing you'll be saying, 'from unimpeachable sources.'"

"Well, I could. I'd tell you, except that a good reporter never reveals her sources."

"That's enough. Sister, you're talking to an old party."

"That's true. My name isn't sister."

She had that prim-lady look she got ever so often. More so lately. Well, you've got to let the young do a certain amount of bragging. She looked out over the becalmed sea and, in her style, was off in another direction.

"Out here—why, it's just lovely," she said. "I could live on this boat. I knew we should have started this sooner."

She swallowed some beer. How young she still seemed.

"I'll kind of miss the town. But I guess the big story is over. I'm glad I was here when it happened. There probably won't be another story in Martha for another century."

Then I knew it was coming and knew suddenly how little prepared for it I was. It was going to be a lot harder than I had imagined. I was surprised to feel in me that old, familiar enemy that it seemed I had spent most of my life fighting off: that knowledge of approaching loneliness, of being alone. Of course I had known she had to go, but I had managed most of the time not to think about it. And I had had no idea it would hit me like this. Anyhow, I hadn't thought it would be this soon. In the two months since the Peeper thing had ended, she had mentioned it a couple of times. But she had not pressed it. Now I knew she would.

She seemed to hurry a little. "Listen, I have a lot to thank you for. I've learned a lot from you. At that newspaper. But if you think I'm ready. . . ."

It had been something special, seeing that process. Seeing someone learn a craft I loved and helping out with that. It had brought a satisfaction I would never have expected. In fact, it had been one of the most pleasurable things to happen to me since I had become a newspaperman.

"Yes," I said, "you're ready."

"You mean that?"

"You claim to know me so well. Would I say it if you weren't?"

"No. You wouldn't. Then you'll give me that recommendation?"

"Sure."

"That's really wonderful of you. And it'll work?"

"They know I wouldn't give it for my own sister if she didn't have it. Of course, you'll be on trial for six months. They'll have to have their own look at you. When do you want to go?"

"Why, as soon as . . . well, as soon as you can spare me. You ran that paper without me before. I suppose you can do it again. Do it alone, I mean."

"I suppose I could. But I have no intention of working that hard. I called Whiteside last week. He says he can find me another girl at the marvelous Southern Methodist University journalism department."

"Oh, he did?"

"Yeah. No problem. He says he's got lots of kids who are willing to take any job to get started in the newspaper business. He said he could ship down another girl like you on a week's notice. He says he can easily find someone else who wants to sit at my feet."

"Another girl like me. He says a lot, doesn't he? Well! That's a big load off my mind. I was beginning to feel a little guilty about leaving you in the lurch."

"There's no lurch. You can leave anytime. I can phone as soon as we get back in, and the new girl will be on her way."

"I love it the way you say 'the new girl.' Like you were ordering a replacement part for the Mergenthaler."

"I told Whiteside I'd pay her a hundred and fifty a week. Twice what I pay you. The paper's practically rolling in wealth now. Circulation is up so much since we made it a *real* newspaper, I can afford it."

"How nice for her."

I looked out across the sea. "No, I'm not going to make the mistake I did with you. I've decided to add some fringe benefits to the job. In these modern times you've got to have those benefits if you're to hold on to your employees. You can't expect them to stay because they're grateful to you for putting all that time and effort into training them. I'll have to make it so attractive to her she'll never want to leave. One thing, I'm going to take the new one out on this boat with me every weekend. If she wants to go."

"I'm sure she will."

"She can sit at my feet out here as well as she can in that office. Maybe she'll like that."

I stood up. I looked at the sun. It was time to go.

"I think we better head back in," I said. "Now that it's all settled."

She got up. "Not just yet," she said.

She looked up at me. She hiccuped.

"You're lying. All that about another girl. That's a big lie. You haven't even *talked* to Whiteside. You just said that to try to get me to stay. You fraud. Playing on my jealousy like that."

"Your jealousy? What is there to be jealous of?"

"All that about the huge effort of training somebody. Playing on my sympathy. Taking advantage of my sense of gratitude. All that about doubling the salary of the new girl. All that about *her*. About fringe benefits. You big phony." Her hair bounced. "Even all this business today of teaching me about the boat. All deliberate and calculating. You knew I'd love it. You *want* me to stay."

"Well, no one likes breaking in someone new on something as complicated as a small-town newspaper. Having to teach someone else everything I've taught you. Teaching her how to cover a story, how to write a story, if she's like you teaching her how to *dress*, for God's sake, how to—"

I stopped because I could hear the catch in my voice. Then I tried again.

"How to be a . . ."

I never got any further in enumerating all the many things I had done for her. I felt a dampness just in the corners of my eyes and felt her fingers reaching up to touch it away. I was vaguely aware of *My Last Duchess* tugging gently in the sea against her anchor, aware that Jamie was standing on her toes. It was not a great amount of kiss, but it was fresh and sweet.

And then she was holding me. Her small body folded into me, her hands digging into my back.

"Why didn't you say so." She was talking into my chest. "Why didn't you ever *say* so?"

"I'm much too old for you," I said.

"Of course you are."

I could feel her body against me, small, my arms around her. Feel her warmth, taking away all loneliness. I could see the sea over her head, and everything in my life that I had felt was important seemed to deliquesce into the pale waters. I held her and stroked her hair. I could feel her holding tight to me. Then she was talking into my chest again.

"I just decided I need a little more experience," she said. "About two or three months. Give or take. Then I'll reexamine the whole situation."

She looked up at me with those huge eyes, the pupil and iris of the one brown color seeming to make you look into them. "But don't you ever get the idea I'm giving up my goal. I mean of being a *big-time newspaperman*. I don't mean the Martha *Clarion*."

I looked down at her. "I would never dream that the Martha *Clarion* could hold on to a big-time newspaperman like you forever."

She giggled. "Baxter, sometimes I actually like you. You make me laugh. That's so sweet of you, doubling my salary. I think you'll discover I'm worth it."

"Doubling your salary?" I said, shocked.

"Of course. All that money the paper's rolling in. Well?"

I sighed. She was in control. I guess she had been from the beginning.

"Double it is," I said.

"Then that's settled. Baxter?"

"Yes?"

Her head was back in my chest. "Getting all those groceries. That was part of it too, wasn't it? You big con."

"Why, I just thought . . . that is . . . I thought you might like for me to show you Mexico. Don't forget, I speak fluent Spanish."

"Mexico?"

She raised her head and looked right up at me. It was a different look from any I had ever seen there.

"Maybe in Mexico," she said, "you can start showing me what all those fringe benefits are."